Entrance to Dark Harbor

Dark Arrow Trilogy
Book 2

Mathias G.B. Colwell

Published by
Melange Books, LLC
White Bear Lake, MN 55110
www.melange-books.com

Cover Design by Stephanie Flint

For Billy, one of my earliest encouragers and a wonderful source of feedback as a writer. The concept of "Dark Harbor" was really the point at which this trilogy began to take shape in my mind, thanks in large part to you, Billy.

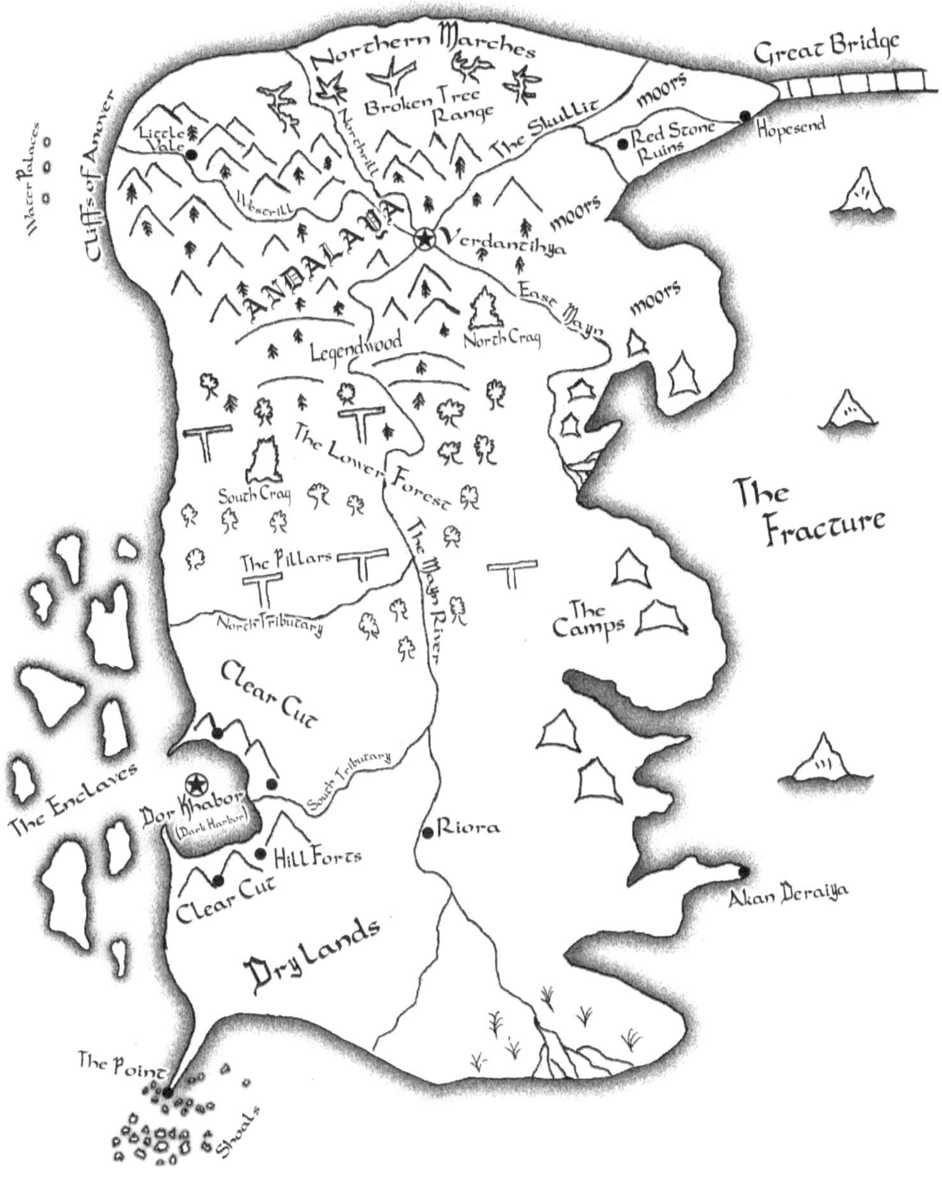

Northern Marches
Great Bridge
Broken Tree Range
Northrill
The Skullit
moors
Red Stone Ruins
Hopesend
Little Vale
Weserill
Water Palaces
Cliffs of Anover
ANDALAVA
Verdantihya
moors
East Mayn
moors
North Crag
Legendwood
The Lower Forest
South Crag
The Fracture
The Mayn River
The Pillars
North Tributary
The Camps
Clear Cut
South Tributary
The Enclaves
Dor Khabor
(Dark Harbor)
Riora
Hill Forts
Clear Cut
Akan Deraiya
Drylands
The Point
Shoals

Prologue

Half-Mask sat languidly in a throne-like chair of worn walnut, the wood a deep, rich brown. He supposed that if he felt any deep connection to the land whatsoever, that the color might remind him of earth and life and growth. But he had forsaken those things long ago. Except, perhaps, for growth, but only in the manner of expanding his lands. However, the time was not yet ripe. Soon. Soon, he would retake what had been lost, and more. Half-Mask had a plan, a plan that was bound to yield the fruit he wanted. Power. That was what made the world turn. Nations rose and fell, people overcame obstacles, races were subjugated, all for the sake of power. Power was freedom. It was the truest kind of freedom there was, over yourself and the freedom to take away the liberty of others.

Half-Mask smiled at that thought and hooked one lean leg over the arm of his chair in which every leader of prominence among the Departed had, at one time, sat. His leg poked out from the long black cloak that had fallen open, but the hood was still shrouding his face in darkness. Southern elves of prominence were often known for wearing heavy, ermine robes, but those robes were ungainly and hindered Half-Mask's ability to move freely and quickly. Not that he feared attack in the heart of his people's kingdom. No, in the palace at Dark Harbor, he was completely safe. Yet he was nothing if not calculated and prepared. He would not allow himself to fall prey to the dangerous politicking of his people. He was much too clever for that and wouldn't bow to expectations when a cloak could be removed much more quickly than robes, if necessary.

The wide window presented a view of the west, over the harbor, and on towards the ocean and the Enclaves. The Enclaves stretched into the western sea, an archipelago of island keeps, fortresses, and small port cities that his people populated. His people were the Departed—those elves who, in the great schism of the past, had abandoned their connection to the land from which they came, leaving behind culture and tradition. Unlike the Highest, as their northern kin referred to themselves, who remained perpetually enthralled to Creation, enslaved by it—bonded as they called it. He sneered as he thought of those fools to the north. Unable to adapt to the times, the northern elves were doomed to the role of slavery, if not outright extinction, once he implemented his plan to assert control over everything this side of the Fracture, the impassable and hazardous sea to the east that separated this continent from the human lands. The thought brought him a small sense of delight. A black fire of hatred for his northern kin smoldered within him.

A small table sat to the right of his miniature throne, and on it rested a mug of dark liquid. Half-Mask idly swirled his slender, smallest finger in the cup as he gazed out over the harbor and watched the reluctant, yet diligent, toiling of his many slaves. They were all formerly of the Highest, the fair northern elves, but his slave masters dutifully enforced the principle that the northern slaves were no longer higher than anything. In fact, if they wanted a name, then in truth they should refer to themselves as the "Lowest" to reflect how far from power they truly were.

Half-Mask lifted his mug, took a sip, then placed it carefully back on the stand table. It would not do to spill. He briefly felt something close to reverence—as close as his heart was capable of producing—as he considered the dark liquid, but then it was gone again, dulled by his incessant thirst for domination and control. It was a thirst that left it difficult for him to revere anything other than his own plans to achieve those ends.

The small table was new—he usually had one of his personal attendants hold his cup while he was not using it—but he had desired solitude. Today, he held his cup himself, or placed it on nearby furniture. How odd it felt to do so, how utterly mundane. Half-Mask was the opposite of ordinary. He was brilliantly vicious, violently powerful, vividly clever, and strong willed. In short, he was remarkable.

As he set the mug down, he resumed the gentle swirling of his finger in the dark liquid. Small puffs of black, smoky steam rose from the cup, making it appear to be piping hot, though it felt neither hot nor cold. It was some strange mix of the two sensations. Icy cold and burning hot and neither at the same time, all rolled into one. The vapors rising from the liquid were more akin to smoke than anything else. Yet even the emission of smoke in itself was strange, since smoke was derived from fire and most liquids did not burn. He lifted and sipped again, loathe to allow too much time to pass between sips of its deliciously potent contents.

He stirred again, glancing down at his finger in the liquid. As he withdrew his little finger, a tiny fleck of golden light streaked from the tip of his finger just as it broke from the surface and was absorbed by the dark liquid. Surprise shattered the void of his detached musings. It had been a long time since anything other than darkness had left him. He had thought that all the light had long since been leeched from his body. Unease flickered through him. He did not like the light. He preferred his darkness.

Footsteps sounded as someone slowly advanced up the stairs with obvious trepidation. He had deliberately told his attendants that he wanted time to think, time to brood. If they were disobeying and approaching him, it meant one or both of two things. Either someone was going to die, or the messenger approaching carried news of the utmost importance, in which case he still might die for disobeying. Principles were principles after all. However, Half-Mask decided—rather magnanimously he thought—to reserve his decision on the fate of his approaching servant until after he heard the news.

A knock sounded at the oaken door. He didn't respond and waited for another knock. Let them sweat. The notion of their fear and worry growing with each progressive knock gave him perverse pleasure. His solitude about to be interrupted, he picked up the only other item on his stand table, the object after which he'd taken his name—his black mask, perfectly crafted to fit the left side of his tanned face all the way from his forehead down to the jawline. It covered his cheek completely, but left the nose bare and featured an eyehole for him to see. The mask covered the splotchy, diseased-looking left side of his face that was pocked and scarred, as well as freshly broken with ever-present sores. He was not ashamed of his face—it was the price he had paid for his power. Yet, a modicum of vanity still held sway over him. Oh, he had modified other aspects of his appearance, he had only to run his tongue over the needle sharp teeth in his mouth to remind him, yet those changes in appearance were by choice, and the patchwork on his face was not. For that reason alone, he covered his diseased-looking blemishes. He placed the mask onto his face.

The knocking continued. After a minute or so of mulling over painful punishments, Half-Mask graciously gave the command to enter. A nervous slave—a southern elf, properly tanned instead of fair like the northern kin—opened the door and shut it quietly behind him. Like Half-Mask and the rest of the southern Departed, the slave had elegantly pointed ears, and a strong muscular frame, unlike the lean northern elves. The slave's hair was cut short to match his station, not like the long, luscious black locks that adorned Half-Mask's head beneath the hood of his cloak. His upper teeth were filed sharp, signifying that he had once been a warrior. But there was little fight left in the slave now, having probably been demoted to the lowest rank in the kingdom for some grievous mistake. If there was one thing the Departed society was good at, it was breaking the spirits of their captives. In the southern capital of Dark Harbor and its surrounding territory, "once a slave, always a slave" was a phrase often spoken. However, this adage had less to do with the physical practicalities of imprisonment and much more to do with the mentality enforced upon those unlucky enough to become captives in the south. Half-Mask's slave masters knew exactly how to break the will of their captives and there were enough slavers on hand to individually target those slaves who showed more resilience. No one maintained their inner fortitude for long as a slave of the Departed, they all broke sooner, rather than later, and devolved into cowering and cringing before the wrath and wishes of their deserved masters.

Half-Mask stared silently at the servant who fearfully alternated between staring at the floor and quick, nervous glances upwards towards Half-Mask. The attendant opened and closed his mouth to speak, but words wouldn't come, too great was his anxiety at being in the presence of true majesty and power.

"Out with it," Half-Mask exclaimed in exasperation, after the initial enjoyment of watching his subject stutter lost its appeal.

The slave finally found his voice, a tiresome, cracking sound, and spoke. "Yes, of course, Prince of Darkness."

No one called Half-Mask "Half-Mask" to his face. The term was not derogatory—Half-Mask embraced all aspects of himself. In fact, he had not heard his original name in so long that it was like a fleeting memory of a long lost dream from his childhood. No, "Half-Mask" was who he was now more than anything else. However, at some point, his people had assumed that the nickname would displease him, by reminding him of his unwanted diseased face. This had been before his plan was truly set in motion. Ironic now that many of the Departed had similarly diseased appearances—appearances that marked them as Half-Mask's handiwork, as the Unsired, reborn not from the land itself but by other means entirely. His means. But years ago, when the nickname arose—when he was only beginning to delve into dark secrets and earn the marks on his face—that had not been the case. Half-Mask had made no move to correct them then and allowed usage of the new name, yet they referred to him formally as the Prince of Darkness, which was also an acceptable title, apt and fitting.

Having steadied his nerves somewhat, the slave attendant continued. Half-Mask listened to the news that was important enough for his attendant to have disobeyed an explicit order. "Fresh runner from the north, my Prince, bringing rumors of strange tidings. Shall I bring him in to report? I think it would be best to hear it from his mouth." The slave faltered when he realized that he had just given unwanted advice to Half-Mask. Annoyance at the intrusion, and the temerity of the slave to suggest a course of action without being prompted, puckered Half-Mask's face sourly, leaving him perturbed and wanting to diffuse his anger. The slave would pay for that mistake later. But for now, it could wait. Half-Mask waved his agreement and the slave quickly slipped back out the door and down the tower steps to retrieve the messenger. It would have been beyond presumptuous to bring the messenger up to the turret room in which Half-Mask sat, unannounced.

A minute passed as the attendant and runner hustled up the steps of the tower. The entrance door swung open and shut again as the slave ushered in a weary looking runner.

"Prince of Darkness, this is…"

"It matters not his name," Half-Mask dismissed the introduction haughtily. What care did he have for the names and faces of his minions? Control the elite and you controlled the population. He did not clutter his mind with the unimportant throngs of his followers.

The slave clamped his mouth closed midsentence and then left at Half-Mask's dismissal, leaving the runner from the north in his place.

Half-Mask curled his lip and opened his mouth into what was supposed to look like a wide smile. He laughed inwardly as the messenger flinched at the presentation of what many spoke but few had seen.

While it was common for the warriors of the southern elves to file the tips of their upper teeth into points suited for tearing and rending of flesh, no one had gone so far as Half-Mask. Half-Mask's molars and side teeth were normal, maintaining his jaw's ability to close, but the front teeth, both top and bottom, were filed into needle sharp points, thinner and meaner than any of the other Departed. The teeth were not thin enough to be brittle—instead they looked dangerous, otherworldly. They looked like the teeth of the deep-sea fish caught by the drop-net fisherman who sailed beyond the Enclaves and beyond even the Outer Rim islands. Those fishermen dropped weighted nets so deep that they hauled up all manner of ghastly fish suited for the lightless world far beneath the ocean's surface. Half-Mask's front teeth were filed so they resembled the maws of those fish. He had seen them on his tours of the kingdom, fish that had glowing embers of luminescence hanging in front of their mouths to attract tiny prey for feeding.

"My Prince," the runner stammered, "I have urgent tidings from Andalaya."

"From where?" Half-Mask asked, his voice dangerously quiet. His people were expected to remember his dislike for the name of the northern kingdom. It was shattered, broken. That result was the only possible silver lining to the arrival of the humans two decades past. The humans were a filthy, thieving sort. They were ignorant and weak, but numerous and had some within their ranks who knew how to harness power and use it to their advantage. Half-Mask hated them, yet the shred of relief he felt at their presence had everything to do with the fact that he hated his northern kin with an even greater, unrivaled passion. Andalaya's downfall had been precipitated by the arrival of human armies and the tentative alliance between them and the Departed.

The runner grew increasingly terrified after realizing his slip of the tongue. "From the north, Dark Prince. There is urgent news from the north," he amended.

"Continue." Half-Mask inclined his head. He would make the runner pay later if he chose. "What was so vital that you felt the need to interrupt my solitude?"

"It regards Silverfist, my Lord."

"Oh really? And tell me, what has my traitorous subject been doing to cause so much commotion that you felt the need to inform me immediately?" Half-Mask waited for the answer. The messenger paused a moment as if not sure how to proceed. Half-Mask took a sip of his black drink.

"He's dead."

Half-Mask's lip curled into an intimidating snarl of anger, flashing his otherworldly teeth at the messenger. The messenger paled slightly.

"How?" Half-Mask said tersely. He bore no sentimental attachment to Silverfist, but neither did he enjoy being startled. Half-Mask could not deny that he was surprised that someone had finally bested Silverfist. The Traitor had been wilier than most. To himself, Half-Mask had even conceded—with grudging respect—that Silverfist was likely more dangerous than just about anyone in the land other than himself and, of course, his father, the king. Silverfist's poisoned metal hand had inflicted death on many who had doubted his prowess. It must have been a formidable opponent to best him. And in that case, Half-Mask wanted to be made aware of who had the type of power and expertise to do so. Half-Mask did not encourage murders, but neither did he outlaw them. He promoted ambition, however that could be achieved. He did not want to punish whoever killed Silverfist—if you died then you deserved to die—because the strong found ways to survive. Yet he needed to be made aware of any power plays that were going on in his land.

"How did this happen?" He repeated his question forcefully as frustration welled up within him. This information must be weeks old by now.

The runner swallowed. "They say a wild youth of a boy killed him. There are murmurings that he has powers like no one has seen. Unlike even..." The messenger trailed off in terror as he realized he had almost repeated what was being said on the streets in Half-Mask's presence.

Powers unlike even Half-Mask himself possessed. Is that what they are saying? He mused thoughtfully. He was inclined to dismiss the rumors. Silverfist had possessed a certain aura about him. Anyone who killed him was bound to make a name for himself and build a formidable reputation. Likely, it was a warrior who had prevailed by no small portion of skill and was now being elevated to a higher status than he deserved. That must be it. After all, Half-Mask was powerful beyond what people knew. He would know if any in his kingdom, other than himself and his father, possessed similar abilities.

Half-Mask sneered at the messenger as the Departed runner locked his jaws tightly together in fear of saying anything else that might provoke Half-Mask. Half-Mask had a fearsome reputation for being short tempered.

"What? More powerful than me? Do not presume for a second to think that any of our people possess the power that I do!"

"Of course not, Prince of Darkness, I would never, ever think such a thought." The messenger opened his mouth as if to speak further, then closed it again.

"What now?" Half-Mask grated in frustration. "Out with it, whatever it is. I command you, speak."

"My Prince, it is just that as you say, no one in the land has the power you do. Yet, this youth is not one of our own, not of our people. He is from…the north. They say his name is Wintermoon."

"Wintermoon, Wintermoon," Half-Mask muttered to himself. Where had he heard that name before? Ah yes, the surname of Adan the Green, once famous defender of the walls of Verdantihya, the broken northern capital.

"Tell me more," he commanded.

The runner complied, although he did not have much more to say. "It is rumored that the Wintermoon youth and another northern elf destroyed entire companies of our slavers. Hundreds of them, singlehandedly. The rumors are not precise, but they do confirm two things. The elves had extraordinary power and that Silverfist is dead. Beyond that, I have nothing else of fact to report."

Half-Mask stood in a fluid motion. He lifted the cup to his lips and took another delicate sip of the dark liquid. He then calmly replaced the cup onto the table. He needed a release. Silverfist's death was an unfortunate inconvenience. Silverfist was never to be trusted, always to be kept at arm's length, never privy to important plans. He was traitorous once, who was to say he would not betray again? Yet, for all that, he had been useful, one of Half-Mask's most invaluable assets. It vexed him that Silverfist was dead.

Half-Mask felt the rage surging upward, his throat a bottleneck for the fury that desired release. He had to channel the energy somewhere. Silverfist dead! The one-handed elf had been important to the plans that Half-Mask had been cultivating for years. The fury was a whirlwind within him.

In a swift movement, he crossed the distance between himself and the messenger and clasped the elf's throat tightly, cutting of his air supply. Tendrils

7

of black, hazy substance wafted from the fingertips of Half-Mask's hand like smoke as he did so. The runner flapped his hands uselessly, struggling to no avail. Strangling wasn't enough. Half-Mask needed pain, he needed blood to slake his thirst for any kind of retribution for the death of his tool and his plans gone awry.

He bared his needle-sharp teeth and sank them into the eye of the messenger feeling the organ pop. It was an awkward bite, his jaws forcing their way into the eye socket, but it felt right. Blood and other unknown fluid flowed and the dying Departed messenger tried to scream, but his gurgling cries were stifled by the hand around his throat. Half-Mask bit again, this time at the neck, finding a pulsing vein and blood burst forth in earnest. After that, the elf died quickly.

Half-Mask wiped some of the blood from his mouth and let the dead elf drop to the stone floor. He returned to his polished wood chair to think. Almost subconsciously, he drank again from his cup, deeply, this time to slake a different thirst than the blood lust and anger he had sated a moment earlier. This thirst was deeper and only the blackness in his cup could satisfy it.

What to do? Silverfist dead. The messenger, now dead. Thoughts flitted idly in his mind. One thing became certain, retribution was needed. Not to avenge the Traitor, he could care less about Silverfist as an elf. But principles were principles. This youth had interrupted Half-Mask's plans by killing Silverfist. That could not go unpunished.

"More powerful than me?" he murmured. That was not possible. Half-Mask controlled the Unsired, at least as much as they could be controlled. Who in all the world could say that, other than him?

"More powerful than me?" This time, his voice was expelled in an enraged outburst. "I'll show them. I'll show everyone. I am hardly impotent, even here, far from where Wintermoon is amongst the shattered ruins of Andalaya."

Half-Mask dipped his finger into the dark liquid again. This time, he did not let his forefinger drift listlessly through the liquid. This time, he stirred with purpose, a decisive motion that was more evident in the look on his face than in the actual motion of his hand.

Shapes began to emerge on the surface of the liquid as he stared with auger eyes at the cup of dark black fluid. The shapes piled up on each other, breaking the surface, rising up like tiny waves and then collapsing in upon each other.

"Arise," Half-Mask whispered. "Awaken."

He stirred more. The shapes solidified into discernible images, creatures of darkness. "Arise." This time, one shape solidified completely, and a single image formed within the liquid. A fluid black tree grew out of the darkness, and a squat powerful creature, gnarled like the strong roots of an oak, uprooted itself from where it had been sleeping. An Ogre. The creature's eyes burned reddish orange and it snarled evilly as the blackness of its shape merged, coalesced, and then separated from the tree beside it. The shapes were merely representations of reality, rather than new creations, though they did not appear as liquid black in the world. But this was his creation point. The dark liquid was his means of bringing about awakening, and for this awakening he'd fused purpose into this creature's consciousness as he had coaxed it into a state of alertness. It had a purpose, and that purpose made Half-Mask smile with dark glee.

"Wintermoon," he whispered to the creature, as the tiny shape in his cup collapsed back into the liquid. A dirty chuckle sounded from his lips. It would carry out his orders. It would obey him. Half-Mask had the power.

He had all the power. He had more power than anyone. He was practically bursting with it. More power than his father, the king? The thought carried a note of uncertainty. The King of the South was the only one on par with Half-Mask. And the time had not yet come for a confrontation. Perhaps the time would never come, he thought in a moment of unforeseen loyalty. Then again, he amended his previous thought with his typical, ruthless hunger for absolute control, perhaps the time would come, and come soon. But there was no need for that yet. The King and Half-Mask worked well together. They knew which roles to assume. They were both dangerous. The king had chosen darkness, and that decisiveness lent him a wily intentionality that could outmatch Half-Mask if he was not careful. Half-Mask had been born into the darkness, he hadn't chosen it. He was a creature of the blackness in his nature, down to his very core, and because of that, his mind functioned much more clearly than most, even more clearly than the king's. Those who touched true darkness often became tinged with madness, including the king.

Half-Mask drank deeply from the mug, slightly tired from the mental exertions related to the awakening. The liquid was cool and fiery, both thirst-quenching and bone-warming. It was the energy of death.

He dipped his mug into a pot of the dark liquid that sat on the floor beside his chair. Upon refilling his drink, he stirred the liquid in his cup with his finger again, and again whispered, "Wintermoon." This time, he did not speak to the creature. It had already risen and was following the precise urges implanted into its mind by Half-Mask. No, he spoke the name of Wintermoon to himself. The name of a youth who had accomplished the great achievement of killing the original traitor. Wintermoon was the name of a filthy, northern elf, a warrior of the Highest, of considerable skill perhaps.

Wintermoon was the name of a foe that was about to die.

Chapter One

Late summer heat sent a trickle of sweat down Miri's neck. The bead of liquid trailed through a light coat of dust that had collected on her collarbone until it met the cloth of her forest-green tunic and was absorbed into the fabric. Her body felt wrung out, tired in the best possible way, after an afternoon spent moving through the woods on game trails and hidden tracks with Elliyar. Ell walked beside her, graceful and elegant in his strides in a way that she never could achieve. He was beautiful. With his wavy blond hair hanging shoulder-length and pulled into a loose tail with a leather thong, his lean, hard facial features were exposed. Eyes blue enough to make her breath catch and a body healthy and hale enough to make any elf jealous. Lips perfect for kissing. Their pace slowed as they neared their destination, a small tent—their own personal camp—erected a few hundred feet away from the rest of the company. She and Ell valued privacy these days. A flush touched her cheeks at the thought, but she didn't care. If Ell noticed, he would likely attribute her rosy complexion to the exertion of the hike and she would not have to explain her mental sensual meanderings.

The narrow game trail on which they trod widened in front of them as it met a more common thoroughfare through Legendwood. The wider path ran for only a few feet before it reached their tent. The small tent was erected in a sunny little glade surrounded by trees. Afternoon light filtered through the trees in golden strands as Miri sat down on a flat rock and lay back, stretching her arms out to the side, basking in the warmth of the rock and the sun. It was almost too hot after working up a sweat walking, but it would not be summer for much longer and Miri chose to embrace the heat before it was gone altogether. Seasons changed and a person had to know how to seize little moments of beauty that might soon disappear. Something told her that their summer of rest was like the heat of this rock. Warm and soaked into the core, but not to last much longer. Already, Ell's sapphire eyes were beginning to grow restless. Indiria's Emerald—or Little Vale as it was commonly referred

10

to—was a few months and many miles behind them. Little Vale held happy and sad memories. The destruction of the village and the deaths of so many of her friends in an attempt to staunch the flow of slavers attacking with their catchpoles and spears was balanced by the memory of her and Ell's Joining. Their coming together had been a bright spot, a reason for celebration in the aftermath of the misery inflicted by the now-dead Silverfist.

"What are you thinking about, Miri?" Ell asked, his curiosity seeming idle rather than pressing. As if he were simply making conversation for the sake of conversation.

"Nothing important, love," she said, as she sat up to look at him. He stood in front of her, wearing tightfitting breeches the color of dry soil. Perfect camouflage for summer surroundings. He had pulled off his green hooded tunic and hung it on a branch to air out.

Miri reached down and massaged her crippled leg. The old wound slowed her down considerably, but she was building strength around it. She would never be able to maintain the pace of a normal, healthy elf like Ell and the rest of his family, but perhaps she could become less of a hindrance to Ell when they traveled together. Not that he would ever admit to that, not in a thousand years, but sometimes she saw the eager look in his eyes as his body itched to run farther and faster than hers would allow. He always adjusted his pace to hers. Those were the only times when she ever really grew wistful for a better leg. Most of the time she was so used to her lameness, that she hardly noticed it, her body and mind adjusted to her own needs in a manner that made everything in life feel normal. But occasionally, Ell's manner of moving—more graceful than even the rest of his war-trained family—made her wish for an alternate past. A history in which she was never injured and her leg remained whole and healthy. It was a dream. She rubbed her leg and placed her mind firmly back into reality.

And reality was beautiful. Ell kneeled down in front of her, bare-chested, and took over the job of massaging her crippled muscles unasked. He quirked a mischievous smile with the corner of his mouth, his reaction to the way her eyes rolled in appreciation at the feel of his hands on her body.

"Mmm. That's wonderful," she half murmured, half groaned, as he continued his rubbing.

A silvery peal of laughter emerged from Ell's mouth at her response and it was a joy to hear. Their summer together had been near bliss. When they were alone, at least. But anytime they had shared the company of his uncle Dacunda or his mentor Arendahl, Ell had been filled with rage. He had always been passionate—since the day they first met, she had known he was full of strong emotions. And she had also known that much of his passion was channeled through anger. It fueled him, burned within, and made him the fighter that he was. But this was different. She knew he felt betrayed by Dacunda's withholding of the truth about his family, but she wished her mate could think more clearly about the scenario. However, Dacunda's perceived betrayal had wounded him deeply enough that he only fully let his guard down around her, now. So it was his genuine laughter that made her smile and pray her thanks that he was not too angry to find the joy in their new union.

Miri leaned forward and pulled his face close, silencing the beautiful laughter with a kiss. A long, lingering kiss. A part of her wished he wouldn't stop massaging her leg, but another part felt grateful that one kiss from her could stop him in his tracks and distract him from whatever he was doing. She pulled away and grinned wickedly at Ell.

"And what was that for?"

"Do I need a reason?" she countered brightly.

"No, you most definitely do not," Ell exhaled lustily as he resumed his massaging of her crippled leg. Whenever they took a long hike or traveled from one place to another, it was important to loosen the muscles around her old injury, or they could cramp and she could find it even more difficult to move for days afterward. Those days of hampered movement were never fun. So tending to her body had become second nature to Miri. Well, tending it or allowing herself to be tended.

"Good. And even if I did need a reason, I could always attribute the kiss as your reward for dutifully tending to the weak leg of your loving mate." She winked and grinned at him as she finished talking. Making light of her old injury had become second nature to Miri by now.

Ell didn't smile in return. He found it much more difficult to laugh at misfortune. And he was especially touchy when it came to her leg.

"Don't," was all he said. Ell could go silent suddenly or speak for long stretches of time in almost completely one-syllable words.

Miri sighed. "What, love?"

"You know what."

She tilted her head to the side and stared at him complacently. If he wanted to make an issue of her self-deprecating little joke, then he would need to actually discuss his own frustration.

He pursed his lips and shook his head slightly from side to side. "You know what I mean. I don't ever view you…your leg as a burden," he finished awkwardly. In stereotypical male fashion, he sometimes found it hard to express himself.

Miri laughed then, a light laugh, as she clasped his face between her hands. "I know, my love, I know."

"Do you?" The intensity in his eyes gave weight to his question.

She stared into his eyes and saw a depth of passion burning there that was reserved only for her. She saw a passion that *was* her. And there were moments when she felt like his passion might consume her. It was these moments when she fell in love with him all over again. Passion was one of the most inspiring of emotions. And her mate was full of it.

She nodded her head solemnly in answer, all teasing of Ell burnt away by the heat of his gaze.

"Good," he said firmly, kissing her with a welcome ferocity. He pulled back again and looked at her. "You're my balance, you know. You're never a hindrance. Never. You keep me sane, you make me whole. You're my balance," he repeated, as if even he wasn't quite sure what he meant by it, but said it anyway because it felt right.

"Who says I'm balanced?" she quipped breathlessly, a fire of her own awakening in her breast as her eyes saw the passion in his face and then trailed down his lean, toned chest.

She moved quickly and pulled him close in a tangle of limbs and an ache of desire. She wrapped her legs around him and melded her lips to his, feeling his pulse quicken in response to her body. They spent an unknown length of time lost in the kiss until they found themselves on the mossy ground without having had any intention of reaching it.

Ell pinned her beneath his hips and trailed his lips from her mouth to her jawline and down to her neck until finally he ran out of skin at her tunic. He paused only long enough to allow her the space to arch her back to enable him to remove her tunic before he was kissing her again, their bare bodies pressed closely together.

It was minutes. It was a lifetime. It was her life and it was glorious.

Miri pushed with her body, pressing it closer and closer to his. She pushed with her mind, her emotions. She pushed with the love she possessed. She wasn't even fully aware of what she was doing. It was instinct guiding her. Something primal, something deep within her told her to push herself into him. At varying times all summer long she had felt this same, strange impulse to meld herself into Ell. It wasn't possible, she didn't even know what her impulse meant, but she pushed herself, her consciousness, forward anyway.

Their bodies were joined and they reveled in the heat of the day matching the heat of their passion. Sweat trickled between them.

And she stretched. Miri stretched her mind out and pushed it towards Ell.

They rolled and suddenly she was on top of him. She bent herself close to kiss his lips and tasted the Lemonberries on his tongue. She smelled the musk of his scent. Her love felt huge, it felt immeasurable, and it felt like it needed to escape from her somehow, like energy transferring, like boiling steam bursting out of a pot.

Miri didn't know if it was possible for two souls to merge. But she pushed anyway, surrendering to her instincts and relinquishing thought. She yielded her very self to the passion and pleasure of the moment.

And then, in the moment that their romantic vigor was spent, it happened.

The air around and between them shook with a concussion so strong, it felt like a thunderclap—even though some part of her knew that no storm had ruptured the sky. The force of her consciousness forked and she was no longer aware of only herself.

For an instant, she was aware of them both. She was aware of him in a way she hadn't known was possible, in a way she had never experienced.

Chapter Two

Elliyar Wintermoon felt the air leave his lungs and he gasped for breath. The concussion of the air stunned him. Suddenly, it was as if there was more than one of her. As if she were in more places than one. One moment Miri was laying beneath him, and the next she was *in* him. With him in body, yet also in his head, his consciousness, his soul. He felt her love for him, and the way she saw all of his faults. He felt her acceptance of his bitter anger at the Departed, at the Humans, and the war in general as well as his feelings of disgust and betrayal by Dacunda and Arendahl. Yet she loved him, even more fiercely, in spite of it all. Because of it all. She loved his imperfections the way he loved hers. They had been intimate many times since their Joining, but this was different. It was much more potent than the sensation of physical intimacy

He felt disoriented, dizzy almost, even though the world didn't spin the way it would for a person who was light-headed. It was difficult to put into words what he was feeling.

Air rushed back into his lungs and he breathed shakily as the event passed. He swallowed, not sure what to say. What had happened? The awareness of her consciousness was gone, but the memory of it lingered. He looked into Miri's eyes and saw the same confusion he felt. Except she had a look of wonder on her face as well, as if she was experiencing something fantastic.

"What just happened?" Ell finally asked of her as Miri cupped both his cheeks with her hands.

"I do not know, love. But I think it is something wondrous."

Ell swallowed again, his throat dry. She was beautiful, his Miriyah, her cheeks flushed from the exertion of lovemaking. Her blond hair was wavy like his. Normally it was braided at the wings, with the braids pulled back and tied together, and speckled with wildflowers in a sort of woodland crown. But now it hung loosely and spilled out onto the mossy ground as she lay beneath him.

The northern elves, The Highest, were fair skinned and Miri was typical in that manner just as she was lean of frame. Yet she was dissimilar to the rest of her race in other ways. Their people, the Highest, tended to carry an air of elegance and immaculateness about them that she did not possess. No, she was beautiful in an earthy way. Perfectly imbalanced, with a nose that was just slightly too wide to ever be called refined. Her green eyes, normally full of alternating amounts of tranquility and mischief, were, at the moment, stunned and wide as they gazed back at him.

Ell pecked Miri's lips with a kiss and then rolled off onto his back to lie beside her. They lay in silence, both processing what had just happened before speaking further. Ell wasn't sure how he was feeling. Surprise and shock still dominated his emotions. He had not known it was even possible to share consciousness with someone like that. But another part of him was slightly uncomfortable. He loved Miri. She was the most important thing to him. Yet, there were parts of himself that he did not show even her. Emotions so often roiled within him and he did not always want to share them. He had felt Miri's acceptance of his faults during their moment of merged thought, and he loved her for it, but he was not sure he would want her to always have that access to the deepest nooks and crannies of his soul.

Miri grabbed his hand lightly, tenderly, but stayed silent. They lay there, quiet for no more than a few minutes, but it was enough time for Ell to collect himself. He gathered his shock and then pushed it aside. He had seen and experienced enough impossibilities in the last half-year that one more unforeseen occurrence would not be able to permanently unsettle him. Riding an Icari, discovering his abilities as a Water Caller, and to top it all off, hearing Silverfist's terrified admission that Ell's family was, in fact, alive had all been shocking. In comparison with those events, this merging of his consciousness with Miri, even for only the brief moment that it had occurred, was at least something he could wrap his mind around and accept. He convinced himself of that to shunt away the nagging fear and worry that tried to seep into his thoughts as yet another unexplained phenomenon presented itself in his life.

"Are you alright?" Miri asked tentatively. She could probably sense his shock and small worries. She was perceptive, especially with regards to him. They were Joined after all, united in the traditional Highest ceremony by Arendahl. Even though that had taken place a mere few months ago, it stood to reason that she would know him better than most.

He gathered his thoughts closely before responding. "Yes, Miri. I am fine. A bit startled is all." It sounded convincing. Hopefully she wouldn't pick up the level of uncertainty and discomfort that had accompanied the general wonder at feeling the depth of her love in such a tangible way. What did it all mean though? Ell couldn't shake the frequent reminder from Arendahl that actions had consequences. Both intended and unforeseen. Those consequences might be good, but they could also include negative results, as well. What would be the fallout from this latest unexplained occurrence?

"You're lying, my love." Ell heard the smile in her voice more than saw it. She wasn't angry, just letting him know that she knew he was hiding something.

Ell nodded his agreement. "I am fine. Truly. But…I just cannot help but feel nervous about something as foreign as what just happened. I have experienced enough shocks in recent times to last me a lifetime."

"Was it negative for you?" She spoke quietly, gently probing him for his experience of the event.

Ell answered just as carefully. It would not do to outright reject something that Miri had clearly enjoyed. He took care of her—body, heart, and soul. From her lame leg to her emotions.

"Of course it was wonderful," he murmured, turning his head to speak into her ear as she gazed at the sky. "Feeling you, your emotions and thoughts, was incredible."

"But…?" She trailed the question, waiting for his response.

"But, there are parts of myself I am not proud of. Emotions, fears, moments of pain and angst that I am not sure I would choose to show even you. Besides, there is something that worries me about what just happened, about its implications for our future. Call it my intuition or instincts for lack of a better or more apt description."

"But it wasn't all bad." Miri repeated his initial stance on the event, as if to reassure herself that he wasn't hurt or angry.

"No, of course not, love. Much of it was incredible, difficult to even describe with words." He did his best to soothe her worries. It was strange, she wasn't usually so preoccupied with this fear of rejection.

"Good," she responded. "Good. I would hate for you to feel like it was all bad, what just happened. Because I thought it was marvelous."

"Of course I do not. I would never think that," Ell replied. "Besides, who can say what just happened? Even if it were negative, it was neither of our faults."

They stayed silent again for a long minute. Ell tried to think what to say. He wasn't always the best at expressing himself. He wasn't sure if his comments were helping or hurting the moment.

"I'm not so sure." Miri's voice was faint.

"What?"

"I said I am not so sure it wasn't my fault. Or at least my doing," she amended nervously. She was more anxious than he could ever remember her being around him. Certainly, she had not seemed this nervous or worried in his presence since their Joining.

"What do you mean?" Ell prodded.

"I…" her voice faltered, then rose again. "I have been feeling this… impulse all summer. This urge. An urge to push my consciousness into yours. I don't always give in to it, but at other times, I do." She paused, turning her head to look at him and gauge his response to her statements.

"Today, I surrendered completely to the impulse to stretch myself into you," she said, staring into his eyes vulnerably. He could see the silent prayer in her eyes that he would understand whatever she had done, or thought she had done.

"Alright," he said finally. "So you gave in to this impulse, whatever it was."

"Yes, I did. And right after that it… happened."

There was logic to what she was saying. Ell had learned that most strange occurrences were precipitated by someone or something. Coincidences happened but they were not nearly as common as many people believed.

"So?"

"So, I did this." Miri answered, waving her hand back and forth between the two of them to symbolize whatever had just happened.

"And?" Ell prompted, feeling a misplaced sense of amusement that for once it was he trying to drag the words out of her and not the other way around.

"And I can tell you're unhappy with whatever just happened!" she burst out in frustration. Tears threatened to fall from her eyes.

Ell had fought in battles, faced dark creatures, and killed the elf who had betrayed his nation and doomed the people of Andalaya to wander nomadically, hunted and enslaved. He had faced all of that with stillness in his heart, without fear. But the sight of his mate in anguish was something his hardened heart could not abide.

He rolled up onto his elbow and looked down at her, tilting her jaw up with his free hand, so that she was forced to look him in the eye.

"Do I look unhappy?" He raised his eyebrows questioningly.

Miri didn't answer immediately, so he asked again.

"Do I?"

"No," she said in a small voice. "Not really."

"Not at all," he corrected firmly, and then kissed her soundly. Then, just for good measure, he lengthened the kiss until her breath raced. He tasted the sweetness of lily water on her tongue, and pressed his mouth to hers even more tightly in enjoyment.

After a long few minutes, Miri pushed him up and off of her slightly so that they could catch their breath. She giggled at his passionate exuberance.

"Again? Really? It's only been a few minutes."

Ell laughed with her and then shook his head. "No, you wore me out the last time." He flopped back onto his back in mock exhaustion and stuck his tongue out of his mouth jokingly. She laughed again, and the moment of levity seemed to breach whatever worry or crack had briefly formed between them.

"Later then," she said with a wink, and he grinned his agreement. He had known that he was completely in love with Miri before the ceremony. But, Joining with Miri had been even more fun than he could have possibly imagined. Life with her was bliss.

"We should probably head over to camp and see about the others." She emphasized camp to indicate that she meant the communal camp, rather than their private camp. The camp with Dacunda, with Arendahl and the others.

Ell's momentary mental description of the last few months as blissful was almost entirely related to his time with Miri. The rest of the summer had been rather bitter. His relationships with his uncle and his teacher had soured considerably. So much so that he avoided them as much as possible. As much as one could when a person traveled in the very company of the people he wished to avoid.

Ell sighed and stood up, pulling on his breeches and taking his tunic off the branch on which it had been airing out. He slipped it over his head and then extended a hand down to help up his mate. Miri stood and dressed as well, then they headed up the path, crossing the few hundred feet of wooded trail between their small private encampment and the group camp populated by his family.

Chapter Three

The camp looked exactly how Ell expected it would. His cousin Ryder was lounging against a log covered in moss and lichen with a handful of foraged nuts. Ryder ate all the time, more than anyone Ell had ever met, and he usually preferred a full meal that included some type of hunted game. However, he was more than willing to snack on whatever was at hand, which was often what could be gathered as the company traveled, usually nuts, fruits, berries, and various assortments of edible greens that grew in Legendwood. Ryder appeared lazy, his light brown hair pulled back behind his head in two braids as he lounged on the ground. But anyone who mistook his apparent indolence for ineptitude in action would be sorely mistaken. Along with his penchant for resting as often as possible, he was also one of the most fearsome warriors Ell had ever seen. Ryder wielded a long axe with not only clout, but a dexterity that most warriors could only muster with a dagger. The largest of Ell's family members, there were not many who could better guard your back than Ryder.

A few feet from Ryder stood Ell's sister, Valerihya, or Rihya as she was called. She was tossing multiple knives into the air simultaneously and catching them before quickly flinging them up again. Juggling blades was a favorite pastime of hers. Not only was she as fearless as anybody Ell had ever known, but she also had the shortest temper. She kept her hair shorter than his, covering the tipped ears she possessed like all of the Highest. Her hair was dyed green—how she managed to make it that color, Ell wasn't sure—and while one could argue that the color would help her blend into the forested environment in which they lived and fought, Ell knew that camouflage wasn't what his sister had intended when she dyed her hair. Rihya wanted flair to accompany her quick temper and fast hands, and the green hair met that purpose. Honestly, Ell thought it suited her well. Ell had never seen another of the Highest dye their hair, but the affectation made her stand out, and as his only immediate family, he was convinced that she deserved that prominence. Well, she the only family he knew. Somewhere to the south, there might be others of his family alive and enslaved. Ell felt a rush of anger at that thought, the way he always did when thinking of the lies of his uncle that had shaped his life, but he felt guilt for feeling angry. His uncle and cousins were the only family he had ever known. It was selfish of him to feel so angry and bitter towards his uncle. Wasn't it? Ell's thoughts and emotions had been mercurial all summer attempting to reconcile his feelings about his uncle.

The only other people in camp were the wizened old elf Arendahl, Ell's teacher and mentor, and the young lad Artorious. Arendahl was instructing the ten-year-old how to properly throw a knife. The stump they were using for practice was riddled with chips and holes, accompanying growth that was trying to overcome it. His uncle, Dacunda, and Ell's oldest cousin, Dahranian, were not in camp.

"The lovebirds emerge from their blissful cocoon," Ryder quipped lightly, as he saw Ell and Miri approaching.

Rihya snickered at the comment. The joke at his and Miri's expense might have bothered Ell a few months ago, but now that he was Joined, it seemed unnecessary to dispute his attachment to Miri. They were mated for life. Of course they would often be together. As such, he merely grinned good-naturedly at his cousin and clapped him on the shoulder. Perhaps some of Miri's tranquil qualities were rubbing off on him. Ell had always been considered rash by his family, but around Dacunda and Arendahl he was even more volatile than usual, even with Miri's mitigating effect on him.

He snatched up a few of the nuts from Ryder's hand and popped some into his mouth nonchalantly before flicking the rest at his still chuckling sister.

"Robbing an elf of his sustenance is tantamount to murder," Ryder protested melodramatically at Ell's theft.

"I don't think anyone is capable of denying your mouth food, Ry," Ell joked back amiably.

"True," his lean and powerful cousin admitted. "I count it as one of my best qualities."

"For you, maybe, but not for the traveling companions you deprive of provisions," Rihya interjected, never one to miss the opportunity for a jab at one of her male family members. "That is why Dacunda and Dahranian must hunt all the time, to fill your belly." So that's where Ell's uncle and eldest cousin were. Of course Dahranian would be doing something useful. Ell loved his cousin dearly, but there was no denying that Dahranian took responsibility seriously—almost to a fault. He resembled his father in more than appearance that way.

Rihya eyed Ell dangerously, switching her object of attack. "And you, my brother, should be wary of to whom you are casting food." She picked up one of the fallen nuts, tossed it up in the air, and then in one sweeping motion whipped one of her knives upward and across in a diagonal to meet the falling nut, just in time to slice it in two. It was not particularly difficult, Ell was sure he could master that aim and skill with some practice, but nevertheless, it was a demonstration of her adept blade work.

He laughed wryly. "Give over, Rihya, I've got enough scars from you already, I do not need any more."

"Then don't annoy me, Ell," she said, rather pointedly. Ell had felt the nick of her steel on more than one occasion. His sister and her temper had a way of lashing out with the edge of her blades when she was particularly vexed or unhappy. Not enough to cause serious harm—she was too precise for that—but enough to warn whoever was harassing her at the moment that he had better stop what he was doing. She was touchy, his sister.

Ell raised his hands and backed away slowly in mock fear of his sister. She just sniffed, clearly unimpressed with his disregard of her pointed display of knife work.

"I thought you would have tamed him by now," Rihya called towards Miri. "He needs to be taught some manners."

In typical older sister fashion, Rihya was perennially convinced that he was in need of some lesson. Although if Ell was any judge on the matter, cutting anyone who crossed you was far greater grounds for dispute and altercation. Sometimes he thought she was in much greater need of education than he.

Miri laughed throatily. "Not tamed yet. Not by a long shot. Though not for lack of trying. In fact, I was just trying." She smiled conspiratorially at Rihya until Rihya's sly smirk made a blush grow on her cheeks. Ell raised his eyebrows at his mate. She was growing bolder by the day. He liked it. She constantly surprised Ell, part of what made their Joining so great.

However, if they were going to begin discussing what he thought they might, then he wanted to be elsewhere. Rihya and Miri were opposites in almost every way. Rihya was mercurial quicksilver to Miri's calm. His sister was a waterfall to Miri's tranquil river. But they had grown increasingly close during these summer months and talked about nearly everything, even things that involved him. Ell cleared his throat awkwardly and edged away from the conversation.

Ryder guffawed through a mouthful of food as he saw Ell begin to slide away. "Wise choice, Cousin." Ell pursed his lips wryly and nodded his agreement as Rihya and Miri put their heads together and began to talk quietly, casting frequent looks in his direction.

The only other place to go in camp would force him to interact with the very person he would least like to. But then again, Ell did need his advice, so perhaps he should face his anger. At least for now. Anything to get away from the giggles emanating from the two females.

Ell approached Arendahl and Art slowly, unsure of what to say. When his feet brought him beside the oldest and youngest elf in their party, he paused and stayed silent, watching the little elf cast the knife end over end to stick into the stump. Art threw his hands up in triumph as he succeeded in his task.

"I need your advice." Ell finally broke the silence lamely, casting his comment in Arendahl's direction.

Without directly acknowledging Ell, Arendahl muttered some directions to the boy, and Art happily went off to a new corner of their camp with a new target in line for his throwing practice.

Only then did Arendahl swing his gaze to Ell. "So we're talking now?" The words were gruff, almost stilted, biting of his sentences in the way the old elf always spoke, like someone who'd been alone for so long he was unaccustomed to conversing.

"Of course we are," Ell responded. "We have always been speaking."

"Hardly."

"What do you mean?"

The old elf slammed his granite gaze into Ell's eyes, somehow making simple visual contact feel physically forceful. "I mean, you haven't said more than two words to me outside of training, boy. All summer, like this." Arendahl referred to anyone younger than Dacunda as 'boy'.

Now it was Ell's turn to feel the frustrations of the past months boil over. "What did you expect? You lied to me, manipulated me. Both of you."

"Lied to you? No. Withheld information. Yes."

Ell puckered his mouth into a sour grimace. "Don't mince words with me. Lying by omission is still lying. And besides, Dacunda did lie to me outright."

"Heh, well then perhaps you should be having this conversation with him."

"Maybe I will." Ell responded belligerently. All summer, he had attempted to keep the peace in his small family by avoiding interactions with Arendahl and especially with his uncle.

"Stupid, boy. You are too old to be acting this foolishly." Arendahl spat the words out so violently, it was as if they actually tasted bad. "We, *he*, kept you safe by lying, Elliyar. If he had told you before that your family might still be alive, you would have long since run off to the south, to Dor Khabor"— Arendahl used the ancient name for the southern port capital of Dark Harbor— "and you would have been killed or worse, ended up as a slave." He almost shook with anger, his lank grey hair clinging to the sides of his thin face.

Ell had no counter to that argument, but still responded bitterly with one final jab. "Still, he should have told me. I had to find out the truth from my enemy. It's my life, my family, and he had no right." He finished a bit petulantly, lacking the bite he desired.

Instead of responding gruffly with tough advice like usual, the old elf switched tactics. His voice softened. "It was his family too, boy. His first. Remember that next time you are feeling so very righteous and slighted."

Arendahl cleared his throat and switched tacks again. "So," he said brusquely, "what do you need to speak with me about? Come on then, boy, don't waste my time."

Ell gathered his thoughts ignoring his elder's impatience. Weren't old people supposed to become more patient as they aged? Arendahl was the oldest member of the Highest, that he had ever met, and the most impatient. However, Ell would not be rushed during this conversation.

"Something happened. Something strange," Ell began slowly.

"Well…?" Arendahl prompted, indicating his desire for Ell to elaborate.

"It happened earlier, while Miri and I were…being intimate," he tried to force down the blush that grew in his cheeks from discussing this with his mentor.

"Ha!" The old elf barked a laugh as he wrongly predicated in which direction the conversation was going.

"No!" Ell exclaimed immediately, heading off any such questions that might arise from that line of thought. "Nothing like that. Everything is fine between us. It was something else entirely, and it just happened to occur at the same time as the other thing."

Arendahl nodded knowingly, but the old elf's impatience had worn too thin. "Out with it, boy."

Ell proceeded to describe what had happened, the merging of his and Miri's consciousness, the way he had felt her emotions and thoughts and she, his. And how it had only lasted a moment before fading and leaving him breathless, disoriented.

He concluded with an uneasy question. "What happened?"

Arendahl's eyebrows had risen during Ell's description of the event. "Well, well, well. That hasn't happened in centuries. It appears the girl is full of surprises."

"So you know what it was, what happened?" It was Ell's turn to be impatient.

"Sounds like she Grafted you, lad. Heh, she is full of surprises, indeed!"

Grafted. What was that? Ell had never even heard of it before. "It wasn't bad, but it wasn't exactly comfortable either," Ell said, trying to verbally process his way through the event. "I didn't ask her to do it, to Graft me."

Arendahl shook his head and rolled his eyes at Ell. "Did you think she was just going to only do everything you ever said, boy?"

Ell ignored that comment and pressed for more information. "What does it mean, this Grafting?"

The old elf paused to think. Ell could tell he was organizing his thoughts. If he needed to do that, a miniature lesson would be at hand. After a few moments of contemplation, the old elf began. "Grafting is an ancient practice, or talent, if you will. She has folded a part of her consciousness into yours. She has forged it in." Ell grew uneasy. For all the wonder of the moment, his intuition had been right. It was going to cause problems. "She will be able to experience important moments or events in your life."

"Can I do it? Or did I help create this... connection somehow, with my powers, I mean?" Ell interjected.

Arendahl snorted. "Don't try and claim credit for this one, boy. No, to Graft your consciousness into another's takes an incredible force of will. A force of love. You had no part in it."

"Tell me more. This 'forging' of our consciousness sounds almost violent," he said uneasily.

"It is, boy. Did you think Miri was all willow and no oak? Love is forceful at times. Did you think love was all butterflies and flowers? It can be painful and even violent. And Miri loves as fiercely and as fearlessly as you've ever fought in battle."

"Well...is it good?" Ell asked, searching to understand Grafting, to label it somehow, to fit it neatly inside a box somewhere.

"Good?" The old elf tilted his head and narrowed his eyes. "It can be useful.

Ell's uneasiness grew. "What aren't you telling me?"

Arendahl sighed, seeming to truly regret what he was about to say. Ell tensed.

"She will sense, even see through your eyes, some of the more important events in your life. Not all of those moments will be good or happy ones." The old elf pointedly eyed the dueling daggers that Ell had strapped to his outer thighs.

Terror clenched Ell's belly as he realized what Arendahl meant. Important moments. Warriors faced pain and death. Ell thought of the truth of the three realities. The First Reality was this world, the physical world in which they fought and labored, loved and died. The Third Reality, where his people went after they transitioned onward from this existence. And then the Second Reality, somewhere in between—a difficult reality to understand, where conflicting and coexisting truths such as good and evil, chaos and fortune, collided and intertwined. Every warrior knew that eventually he would depart this reality, the First Reality for the next—the Third Reality. Miri would likely be exposed to his final moments, his death. More than anything, he did not wish for her to suffer that.

"Can I make it go away?" he asked desperately. "Can I sever this connection? I saw her emotions too, so perhaps it is a two-way link. Perhaps you are wrong, Arendahl, maybe I have more control than you think."

Arendahl shook his head sadly. "I suspect you experienced her emotions and thoughts only this first time because it was the moment of forging, the initial instant of Grafting. From here on out, legend says you will not experience that again. It will only be the one who Grafted the other that will be privy to seeing into the other's head—feel what they are feeling, and see what they are seeing." Arendahl put a hand comfortingly on Ell's shoulder. "I am truly sorry, Elliyar. There is nothing you can do. What is done is done."

Ell shrugged his shoulders trying to make it appear as if it was of no concern, but he knew he wasn't fooling is old mentor. He needed time to think. Time alone.

Perhaps a hunt would clear his thoughts.

He thanked Arendahl and before anyone else could speak to him, he left the camp. He would return to his small camp with Miri, grab his bow and be off on the hunt to think, and to just be. Some time to clear his thoughts would serve him well.

Chapter Four

Ell's black yew bow and Dreampine arrows felt good in his hands. He pulled an arrow from the quiver over his shoulder and fit it to the string as he sighted his prey. Dark arrows. Black arrows. Their hue was normal to Ell. He was a warrior who fought from the shadows. The northern elves of Andalaya were scattered to the four winds, too disorganized to field an army, with no one to lead them even if they could. The few who still fought for Andalaya did so with guerilla tactics. The majority of Ell's nearly two decades of life had been spent in a series of ambushes. He and his family fought as a unit. They ambushed the humans to the east with their cut-and-run tactics, they tracked and followed small parties of Departed slavers that had come up from the south, and they picked them off in small, manageable increments.

Ell had cut his teeth on combat. However, until the battle at Little Vale, three months gone, Ell had never truly experienced a conflict on a larger scale than a handful of dead at a time. He and his family had dug in with the villagers and defended the earthen bulwark erected at his uncle's direction. He remembered that day in flashes. So many had been lost. Silverfist had come with many bands of slavers, a small horde compared to those of the Highest who fought for their lives and freedom. But Silverfist was dead, killed by Ell had killed him in a contest of arms and will, yet the repercussions of his actions would resonate onward through time. Silverfist had betrayed Andalaya, turned over the capital city Verdantihya and the Source to the humans, and that had been the doom of Ell's people. It had been before his time, but he still felt the bitterness, the sore ache in his throat all the Highest felt at the thought of all his people dead and captured. The fabled walls of Verdantihya brought low, the river of Source Water released by Silverfist's traitorous actions to burst the city gates open from the inside.

Ell focused on the shot ahead. Now was not the time to agonize about what could not be changed. He fought with black arrows, from the shadows, unlike his forefathers, the Andalayan heroes of old who had stood proudly shoulder-to-shoulder with their brothers in arms defying their enemies to their face. That life, those battle tactics, were not for Ell. He would not survive long if he did not adapt to the current circumstances.

He drew the black Dreampine arrow back to his ear as he sighted the stag he had been tracking since he left camp. Ell breathed in and held the air for a moment to stabilize. Hunting was a good distraction. It allowed the body to work and the mind to fall into the mundane details of tracking, sighting, drawing, breathing, and loosing.

Ell exhaled slowly and prepared to loose his arrow. A flicker of movement at the corner of his left eye caught his attention. It was just the barest hint of motion, but his instincts hardened to a knife's edge as he appraised his surroundings with his peripheral vision. Ell stayed absolutely still, his only movement the shifting of his eyes as they surveyed the scene.

Once Ell had appraised his surroundings, he swung his bow and arrow swiftly and smoothly to the left and loosed his arrow all in one motion. The stag, startled by his sudden movement, burst into flight and disappeared into the underbrush, scaring a few quail into flight. But Ell's arrow flew true and found an even more apt prey as, with astounding force, it pinned a Ghoul to one of the giant Evergrow trees that were scattered throughout Andalaya and Legendwood.

Filthy creatures. Ell spat in the dead Ghoul's direction. He hated that they were filtering out of the northern marches, out of the Broken Tree Range, and down into Andalaya proper. They were vile, opportunistic hunters who lived and hunted alone, eating whatever they could, even each other. But what could he do other than this? He killed them when he could. Just like he did with the humans. Just like he did with his people's dark kin to the south. Fighting a war on two fronts wasn't possible. And yet fighting on only one front wasn't even an option. The plight of Andalaya, once great and beautiful, now plagued on all sides by greedy invaders, ancient enmities, and the brutish nature of the dark creatures from the First Days that were growing in number.

Ell walked forward and wrenched his arrow from the chest of the Ghoul and warm black blood gushed forth. The Ghoul had a typically slender body and was only somewhat shorter than Ell. The creature's light frame stayed brown in death, matching the tree against which it was slumped, but Ell knew that Ghouls were experts in camouflage had the ability to adjust their skin tone and appearance to match almost any surrounding. They were opportunistic hunters, but very deadly. He used the tip of his arrow to flip over the spindly-fingered hand and gaze at its palm. Idle curiosity really. The palm and fingers were covered with suctions and stingers. Not only would the suctions allow the Ghoul to scale nearly anything with ease, but they also enabled the Ghoul to seize its prey with an almost unshakeable grip. The stingers delivered a dose of toxin that could kill anyone in minutes. Unless you had enough Source Water to heal yourself. But the amount of Source Water that would take would be immense. A person would only underestimate the peril a Ghoul posed at their own folly. Ell himself had nearly fallen prey to the creatures on a number of occasions. Disgusted, Ell let the creature's hand fall back to its body. The mouth was slack in death, exposing its mismatched teeth, some sharp some not. Ell shook his head and turned away. It was a good kill. Killing the dark creatures that plagued Andalaya was always good. Still, he wished the buck hadn't escaped. Ryder ate through their provisions the way a flash flood flushed out a ravine. The extra meat would have been welcome.

He should probably head back to camp. The others might grow worried if he was too long out on his own. Not that they doubted his capabilities as a fighter. He was a Water Caller after all, one of the storied warriors from the First Days returned, whose powers were far beyond that of a normal elf. But these were dangerous times and Ell was having difficulty using those powers.

The relief and distraction Ell had felt from the effortless and thoughtless task of hunting evaporated and all the worries of the summer crashed in again. His abilities were growing, but Water Calling was not easy and despite his breakthrough at the battle for Little Vale, his Water Calling abilities often eluded him when he needed them most.

Ell wiped the tip of his arrow clean of the Ghoul's black blood and slipped it back in his quiver. Perhaps he would get lucky and spot a hare to bring down on the way back to the others.

The area in which he had been hunting was full of tall Evergrow trees, pines and firs, but there was also a smattering of alders, maples, cedars and others, as Legendwood spread south and met the Lower Forest. This portion of the woods had underbrush but there were also open spaces. Moss and lichen clung to tree trunks and limbs, even the stones along the forest floor. This late in summer, the foliage was beginning to change and his green surroundings were speckled by some yellow and brown leaves.

An oak tree appeared in front of Ell as he walked lightly back towards camp. Its roots tangled the ground around its thick trunk. Knots and holes patterned its bark and the limbs spread out around it in a tangle of wood. An odd looking tree, out of place it seemed. It was more common to see this type of oak further to the south.

Ell strode on, past, when, to his surprise, one of the roots lifted out of the ground to wrap around his ankle and one root after another freed itself from the dry summer dirt to reach towards him.

Ell tried to kick his way free of the root grabbing his ankle. What was happening? Trees didn't do this! Two knots on the tree trunk flicked open and red holes burned in front of Ell.

This wasn't a tree at all. Furiously, Ell drew and slashed with one of his two dueling daggers. The force of the blow was enough to sever the root grasping his leg, and the tree—the thing—let out an agonized screech of anger. The sound curdled Ell's blood.

He stepped back and set himself to defend. The tree began shifting and undulating in strange fashion before a creature eventually separated itself from the trunk of the tree against which it had been pressed. Only once it was distinctly separate from the tree, Ell's keen senses could discern its nature. The flaming, red-orange eyes were a dead giveaway. This creature was dangerous. Like the flying Icari, the Ghouls, and Stone Ogre Ell had faced with Arendahl in the northern Marches, the red eyes were an indicator of an ancient evil. This darkness was the first darkness, the evil of the First Days reawakening now in greater measure than in centuries, and it was Ell's duty to prevent that from happening. If he could. If, was a big question. The creature wasn't huge. It couldn't be more than a few inches taller than Ell, but as it finished separating itself from the tree behind it, and moved forward, Ell noticed multiple arms attached to it, the way a tree had many branches. It hulked menacingly. It looked like a dwarfed version of the oak tree behind it, all gnarled nobs and bulging joints, surrounding a trunk-thick core of body. The eyes flickered like angry flames as it attacked.

The creature swung one of its many arms at Ell and he dodged lithely back out of its range. He pulled his second dueling dagger, the one recovered off of the body of Silverfist after the traitor's death, and prepared to fight.

The blows the creature rained down on Ell weren't particularly fast individually, but there were too many arms swinging oaky fists at him to dodge them all. An upswing of one dueling dagger sheared off a few wood-like fingers of one of the creature's hands, and a slash to the torso scored the barky body with a long gash that oozed black blood like sap. But a hammer-like hand smashed Ell to the ground. He recovered quickly and popped back to his feet to attack again, but regardless of his attacks, it was still like trying to fight a small tree. The blows that Ell landed were merely chipping away at the tough bark. He fought with precision and pace and power, but he seemed to inflict minimal damage to the creature. The entire time it pressed the fight, advancing on him relentlessly, a desire to kill burning in its eyes.

Ell knew what he had to do. There was a well of power within him, a power he could tap into, the likes of which had been used by the heroes of old who also fought this ancient evil. As he fought, he split his focus, a dangerous but necessary move. One part of his mind, a small part, focused on maintaining his defense. Cut, move, duck, slash. Dance in and dance out of range. It was more instinctive muscle memory than anything else. The other part of his brain sought to tap his abilities. He was a Water Caller, capable of extraordinary feats. He could draw power from the life source of the land, from Andalaya, from the water that could be found in anything and everything. Ell reached his consciousness out and sought to find the water around him. He pushed out with his mind, searching, looking for the connection to the world around him that would allow him the strength to defeat this foe.

Slash. Shear off a wooden hand. Cut. Duck. He went through the fighting motions by rote, his mind far more concentrated on the task of tapping his power. He felt a oneness with the land begin to grow. He was a Water Caller. It wasn't something he had to try to be, to try to earn. He already was one. It was in his blood, his lineage, his heritage from millennia past. Ell felt the power well up within him. He felt the water in the trees, the moisture in the air, ripe for drawing upon. He could sense his abilities right below the surface waiting to be tapped. It was time. He would teach this beast a lesson.

Just as Ell was a finger's width from tapping his powers, a rough fist collided with his face. His focus, his concentration, all of Ell's efforts to reach his powers exploded in a moment of pain and near unconsciousness.

Little details appeared to him in an odd moment of clarity before darkness threatened to overtake him. Details like leaves. The creature resembled a tree but bore no leaves. It was like it only reflected the dead aspect of a tree. Pain. It flickered sharp and red across his vision. His face felt like bloody, cracking ice ready to shatter into a thousand pieces. Details. His cheekbone was likely cracked, maybe worse. These tiny thoughts flicked randomly through his thoughts before he shook himself into a semblance of an alert state.

The tree beast grabbed his limp body and lifted it towards a jagged hole in what appeared to be its face. *Mouth*, Ell thought, fighting for consciousness. The mouth, now gaping in a horrendous array of blunt and blackened teeth, had been impossible to discern before it was opened.

Ell still clung to his dueling daggers. They had been crafted with an ancient skill, long forgotten, forged from one blade and then split into two daggers at the last possible moment in the forging process, lending them an unexplained affinity for one another. Alone, the blades were much like any other. But used together their affinity created an energy of sorts, and the blades would move just a hint faster for its user, lending that warrior an edge in battle. Ell's pair had been passed down his family for generations, and though he was too groggy to try and reach for his Water Calling abilities again, the strange power of his family's dueling daggers, the energy and speed they lent to their user, might be enough of an advantage to save him.

The creature grasped Ell with a few of its many arms and Ell felt the wood-like hands send splinters into his skin and catch on his clothes. In front of the opened mouth, Ell knew he had one moment's chance for a burst of energy and speed to free himself and incapacitate the creature long enough to escape.

The eyes. They were the weakness. The rest of the tree beast's body was hard as old aged wood. But those flaming red eyes had to be vulnerable. It might think that he was limp and finished, but his dueling daggers would be enough to abuse it of that notion. They had to be. Ell prayed that they would.

The beast brought him closer and as the beast widened its mouth to take a huge and fatal bite from Ell's body, Ell spent the last of his energy. In a burst of speed, he stabbed forward with the two daggers, the blades moving in a supernaturally quick arch of silver to plunge into the eyes of the dark tree creature simultaneously. An inhuman wail of pain and fury sent shivers down Ell's spine. The beast wrenched its head away from Ell's blades, tearing the bark of flesh around its sockets even further, causing black blood to fountain onto Ell as it did so. It flung him away angrily. Ell cartwheeled head over foot until he impacted with a tree at his back. It knocked the air from his lungs and as he fell and his head hit a stone on the ground, gashing his forehead. Blood coursed into his eyes, blinding him. The only respite to his pain and blindness was the sound of the angry, injured beast as it thrashed and crashed its way through the woods away from him.

He supposed the fight was a draw. Ell had taken its sight and he was near blinded with the blood gushing into his eyes from the wound on his brow. He pushed himself unsteadily to his feet and sheathed his daggers by feel instead of sight. It was lucky that he had drawn and replaced his weapons so many times that sheathing them was second nature to him, a muscle memory that his body could do reflexively without even the slightest bit of real thought required.

Ell stumbled blindly, trying to wipe the blood from his eyes without much success. He groggily tried to set his course for home, but only made it a few feet before true blackness enfolded his mind and he collapsed in an unconscious heap at the foot of an enormous Evergrow tree.

Chapter Five

Miri was sitting with her back to a log, chatting idly with Ryder. Sometimes, it was a relief to spend time with Ell's large cousin. Ryder was the most lighthearted of the entire company, and his levity provided a necessary balance to the serious nature of his relatives. Ell had told Miri of his past, that he and his family had spent their entire lives fighting. The battle for Little Vale might have been an uncommonly large conflict for them, but the general notion of it wasn't foreign to them the way it was to her. She was not like them. She did not live for battles. If anything, she lived for laughter and the way a burbling brook promised a cool drink on a hot summer's day. Miri had limitations. There was no denying that fact. Her leg inhibited what she could do. Growing up, her priorities had adapted to suit her body. Learning to fight simply hadn't seemed realistic and so Miri had steered as far from of weapons as possible. Oh, sure, she could have learned to hold a bow and throw a knife with relative accuracy and skill. But a leg was more important in even those actions than one might think. Solidity and balance were crucial to success in war, and she was sorely lacking in both. It wasn't to say that she couldn't have achieved some minimal measure of success or mastery of those more stationary methods of protection, it was just that she hadn't wanted to.

She was the opposite of Ell and his family. She loved them, they were her family now, but they focused on things in which she had little interest. Her interests had diverged long ago into the pursuit of simple pleasures. The sun on her face, a breeze that stirred the birds to singing. Those were the activities in which she found the joy that replaced the feeling of running gracefully and with power. Elves were, as a rule, physically perfectly formed in many ways, and Miri was one of the few who was not. Her avoidance of weaponry and all that it required was less a matter of her distaste for battles and more of something else. If she was truly honest with herself, the avoidance of such things as hunting and fighting was to avoid being reminded of her own physical shortcomings. She put on a brave front. And she had lived with her injury for so long that it had become a part of her, but she had also internalized her coping mechanisms.

Ell's family practically breathed battle and all that it entailed. By necessity, of course. Yet it affected their everyday actions. Always training, always preparing, honing their skills for the next battle. Always being useful or productive.

Rihya was the quintessential example. The diminutive elf stood on one edge of camp throwing her knives with deadly aim at a tree some twenty feet away. She did it every day. She was fiery in her temper and her responses to insults and she made sure that she had the skills necessary to back up that quicksilver nature.

Dacunda and Dahranian, were both tall and lean with their light brown hair pulled into a long braid down their backs. They sat together, cleaning their kill from the latest hunting trip. Their brown eyes flicked back and forth as they talked and worked. They rarely smiled, not that they unhappy people, they were just sobered by their constant exposure to war, death, and pain.

Even Arendahl, had his moments of levity, but his jokes were more often than not at the expense of another. He was not unkind. He was a mountain, weathered and beaten down by countless storms and quakes. The result of a lifetime spent killing creatures such as Ghouls had left him with little humor other than the fatalistic kind. Dacunda and Dahranian seemed like they were in a competition to see who could be the most serious.

Ryder was thus often a welcome conversational relief. They were currently having a very important discussion about which meat was, for one reason or another, the happiest.

"Rabbit or hare is my favorite animal to eat because they seem to me to be the happiest of meats," Ryder concluded with a wink and a smile. She was never sure when he was joking or being straightforward.

She laughed. "Ryder, I cannot fathom how you make that assumption."

"Well, hares are always hopping about. It just seems like a happier manner of travel. I mean, please Miri, you try hopping all day and see if you can contain your laughter."

She shook her head and smiled fondly, rolling her eyes the way her new cousin Ryder often made her do. "Fine, Ry. They are the happiest of meats."

Ryder nodded decisively, happy at his success at proving his very important point.

Suddenly, Miri's vision clouded, and her vision filled with flaming red eyes, ugly and evil, bent on her destruction, until blackness and the sickening feeling of the world slipping slowly out of existence replaced them.

"Miri!" Ryder was yelling her name and shaking her. She lay slumped over onto the ground. Miri felt disoriented and confused. Had she fainted? What had just happened?

The other members of their party were on the alert now from Ryder's worried cries. Dacunda, ever the protector, was across the distance and at her side in a heartbeat. He looked into her eyes and felt her pulse and forehead. He lifted and moved her arms, checking for what? Hidden injuries perhaps? For something that might have caused her to lose consciousness? Had she really lost consciousness? Something about the whole experience had felt immediate and personal yet somehow experienced from a distance. It was altogether strange.

Then Arendahl was there, aged and knowledgeable. He checked her over the same way Ell's uncle had, only he asked questions. "What happened?"

"I don't know," Miri answered truthfully.

"Try and walk me through what you were feeling before you fainted." The old elf paused. "Walk me through what you…saw."

From the way he asked, Miri could tell that Arendahl had some idea of what had caused her collapse.

She pulled herself together and shook off the latest pair of worried hands coming to check on her—Rihya's, feeling protective over her new little sister, not believing that anyone could do anything as well as she—and finally freed herself from the worried attentions by pointedly placing her focus on Arendahl and his question. "I was just talking with Ryder. About nothing really, just silly topics, when all of a sudden my vision clouded. Then…it was confusing. It was as if two red eyes filled up my entire vision. It was like I couldn't see anything else. And then there was blackness."

"You mean, then you fainted?" Arendahl questioned shrewdly.

Miri paused. "Not exactly. It was like I sensed the blackness, the unconsciousness from far away, before I actually experienced it myself." She put her hands on her head. "It sounds crazy, I know."

Arendahl narrowed his eyes as he looked at her. "Not crazy at all, girl. Heh. This is going to be complicated if you faint every time he gets injured." The old elf muttered the last sentence to himself so quietly Miri wasn't sure she had heard him correctly.

But some of what he said registered. "Hurt? Are you talking about Ell?" Fear replaced her confusion.

"Peace, Miri. Be still and rest a moment." Arendahl put a hand on her shoulder as she fought frantically to rise. When she wouldn't be still, the old elf shook his head in annoyance and forced her back to her sitting position with an iron grip. "I said be still, girl. You need a moment, so take one." Sometimes, Miri was astounded at how strong the old elf was. But then again, he was the only Water Caller other than Ell. An elf with the power to defeat a band of foes all by himself. Of course he would be strong.

She acquiesced and sat. She focused on her breathing. In, out. In, out. Ell would be fine. He had to be.

"What happened to her?" Dacunda asked Arendahl.

"No time for explanations. Time to find the boy." The old elf brushed aside Dacunda's question without a second thought, his stilted manner of interaction so common now that Miri almost didn't notice it.

"Ell?" Dahranian, the eldest of the cousins, asked.

"What other boy is not here? Honestly, sometimes youths can be so dense." Arendahl shook his head and started along the trail towards Miri and Ell's camp without another word. The rest of them picked up weapons and followed. Everyone but Miri of course. She walked along with them, empty-handed, fear and worry gnawing at her gut as they passed her small tent and followed the almost unperceivable trail Ell had left as he went to hunt.

They didn't have to go far. In a clearing not more than a few short minutes' hike through the woods, they saw a Ghoul dead at the foot of a tree, its black blood crusted and dried around the wound in its chest. They found Ell in the same clearing, face down in the dirt, blood from two wounds to his head pooling under his face. The blood mixed with the dry dirt to create a paste of red-brown mud that still clung to his face when Dacunda and Dahranian lifted him from the ground.

Miri's gut clenched. He couldn't be dead. He couldn't. She kept repeating that over and over to herself, an inner mantra to soothe her frayed nerves. Rihya picked up Ell's fallen weapons—the black yew bow he used, his black Dreampine arrows, and the two dueling daggers he carried on his body at all times. The dueling daggers were his favored method of combat, and it looked like he had used them since they were covered in dark, inky blood. A chill ran through her body. He had faced something other than a Ghoul here. Something that seemed to have gotten the best of him. Not many creatures could outmatch her mate. Only those dark beasts of old, reawakened after having disappeared for centuries might possibly be able to best him. He had faced down Ghouls aplenty, ridden an Icari to save her from the Departed slavers who had held her atop a Pillar—the only northern elf to ever accomplish such a feat—and defeated Silverfist, the most feared traitor of all time. What had he faced here that had left him in such a wounded mess?

Arendahl surveyed the scene. Miri watched his eyes glance from the dead Ghoul, to the blood soaked ground, to what appeared to be a swath of crushed or uprooted underbrush leading away from the clearing.

"He didn't kill it," Arendahl said quietly, thinking out loud. There was no use trying to get him to explain himself until he was done following the maze of his thoughts to its logical conclusion.

Dacunda spoke up. "Come, let us return to camp." Ell's uncle snapped his fingers under Miri's still stunned gaze. "Miri, are you alright?"

Miri shook her head slightly to clear her mind. What was wrong with her? She had seen him wounded before. He had been near death after slaying Silverfist, poisoned by the traitor's poison-ridged metal fist. Arendahl had used his powers as a Water Caller to coax Ell into healing. Miri had tended him until he had recovered fully enough for them to be Joined. Why was she so shaken now? It must be because of the events earlier. That strange merging while she and Ell had been laying together in the privacy of their camp. That was still unexplained to her. Did it have something to do with what she had seen before passing out? Arendahl seemed to know more than he had told her. She would have to find out soon. Determination grew in her breast. She would be told what there was to know about this—whatever this was. Maybe it would help her keep Ell safe in the future.

Miri watched Dahranian hold a flask to Ell's lips, attempting to pour a trickle of Source water into his limp mouth. Dahranian had passed his hold of Ell over to Ryder so that he could use both hands to open Ell's mouth to receive the healing liquid and coax his throat into swallowing.

Source water was the supernaturally potent water able to heal even the direst of wounds if the user had enough quantity at their disposal. The Source was the lifeblood of the land, the heart and soul of Andalaya. It was the raging spring, located in the ruined capital of Verdantihya, from which all major rivers in the land were birthed. The water Dahranian was forcing Ell to drink would be enough to heal him. It had to be.

Arendahl was still surveying the clearing, light from the sky above dappling through the canopy to pattern his face. He was gazing off into the woods along the path of whatever beast had thrashed its way through the undergrowth.

"Arendahl." Dacunda said. "Elder!" Ell's uncle insisted respectfully, but forcefully. "We must get my nephew back to camp and tend to him properly."

Arendahl looked at the younger elf and nodded silently. Ryder and Dacunda carried Ell's limp form, behind Dahranian who walked with one hand on the sword that was strapped to his back. Miri could tell that Ell's cousin was coiled and ready to spring into action should whatever had attacked Ell return. Rihya carried her brother's weapons and kept close guard to Miri as they walked, while Arendahl brought up the rear.

"He will be fine," Rihya said comfortingly. "He has taken worse than this before and been ready to fight the next day. He is strong, my little brother." A note of pride crept into her voice.

Miri nodded, still finding it hard to locate her voice. She was more shaken than usual after the myriad of strange events of the day, especially it's culmination with the discovery of Ell's wounded body.

"He will be," Rihya reassured her steadfastly.

"Hurry," Arendahl said behind them. "We should make haste."

Rihya narrowed her eyes at the way the old elf spoke. Miri noticed there was something strange in his demeanor, almost as if he were on edge. If she didn't know any better, Miri would have said that Arendahl was afraid. But of course that was silly. The old elf was not afraid of anything. He had spent nearly his entire life in the northern reaches of Andalaya, facing the worst kind of creatures imaginable. Nothing could shake him. Yet the odd look about his eyes remained. And Miri saw that Rihya cast frequent worried glances at him.

The trip back to camp took slightly longer than the way there because they were carrying an unconscious member of their party, but it was still over in no time. Ryder and Dacunda set Ell down on soft grass in the camp and Arendahl knelt to check him more thoroughly than he had before.

"Hmm. Yes," the old elf muttered to himself, as his hands poked and prodded the unconscious Ell gently. Arendahl took the flask of Source Water from Dahranian and poured a substantial amount of the liquid into Ell's mouth.

"That should do it." The old elf said as he stood

"He's alright?" Miri heard the catch in her voice as she asked.

"The Source Water will heal the worst of it and a day or two of rest will see him back on his feet."

Miri was finally able to breathe easily. The fear that had strangled her and forced her into an almost numb sensation finally loosed, and she felt a few tears trickle down her cheeks. She wiped them away and settled down by her mate's body to wait for him to awaken.

Chapter Six

He felt the stiffness in his body before he even opened his eyes. Getting thrown against a tree by something monstrous would do that to a body. Ell woke to the sound of talking punctuated by the noise of Ryder's jaws mashing something noisily between his teeth. Ell kept his eyes closed and just listened.

"What was it that attacked him?" Rihya was asking in her regular demanding voice.

"Do you think I'm omniscient, girl?" Arendahl was dodging questions like he always did.

"I think you always know more than you say. That is what I think. And I think it's about time you shared what has you so nervous. I saw how you were acting in the woods." Rihya never was one to be put off.

"Heh, well, that may be true. But you should know better than to speak to your elders in such a fashion, Valerihya." Arendahl's tone was colder than it usually was. The old elf was always stilted and curt, but he wasn't usually cold. The haughtiness in Arendahl's voice was odd enough to force Ell to open his eyes and see what was going on.

Ell shifted his weight and tried to sit up quietly, but the ache in his body prevented him from doing so without a groan emitting from his mouth in pain. It immediately drew everyone's attention to him.

Miri's head whipped towards him and Ell saw the warring emotions of relief and worry battling on her face. Relief that he was awake and moving. Worry at his sounds of pain. However, surprisingly, it was Dacunda who was the first at his side.

"Easy lad, easy. You were out cold for nearly a full day. You need to be gentle with your body." Ell's uncle assisted him as Ell forced the issue and rose anyway.

"Thank you, Uncle," Ell said stiffly, and the stiffness was not due only to his physical condition. He and Dacunda had not shared many words in the past months. It was strange that his uncle was being so careful, even tender with him.

Ell politely shook himself free of his uncle's steadying hands and stood alone, albeit a bit shakily. Rihya snorted back a laugh as she saw him wobble on his feet.

"Ever the proud one, little brother. It wouldn't hurt to accept assistance." She shook her head at his stubbornness with her arms crossed. Miri started forward to help him, but Ell motioned her off.

He eyed the rest of the camp. They were all looking at him as if they thought he might collapse at any moment. Well, he would show them. Ell decided to end the unusually pointed argument that was brewing between Arendahl and his sister by answering her question as best he could.

"I don't know exactly what it was that attacked me, Rihya, but it was strong. And it was evil."

"You are sure it was a dark creature?" Dacunda asked, a serious expression replacing the worry that had previously occupied his face.

Ell nodded. "Yes, Uncle. Those red eyes are unmistakable. Added to that, it tried to kill me unprovoked and that it was also keeping company with a Ghoul, so I would say the odds of it being evil are nearly certain."

"Keeping company with a Ghoul?" Arendahl interjected. Ell nodded his affirmation to the question.

"What?" Rihya asked the old elf sharply. Ell had to agree with her previous assertion. Arendahl clearly had some idea of what was going on.

"Tree Ogre." Arendahl harrumphed his answer.

"What is a Tree Ogre?" Dahranian joined the conversation.

Arendahl addressed them all. "Tree Ogres, or Wood Ogres as they are also called, are another of the creatures our ancestors battled in the First Days," the old elf said, using his teaching voice that Ell knew meant he was about to spiral into a lecture of sorts. Arendahl continued, recapping the highlights of the story of the Highest and the roots of Ell's people. "Our race was birthed into a land obscured by shadow. Creation itself spun us out from the Source to right its wrongs. We were born into a land of chaos, a world we had to subdue in order to save."

"I remember you telling us this story in the northern region some months ago," Ryder interjected.

"Don't interrupt me, boy." Arendahl's voice broke peevishly from the almost hollow intonation of his storytelling voice. Ryder lifted his hands and made a slightly guilty face that Ell couldn't help but laugh to see. Dire events were transpiring, Ell had nearly been killed by a Wood Ogre, but somehow his cousin Ryder could bring levity to any situation, whether he meant to or not.

"As you say, I've told the story to you before so I'll keep it short this time.

Our race, the Highest, was born to fight and vanquish the dark creatures from the land. We were born to combat the Unsired, those terrible warlords of old who had a power over the evil beasts, over the darkness. The Unsired had rejected Creation, their sire, and embraced evil. Evil ran rampant and we, the Highest, were the balance that fate spun out to correct its mistakes. Tree Ogres, such as the one Ell fought yesterday, were just one of the dark creatures under the thrall of the Unsired."

"Why have we never heard of Tree Ogres before?" Ell asked curiously.

"Unlike Stone Ogres and Ghouls, the Tree Ogres lived within the boundaries of Andalaya proper. After the First Days ended, many of the dark creatures disappeared gradually until they were thought to be gone. Until recently. However, the Wood Ogres were hunted to extinction almost immediately because they lived so close to our people's homes." Arendahl gave his explanation quickly as if wishing to be done with the subject.

"Anything else of note that we should be made aware of about these Tree Ogres?" Dacunda asked.

The old elf responded. "The Wood Ogres were always rare, even in the First Days, and they were known for being particularly vicious. Ghouls often followed them because these Ogres did not always kill their victims. They were known to mangle their foes and then leave them in a bloody pile for the Ghouls to feast on afterwards."

Ell shuddered to think about what might have been his fate had he not seen and then killed the Ghoul ahead of his fight with the ogre. He could well have become a meal.

Arendahl seemed to sense his line of thought. "Aye lad, it was well that you killed the beastie before you fought the Tree Ogre, else there might have been naught but bones for us to find when we came looking."

Miri had slipped over to his side and grabbed his hand, holding it lightly. Ell's clammy, still-recovering grasp didn't seem to bother her, for which he was grateful. Ell swallowed, suddenly feeling exhausted after only a few minutes of standing. He stumbled over to a log and plopped down unceremoniously. Miri sat with him, staring worriedly at him.

"I am fine, Miriyah," Ell said using her full name to impress upon her his sincerity.

"Of course you are." Her response did not sound as certain as he had hoped it would.

"You need rest, boy. Try not to be a complete fool about your recovery." Arendahl deftly poked holes into Ell's ego.

Ell waved off the advice half-heartedly. His gesture could be construed as weary acquiescence to the old elf's advice. He hoped that was how Arendahl had interpreted his wave, because he was in no mood for an argument now.

However, Rihya was not as weary as Ell, and she had questions left unanswered. "That cannot be everything, Arendahl." She turned to Dacunda. "Uncle, please convince him to tell us what else is going on. I can tell there is something more than just this incident with the Tree Ogre. You and Arendahl have been treading lightly around us all summer, whispering together, and more anxious than I have ever seen you."

Ell was startled. He had not noticed the things that his sister was mentioning, but then again, he had done his best to avoid his elders this summer, so it was no wonder that he had missed these developments.

Dacunda looked to Arendahl for advice on how to answer. Rihya rolled her eyes at the action, and crossed her arms waiting impatiently.

Arendahl shook his head slightly at Dacunda. But Dacunda, for once, did not do what his elder and mentor told him.

"It is time, Arendahl. It is time that we told them. They have a right to know."

"What is it, Father?" Dahranian asked. He, unlike Ell, was not used to Dacunda keeping him in the dark about anything.

Dacunda didn't directly respond to his son's question. Instead he addressed the old elf again, this time more firmly. "Arendahl, you must tell them. It cannot be hidden any longer. And we need them to know, we need them to be prepared for what is coming."

Arendahl sighed almost regretfully as if he was breaking sad news. Perhaps he was. Ell's stomach clenched. He was not often frightened, but seeing his uncle—and especially Arendahl—so concerned, so unsettled by whatever information they possessed, sent a chill down his spine. What was it they were hiding? Miri tightened her grip on his hand. Her presence and touch were a comfort.

And then, in typical fashion, once his mind was made up to do something, Arendahl just did it. Without preamble he simply told them.

"The Unsired are back. They have returned to the land. And with their return, the darkness waxes full, and the beasts return."

Ell heard gulps from his family members. It was not often that you received news that the nightmares of old had returned to life. Lore was supposed to stay ancient, lost in some dim recess of the past, forgotten in all but history records. It was not supposed to return to haunt you. And yet, for some reason he did not feel shocked. Oh, he was worried, to be sure. The gravity of the matter was not lost on him. But he also felt calm, as if it all somehow made sense. After all, he was a Water Caller and his kind had been created as a balance to the Unsired, had they not? Was that not what Arendahl had said? It only made sense that his kind, those of his supernatural lineage, would return to thwart the Unsired and their sinister purposes once again. It was as if his purpose for existence became clear. He was made for this battle.

Ell felt a smile grow on his face. He did not try to quell the anticipation he felt welling in his chest. Adventure waited. His destiny was waiting for him. He would meet the enemy head on. Ell could feel himself looking forward to the coming conflict.

Arendahl's eyes landed on Ell's face and Ell saw the old elf's eyes widen in surprise as he surveyed his protégé's reaction to the terrible news, but Ell couldn't contain the strange delight he experienced as he felt his purpose click into place. He knew he shouldn't feel happy at this news, and yet he did. Ell gazed back at Arendahl and Ell saw the old elf's disposition switch. Arendahl had been nervous, worried as he divulged this terrible news, and if Rihya was right, the old elf had been anxious all summer and with understandable reason. Yet as Arendahl stared at the light in his young Water Caller companion, Ell saw the pressure and fear release from the old elf. Arendahl would not be alone in this endeavor. There were two Water Callers now and they would both fight for Andalaya. A smile creased the old elf's weathered face.

The others recovered from their shock and started clamoring with questions. Arendahl sorted them out and answered them as best he could. "No, I do not know how long they have been back. I suspect some years. Long enough to grow in power but not long enough to fully assert control over the land yet. No, I did not discover this entirely on my own. Dacunda brought me hints of strange occurrences and I followed the scent of the Bonewinds south where my questions found answers. We kill them like any other beings. In fact, you have fought some of them already at the battle for Little Vale. They are being formed again somehow from the ranks of the Departed."

Ell sat to think now. Events were crystalizing for him. All the strange encounters over the past months with members of the southern elves were beginning to make sense. The sickly appearance of some of the Departed that he had fought both on raids and during the battle for Little Vale, the black blood that had rushed from the veins of many of his Departed enemies, was no longer a source of confusion. The conundrum was answered. They bled black because they were the Unsired. Their bodies and minds had warped to adapt to their new and darker natures. The real question was, how were they changing? Was it just happenstance that many of the Departed were shifting in nature? Or was something more sinister happening? Was something or someone creating the Unsired?

These were all thoughts that threatened to clog Ell's mind. He was a warrior, through and through, down to the core. Ell thought like a soldier, analyzing risks and opportunities, thinking strategically. Yet he had spent too much time around Arendahl to not ask these sorts of questions and at times they threatened to overwhelm him. The vast unknown of so much of what was happening sometimes dwarfed the feeling of clarity he had been experiencing just a moment earlier.

However, the more Ell sat with his thoughts, the more certain he was becoming of one thing. Life was dangerous. He had always known that, always accepted that the life of one of the Highest who still fought would be fraught with peril. That was not a new concept to him. Yet, something about Arendahl's revelation of the Unsired having returned pushed this acceptance and understanding over a new edge. Ell recognized, deep within his soul and his consciousness, that this fight with the Unsired was something he had been born to do. That the conflict with this ancient foe was also very likely to claim his life. Ell had long ago learned to pay attention to his instincts, this and his encounter with the Tree Ogre emphasized that his life was short and precious. He didn't want to die without anything important being left undone or unsaid.

He needed to find his family. Ell had been near death many times with wounds sustained in battle. He was familiar with the way a person's life could play through their consciousness in those final moments, the way the regrets of actions untaken could rob those final moments of the peace a dying elf deserved.

Ell felt committed to never experiencing that helpless feeling of regret. He would make certain that he went into whatever battle lay ahead clear headed and of pure of heart with the knowledge that he had done everything in his power to achieve the important goals deemed necessary to his conscience. That meant finding his family, or at least doing everything in his power to attempt to find them. They might be dead, but Ell didn't want to reach his own deathbed wishing he had listened to his heart and tried harder to reach his enslaved family. These were morbid thoughts, unpleasant, but they were the thoughts of a keen mind of a warrior who had seen his share of death.

"What is on you mind, Ell?" Miri leaned into him and put her head on his shoulder.

Ell didn't answer her question directly. "Walk with me?"

Miri raised her eyebrows as he stood a bit shakily, as if to ask if he was sure he wanted to be moving about, but stood with him. Dacunda also noticed his instability and was quick to caution Ell.

"Nephew, is it wise to be moving about so soon after your injuries?"

"I am fine. I just want to stretch my legs a moment." Ell put his arm around Miri's shoulder, solidly read to support him. "I will use my living crutch to the fullest extent, have no fear," Ell joked painfully. Miri smiled. Dacunda seemed unhappy with Ell's decision but their differences had formed a wall between them this summer and that barrier led the both of them to tread more carefully around each other with a stiff politeness.

Ell and Miri strolled very slowly away from camp. Not far, though. They stayed well within earshot of the camp. Ell was not keen to repeat his encounter from yesterday. He kept a sharp eye out for any other Ghouls or Ogres who might be in the vicinity. Not that it would do much good. He was not a very mobile fighter at the moment. A few days rest and he would be good as new—elves had strong constitutions and their bodies had a tendency to rebound quickly, especially when they used Source water whose healing power quickened their blood and muscles—but until then, he'd need to be careful. However, it was second nature to keep an eye out for danger, even if he wasn't prepared to face it.

"What is it?" Miri asked softly, as a few yellow leaves, hinting at autumn, drifted down around them in the breeze.

"I have been thinking about my family." Ell said.

Miri tilted her head. "What about them?" she asked, looking back the way they had come. "I know you have had words with your uncle and Arendahl throughout the summer. Is that what you wish to speak with me about now?"

Ell sighed at the thought of his deteriorated relationship with his two elders. "No," he responded. "Dacunda lied to me my whole life. He told me my parents were dead. But they were not. Whether he did it to keep me from risking my life is irrelevant. I am old enough to know the truth and decide how to protect myself. And Arendahl, he is too clever for his own good. Lying by omission is no different than lying outright." Ell was surprised at the rush of anger he felt while speaking. The unresolved issues he had left to fester all summer were bearing a bitter fruit.

Miri smiled a small sly smile. "Clearly, you do not want to talk about them." Her exaggerated innocence as she spoke was enough to tip Ell out of his simmering fury and laugh wryly at her sarcasm.

"Alright, I admit, maybe it would be good to speak of these things. Just the two of us," he amended quickly. Ell did not desire another argument with his elders. The summer months had been only too full of them.

"No, what I meant is that I have been thinking of *them*…the rest of my family. If they are still alive," he muttered half to himself.

Miri nodded her head understandingly. "What is it you wish to discuss? You wouldn't have walked me away from the camp unless there was something you wanted to say to me."

Ell nodded sadly. "It is time. I must go look for them. I could not bear it if my death came and I had not done so."

Miri stopped their walk and turned to face him, putting both hands on the sides of his neck as she looked at him. "Why are you speaking of death as if it is imminent?"

Ell shrugged her worry away more nonchalantly than he felt. "It is nothing really, just, yesterday reminded me of how fleeting life can be. I am often in the gravest of peril when we fight, whether we raid the humans or the Departed."

His mate didn't answer, she just stared penetratingly into his eyes. She sensed it was a more serious concern of his, but she chose not to push him. She had Joined with him knowing exactly who he was—a warrior of the Highest, a Water Caller of ancient origin. Miri knew that death stalked him around every bend in the path and she accepted it, even if she didn't like it.

"I must go look for them," he stated deliberately. "I will never forgive myself if I do not."

"And I cannot go with you." Once again, she saw to the heart of the matter, the constant struggle for them. Mated, they wished to spend every day together. Yet Miri was not trained in the way that Rihya was, or the rest of Ell's family. She would never be able to hold her own in a battle. And on top of that she was crippled, and therein lay the problem. Even if she were trained, her weaker leg would never allow her to keep up with them.

Ell pursed his lips sadly as he stared at her. There was no need to answer her. Her statement had not been a question. She knew her limitations.

"I do not like it when you leave me," she said quietly, looking wistfully at her crippled leg.

"Nor do I, but this is important, love." Ell tried to impress upon her the weight of the responsibility he felt, the burning need within him to find his family, or to just figure out if they were dead. After all, they had spent decades in captivity. It was just as likely that they had died in their imprisonment as it was that they were still living and breathing. Even so, just the knowing would release Ell from this sense of duty he felt to find them. Duty and desire. He longed for a father in a way that was hard to express. Ell had spent many an hour this summer indulging in those types of daydreams, imagining how incredible it would be to find his father after all these years and show him the type of honorable warrior his son had grown up to become. Dacunda had been there his whole life. His uncle was as much a father to Ell and Rihya as he was to his own children. Yet for some inexplicable reason, it did not feel the same.

Miri buried her face in his chest. They had spent all summer together, but that degree of close proximity was about to end. Ell felt a grip of longing in his chest, the anticipation of the yearning he would feel when they were apart. He kissed her, tilting her face up gently. Then held her again. They stayed in an embrace for a few long minutes before slowly and silently making their way back to camp.

Ell hobbled into camp, his weight still almost fully supported by Miri. Despite his exertion, the walk seemed to have done his body good. It had tired him out, but it had also loosened his muscles slightly. Oh, he was still sore, but not the deep, aching soreness he had been feeling earlier. This soreness was closer to how he often felt after a hard battle or a long journey. Arendahl really had been right, saying that a few more days of rest would make Ell as good as new.

Ell pulled Rihya aside immediately when they reached the others. "It's time, Rihya," he whispered into her ear. He felt he owed her the courtesy of letting her know what he was planning on doing before the others. It was her family too, after all.

"Time for what?" Rihya asked crossly, her eyes narrowing dangerously. She didn't keep her voice down either, and her response drew the attention of the rest of the company.

"Yes, boy, time for what?" Arendahl pointedly parroted Ell's sister. Ell could practically feel the old elf's eyes piercing the back of his head. Ell sighed and turned around slowly to face the others. If Rihya wanted a public discussion, then it seemed she would have her wish. Ell steeled himself, firmed his will for the confrontation that he knew would soon take place, and gazed at Arendahl and Dacunda calmly. "I think you know what I mean."

"Do not be foolish, Elliyar!" Dacunda shouted, comprehension causing frustration to burst forth from his lips. "It is too dangerous."

"Idiot boy! Not all impossible things are there to be vanquished! Dor Khabor is a death trap." Arendahl growled bitterly as he similarly saw what Ell's intention was. "You will be killed—or worse captured!—and likely for nothing."

"You do not know that for certain," Ell said quietly. "I must find out the truth. With his dying breaths Silverfist claimed their existence—he told me that my parents were alive. Or that they had been all those years ago," he amended. "I must know if that is still true. If they still live. One way or another I am going to find out."

Surprisingly, his sister didn't jump in to add her disapproval to their uncle and Arendahl's. She could usually be counted on to hold Ell in check when his wilder fantasies and tendencies grew too much. But not this time. "I am with you, little brother," was all she said. She spoke firmly, resolutely. Of course, it was her family too. She must feel the same need, the same longing to find them as he. Ell felt a surge of gratitude, nonetheless, at her support.

Dacunda was shaking his head. But Dahranian seemed unsure about what they were speaking of, and Ryder, a handful of nuts poised halfway to his mouth, asked, "What's all this about?"

"My parents did not die all those years ago, Ry. They were captured and taken as slaves to Dark Harbor. And these two have been keeping the truth from me all this time." Ell finished the quick summary by using the hand not draped around Miri's shoulders to indicate the two elders in the group.

Ryder screwed up his face in thought. He didn't seem surprised, but then, not a lot surprised Ryder. He had a way of riding the river of life and going wherever it chose to take him without any difficulty.

"So that is why you have been at odds with my father and Arendahl all summer," he said thoughtfully. Ryder jammed the handful of nuts into his mouth, buying himself time to think as he chewed.

Ell ignored the arguments and pressed his position. "I will leave tomorrow at first light."

"You can hardly walk, Elliyar," Dacunda protested, a valid reason Ell was forced to accept as a twinge of pain nearly made one of his legs buckle. Perhaps it was time to sit. He remained standing. Ell needed a show of strength to convince them of his course of action.

Arendahl was shaking his head with a worried sneer on his face. "And tell me, boy, how will you find them? Do you even have a plan? What will you do if they are not there? They may be years gone for all we know. Many of the slaves the Departed capture are sent to the humans and transported back to their land. What will you do then, if you discover a rumor telling you that your family is long gone and taken all the way to the other side of the Fracture? What will you do then, heh?" The old elf finished his tirade of questions.

The Fracture. A deadly ocean of glacial ice walls and icebergs separating the human land—Etheros—from this continent. Thousands of ships had attempted to sail across it over the centuries and none had ever returned. It was impassable. Only the great land bridge in the north connected the two continents.

Ell's calm finally broke. If they wanted a fight, then they would get one. "I do not know, Arendahl! I only know that if I do not try and find them, then on my dying day I will regret it. And with the world in chaos, that day may be arriving sooner than expected."

"Please, Nephew, do not do this." Dacunda pled with him, trying a new tactic to soften the blow of Arendahl's anger and intensity.

"Do not try to persuade me out of this, Uncle. You knew this day would come—it is the very reason that you lied to me for all these years!"

Dacunda sighed. "I lied to you because your father asked it of me." The statement shocked Ell out of his rant for a moment.

"What?" The anger, the bitterness towards his uncle threatened to evaporate almost completely in his surprise. He held onto it spitefully.

"We made a promise to one another, Elliyar, a promise long ago. If either of us were ever captured and taken to Dark Harbor, we would tell the other's family that he was dead. Neither your father nor I wished for the lives of our loved ones to be risked in a fool's quest for rescue. And it *is* a fool's quest, Nephew." Dacunda finished quietly, but firmly. "It is a suicide mission, and I must try, with everything I have, to dissuade you of it. I must try, for the sake of my vow."

Ell's anger toward his uncle had burned down, but it was still there, still simmering beneath the surface. He better understood his uncle's actions now, his lies, but he still could not quite forgive them.

"I am sorry, Dacunda, but you cannot keep me from going. Join me in this venture or not, but if you accompany me, know this—it will be my expedition and I will make my own decisions. Your lies have earned me that right."

"Why should we obey you?" Dacunda asked.

"Because you owe me. You owe us, Rihya and I!" Ell burst out in response.

Dacunda's face hardened with resolve. "Let us be clear, I do not owe you anything, Elliyar. The only person I owe anything is your father, and to honor that debt I will do as I see fit."

Rihya stepped in close to her uncle and surprised him by nicking him just slightly with her blade. It was an unsavory habit she'd picked up for when she wanted to gain someone's full attention. Dacunda clapped a hand to his arm and gritted his teeth in annoyance as he turned towards his niece.

"That is for being stupid, Uncle. You are the only father we've ever known and you have been lying to us our entire lives. Of course you owe us!" She turned to confront Ell. "But it is true that the real debt he owes is to our father, so grow up, Ell, and realize that he is only trying to do his best." She finished by motioning with both hands for the two of them to continue, as if her statement had somehow resolved the differences between them.

Ell set his jaw and ignored her. He would not budge this time.

"Nephew…" Dacunda began, but Ell cut him off.

"You will follow my lead, Uncle, and do what I say, or you will not come. That goes for all of you," Ell said as he turned his head to address the rest of the group.

Ryder clapped him on the shoulder. "I am with you, Cousin. And when have I ever wanted to command anyway?" He winked at Ell.

"You already know my response." Rihya nodded her head slightly at him.

Dahranian was staring at his father as he spoke. His words were slow, almost difficult for him. "I cannot say I approve of your tone, Ell, or of the way you have hijacked command, but I would not be your family if I turned my back on you now."

Dacunda stared at Ell silently for a long moment before speaking. "If this is the way it must be, then so be it."

All that was left was Arendahl since Ell had already spoken with Miri and knew her stance and Art was too young for a vote. The old elf's eyes were penetrating. Slate-grey they bored into Ell. A moment turned into a minute, which turned into five.

Finally, Ell broke the silence. "I do not need you to come, nor do I need your approval."

Arendahl barked a laugh. "Need me, of course you do. But I will not be joining you on this venture." Ell felt a blow to his gut. It was true, another Water Caller would be invaluable.

"I have other matters of importance to which I must attend. But I'll travel south with you for a ways, to continue your lessons, of course. Now that this is all settled there will be no reason to avoid me the way you have all summer. And boy, I mean to drill you hard enough to make up for a summer of slacking." Arendahl finished and waited for Ell's response.

"Very well." Ell smiled ruefully. "The training will not be amiss," he admitted, thinking of his attempt to tap into his abilities while fighting the Tree Ogre and his subsequent failure to do so.

Arendahl cast a knowing glance at him. As a fellow, albeit more experienced Water Caller, Arendahl would be aware that with full access to his abilities, Ell shouldn't have ended up half dead after the fight with the Ogre.

His mentor gestured him over. "One last word of caution," Arendahl began, speaking quietly in Ell's ear so that only he could hear. "You have set your course and asserted your command. This time will be different. You lead now, and you lead by your own choice. Know this, there has never been a slave freed from Dor Khabor. Never. I wonder, will you be so keen to risk the lives of those you lead when you reach the southern capital? The responsibility for the lives gained or lost on this mission will fall squarely on your shoulders."

And with that, Arendahl turned away and left Ell to slump from Miri's shoulder onto a log to think about the added weight that had settled onto his shoulders and his conscience. It had felt right to demand command of this mission. In a way, it still felt right. But Ell would have been lying to himself if he didn't admit that the responsibility he felt now was discomfiting. He gazed around the camp as his family readied themselves to depart and wondered which of his kin he would lead to death.

Chapter Seven

For all of Arendahl's talk of the burden of leadership now falling on Ell's shoulders, that burden did not begin immediately. The next day when they broke camp, there was no need for anyone, let alone Ell, to direct people. His family had been making and breaking camp together for years, and they needed no reminders of how to do so properly. It seemed that Ell might not taste the bitter weight of command to which the old elf had been referring until later.

After breaking camp, they set out south at a gradual pace. There was no immediate rush and at this point in the journey, they were still slightly encumbered by the slower paces of the child, Artorious, and Miri. However, since the decision to move south and begin the mission to find and rescue Ell's family—if possible—had already been made, there was no real need for haste. There was no timeline to which the company needed to adhere. Dark Harbor would be there whether they reached it in a month or a year. Any rush to do so was only an internal desire of Ell's to find his parents, not a practical need to hurry their expedition. So it was that they moved at a steady pace, often moving at a fast walk, rarely breaking into a run. They were still in Legendwood, and while slavers would often raid right into the heart of Andalaya for their prey— if nothing else, the battle for Little Vale was proof of that—they were not quite so common an occurrence this far north. Their company traveled together all in a group. However, when they left Legendwood and reached the Lower Forest where the Pillars began and the Departed exerted near total control, they would have to send a lone member of their party to scout the trail ahead and report back if there were any dangers to avoid. But for now, it was not necessary. Better to stay close and in a group in case any more dark creatures, such as Ogres, were waiting to attack.

Ell took a swig of water from his waterskin, enjoying the feeling of wetness sliding down his throat. The liquid could not be described as cool, for the weather was still hot enough in late summer to warm the water in its container at his hip, yet it was refreshing nonetheless. At the very least, it washed the taste of grit and travel out of his mouth, a taste that could accumulate after hours spent on the trail with the occasional dust kicked up into the air by the passing of feet.

"Source Water?" Miri asked, as he removed the gourd of water from his mouth and replaced it at his hip.

Ell shook his head. "No sense using our supply on me. I am fit enough for the pace at which we are moving." Source Water was the lifeblood of Andalaya, stemming from the raging spring known only as the Source, which burst from the mountainside and through the gates of the ruined ancient capital of Verdantihya. It flowed into the valley and eventually joined other streams until it split into the five major rivers of Andalaya. The Source represented the birth of their race by Creation itself to right the wrongs of so many millennia ago, and held mystical powers. It was a tangible representation of the elves' relationship to the land and Creation, Its water could be found in a diluted capacity even far from Verdantihya, and could be used by the Highest to heal minor wounds by drinking it or being submerged in its waters. When concentrated, it could provide near-miraculous recovery from fatal wounds. Thus, it was common practice among Ell's people to maintain a waterskin or two of Source Water from Verdantihya—despite the risk of slavers who knew Highest would come there—at all times. Ell and his family had made a number of trips—this time without incident—to the ruined capital and their rations of Source Water were near to bursting. Having eight people in their party made them move at a slower pace but it also allowed them to carry extra skins of water, which was a bonus that could not be overlooked. Ell had lost track of the number of times that a swallow of the Source had saved him or one of his family members from an arduous recovery, or even from death.

"A little drink couldn't hurt our supplies and I hardly think the others would find it amiss if you took a little." Miri said as she walked along beside Ell.

Ell shook his head again. "No, I feel much better today than yesterday. It is not worth the waste. Besides, we may need as much of the Source as we can carry with us where we are going." Ell thought grimly of the southern capital as he finished his sentence. Dark Harbor was strong and powerful enough that the Humans had struck a deal, an uneasy alliance, with the southern elves rather than try to attack it. As long as the Departed had been willing to ally with the humans and betray their northern kinsman two decades ago, the humans had been willing to let them be. The humans assumed full control of the eastern half of the continent while the Departed raided the shattered land of Andalaya for slaves to give to the humans. The humans took three quarters of the slaves that the southern elves captured as part of their alliance, while the rest of the hapless northern victims wound up in Dark Harbor, serving dark elf masters.

Ell found himself praying that his family was there. The only way to the human lands was across the great bridge to the north and it was far too heavily fortified to slip across. No elf, not even the Departed, were allowed to cross it freely. Only slaves were transported from this land to the human continent. Across the great ocean, lay a human world of unknown size where countless members of Ell's race toiled in shackles. Ell thought about what Arendahl had said the other day. What if his parents had been taken across the Fracture? They would be as good as dead if that were the case. Unlike the great Western Ocean, with its warm waters and many islands, the Fracture was impassable. Incredibly strong northern currents swept down from the arctic seas to the north and clogged the middle of the Fracture with icebergs and even floating glaciers that provided giant walls of ice, miles long. It was like that as far to the south as anyone could sail. The northern currents were that strong. Over the centuries, ships had stopped trying to traverse the Fracture since none that sailed far into its icy waters ever returned.

"What is weighing so heavily on your mind that I cannot command your attention for even a moment?" Miri teased him gently. Ell was startled out of his worries and looked at her.

Miri had her golden blonde hair braided at the wings in her usual fashion, the braids speckled with flowers and wrapped to the back and fastened together, forming a woodland crown of sorts. A princess of Andalaya if Ell had ever seen one. Her face was flushed with pink from walking and a bit of sweat beaded her brow in the heat.

"Let's stop here for a midday break," announced Ell's uncle. "If that is alright with you, Nephew," Dacunda phrased uncomfortably. Ell had assumed command of this mission two days ago, meaning that he was in charge—or that his family was humoring him and honoring his wishes. It created an awkward dynamic with his uncle. For as long as Ell could remember, he had jumped whenever Dacunda had ordered, trusting him implicitly. It had kept him alive all these years. It had made his family an expertly oiled weapon, a supreme fighting unit. But that trust was now gone, and Ell wasn't sure it would ever fully return. Ell quietly nodded his head in agreement.

They all sat down on boulders or logs or just the grass and dirt of the earth and drank from skins holding normal water and passed food around. Ryder, of course, took the largest portion of food in his hands and, when Dahranian gestured to this with a slightly humored twist to his mouth, Ryder responded, "Do not worry, brother, I am simply gaining strength for a tremendous hunt tonight. I'll be working hard to bring in game for us all and I need to gather my energy now." Ryder punctuated his comment by thrusting a chunk of dried venison into his mouth and biting down happily. Dahranian shook his head but couldn't help but smile at Ryder.

As they all rested, Ell answered Miri's question from a few moments ago. "I have been thinking a lot about my family. What if Arendahl is right? What if they're not even in Dark Harbor and I have risked our lives for nothing?"

"Well, you will never know that unless you look for them." Miri replied evenly, placidly, a small smile upon her face. She often smiled even when their discussions did not merit pleasure.

"But what if I am wrong? I don't want to leave you. But then again, I have to do this, it's my parents after all." Ell's uncertainty caused him to vacillate from worry to resolve even within the span of a sentence.

"Ell, love, relax. I understand why you are doing what you are doing. I understand, truly."

Ell inclined his head to the side. "Do you really?"

"Have you forgotten that my parents are dead also? Even if yours are only perhaps not." Miri gave him a pointed look. Ell nodded his agreement. He did remember, they had spoken of it often in recent months in relation to the news that his parents might not be dead.

"They died in a slaver raid the day I sustained this wound," Miri indicated her leg, "and what I would not give to have them back. I have family in Little Vale, extended family like you have your cousins and uncle, and over the years I have come to think of the entire village as a family of sorts. But it is not the same."

Ell breathed a deep sigh out. It would be just like her to understand his emotions completely. Just like her to be comforting him when it was he who was pushing to leave her.

Miri put her hand on his arm. "I understand why you must try and find them. And I do not hold it against you." Ell kissed her on the forehead. He was lucky to have a mate as good as she.

She continued. "I'm just glad that I now have this…connection to you, even while you go." Miri paused as if not sure he understood what she meant. But Ell did. His entire body tensed at the mention of Grafting. He puckered up his mouth at the thought of her experiencing his pain, his fear, even his death.

"Look, Elliyar, I know you are not pleased with the connection, for whatever reason that is—" the look she gave Ell told him that she knew there was something about Grafting that he wasn't telling her, something that was making him so uncomfortable, "—but I am pleased with it. So be pleased with me." She ended with a plea of sorts. He glanced at her and saw that she was smiling winsomely at him, batting her eyelashes with only slight exaggeration.

Ell rolled his eyes at the mockery of it, stifling a laugh. Exasperation filled him as he focused on the topic. This was no subject for mirth. The Grafting was bound to end in unpleasantness and pain for her.

"You do not know the half of it, Miri," Ell began, thinking of how to warn her of the potential dangers of Grafting without worrying her too greatly.

Now it was Miri's turn for exasperation. "So tell me then, divulge whatever dark secret about whatever it was I did, that Arendahl told you." Ell could tell from her tone that she was getting frustrated.

Ell sighed. There was no good reason not to tell her now. She knew something was up, and he had hinted at his dislike for what had happened enough times now that there was no hiding it. And according to Arendahl, there was no reversing the Grafting. It was here to stay.

"It is called Grafting." Ell proceeded to explain to her the little bit that Arendahl had spoken about to him the other day. Miri listened in silence, keen eyes hanging upon every word. Ell finished his explanation with, "That is all I know Miri, and it's not much. It's a largely unknown talent, long forgotten in our history since it hasn't happened in centuries." "So you are worried." Miri stated promptly after he had finished.

"Of course I am!" Ell practically exploded and then quieted back down. The others glanced up at the outburst, but sensing they needed a moment of privacy, continued to converse quietly amongst themselves from a few yards away.

"Don't you see, Miri, it is only bound to bring you pain. Sure, you will see important moments in my life, but when I am gone, those moments that are important enough to register with your consciousness embedded within mine will not likely be pleasant."

"I probably saved your life two days ago," Miri countered.

Ell pursed his lips in frustration. "But you had to witness me nearly being killed. I do not want that for you."

Miri turned a steely gaze on him. "My leg may be lame, but I am not so weak as you sometimes think, love." She said 'love' with an edge as if daring him to disagree.

Ell spread his hands, backpedaling slightly. "That's not what I mean, and you know it."

"No?"

"No," Ell said. "Of course not. I just would choose to spare you whatever pain I could, that's all."

"The pain of what, your injury?" Miri said dismissively.

"The pain of my death," Ell responded somberly. The severity in his voice seemed to tell her that, for now, he would not be persuaded. But what did it matter, it was all a moot point. They could not reverse the Grafting now anyway.

Miri looked at him peacefully, but firmly, and said, "I would choose pain, every time, over distance, over having no connection at all."

And just like that the discussion was over. Miri made it clear she no longer wished to speak of it, and Ell appeased her by turning his attention to the rest of his family.

"Ready?" Dacunda asked Ell instead of just telling him what to do the way he would have only a few days ago. "We should keep a steady pace."

"Agreed," Ell responded.

"Alright then, off we go." Ryder slung the strap of his small pack over his head and shouldered his long axe as he stood.

They set out again at an even walk, a pace that Miri and Art could maintain without overly exerting themselves. The land passed by slowly. Ell and his family were in the southern region of Legendwood now surrounded by foothills. The mountains of Andalaya with their pines, firs, spruce, and Evergrow trees and their wide open spaces, had given way to foothills populated more by underbrush-surrounded maple, alder, ash, and elm, more than by pine and Evergrow trees. It wouldn't be long before they would leave the foothills and Legendwood behind and enter the Lower Forest, which was flat and covered by many of the same trees as Legendwood, but with the addition of oak.

Ell walked and enjoyed the view of the greenery all around him. He had never been to Dark Harbor, or even further south of the Lower Forest, but he had heard stories. How the rulers of Dark Harbor had ordered a clear harvesting of the forests surrounding the hills protecting their port to make it more defensible. Much of the south dry and hot and dusty. Ell and his family were heading into unfamiliar terrain, so he took what moments he could to enjoy the yellowing maple leaves drifting lazily to the ground and the sounds of animals scurrying in the underbrush and birds singing in the canopy of leaves above him. The sun drifted onto the path, dappling their way with patches of bright light. An occasional gap in the branches overhead allowed swaths of hot sunlight to make them sweat as they walked. At other times, the green and gold canopy bathed them in shadow and left nooks and crannies of the forest that had retained their dewy morning moisture in the absence of direct sunlight. These areas were often dappled with solitary strands of sunlight that filtered through to create a patchwork of dark and light. It was breathtaking. Ell loved his homeland and everything in it. And he had no doubt that if the humans got what they wanted, they would destroy most of it. The humans were already steadily logging the eastern sections of the forest nearest their camps. Ell and his family had spent the better portion of the last few years setting up ambush after ambush on the cutters chopping down his beloved woods of Andalaya in an attempt to slow the humans' progress.

The day passed in relative ease. There was no real hurry since they were still many miles from where they were headed and they all knew it would not be long before their company would be forced to separate. Arendahl, Art, and Miri would not accompany Ell and his family into the heart of enemy territory. Such an expedition required training and a set of skills that his mate and Art did not possess. This would be dangerous even for skilled warriors, and Arendahl had bluntly informed Ell that he had more important things to do... Ell did not look forward to the parting, and so he pushed it from his mind as they traveled.

It seemed like everyone had a similar idea, because Ell heard only laughter and jokes at every turn. Good spirits abounded, and he even found himself having a civil and respectful conversation with his uncle. Almost an enjoyable talk, really. That had not happened since the day after his Joining when he had confronted Dacunda about what Silverfist had told him. Ell decided to simply enjoy the comfortable ease while it lasted. There was plenty of time to air his grievances another time, but something in Dacunda's demeanor inclined Ell to think that his uncle wished for a peace between them, a truce of sorts as they headed south and into danger.

And so the days passed and they wandered south. The Lower Forest now surrounded them, the cluttered underbrush and moss-and-lichen coated land and rocks of Legendwood having given way to more open spaces between the oak, walnut, and ash trees, and parched ground. It would soon be watered with autumn rains, but for now it was yellow from a long summer of heat.

Ell could see the South Crag to the southwest off to his right as he and his uncle walked in the vanguard position. It was still many miles distant, days of walking at their current pace, but its sharp, jagged form thrust upward from the lowlands around it, a rocky fang piercing the heavens. It was even taller than its northern twin, the North Crag. Ell's memory flashed back to that gusty, stormy night months ago, when, in the midst of a gale with the rocks slippery and the wind howling to rip him to his death, he had defied the odds and done the impossible. That day, he had climbed the North Crag and clashed with the Icari in its sky-high aerie, vanquishing it long enough to secure the passage of flight on its back to rescue Miri from the Pillar. Dacunda thought it was the inspiration of legends, or so he told him jokingly when they had been on better terms.

The southern spire of rock held firm in Ell's vision and he brushed the past from his thoughts. It was not time to dwell on old victories. There was only the present battle ahead. It would not do to forget that what they were attempting had never been done. No one had ever been rescued from Dark Harbor. And yet here Ell was, traveling south with his kin, preparing to attempt to do just that.

"What weighs on your mind so much that you do not even hear me speak?"

Ell blinked and realized that he had been focusing so much on his thoughts that he had ignored his uncle's attempts at conversation.

"Nothing, Uncle.... I was just lost in thought. It was not important."

Dacunda smiled at him for the first time in a long time, and while Ell could see there was still the residue of pain from their falling out, he could also see the genuine care in his uncle's eyes.

"You have never been a very good liar, Elliyar. What is it? What is troubling you?"

Ell glanced at him out of the corner of his eye as they walked. "Nothing is troubling me, exactly. I was simply pondering our course of action when we arrive in the south."

A knowing look flitted across his uncle's face before the older elf smoothed his features back into the unreadable mask he usually wore. Dacunda was nothing if not stoic. "Ahh. The burdens of command. You are wondering about many things these days, are you not, Nephew? What path to take to the south? How to infiltrate the city when we arrive? How to keep everyone safe?" Dacunda asked his last question in a quieter tone of voice, as if he knew only too well its burden.

Ell stayed silent. He felt awkward at the topic of conversation. It was too close to the topics from which their rift had occurred, but Dacunda pressed on anyway, either not noticing, or blatantly ignoring the uncomfortable silence from his nephew. "I know these queries. They are the sort of speculations that keep me awake at night. How to fight effectively and cause damage to the enemy while still ensuring my family's safety? Elliyar, I know what it is like to lead. And I do not envy your position in this venture, but I do hope that you look to me for guidance." Ell knew that this wasn't full acceptance of the task that lay ahead. Dacunda had fought him tooth and nail last spring and into the summer to prevent him from setting out to look for his father. And his uncle was clearly not completely on board with this venture, but it was a comfort to know that he might have someone to talk to about his worries as they drew closer to their destination.

Again, Ell didn't know exactly how to answer. He just nodded. Dacunda seemed to understand that there was nothing further to be said at the moment. Dacunda was accustomed to being the leader, at least when Arendahl was not around, and he must feel somewhat out of place at the moment. But he was clearly willing to offer advice when it was needed and for that, Ell was grateful.

Dacunda brought a close to the topic by gesturing to the rest of their group.

"Do not worry overmuch, Elliyar. At least not today, not for the moment. Enjoy the fact that your family is yet whole and happy." Ell took a moment to appraise the scene. Dahranian was showing Art the proper grip on the handle of a sword, wielding the blade lithely as he walked, his skill preventing danger from befalling himself or the boy. Art was eagerly lapping up every piece of information that Ell's cousin provided.

Ahead of them, Rihya and Miri and Ryder were locked in some kind of heated, yet comical debate. No doubt Ryder was espousing some nonsensical theory or story while the two females laughed and poked holes in his logic.

Arendahl was keeping a steady vigil on the land surrounding them, ever watchful of the nearby woods as he led the way. However, a small smile played at the corners of his mouth as he watched and listened to the lesson Dahranian was giving to the boy. Ever a teacher, Arendahl must enjoy observing the educating spirit apparent in someone other than himself.

Ell tilted his head and smiled. The scene before him was a good one. Yet it could not distract him from the fact that they were heading south, into danger, into the heart of enemy territory. How could Dacunda want him to forget about all that?

"It is hard to shake the worry from my mind, Uncle. And I am not sure that I should. It seems imprudent to simply focus on laughter at a time like this."

Dacunda changed the direction of the conversation. "Do you remember what I told you last spring when Silverfist was on our trail and we were heading back to Verdantihya after raiding the humans? You had just fought a strange Unsired and burned the body, thinking it was diseased."

Ell struggled to remember. It had been a normal raid until he found himself face to face with what he now knew to be one of the Unsired. Powerful and strong, yet blank-stared and unpredictable, with a face that looked ravaged by a plague, the Unsired had been a worthy foe. Ell remembered the trek north into Andalaya afterward.

"I was angry."

Dacunda nodded soberly. "And what did I tell you?"

"You told me to channel my anger, let it fuel me. But you said I must be careful not to let it consume me."

"Yes, Nephew. You are still angry. I can see that. And now much of that fury is directed towards me. But you must not let it consume you now. You must not let it drive you to make bad decisions. The worry you feel is your heart letting you know that you have chosen a course of action and do not yet have a plan. You worry for our safety because you know you have not prepared strategically for this venture."

Ell felt his face harden and his mouth purse defensively. He opened his mouth to disagree, to debate any and everything his uncle was saying, but Dacunda continued without letting Ell speak.

"Just listen, Elliyar. Listen to me. You lead now, you have made that clear, but you must still be wise. It is important to tap into your anger the way you tap into your abilities as a Water Caller. Channel the anger towards a purpose, towards creating a plan. It is important to do these things, to take the responsibility of leadership seriously. Your anger has often made you a serious lad," Dacunda said, referencing the past, "but you must also learn when to let go. When to notice the moments to enjoy. Now, with laughter all around us and a healthy family before you, is a time to simply enjoy the moment. There will be plenty of time for planning and strategy later. Tonight, perhaps, or tomorrow, but not now."

Ell looked ahead once again. Miri happened to cast her gaze back towards him at just that moment and flashed a white, toothy grin at him. And suddenly, Ell found himself in complete agreement with his uncle. Dacunda was right. For now, for today, it was better to enjoy the moment than get lost in the anxious musings of his mind. There would be plenty of time for brooding as they traveled south. There was still a long way to go before they reached their destination. Ell smiled back at his mate and nodded to his uncle that he understood. He breathed in deeply the fresh air around them, felt its dry warmth as it rushed into his lungs, and determined not to think of anything important for the rest of the day.

Chapter Eight

He knew immediately what the scent was when it wafted past his nose. There was not a moment's hesitation this time as there had been when Ell had smelled it before. Ell turned his gaze to Arendahl and the old elf had his own nose lifted and crinkled to the wind like a wolf. The grey haired elf looked at Ell and nodded once before saying what they had both realized.

"Bonewinds." Arendahl stated calmly. The smell elicited a different response from the rest of the party.

Ryder swore and brought his axe up in a tight, ready grip. His long axe, like many of the weapons of Ell's race, had bits of moss and lichen clinging to it. The Highest were one with the land around them and their weapons illustrated this connection.

Almost as one, Dacunda and Dahranian drew their swords from the sheaths over their backs, silent and tense. They did things in unison, those two. They did not swear the way their kinsman did, but they were a coil of muscles and steel waiting to explode. They widened their stances and glanced around the light woody terrain that was ushering their path southward.

"Where?" Rihya asked urgently of Arendahl, as she twirled two blades that had immediately found their way into her hands upon the elder's warning. She too knew what the Bonewinds meant—knew that they were an ancient alarm for those of their kind who knew how to read the signs and warnings that preceded their enemies of old. The Unsired.

Arendahl shook his head. "It doesn't work like that," he said impatiently. Not wanting to explain himself now. "The scent just warns us they're near."

"Boy, quick, climb a tree and give us a lookout of the area. Well, hop to it!"

Ell knew better than to argue when Arendahl set his mind on something. For all that Ell had decided to assume control of this expedition, there was no denying the fact that Arendahl commanded obedience like no one Ell had ever met. Almost without thinking, Ell found his feet moving and he was already hoisting himself into a tree by the oak's lowest limbs by the time he realized that he'd obeyed automatically. He smiled ruefully to himself as he climbed. He still had a bit to learn about leadership.

The climb to the top of the oak was quick and it yielded results. The tree was not exceptionally tall, but luckily it rested on slightly more of a rise than the woods surrounding it. A small clearing could be seen just to the south of where he and his family now stood. And in the clearing was the source of the smell—the southern Bonewinds gusting up faintly, dry and rotten, the smell of disease and death that heralded the Unsired. And there were certainly Departed in the clearing ahead of them.

Ell didn't bother to climb down, he just dropped lithely to the ground, landing in a crouch, before straightening and reporting to Arendahl in the same manner he had always done when relaying his reconnaissance to Dacunda, having often functioned as a scout over the years. "Small band of Departed in a clearing just to the south. Maybe ten of them. Some of them must be Unsired for us to be smelling the Bonewinds," he nodded his affirmation to everyone's questioning looks. "Doing what, precisely?" Arendahl spoke in a clipped, hurried tone.

"Chasing someone. Human by the looks of it. A slave maybe?" Ell responded. "They will catch him by the time they reach the end of the clearing, if we hurry, we can set up an ambush at the far end and catch them unawares."

Ell had already turned to make his way to the far end of the clearing before Arendahl spoke.

"No. This is none of our concern. We should avoid the confrontation."

Ell stared at the old elf incredulously. Avoid a chance to kill the Departed. What game was Arendahl playing at?

As if reading his thoughts, the old elf answered simply. "It is too rushed. And we owe nothing to the humans. What do we care if they run afoul of each other? Besides, they outnumber us."

"We have ambushed greater numbers than ours many times," Ell replied fiercely. "And each time, we have emerged victorious."

Ryder voiced his support for Ell's statement, yet the rest of the group remained silent, watching the two of them to see who would win this small struggle for power. Suddenly, frustration welled up in Ell. He had specifically said that he would be in charge of this expedition. He didn't have to listen to his teacher at every turn. Part of him knew he was being petulant, petty even, struggling for control, but another part of him just wanted to kill the Departed and rescue a slave. Was that so bad?

"You do not tell me what to do, Arendahl. I am leading us now. And we will set up an ambush. We must go now for us to be able to reach the edge of the clearing in time to accomplish it and achieve success." Ell's voice cracked out coldly, and more commanding than he had ever heard it sound. Something about Arendahl sending him scrambling up into a tree like a squirrel without a second thought on his part rubbed him in the wrong way, and he wanted to assert his ability to lead.

Without waiting for confirmation, Ell turned to Ryder, Dacunda, Dahranian, and Rihya. "Come. We must go now if we are to reach the perfect spot in time."

Arendahl was staring at him shrewdly now, watching as his kin hastened to comply with his commands.

"You will stay here and protect Miri and Art, Arendahl." Ell gave the old elf another order, well aware that he was pushing his luck to make him comply the way the others had.

"Will I now?" The old elf mused out loud, but he stayed all the same as Ell and his family turned away and sprinted lightly through the forest to reach the woods at the end of the clearing in time to set up the ambush. They ran lightly, in great leaping strides, covering ground quickly, yet hardly setting a leaf or branch out of place at their passing. As they ran, a loud concussion rocked the clearing, a sound unlike any other that Ell had ever heard. It was like thunder in the forest. Unable to spare time to worry about the unknown, they ran onwards.

They reached the end of the clearing, circling just outside the edges so as not to be seen in their approach. Ell motioned for them to stop and spoke quietly, "Simple seems the best way. Bows and arrows first and then we will finish off whatever we do not kill with first shots with our steel. Rihya and I will target the frontrunners."

Ell leaned against the trunk of a wide oak, his back to the clearing, his body concealed by the tree. The others were fanning out and doing the same. They all nodded their agreement to his plan and lifted bows off their shoulders and fitted Dreampine arrows to their black yew bows—weapons characteristic of the northern elves' tattered guerilla resistance.

One minute passed and they heard the heavy breathing of a tired runner. The human no doubt. Humans did not have nearly the endurance and stamina of an elf. An elf could run all day with hardly a rest, but the same was not true of a human. Ell heard the war cries of the Departed behind the slave and looked over at his companions—his family with whom he had executed hundreds of ambushes exactly like this—to see if they were ready. They were. And when Ell judged that the targets were within range by the sound of the running, he gave the nod to his family and as one, they stepped from around the trunks of the trees and raised and loosed their black arrows from the shadows, as if all in one swift and sure motion.

The arrows flew true and found their marks. Five of the Departed dropped to the ground in the first flurry, clutching arrows that had pierced throats, eyes, and hearts. The remaining five froze as if trying to decide whether to run or attack. Surprised and in disarray, two fled and were feathered by Dahranian and Dacunda, falling to the ground with arrows in their backs. The three that had charged were met by Ryder, Rihya, and Ell. Ell could tell by their blank gazes and sickly faces that these three were most definitely Unsired. They moved powerfully, with the wider and more muscular frames of the southern elves, but their movements were jerky. It was hard to put a finger on what made their movements so strange, it was recognizable on an instinctual level by the way they moved and the way they fought.

One rushed at Ell and swung a heavy, cruel scimitar at his head. He ducked and darted in close, freeing his dueling daggers from their sheaths on the outsides of his thighs to eviscerate the Unsired in one quick cut. He heard more than saw the thud of two arrows planting themselves in the chest of the Unsired he had just disemboweled. His uncle and oldest cousin were cleaning up after the hand-to-hand fighters.

Rihya had thrown a dagger into her assailant's eye then dashed around to hamstring him and he crumpled to the ground. His sister darted in close and finished off the Departed—the Unsired, Ell corrected himself—by cutting its throat. Black blood fountained out over her hands and onto her wrists, eliciting a disgusted look onto her face.

Ryder, having faced off with the last of the three, and was having the hardest time. He had engaged with the biggest of the Unsired and the thing that had once been a southern elf fought Ell's cousin violently with a long spear and a small shield. He was catching Ryder's axe blows on the shield with one powerfully upraised arm while delivering snakelike strikes with the tip of his spear, forcing Ryder to dodge and move out of the way continually. Dacunda and Dahranian gave Ryder a shout to get out of the way and began loosing shaft after shaft of black arrows into the Unsired. One arrow pierced its shoulder, another its eye, but it fought on and turned to engage the two shooting at it. The Unsired were an ancient evil and while some died as quickly as the Departed they had once been, this one seemed to have gained supernatural strength to resist its wounds. It didn't howl in pain, it just stared blankly ahead and adjusted its course to attack the new assailants. In the end, Dacunda cleverly targeted its legs and stuck enough arrows in it to make it collapse, unable to bear its own weight. Ryder stepped in quickly and lopped off its head from a fair distance with his long axe.

"Couldn't let you steal my kill," he managed to say with a straight face, only ruining his serious display with a wink to Ell. Dacunda and Dahranian, accustomed to their kinsman's antics, ignored his joke and began retrieving their arrows and checking to make sure the dead would remain unmoving.

It wasn't until Ell retrieved his arrows and cleaned them before putting them back into his quiver, that he remembered the human. Ell turned his head quickly, surveying the scene and saw a human head poke itself out from behind the trunk of one of the trees. Ell walked toward the human, who had now stepped fully into view, seeing that the Departed were dead. Dacunda and Dahranian, seeing where he was walking, stopped checking the dead and rose to flank him. Ryder and Rihya continued retrieving arrows and wiping ink-black blood off of them onto the withered yellow grass and the soiled clothes of the dead.

The human walked toward them carefully, hands raised in the universal signal to show he was unarmed. He was of average height for a human, just about the same height as the elves, but he was broader in the shoulders and thicker in the waist. He was also swarthy like the southern elves, with dark tanned skin. However, unlike either of the races of elves, he had hair cut closely to his head and a black, finely groomed goatee cropped close to his face.

"Who are you?" Dacunda took the lead out of habit, stopping to stare at the human from a few feet away.

Ell flicked his eyes towards his uncle in annoyance. He did not wish to appear petty, but his attained control of his own life and actions felt very flimsy right now. One minute, he was making decisions, the next, it seemed like he was barely keeping control of the expedition as Arendahl or Dacunda questioned his every move—like his decision to ambush the southern elves.

"I am Kalabi," the human answered politely, keeping his hands raised to show them he meant no harm.

"What are you doing here, this far from your own kind and pursued by those with whom you have an alliance?" Ell asked. The humans and the dark elves had enjoyed an uneasy truce, an alliance of sorts, for the past two decades.

"I am running away, of course." Kalabi responded as if it should be perfectly clear, his brown eyes wide with innocence—and gratitude. Ell could see genuine gratitude there swimming in his expression.

And perhaps it was obvious. Ell took a closer look at him, letting his gaze drift away from the human's face. Trailing down, he saw a finely worked golden collar around Kalabi's neck. Slave. He was a slave. But then Ell saw his garments. A flowing white linen shirt with similarly loose white linen breeches, were no ordinarily woven clothes. They were very fine, if soiled from travel. They did not look like any of the clothes that he had seen human slaves wearing on previous occasions. Ell's suspicion returned in full force. Dacunda had drilled caution into all of them from an early age.

"I see," Dacunda said. He seemed about to speak further until he closed his mouth abruptly and looked to Ell. It was still odd, Dacunda looking to Ell for directions, yet it was what Ell had forced upon him if he wished to accompany Ell—and subsequently all the family he had—south. Ell resolutely and firmly regained the lead in the situation.

Ell motioned for Kalabi to follow them. "You will come with us for the moment. We have much to ask you, but we cannot stay here." Ell looked around at the miniature scene of carnage. There were only a handful of bodies, but already the smell of death permeated the air, much more strongly than when he and Arendahl had scented the Bonewinds earlier.

They jogged lightly back towards Arendahl, Miri, and Art. Ell ran at the front with Dacunda and Dahranian to his left and right. Kalabi ran in the middle and tried to keep up with their pace, although Ell could tell by his breathing that he found it difficult, even though it was an easy pace for the elves. Rihya and Ryder carried the rear, watching their backs, but also keeping an eye on the human to make sure he didn't try to run. Not that he could get far even if he did.

It was only minutes before they had returned to the rest of their party. Arendahl paced impatiently while carefully surveying the woods around him. Miri sat on a log with Art talking quietly and keeping the boy occupied while they waited.

"Took you long enough. What was the hold up?" Arendahl barked at Ell.

"You are the leader?" Kalabi directed his half statement, half question towards the old, grey haired elf.

Ell puckered his lips in frustration, but couldn't really blame the human for his thinking. Other than Art, Ell was the youngest one, just entering the year of his twentieth name day, same as Miri.

Arendahl laughed shortly and then flicked an amused glance at Ell. The old elf shifted his gaze back to the human and spoke.

"Not today. You'll need to address yourself to Elliyar." He indicated Ell with a gnarled old finger.

Kalabi turned towards Ell in surprise. "My apologies. I did not mean to offend by my mistake."

Ell brushed it off as best he could. "It is of no importance. But I do wish you to provide me with answers."

"Of course," Kalabi replied promptly.

And so Ell began interrogating him with simple questions. "Are you alone?"

"Yes."

"You say you are running from the Departed?

"Yes."

"Why?" Ell asked Kalabi bluntly.

Again, the human looked at him as if it were clear. "I am a slave. And I do not wish to remain so." He tilted his chin up so that the sun glinted off the gold collar.

"You do not look like any slave we have ever seen," interjected Dacunda, before retreating into annoyed silence again at Ell's cold stare.

Ell repeated his uncle's statement. "You look different than the others we have seen."

Kalabi spread his hands wide. "That is because I am a Maker. We are highly prized and not sent into combat or work duty along the front lines."

Maker? What was that? Ell filed the question away for later. "Then how did you come to be here, all the way across the continent, near the edges of Andalaya?" He pressed his questioning.

"I told you, I am a slave, so I ran. I came to be here on my own two feet. I simply escaped and got as far away as I could. The southern elves saw me and chased me. I knew that if they caught me they would either kill me or send me back to my enslavement." Kalabi was now growing frustrated with having to repeat himself.

Ell went back to the bit about apparent types of slaves. "What is a Maker? What is this type of slave?" All of Ell's family leaned their heads in, interested but remaining quiet as the human responded.

Kalabi took a breath before answering. "We are the most prized among the slaves. We are given all that we could wish for, jewels, fine clothes, women, drink. In exchange, we create. We make their tools, their war weapons. We invent many things, including the machines with which they make war to further their progress. We are selected at a young age after completing aptitude tests, to be trained as Makers."

Ryder barked a laugh. "Doesn't sound so bad. Why would you want to leave all that privilege and luxury behind? Females and wine can't be all that terrible."

"Yes," Ell narrowed his eyes suspiciously. "I must ask you again, why did you leave?"

"I may have had everything," Kalabi stated plainly, coolly, "but I was still a slave. There is no substitute for freedom."

Ell felt a rush of admiration for the man. It appeared at least some of the humans had dignity, and nobility.

"Alright, supposing we accept all that you have told us," Ell suggested, emphasizing the doubt to make it clear that he was far from trusting, "what other information can you give us? Are there any more humans around? Did you see any other bands of Departed?" He fired the questions quickly at Kalabi.

Kalabi spread his hands again in regret. "I saw no one other than the ones who chased me. I have seen no one for the many weeks it took me to travel from the camps to the east. But while I have done enough to elude my captors this far, I must admit, I am not a skilled woodsman and my skills of observation might be lacking." The human slave—ex-slave Ell corrected himself—admitted it freely, unashamed of his lack of ability in the wild.

Ell paused. He glanced at Arendahl and Dacunda. He wished to consult with them, but he did not want to appear as if he were regretting or relinquishing his command of the expedition. In the end, for once, Ell's better sense won out over his pride and he motioned for his two elders to come with him a few feet away. In hurried, quiet, voices he asked their opinions.

"Seems to be telling the truth," Dacunda volunteered without batting an eye at Ell's request for advice. Ell nodded his agreement.

"Remarkably straightforward for a human," Arendahl said. "I did not expect to meet one of their race so honest. We should take him with us, he could be useful."

Ell wasn't sure he liked that idea. Kalabi might seem trustworthy and his story seemed to make sense—Ell had seen the look of outrage and anger when he spoke of slavery—yet, the safety of Ell's family and his parents' hope of freedom depended upon this venture. Did he want to take a risk on a stranger?

"I do not want him to accompany us," he whispered to Arendahl and Dacunda as he came to a decision. "We know too little about him. He could be a danger or a hindrance."

"Don't be foolish, boy!" Arendahl immediately disagreed. "He'll be useful. Mark my words. The Maker caste of slaves. They sound like they would be very convenient to have around."

"No," Ell disagreed.

Arendahl shook his head. "Foolish! Did you figure out what caused the clap of thunder? He may know." The old elf shrewdly pointed out. In the adrenaline and the heat of the skirmish, Ell had forgotten all about the concussion of sound that had shook the clearing. Ell's embarrassed silence was all the answer that Arendahl needed. The old elf snorted.

Dacunda spoke up again. "Elliyar, you fought so hard to rescue him and now you wish to leave him on his own. We are entering enemy territory. He will be taken or killed in a matter of days, most likely. You are effectively sentencing him to death. Besides, do you not feel that Arendahl may have a good point?" His last question dug at Ell, nettled him.

"We are not responsible for him. We saved him once. We do not owe him anything." Ell found himself fighting back, arguing for the sake of arguing.

"Come, boy, one night at least won't hurt. I know a place not far from here. We'll make camp and make the decision there. A few more hours with him and we may be able to glean some useful information." Arendahl's patronizing tone made Ell grit his teeth, but he had run out of logical arguments. One night at least wouldn't hurt anything.

"Fine," he muttered.

They walked the few feet back to the others. Everyone looked up at them to see what decision had been made. Kalabi looked up expectantly.

"You will accompany us to our evening camp. Beyond tonight nothing is certain, but for now you will be safe with us." Ell spoke directly to the human. Kalabi inclined his head politely and gratefully.

"I wish to stay with you longer than tonight. I can be useful," Kalabi volunteered with a cautious, but hopeful expression on his face.

Ell appraised him. "That will be decided upon later. But you should know, we do not make a habit of letting outsiders join us."

"Well, that is that. Follow me then," Arendahl said brusquely. "I know a place not far from here—although far enough to be a safe haven for tonight." The afternoon light was fading as the sun sank lower in the sky. His hair glistened silvery in the golden light as opposed to its usual lank grey appearance.

"Where will we make camp?" Rihya asked, ever inquisitive.

"We will go to the ruins of Castan Yol," the old elf replied, with an odd tone in his voice.

Chapter Nine

Half-Mask peered out over the city he held in his fist from the window of his high tower room. Dor Khabor—or Dark Harbor as it was most frequently called—was spread across the island on which it lay. In the distance to the east, he saw the mountains that ringed the bay from the land. In between each peak, mountain fortresses had been constructed, rendering the narrow valleys nearly impassable. Nobody worried of attack by sea. The island was covered by the city to the inch, and much of their fighting force was in their long ships and sea warriors. In fact, many of his people were more comfortably with a deck rolling beneath their feet than on solid ground. His own brother was one of them. Half-Mask shook his head in disgust. If it were up to him, he would just kill his brother and have done with it. But it was too early for that to occur. Too early in his plan. For now, he had to maintain a semblance of appearances and killing his royal brother would not further his cause. Besides, his brother did fill an important role, and he performed his duties admirably. Nevertheless, Half-Mask despised him. His brother's principles made him weak.

Why had his father chosen now, of all times, to come back to the capital? The King of the South hadn't left his Enclave for years. Half-Mask paced impatiently across the length of his tower—impatiently, not nervously. He was never nervous, not that he ever admitted, even to himself, at least. His gaze drifted from window to window as he looked at the ramshackle state of his city. The tower windows were huge, meant for viewing, and the walls around him obstructed less space than the windows covered. His city was a maze, a warren of activity, buildings erected on top of each other in a haphazard manner, in the way that only happens when a city is confined to a limited amount of space and that space runs out. The only option is to build up and over other buildings. This ramshackle approach to the city construction meant that wooden and stone houses, shops, factories, and more leaned outward, over balancing, in many cases gaining slightly in width and scope as they rose. This left the narrow tangle of streets shadowed by overhanging edifices, perfect, dark alleys, and corners for all sorts of criminals to lurk. Half-Mask smirked. He appreciated the danger of his city. It embodied his vision. The strong survived. One had to stay alert and ready at all times in Dark Harbor else they were likely to run afoul of a blade in the back or at the very least lose a purse after traversing its jumbled streets. It was dark, shadowy, just as he was.

Where was the king? Frustration was building. Half-Mask was not one to wait on anyone. How dare his father keep him waiting thus! He flexed his fingers like claws and lightly tongued the needle sharp points of his front teeth, a habit he had developed over the years, a simple reminder of the potential for violence that he possessed with merely his bodily form. A tiny, nagging voice murmured caution in the back of his mind. Careful now, it said, careful. It would not do to meet his father full of rage. No, it would not do at all. The King of the South was not to be taken lightly.

Finally, steps could be heard climbing the ancient stone tower. No one would announce his father, the King needed no introduction, and it could be worth as much as one's life to spend time in his presence. He could be even more fickle than Half-Mask in that way. Likely, this was due to the madness.

The door opened eventually. The worn, iron-banded wood swung inward and the king swept in slowly. He was tall for an elf, and wore a dark cloak with the hood up, veiling his face in shadow. His hands protruded from the sleeves of his cloak and carried the same diseased appearance that Half-Mask's face did. Unfiled white teeth flashed from the darkness under his hood as Half-Mask's father spoke.

"You should not pace so, my son, it only shows weakness to appear so…anxious." The king spoke in a dead voice, seemingly devoid of all emotion. Yet Half-Mask heard the faint humor attached to the statement, the jest at his expense.

Anxious! Half-Mask seethed inside. He would show his father what worry truly looked like by turning the King's face to a mirror when Half-Mask finally had his way with him. Calm. The voice burned like a coal in the back of his mind. Not yet. Not yet. Even so, Half-Mask merely sneered in response. "I will pace if I see fit, Father."

"So you will," the king said, in that same dead voice, and changed the subject as if it were the dullest topic he could imagine. "You have mismanaged events in my…absence."

Half-Mask narrowed his eyes. "How?"

"The Traitor is dead. Even in my seclusion, word of that loss has reached my ears. He was central to many of my plans." The king's voice did not lose its deadened quality, yet Half-Mask could hear the edge creeping into it.

"Your plans?" Half-Mask snarled the question.

The King of the South inclined his head in response. "Very well, our plans then. Yet do not forget, my son, that it was I who brought you into this."

Oh, he would not forget. Never would Half-Mask forget that moment, not long after his birth, when his father had torn him from the arms of his mother and suckled him with the dark liquid that was now Half-Mask's only drink of choice. How he remembered that moment, as nothing more than a baby, was a mystery to Half-Mask, yet perhaps it was such an important moment that it had imprinted itself upon his consciousness forever. He did not resent his father for that choice, for giving his son to the darkness. It was a dark blessing, the life Half-Mask led. But he would not be an inferior. No. That time was long passed. One day…

For the first time, a smile played at the corner of his father's mouth, just for a moment before his face receded into its usual blank mask of nothingness. As if he could tell what Half-Mask had been thinking, the King asked in a neutral tone, "Is it time, then?"

Half-Mask's breath quickened with excitement and anticipation. He felt his mouth slack open, just slightly anticipating the kill, the blood, the death.

The King of the South trailed a finger idly along the wooden table at the center of the room as he watched his son, waiting. The finger emitted a smoky, insubstantial darkness from its tip, wisps of blackness wafting up, leaving a trail in the air between them, the way smoke wafts from a chimney.

Half-Mask controlled himself. The blackness trailing through the air brought him back to reality. It would not do to underestimate his father. Oh, it wasn't fear—he told himself—it was caution. He forced his pulse down, calmed has mind, and he affected a smile. No, not fear. But in all the world, if there was one person not to be taken lightly, it was the King of the South. Half-Mask would bide his time and wait.

"Not yet, Father."

"Very well then, back to business." His father spoke as if getting back to business could not possibly be any more boring. He spoke with the numbness that only one who was half possessed by death could do. "You have mismanaged things. Not only did the Traitor die, but the manner in which he died is most…inconvenient."

Half-Mask's nostrils flared, but he kept his voice civil as he stared into the pure black eyes of his father. "I am dealing with it."

"Are you? It has been months since Silverfist was slain by a northern boy rumored to possess strange powers, hidden talents. Not only did he kill the Traitor, but he led the slaughter of hundreds of our people."

"Slavers can be replaced without issue." Half-Mask responded in angry annoyance. "It is of no matter." He waved his hand dismissively.

"You are wrong." The King of the South spoke with dead certainty. "There are rumors of powers beyond that which we possess. Those rumors need to be squashed with the utmost ruthlessness. We rule by power, my son, we rule by the abilities we possess…" the king emphasized his point by suddenly growing hazy in appearance, a dark specter of insubstantiality before flickering back into focus, into solidity, "however, most of all, we rule by fear. And fear is only absolute in the absence of hope. These rumors from Andalaya must be destroyed because they cause people to wonder, to think about what they might mean. They cause people to hope."

Half-Mask gritted his teeth at the naming of that filthy, northern kingdom. Even shattered as it was, he hated the reminder. But his father spoke sense. Half-Mask had never doubted his father's ability or his cunning.

"Then we will crush those rumors."

"Good," his father said. "Then do it."

The king issued the command with a finality that said there was no other option but to succeed, and then swept back out of the room and began descending the steps of the tower. Half-Mask abhorred being told what to do, but he knew it must be done.

He grabbed his goblet of black drink and sipped, savoring the rich flavor, in one instant bitter, the next so sweet it was sickly. He held it near his mouth and let his tongue loll out, delicately dancing on the surface of the drink. It was ecstasy in a cup.

After a minute he pulled his focus back, stuck a smoking finger into the goblet, and began stirring the dark liquid. Half-Mask whispered. He cajoled the darkness. Before long, shapes began to emerge. They rose up out of the surface of the liquid, climbed down the sides of the cup and dashed back into the center, roiling in upon themselves. Little waves of blackness rose and fell as he murmured. Finally, shapes solidified. Narrow, thin bodies of black began climbing the sides of his cup as if they had suctions on their hands and feet. More and more, a small legion of them rose out of the blackness, at his Awakening, and began climbing over and around each other.

Not for the first time, Half-Mask uttered the name of an enemy into the cup. "Wintermoon."

The thin dark shapes of creatures froze as he whispered the name, as if hearing it and processing the information.

"Go," Half-Mask commanded and the shapes leapt from the walls of his goblet back into the dark liquid and disappeared into its mass.

Half-Mask drained the drink in one giant gulp.

Chapter Ten

"Good, boy, good. I want you to focus. Do it by choice not instinct. Otherwise instinct will be all you have to guide you when the power comes. I want you to be bursting with it but still able to think clearly. And I don't want you to pass out from fatigue afterwards the way it has happened when you access your abilities by accident and without intention." Arendahl was issuing a series of commands, hardly waiting for a response before barking the next order.

Miri listened to Ell's training with Arendahl. They always stepped a few feet away from the rest while they practiced, but Miri positioned herself strategically along the edge of the camp, so she could overhear them as they worked. Ell had described his powers as a Water Caller to her—the way he drew upon the power of life, the power of water, ever-present throughout Creation around them. He spoke of the way it swelled suddenly within him when he accessed it, how much of the time he tapped these abilities accidentally, leaving him exhausted and drained when they finally left him, as they had after rescuing her from the Pillar. Ell had told Miri also about how, at the battle for Little Vale, he had finally accessed his powers deliberately. It had occurred by finally accepting himself as a Water Caller, by not trying to struggle or work for it, but rather realizing that it was simply who he was. That acceptance had allowed a shift within, making it easier to access his abilities.

Yes, Ell had told her all of these things, but Miri still found it interesting to listen and watch as he learned as much as he could from the wizened elf. They had been training like this every evening after camp was made. It was the only reason that Arendahl was still with them instead of tending to other important matters. Or so he said.

"That's it, boy!" Arendahl urged his pupil.

Ell let out a grunt of effort and then a vexed sigh. "I had it, Arendahl. It was there, just beyond my reach, and then I grabbed it. I felt it swell inside me like it always does, but after a few moments it was gone." His dejection elicited a wave of sympathy through Miri. Her mate was so serious, so focused on being and doing all that he could. Often, she thought of it as her own personal mission to make sure he did not take life too seriously. Her mission was to make sure he remembered the lighter and brighter side of life whenever possible. Otherwise, she had no doubt that the pressures and responsibility of being the second Water Caller in centuries would swallow Ell whole. She would prevent that from happening. Somehow she would do it. She promised herself that.

She kept listening and heard the old elf utter surprisingly encouraging words towards Ell. Arendahl was usually a curt, unyielding teacher, not giving much praise and more apt to pick out the details of what you did wrong than right. But, perhaps sensing—as Miri did—that after a huge breakthrough in his abilities at the battle for Little Vale, but following a largely unproductive and disappointing summer of near-futile attempts, what Ell needed most right now was reassurance and some encouragement.

"Don't worry. It'll begin to happen soon enough. You're making progress." The old elf spoke gruffly in his stilted manner, as if he was not comfortable giving compliments.

Miri kept herself angled toward the rest of the group, camped just within the borders of the ruins of what must have once been a small city, arrayed around a small, partially concealed fire. However, she kept her ears trained on the conversation behind her.

"Am I, though?" Ell asked. "I had such a breakthrough moment during the battle. It was as if everything made sense, I knew deep down to my core that this is who I am, that I am a Water Caller. And yet, now…" Miri heard her mate's voice trail off into silence.

"Now what, boy?"

"Now it feels like I am back to the first step, where I can barely access my power whether by choice or by accident. You know, I tried to grab hold of it when I was attacked by the tree ogre, but I lost focus and it slipped away."

"I figured," the old elf grunted. "There's no way that thing would have troubled you if you'd been bursting at the seams with power. But even so, just the realization that it is close, that it was there before you lost it, that's progress, lad. That's a long sight better than not being able to sense it at all."

A burst of laughter erupted around the campfire as Ryder told a ridiculous joke. Even Dahranian, the most serious of the bunch cracked a wide smile at his brother's antics. Rihya was keeled over on her side, gasping for breath, Art was laughing and staring at Ryder adoringly, and Dacunda was shaking his head despite a small smile playing at his lips as he tended the spit above their fire. Miri had missed whatever had entertained them, but she was more interested in the conversation behind her than the humor around the fire.

She kept her eyes trained on the tunic she was mending as a guise for where her focus lay, but her ears drank in the training discussion like a thirsty soul. Ell was forthcoming with her, he told her much, but hearing the session was different. It was like seeing a new side of him.

Ell was now back to reaching out his consciousness. "Stretch it out, feel the land around you. Feel the water in every particle, the morning dew absorbed in the ground, the roots of the trees, packed full of water to sustain the tree. Feel the streams and creeks all around."

Ell did as he was told. Miri chanced a glance behind her and saw in the fading light of evening that Ell's eyes were a cloudy, foggy color, rather than their usual clear blue. A faint condensation was clinging to him as if it was misting right around him.

Ell smiled abruptly. "I've got it!" He exclaimed. "I can feel it. Such power right at my fingertips." Miri smiled in silent joy. She could hear the elation in his voice. He had been so angry all summer, with both his elders, but also at himself. He hadn't said it, but she knew that his failed attempts to reach his powers had left an injury of sorts on his psyche. She hoped it was now mending.

Just as she thought that however, Ell swore and puckered up his face in disgust. "It is gone. Just like that. There one moment and gone the next." The dejection in his face was painful to witness.

"What were you thinking of when it left?" Arendahl always asked shrewd questions.

"What...?" Ell seemed to be caught off guard.

"I said, what were you thinking about, what was occupying your mind when you lost it?"

"I..." Ell trailed off, clearly embarrassed by something.

"Out with it boy," barked the old elf impatiently. "I've no time for your embarrassed dawdling."

Ell sighed and responded. "I was elated right when it happened, but then I heard my uncle say something and..."

"You are too angry at him, Elliyar. It is painful to watch. It is killing him inside, you know. He sees you as a son, and now you act as though you hate him. Is forgiveness really so hard to give?" Arendahl waited for an answer to his question, but Ell stayed silent, a firm, stubborn look on his face.

"Very well. How about this to make you think? I believe that your anger is causing you to lose focus. You are too consumed by it, boy. Rage can be channeled. But our abilities tap into Creation itself and Creation is not angry. The land does not hate or feel fury. It simply seeks balance. We, the Highest, and especially the Water Callers, were spun out by fate, by Creation to right the wrong in the world, to mend the evil. But Creation did not make us out of anger, it made us to correct an imbalance." Arendahl paused for effect. "You must control and master your emotions, lad, else I feel it will continue to be hard for you to grab hold of your abilities."

Ell nodded sourly. Miri would have laughed at the funny expression on his face if it had not been so sad to see him this angry at his uncle. She alone knew how hard the summer had been for him.

"Now, again." The old elf said briskly, motioning Ell back into training action. Ell dutifully complied. They had only been training for a short while and would continue for at least another hour.

Miri split her focus again and looked around the fire. The newcomer, Kalabi, was engrossed in conversation with the boy Art, teaching him some sort of skill or another. Kalabi clearly had a brilliant mind. Just a short time speaking with him and she had been convinced of that.

Dacunda and the rest of his family were now passing around some freshly cooked rabbit that Dahranian had skewered with an arrow as they traveled. Ryder tossed her a piece of the meat.

"There you go, cousin!" He practically shouted delightedly. "Don't wait for it too cool, it's best when hot." His toothy grin made Miri smile, and she dutifully took a bite, even though it was so hot that she was juggling the piece in her hand just to avoid discomfort.

Finishing her portion of the meat, Miri receded back into the guise of mending in order to listen uninterrupted once more. But a thought struck her. Ell was training, so why didn't she? Miri cautiously pushed out her own consciousness, but not towards the land as Ell was doing, but instead towards him. Miri focused all her mind on her mate, on his thoughts, his emotions, she pushed her consciousness out like she had in the moment of the Grafting…and nothing. Miri felt absolutely nothing. Determined, she tried again. Miri tried to recall all the information about Grafting that she had gleaned from her conversations with Ell and Arendahl. What had Arendahl said? He had said it was a one-way connection, that much was certain. So she alone would be able to experience Ell's thoughts and emotions, and sometimes even see through his eyes. But only in important situations. Momentous events were required to stimulate that part of her consciousness that she had folded—had forged—into his. Otherwise, nothing would happen.

Miri pushed until she felt like she would get a headache. Nothing. Disgruntled, she felt like she understood a bit how Ell felt when he didn't tap into his abilities as a Water Caller. It was frustrating to know that there was something outside her realm of control, something so personal as a window into her mate's soul, but beyond her ability to access.

She wouldn't tell Ell what she was doing, that much she was certain. He was still too worried about some potential for future suffering to see the Grafting for what it was—a blessing. It was a way for them to stay somewhat connected even though Miri knew they would soon be separated by many miles.

"Yes!" Ell burst out, interrupting her line of thought. "Yes," he repeated jubilantly.

"Now hold on to it, boy. Don't let it go." The old elf muttered his encouragement.

"It is here to stay this time, Arendahl. I can feel it, I can feel the connection to the earth. For now, I can hold it without fear of losing it."

Miri heard the pride in Ell's voice as he achieved success that had eluded him for months since the battle for the valley. She smiled and pushed out her own consciousness... Nothing. Apparently, this wasn't an important enough event to enable her to access the Graft. Or perhaps she just did not know what she was doing.

Ell, having just done what he had set out to do and clearly feeling pleased with himself, felt comfortable enough to change the course of discussion. "I forgot to ask you, Elder, why do we—you and I, Water Callers—smell the Bonewinds so much earlier than the others?"

"Well, the Bonewinds are an ancient warning from Creation itself that our enemies are near. It makes sense that we—Water Callers, the leaders of the fight against that evil—would be most attuned to that warning, eh?" The old elf answered the question, but seemed more interested in continuing the lesson. "Now, you're still holding your ability right, you haven't lost it yet?"

Ell nodded his affirmation, but then stopped cold and his expression was suddenly more alert than ever. Arendahl also froze and tilted his nose up in the air.

"Speaking of Bonewinds," murmured Arendahl cautiously, and then he and Ell both made eye contact as if realizing something simultaneously.

"To arms!" Cried the old elf, drawing his sword in the blink of an eye.

In a flash, Ell had drawn his two dueling daggers—holding one point up and the other tip down, in his typical fighting manner.

The others had but a moment's notice afforded to them by Arendahl's warning shout before a mass of shapes began swarming out of the rubble of buildings around them. Through the growing darkness, Miri watched as more Ghouls than she could have ever imagined raced towards the camp. Some of the Ghouls scampered along on all fours, others loped in the direction of the camp on their hind legs, while even more of them skittered spiderlike along the sides of broken walls, the suctions on their hands and feet allowing them to pass along the vertical objects as if it were no more difficult than running on the ground.

Ryder and Rihya were both swearing as they pulled steel from sheaths and picked up secondary weapons. Dacunda and Dahranian smoothly drew the swords strapped to their backs in unison, stoically facing the veritable horde of dark creatures boiling towards them over the rocks and rubble of the ruins.

Arendahl was barking orders. Whatever pretense he'd made about Ell assuming command, it was clear that he was prepared to take control of the situation when he thought it was required.

"Form up now, hurry, we don't have more than a few seconds!" Miri watched as the old elf directed her new family into their fighting positions. "Dacunda, Dahranian you hold the center of the line, Ryder the right, Valerihya the left. Miriyah, Artorious and, you, newcomer, get behind us and stay back. Elliyar and I will step right into their midst and take the fight to them. You all clean up the scraps that get through." To a bystander it might seem arrogant, even suicidal, to declare that two elves were going to charge into the midst of a swarm of attacking Ghouls, but that bystander would not be aware that the two lanky elves—one young, one elderly—were born for it.

Everyone, even Ell, obeyed the old elf's barked commands without a moment of hesitation. Miri clambered over a few fallen stones and quickly moved behind the defending fighters, clasping Art's hand as much to comfort herself as the boy.

"Well, boy, still tapping your abilities? Remember, avoid the stingers..." Arendahl was saying to Ell.

Ell only had time to give a vigorous nod of assent before the beasts were upon them and Ell and Arendahl leaped forward into the fray with a whirl of steel and blades.

Miri had seen Ell in combat before, while he was fighting to rescue and free her from the Pillar, and she had also watched him take on an Icari all by himself, but she had never truly seen him in the midst of battle—having not witnessed the desperate fight to save Little Vale herself.

It was overwhelming to watch it now, almost terrifying. He was her mate, but he dealt death like nothing she had ever witnessed. Ell was a vortex of death, a whirlwind of mayhem. He and Arendahl cut a swathe through the Ghouls, leaving thin camouflaged limbs and heads lopped off of bodies to fall to the ground. The strange keening cries of the Ghouls as they fought and died sent a shiver down her spine. They were otherworldly, frightening to hear.

However, the fight didn't go as one would expect. Even Water Callers, fighting with their increased strength and reflexes, their heightened agility and speed, would have missed a few. Some of the Ghouls should have bypassed Arendahl and Ell and begun to attack the rest of them. But this wasn't the case. The mass of Ghouls, maybe one hundred of them now swirled around the two Water Callers doing everything in their power to just touch them, to simply place a hand full of deadly, venomous stingers on bare skin and pierce the flesh.

Eyes fogging in the manner they always did, Ell fought and slashed with a beautiful elegance. Condensation misted into the air around only him and dewy droplets of water wicked off his blades as he wielded them with incredible accuracy. But the strangeness of the fight increased. Even Arendahl appeared to be getting ignored by the Ghouls, such was their continued focus on Ell. All of the dark creatures focused so intently on Ell, that even with all his supernatural talent and ability, he began to waver before the onslaught. The beasts were quick and agile in their own way, leaping up to walls and then back down to attack him from above as well as from the sides. Arendahl slashed at their backs and a few of the Ghouls turned to try and deal with the lank, grey haired elf, but his gnarled hands gripped his sword and dispatched them with relative ease, yet for all his efforts he couldn't quite get through the mass of creatures separating him and his young protégé.

Dacunda, Ryder, Dahranian, and Rihya shared uncomfortable looks as they watched the youngest of their family fight gracefully, lithely, but also desperately for his life, against the swarm of venomous evil. Arendahl had told them to stay put, to mop up the scraps, but the old elf could never have envisioned a scenario like this where every enemy made it their utmost task to kill only a single foe.

"That's it, I've seen enough," declared Rihya angrily, and dashed into the fray. Of course, she would never willingly watch her brother be worn down by numerous and dangerous foes.

The three other trained fighters shared a quick look, as if to ask each other silently whether they should obey the order of their elder or follow the lead of their young cousin.

"Right, you two go," Dacunda said gruffly.

"As you command, Father," Dahranian responded respectfully.

Ryder winked at his father. "I thought you'd never say so."

The two brothers advanced into the backs of the Ghouls boiling around Ell, joining Rihya in an attempt to draw some of the pressure off her brother.

Dacunda glanced behind him at the three non-fighting members of the group. He was clearly staying back to guard them, should one of the Ghouls act more naturally and attack them. However, sitting out of the fight was no easier for him than for his sons, and his face was constricted in a grimace of anxiety and frustration.

The fight continued in earnest and Miri watched her family kill Ghoul after Ghoul. But their energy was waning, the numbers of the Ghouls were just too many.

Kalabi grabbed Dacunda's arm and whispered urgently in his ear. Miri heard Ell's uncle say, "Are you sure?" and Kalabi nodded assuredly and with emphasis.

"To me, brethren to me!" bellowed Dacunda. Elf heads swiveled quickly and began making their way to the call of Dacunda. Ell, the hardest pressed was the last to reach their ranks, standing just in front of the rest.

"What are you planning?" Arendahl asked Dacunda, as the old elf fended off a Ghoul with a slash and then skewered another.

"It is not my plan," Dacunda responded, cutting and slashing, standing his ground against the dark foes. "It is Kalabi's idea."

Miri turned her head to watch as the former slave dipped a hand inside his flowing linen clothing and pulled out a small packet. The human lobbed the pouch over the elves in front of him and into the midst of the thinned, yet still formidable, attacking force of creatures. Red eyes of the Ghouls gleamed in the moonlight before the pouch impacted the ground and the scene in front of Miri erupted like nothing she had ever seen. A concussion like a small ball of thunder shook the ruins, and fire flamed up and outward in a spiral of death. Body parts of the Ghouls flew through the air and charred pieces of meat and bone sprayed everyone. Only a few of the swarm of dark creatures survived the blast and they were quickly dispatched by the two Water Callers with ruthless efficiency.

When the dark creatures were dead and bodies had been checked to make sure of it, every eye turned to Kalabi. Eyebrows were raised in surprise, and Ryder clapped the former slave on the shoulder in excitement.

"What a show that was!" Ryder exclaimed enthusiastically. "I have never seen the like. It was like a tiny fire mountain erupting."

Dacunda and Arendahl eyed the slave with narrowed, appraising eyes, but they too offered thanks and appreciation.

"We call it handfire." The former slave explained to their questions about what he had just used to kill the Ghouls.

"Well, it is very effective," Dacunda allowed.

Kalabi nodded politely. "It is newly developed. And most of the research and composition was developed by me." The human pointed delicately and humbly to his chest. The rest of the group gazed at him with added respect.

"Well anyone who can invent something that kills that many of those sticky bastards at once is good in my book," Ryder proclaimed. Kalabi grinned in appreciation.

Ever watchful, ever serious, Dacunda was the first to shake free of the shock of what they had just witnessed and suggest the next course of action.

"We should move camp. Not out of the ruins altogether, but to the other side of the city at least. If that is alright with you that is, Nephew."

Ell inclined his head in agreement. They gathered their few belongings and began walking towards the southern end of the ruined city of Castan Yol. Ell stayed quiet as they walked, the moonlight playing across his wavy blond hair, his blue eyes no longer cloudy since he had let go of his Water Calling powers.

"You have not collapsed with exhaustion." Miri noticed. Ell blinked and looked in surprise at her after her comment.

"What? Oh, right, well, it's because I tapped into my abilities consciously, rather than instinctively. It was fortunate that I was training with Arendahl and was already holding my powers when the Ghouls arrived. Otherwise, I might not have been as much use."

He stayed quiet. Something was amiss. "What is wrong Ell, other than the usual worry that a battle evokes?"

Ell responded slowly. "It's not battle really. I am accustomed to such occurrences. It is more the manner in which it was fought." He trailed off without specifying what he meant. However, Miri knew.

"You mean the way they all targeted you?"

"You noticed?"

"Everyone noticed," Miri snorted, somehow managing to find humor and joy in the moment, despite the terror of the previous situation.

"I suppose that is true," Ell admitted. He seemed shaken, very uneasy.

"Talk to me, love," Miri prodded him. He needed to know she could be there, could handle whatever it was that was worrying him. Her body might be weak, but her spirit was strong.

He gazed at her in silence for a moment then smiled slightly. "Very well. I am worried, you are correct. It's the Ghouls. I have never seen more than a few at once and even then they hardly worked in unison. This was unheard of, hundreds of Ghouls fighting in tandem."

"Not unheard of," Arendahl clipped, interrupting. "Happened in the First Days, or so legends say. Entire armies of creatures fighting along the Unsired, obeying their command."

"But there was no Unsired here tonight." Miri contradicted the old elf.

He appraised her with a keen eye. "Smart girl. No, there wasn't. And that is why your young Elliyar is worried."

Ell nodded his agreement as they continued walking. Everyone, now listening to their conversation, had rapt looks upon their faces. "What do you think it means?" asked Dahranian of the old elf.

"I have ideas," Arendahl said, hinting at a dark mystery, but volunteered no more. As much as they tried, the rest of them could get no more information out of the old elf. They tried and tried—all except for Ell, who walked in brooding silence—until Dacunda raised his voice and finally put a stop to it.

"Enough! He will speak on this when he is ready. Show respect for your Elder." Dacunda set his things down. "This is far enough for tonight. We will make camp here. No fire this time. I do not want the added attention." He clamped his mouth shut as if realizing he had subconsciously assumed command again, but this time Ell didn't seem to notice or care because he was too lost in thought.

They set their packs and weapons on the ground and made ready to sleep for the night. Ell curled his body around Miri's, his breath in her ear, stirring her hair ever so slightly. Before they had time to fall asleep, Ell spoke once more.

"Do you still wish to accompany us, human, or has this taste of darkness been enough for you?"

There was no answer from Kalabi, just the steady breathing of people thinking deeply as they fell asleep.

Chapter Eleven

The ruins of Castan Yol were not like those of Verdantihya. Even after its destruction, Verdantihya captured one's breath, the way the trees sprouted just so and how the stones of the roads curved around them, spoke of a melding of sentient creation and the natural explosion of life from the earth, an unbelievable mix of nature and architectural genius. Castan Yol resembled more normal ruins. Even as a broken and sacked city, Verdantihya captured one's breath, Castan Yol had nothing of this. It was old, certainly, and it wore its age with pride and dignity. The beauty of its architecture, what was still visible and not rubble, could be easily attributed to the careful crafting of builders, unlike the supernatural craft and quality of Verdantihya. But despite its differences from the capital of Andalaya, despite its diminished impressiveness, Ell still found Castan Yol to have a charm to it.

Ell awoke just before dawn, having slept fitfully throughout the remainder of last night. The early rays of light crept over the broken walls of buildings and glistened in bright streams through solitary arches, bound with ivy and creepers. Yes, this ruined city had a beauty to it. It spoke of centuries of elven history, and it reminded Ell of just how much of that history had been lost and destroyed, even before the humans arrived. The conflicts between his people and the Departed had been occurring for many generations before the doom of the last two decades.

Ell shifted his body, trying not to wake Miri. Let her sleep, he thought. It had been a wearying night even for those who had not fought. Ell's eyes roved the campsite which was nestled in the corner of a roofless stone building, protected by the remnants of the only two walls that were even remotely left standing in the immediate vicinity. His gaze found Dacunda, who looked back at him with steady eyes. Ell raised a finger to his lips, motioning for silence, hoping his uncle would understand his desire to let people rest, to let them sleep. They would all be the better for it. Miraculously, not a single Ghoul stinger had found elven flesh last night, so their stores of Source Water had not been depleted. Yet, the battle had been exhausting, even nerve-wracking, for its sheer unpredictability. Who would ever have imagined Ghouls appearing and fighting in those kinds of numbers, and with such focus? With such focus and with such singular purpose, he thought grimly, for his destruction. But why had they focused on him alone? He was not the only Water Caller. The answers to his questions eluded him.

Dacunda seemed to understand his gesture for quiet and nodded back at him. He had led for years and understood the need for good rest after a skirmish. Ell's uncle continued what he had been doing before Ell awoke, mending a rip in his breeches.

Ell didn't go back to sleep, but he wriggled himself closer to Miri's back and nestled his face between her shoulder and her neck. Her golden hair tickled his face, but it felt nice all the same and although she murmured and shifted her weight slightly into his, she did not seem to wake. Ell closed his eyes and simply existed in the moment for a while. He breathed in and out. He imagined what it would be like if no responsibility weighed on his shoulders, if his family were all whole and safe together, none of them trapped in decades of captivity. He imagined if their elven nation hadn't been shattered before he was born, and peace rather than war was the norm. Most of all, Ell imagined a life where he and Miri never needed to be separated. That world seemed nearly perfect to him. But it was not reality. He would soon have to leave her behind. They would need mobility and the ability to move quickly once they reached the region fully under the control of the southern elves. Miri and Art would be a liability, a hindrance, and Arendahl had already declared that he would not be accompanying them much further on this mission. Ell hoped he would take good care of Miri. No, he knew he would. As cantankerous as the old elf was, Ell could see that he had developed a genuine fondness for Miri, much like the rest of Ell's family.

"What is it burning a hole in your skull? I feel like I can practically hear your thoughts running wild." Apparently, Miri was awake. She did not turn around to lie facing him on her side, but rather nestled herself in closer to him in the position they already were in.

"I thought you were asleep." Ell countered, not really wishing to discuss the thought of leaving her just now. "And how could you tell I was awake without looking at me?"

Miri's laugh tinkled quietly into the dewy morning. "I was asleep, but I woke up a few minutes ago. I can always tell when you are asleep. Your breathing is different than when you are awake, a bit smoother, deeper."

"I suppose that just proves you are more observant that I." Ell complimented her, his smile pressing into her skin, keeping his voice low so that others could continue sleeping.

With his cheek pressed against Miri's he was able to feel her smile. "In some ways, Ell, but not in others. I would be hard pressed to claim even a remotely close level of observation to you in areas such as reconnaissance or in the heat of battle, for example." Now she finally did turn her body around to face him. "But I know you, I know your little quirks." She looked at him confidently, knowingly.

"Oh, do you?" He teased.

"I do indeed," she breathed, completely serious.

On that note she changed the subject. "Well, Ell, if you do not wish to tell me what was occupying your mind then I think I will close my eyes again and see if I cannot take advantage of this unusually luxurious respite to our morning routine." And with that she closed her eyes again, burrowed her face into his chest, and promptly fell back asleep.

The rest of early morning passed in a haze of dreams and dozing. Ell was not sure whether he fell completely back to sleep, but he drifted in and out of full consciousness for some time. He heard others do the same as he, shifting their weight, and moving slightly, then realizing no one was rising and closing their eyes again. The only exceptions were Dacunda and Arendahl. Arendahl had disappeared before Ell had even awoken the first time, likely off scouting their surroundings, and Dacunda kept a sharp vigil over the camp, allowing the rest of them to sleep.

Finally, with the sun high and late morning fully upon them, people began to arise from their lazy slumber. They broke their fast on dried meat, berries, and nuts. Everyone seemed keen to congratulate Kalabi on his handfire since it had broken the Ghouls' attack last night. The human slave accepted the slaps on the back and the eager congratulations with a bemused smile on his face.

Kalabi ended up sitting next to Ell on the first step of a ruined staircase that spiraled up but led to nowhere, the walls of its former building long since collapsed around it, leaving it entirely alone. For the first time that morning, Ell noticed that the human seemed uncertain. Kalabi had proven himself to be composed, if nothing else. Even in the face of a pursuing Departed or a small army of Ghouls he had shown the ability to think quickly and act with assurance. Yet now he appeared almost nervous.

"What were those…things last night, Elliyar?" Kalabi asked in a shaky voice.

Rihya, sitting close to overhear the question interjected. "What? Ghouls? Have you never seen a Ghoul?" The surprise in her voice was clear.

"Ghouls." Kalabi mouthed the word slowly as if tasting something new or foreign. He furrowed his brows in thought. "No, I have never seen them, nor heard of them. They must not come near the human camps, else I would have heard reports. But then again, I was kept under close watch and not often allowed outside my sleep or work tents so I suppose I cannot claim to be abreast of everything." He said the last bit with a small, self-deprecating shrug of his shoulders, to compliment his return to his usual manner of composed and polite speech.

"They frequent the northern regions of Andalaya," Ell said, hoping to supplement the human's lack of information. "But they have recently been moving south in greater numbers. Although nothing like last night," he muttered.

"They do not seem incredibly fearsome, at least not if they were alone," Kalabi mused.

Arendahl, the reigning expert on all aspects of the dark creatures, especially Ghouls, had arrived from patrolling and joined the conversation. "Heh," he grunted. "That's because we got lucky, not a one of them grasped us. They've got stingers, boy," Arendahl explained. "Deadly little bastards. Normally they don't attack in numbers. They just sit camouflaged in the shadows and wait until you're within arm's reach and…" Arendahl thrust out his arm in a snatching motion, startling Kalabi who had been drawn into his description.

"And?" Kalabi recovered from his startled moment.

"And once they've touched you, boy, you might as well be dead. Deadly venom, kills you in no time at all, just in time for them to have a nice little snack." Arendahl leered nastily.

"I despise Ghouls," Dahranian grunted, as if just talking about them was enough to set his teeth on edge.

"Who doesn't, Dahranian?" Rihya rolled her eyes. She hated when people stated the obvious. She turned back to Kalabi. "I still cannot believe you have never seen them. How is it possible that humans have never seen them? Your slave route passes to the north along the Great Bridge. It seems impossible that not a single human has ever been attacked."

Kalabi lifted his hands palm up and spread them just slightly. "I do not know, Valerihya." Kalabi seemed uncomfortable calling anyone by anything other than their full and proper name. Rihya's mouth twitched as if she wished to correct him and tell him that just Rihya was fine. But she didn't.

Something about this topic of conversation made a deep feeling of foreboding grow in the pit of Ell's stomach. Indeed, his sister was right. It did seem incredible that in nearly two decades, Ghouls and other dark creatures would not be common knowledge to the humans. What possible explanation could there be? And then the truth hit Ell like a war hammer. Of course! The ones controlling the dark creatures, the Unsired, were engaged in a temporary alliance with the humans so it stood to reason their minions would not attack their allies. But it did not explain why they would keep their allies completely in the dark about their strength of war and their capabilities for violence. Unless…Ell followed the trail of a worrying thought. Unless, the Departed—the Unsired—had kept their ability to control the dark creatures secret because they were planning on breaking the alliance. Ell hated the alliance between the southern elves and the humans. It had broken his people's back, crippled them. But the thought that the Unsired might be nearly strong enough to throw off the yoke imposed upon them by the humans with their vastly superior numbers, was a thought nearly as worrisome as any Ell could have imagined. Were the Unsired that close to regaining power?

Ell's thoughts were interrupted by a change in conversation. The group was clamoring to hear about handfire.

"Yes, tell us how you make it," Ryder was asking eagerly.

"Can you make more handfire?" Dahranian interjected intently, obviously imagining what it would be like to carry it with them into battle.

"And why have we never seen it before?" Rihya flicked her own quick question towards Kalabi.

Kalabi laughed and raised his hands. "One question at a time, please, I cannot speak to each person simultaneously." He looked towards Rihya. "I will answer your question first. You have not seen handfire before because it is a new invention. Invented by none other than myself." Kalabi placed a hand in pride on his chest.

"As for you two brothers," he directed towards Ryder and Dahranian, "your questions are similar. I can, in fact, make more handfire, if I have the essential ingredients. They can be difficult to find, but not impossible. Those ingredients, to keep things simple, are the combination of certain combustible minerals and substances, the details of which we can get into at a later time. Also, small pieces of mineral stone, such as flint, worked into the substance so that upon impact they catch and ignite tiny sparks, setting off the combustion."

"Those would certainly be useful," Dacunda mused, speaking for the first time that morning.

"A moment, boy?" Arendahl jerked his head to the side of the camp. Ell stood up, leaving the group to discuss the possible benefits of handfire, and stepped a few yards away for a private discussion with Arendahl.

"What is it, Elder?"

Arendahl looked at Ell with a flat gaze, lips mixed between a purse and a pucker. "So it's Elder now, is it? Not giving me orders anymore?"

Ell felt a flash of embarrassment. He knew that if he wished to keep control of this mission and make decisions regarding the future of his family—decisions he deserved to make!—then he had to assert himself. But Ell couldn't help feeling slightly ashamed of how he had talked to Arendahl the previous day before the ambush. Elders were revered in their culture. Not to mention the old, grey-haired elf was Ell's only available teacher as a Water Caller. It would not due to alienate himself from Arendahl.

Ell chose silence and tried to assume a contrite look. Well, Ell wasn't sure he had ever managed to be contrite in his entire life. He settled for what he assumed was a calm and respectful look.

"Arrogant boy," Arendahl snorted, but seemed satisfied enough that Ell had not argued back. "Enough of this. I will not be with you much longer, I will have to leave and attend to other matters." He said it slyly, as if it were something he wished to remain hidden from Ell. "That means we must make the most of these opportunities together. Come, let us train some more. I want you to practice some new things."

New things? The thought that the old elf had been holding out information on Ell made him frustrated, but excited. However, another thought crossed his mind. "One thing first, Arendahl."

Arendahl tilted his head to the side and raised his eyebrows, waiting.

Ell decided to convey some fears he had been experiencing lately. Who better to talk to than Arendahl—the elf was old enough not only to have fought in the fall of Verdantihya, but also to be able to refer to Ell's uncle as 'young Dac'.

"There has been something on my mind since last night. We know the Unsired can control the dark creatures, bend them to their will?"

Arendahl nodded promptly, eyes narrowed. The old elf was always eager to train, but he also knew the value of seeking to attain answers to important questions.

Ell continued. "Yet, there was not a single Unsired among the bodies of the dead last night." Ell had looked specifically for the body of at least one of the Departed but had seen none.

"Could have been the explosion," grunted Arendahl, noncommittally.

Ell tilted his head, a gesture that looked in askance of the old elf. "Please, Arendahl, we both know we would have noticed one during the fight. Somebody would have." Ell pressed forward with a morbid eagerness to convey the theory that had been forming in his mind for some time now. "Arendahl, why are there so many of the Unsired? We have seen them in great numbers these last months, yet there are only two of us—two Water Callers? Are we not the balance to the evil you said?"

"We are the balance, but the Highest as a people, as a race, are the balance to the Unsired." Arendahl spoke slowly, his eyes narrowed.

"Yes," Ell said with a sinister excitement. "Yes, exactly! You said we are a balance. But if our people are the counterweight to the Unsired, then what are we the balance for?"

The old, grizzled elf just stared at Ell for some time. Ell felt a nervous anticipation. "Come, let us train."

"No!" Ell spat. "Do not treat me like a child. I want to hear your opinion on this, your honest opinion."

"Fine," Arendahl responded through grated teeth. "But this stays between us, for now. I have no proof and it would only dishearten people."

"What is it, Elder?" Ell composed himself and asked politely.

Arendahl glanced around to make sure others were not listening. "There is sense to what you say, Elliyar. I do not deny that. In fact, if you dig deep enough in lore, there are hints, just the vaguest rumors of something...else. Something worse. Beings much more powerful."

"Worse than the Unsired?" Ell whispered. It was hard to imagine that.

The old elf nodded solemnly. "Indeed."

"So whatever these worse entities are, they must be able to control dark creatures from a distance, not even needing to be present to exert their influence over them. That is why there wasn't an Unsired at the fight last night. Something else was in control of the Ghouls." Ell was thinking quickly now, connections firing in his brain.

"It is all speculation, Elliyar. I don't have the answers to these ponderings, only possibilities."

"But why the secrecy, Elder?"

"I told you, boy, it would dishearten the rest. We have been fighting a losing battle for twenty years now. Our people are scattered, our kingdom is broken, and our armies destroyed. For the first time in a long time, there is hope. You, Elliyar. A Water Caller, born of the ancient lineage. You killed Silverfist, you slew many bands of slavers. Word is already spreading through Andalaya, whispers and murmurings of a boy who can accomplish the impossible."

"But that is crazy, Arendahl. You are a Water Caller also. You have been for years. Also, you helped me do all of those things, not to mention my family. I did not do any of that on my own."

Arendahl smiled a rare smile, the sort he reserved for Ell only on occasion. "You are a strange mix of arrogance and modesty, boy. One minute assuming control of everything and demanding respect, the next claiming you are not special at all."

Ell opened his mouth to object, but the old elf over rode him and kept speaking. "Did I fly on the back of an Icari and survive? Did I free prisoners from a Pillar for the first time in history? Did I kill the betrayer of our people?"

"You could have," Ell mumbled, almost embarrassed now.

"But I did not, Elliyar. And I am old. Am I not the oldest elf you have ever seen?"

Ell was forced to nod his acceptance. It was true, grey hair on an elf was almost unheard of. "But, what do you mean by all of this?"

"I mean, Elliyar, that you are a catalyst for our people, word of you brings a new hope, a belief in something better, a rallying point to galvanize our people. If word gets out that not only have our ancient foes, the Unsired, returned, but that the Unsired are not even the worst of our concerns, that hope will vanish like a puff of smoke. We cannot let that happen. So for now, stay quiet. Agreed? Arendahl bored holes in Ell's head with his stony gaze.

"Agreed," Ell said reluctantly. "But at some point we will have to tell them. At least my family. They deserve to know." The anger he'd felt at his elders for keeping secrets, the anger he had felt all summer flared up again. "They have a right to know the truth!"

Arendahl stared at him complacently and ignored his last statement. "Alright boy, ready to train and learn about something new?"

Chapter Twelve

"So far, you have only accessed your abilities in a general way. You have finally grown more accustomed to the notion of yourself being a Water Caller and have come to accept it as an identity rather than something you must work to become. That's why, even though you still have some trouble accessing your powers, you are able to intentionally call upon your powers much more frequently." Arendahl got straight to the point.

"Doesn't feel like I am making any progress," Ell grumbled, and immediately regretted his tone of voice. He sounded whiney and petulant. Someone claiming leadership shouldn't speak in such a way. Luckily, the old elf chose to disregard his comment and press on with the lesson.

"You have learned, Elliyar, to extend your consciousness out to the land, to find a oneness with Creation, to put yourself in harmony with it. It is only natural because we, the Highest—and particularly Water Callers—were spun out by Creation as a balance, a correction, to the disease of Unsired and darkness that was plaguing the land. It only makes sense that we should put ourselves in tune with the land around us in order to access our powers."

It was funny, Ell mused silently, how Arendahl spoke so differently when he was teaching. Any interaction with the grey-haired elf was usually characterized by Arendahl's stilted, choppy speech, almost an inability to hold a normal conversation. Yet that trait disappeared when he lectured. When the old elf lectured Ell on what it meant to be a Water Caller, he spoke in lengthy, long sentences, with full descriptions. It was an odd discrepancy in the elder's behavior.

"I know all of this, Arendahl."

The old elf harrumphed, and made a sour face at his young charge. "Impatient, boy, so impatient." As if Arendahl himself wasn't the height to impatience. Ell snorted and received an even sourer grimace from the old elf before the teacher continued.

"I am setting the stage for what I am about to explain to you. We have put ourselves in contact with the land around us, touched the essence of Creation. This has enabled us—you Elliyar—to touch your powers in a general way. Even by intention, which is progress for you, it has still been general."

"What do you mean?" Ell asked, removing his attention from the high-standing sun shining down through the scattered oak trees that had grown in and around the ruins of Castan Yol.

"Speed, strength, agility. All these things come naturally when you access your powers. But there is much more to touch in terms of the abilities available to a Water Caller."

"Like what?"

"Well, boy, did you ever wonder how I brought you back from the brink of death last spring after your fight with Silverfist?"

Ell pondered this a moment. "I though you used Source Water."

"Of course I did boy, but poison that deadly and flowing that freely through your blood by the time I found you would have required more than just our supernatural healing water. Oh, of course the Source Water was an aid, but I also tapped my abilities as a Water Caller." Arendahl's eyes gleamed the way they always did when he instructed. Ell almost smiled at how enlivened the old elf became when he did what he enjoyed best, but at the last moment Ell refrained, assuming that Arendahl would likely view a smile as distraction.

"So what exactly did you do?" Ell asked.

"Well, Elliyar, our powers as a Water Caller include a number of different aspects. One of those is the power to heal, when we are able to channel our minds and powers, when we focus on such an outcome."

"But how does it work?" Ell was confused. He could see how the latent power of the water in all Creation could have a store, a wealth, of energy just waiting to be tapped for use. But how could healing come from that same energy?

"Think, boy! We draw our power from Creation—we were birthed by the land, just like the Source in Verdantihya. The water from the Source heals, and it flows everywhere, absorbed out of rivers and streams, evaporating and then falling from the sky as rain. It is more diluted, the further along it moves through the process, and to experience the utmost of its healing capacity a normal elf is best served by drinking from water gained directly from the source." Arendahl was animated now, using his hands and waving them around excitedly as he spoke.

"I know this Elder." Ell tried to politely nudge his teacher to reach the point. "It's why we carry flasks of water from the Source. It is not a new concept to me."

"Of course, it isn't," Arendahl replied gruffly. "But think, all that water from the Source is dispersed throughout the land, absorbed and dissipated everywhere. And think, also boy, what do we do when we access our abilities?" The old elf asked the guiding question.

Ell furrowed his brow. "We stretch out our consciousness into Creation, into the land, and feel the water that is everywhere."

"Yes! We do. Do you not see? That is a lot of water we are accessing. The Source Water might be diluted in that fragmented and dispersed state, but we are accessing large portions of it—maybe all the water in the land—at once. And even in that dispersed state, when you add together all the dispersed Source Water in that quantity it provides a concentrated enough dose of Source Water to channel through our powers to heal in an even more powerful way than even drinking directly from the Source itself would do. Do you see?"

And Ell did understand. He began to imagine all those tiny droplets of water, all the latent water in the air and the earth containing only a miniscule dose of healing potential, but when added together it equaled more than a strong dose of the Source Water.

Ell nodded his head. "How do you focus the power to be able to do that?" It seemed a difficult task indeed. He had enough trouble at times just accessing his powers in what he now knew to be only a general way.

"Give me your hand." Arendahl ordered.

Ell stuck out his hand without question, and jerked it away hastily after Arendahl had whipped out his belt knife and sliced Ell's palm with lightning speed.

"Why did you do that!" Ell exclaimed with a grimace. The cut was not deep but it stung, and the unexpected injury put him in a bad mood immediately.

Arendahl snorted. "Don't be foolish boy, the best way to learn is by practical application. I am going to fix you up in a moment." Ell kept his mouth shut in sullen silence and watched the old elf take his hand. Arendahl was already holding his powers as a Water Caller and as he grabbed Ell's hand, Ell felt a jolt of cold wash over his senses. A bite of pain accompanied by another cooling sensation and the wound closed up and healed completely right before Ell's eyes. No scar was left, no mark, nothing but fresh skin, if only a tiny bit more pink than before.

Ell's eyes widened as he watched. "Impressive," he breathed.

Arendahl grunted his agreement. "Useful little talent, isn't it? But mind you, that was a very minor cut. Not deep at all. Bigger, deeper wounds, and wounds left untended for longer, are much more difficult to deal with. Sometimes even this power we possess isn't enough to save someone."

Ell nodded his head, still staring at the healed palm, flexing his hand and marveling at the fact that he felt no pain. He reached eagerly for his own belt knife. "Can I try now, on you?"

"Don't be an idiot, you're nowhere near ready to heal someone. I'm not letting you slice me open." Arendahl shook his head in disgust and muttered something else that sounded like 'impulsive' and 'rash'. Ell stared flatly at the old elf, but kept his peace.

"No, what I want you to do is hold your power and then focus it. Usually, when you tap into your abilities you become like a raging storm, all surging tumultuous energy eager to burst forth. Does that sound about right?" He raised his eyebrows in question at Ell, waiting for a response.

"More or less, yes." Ell responded slowly after a moment of thought. It was true, when he was filled with his power it felt like he was bursting with it. It felt like he had all the energy in the world at his fingertips and that energy was just waiting to be put to use. Often, through violence. It was nice to imagine that there was a balance to his violent potential in an ability to heal.

Arendahl took his assent and continued. "Well, go ahead tap into your abilities."

Ell dutifully stretched out his consciousness. He focused on how he was already a Water Caller, it was him, it was who he was, his identity. He was created by the land, for the land. Creation was connected to him. Surprisingly, his powers flooded into him in a matter of moments. His eyes fogged slightly, and Ell gazed at Arendahl through that odd, wispy, clouded sight that that felt both strange and natural.

"Got it?"

"Got it," Ell responded.

"Good. Now this time, instead of letting the power within rage like a storm out of control, I want you to focus it. Sharpen your focus, sharpen your power to a fine point. You are taking your general abilities and making them into a tool for a particular use. Sometimes it is helpful to imagine that your powers are a weapon. Visualize the point of a knife or a sword."

Ell tried, but found it difficult. Focusing his powers to a point felt like trying to subdue a flash flood. He tried and tried but found no success.

"Well, I didn't expect you to get it on the first attempt." Arendahl clapped a hand on his shoulder. The old elf smiled. "That's why I didn't let you cut me. It will take practice to get accustomed to focusing your power. But once you do, more than just healing will be within your reach."

Ell's interest was peaked again. "What else?"

"Along with healing, you may eventually be able to leech water from objects, manipulate the actual physical essence of water, sense things in the water like I did the night I found your family in the rainstorm in Verdantihya.

You may be able to do many things, Elliyar, but I will not reveal them all at this moment. For now, you must simply practice focusing the powers you possess, which will enable you to be ready for the next step of accessing a specific ability."

Ell wasn't sure how leeching liquid from different objects would be helpful, but he could see how manipulating the substance of water itself might definitely be useful. Suddenly, a thought crossed his mind, a memory of a dead Departed elf who had looked sickly, diseased. Ell had just finished a raid with his family, he had chased the Departed into the woods and killed it even though it had been acting strangely. It had been his first encounter with one of the Unsired, although he had not known it then.

Ell remembered reaching down to touch the diseased face almost instinctively and seeing the face flicker back to a healthy complexion before the moment passed and the southern elf returned to its sickened appearance. Ell recounted the event to Arendahl. The grizzled elf's face took on a deep, thoughtful look.

"What do you think happened? Did I almost heal it maybe?" Ell asked, searching for answers.

The old elf took a moment before responding. "I do not know what that means, Elliyar. It could mean many things or it could be nothing more than a figment of your imagination. You were very surprised by the way the Unsired fought, so it is possible that you thought you saw more than you did. But then again, maybe you didn't, maybe it was something very meaningful indeed."

"That is a lot of maybes and ifs," Ell said more grumpily than he intended. He hated not having the answers to puzzling questions.

"I do not know everything," Arendahl snapped back. "I can only tell you what I know for certain, which is very little in this case." The old elf shook his head as if to clear it. "Enough. Enough, for now. Let us return to the group."

Ell was drenched in sweat from the mental exertions of attempting to focus his powers down to a fine point, honed and ready for specific tasks, and the suggestion of a rest was agreeable. They walked together back towards the others.

Just before they reached them, Arendahl pulled on his arm slightly to stop him. "I will not be with you much longer in this quest to reach Dor Khabor, Elliyar. You must promise me that you will practice, not only accessing your abilities in general, but also focusing your powers as well. There will come a time, and that time will likely be soon, where you will need your powers for more than just the typical speed and strength it provides. You must be ready for that time, prepared for when it happens."

"Why must you leave, Arendahl?" Ell asked, frustrated.

Arendahl smiled sardonically. "Regretting leadership already, boy? Wishing I was sticking around after all?"

"That is not what I mean. By assuming command of this expedition I did not intend for that to mean you would not accompany us," Ell said with exasperation.

"We don't always get what we want, boy. You asked for command, and now you've got it. Besides, I really do have important matters to which I must attend. My mission is likely much more vital for our race than the rescue of your family."

Ell didn't have any response to that comment. It was likely true, rescuing a few of the captive Highest wouldn't do much in the grand scheme of the war. But it mattered to Ell, and for now that was all he could manage. He had to rescue his family, no matter the cost.

Chapter Thirteen

"—And then he stuck himself with his own sword, so I said, 'doesn't the pointy end go in your enemies?' You should have seen the look on his face. Well worth the seconds I waited to ask him that question before I killed him and put him out of his misery as a fighter." Ryder was finishing telling some jest of a story as Ell and Arendahl approached the group. Ell's cousin was garnering differing amounts of support for his storytelling antics. Ryder had managed to elicit a few unusual chuckles from Dacunda and Dahranian, and Rihya was rolling on the ground laughing. But Kalabi was just smiling politely, and Miri was clearly unsure whether the story even merited laughter.

"You telling the one about the clumsy general again, Cousin?" Ell asked. He already knew the answer; he had heard it enough times to identify the story by its punch line.

"The very one!" Ryder roared enthusiastically. Ell's cousin then turned to Kalabi. "My apologies, my friend. I know the brunt of this joke is one of your kind, but I mean no personal offense by it. It's just that you humans can be so ungainly and blundering sometimes."

"None taken, Ryder. I, myself, have noticed the very same thing on many occasions." Kalabi retained his calm, pleasant façade, but Ell noticed a faint strain showing around the edges of his smile. He might be an ex-slave, and bear no good will towards his former masters, but that didn't mean he would enjoy enduring Ryder's innocent, yet clearly ill-mannered teasing at the expense of his race. The dynamics of the group would surely switch slightly from here onwards now that it was mixed race.

Ell decided to step in. "That's probably enough, cousin. I am sure you have regaled them with enough stories by now. Give them a break, why don't you?"

"But I've only told them seven stories, Ell." Ryder declared.

"Seven is quite enough," Arendahl interjected, and then muttered to himself, "I don't think I've ever met someone who likes the sound of his own voice so much."

"Hey!" Ryder cried indignantly.

"Give it a rest, Ry," Rihya said, still wiping tears from her eyes. "Why don't you quit while you're ahead? This way we will be more likely to want to hear your tales again the next time."

Ell sat down on a moss-covered stone next to Miri as Ryder huffed his way over to the food stores.

"Do not eat through everything we have, my son," Dacunda said with a faint smile on his face.

"Do not worry, Father, if we run out of food I'll get us some more," Ryder grunted sourly and then dug his fist into a bag and came up with a huge handful of nuts.

The rest of the group had already eaten a midday meal, so Arendahl and Ell were left to eat alone—with Ryder and his constant in-between munching. Ell pulled out some dried meat and berries and began working through them at a surprisingly rapid pace, unexpectedly hungry after a few hours spent training.

"Worked up an appetite, eh?" Arendahl asked, as he spat out the pit of a small fruit he was eating. Ell just nodded and put another bite of food in his mouth.

They ate in silence for the next few minutes, but after Ell and Arendahl had eaten their meal and washed it down with some cold water from a nearby spring, Ell decided it was time to take care of a few details.

He turned to Kalabi. "We should talk about what you said, about wanting to accompany us." He expected a response from Kalabi, but the human just waited patiently, his gold collar glinting in the afternoon sunlight.

Ell pushed on. "It will not be safe. You saw what last night was like, those Ghouls are menacing, but they are little more than the least of our concerns. We are headed for Dark Harbor, the southern elven capital, and I believe you know its reputation." Ell needed nothing more than to see Kalabi's shudder at the mention of Dark Harbor to know that the human had heard the rumors. It did not surprise Ell. As a former slave, it would stand to reason that he had heard tales of the worst place on earth to wind up a slave. The humans might have struck a deal with the Departed that guaranteed them the greater share of slaves that were captured, but the slaves that reached the human camps knew nothing of the suffering that awaited those few selected to stay in Dark Harbor.

"I am aware of the risks," Kalabi finally responded, after listening quietly to Ell's warning.

"And?" Ell asked.

"And my decision is the same. I wish to accompany you."

"My uncle thinks that we are on a suicide mission. Isn't that right, Uncle?"

Ell turned his head to see Dacunda staring at him with narrowed eyes.

Dacunda inclined his head. "I do not deny it. It will not surprise me in the slightest if none of us reach the end of this journey alive," he said somberly. Ell felt a cold fear wash through him at his uncle's matter of fact discussion of their demise. He fought to ignore the tiny voice in his head that whispered it would be entirely his fault if they died on this mission.

"Knowing all that you know, why do wish to accompany us?" Ell changed his tactic slightly.

Kalabi responded quickly and sincerely. "Despite what you say—and despite your cousin, Ryder's, continued jesting at the expense of my race—," Kalabi turned a quick smile towards Ryder to show that he was not offended, merely joking, "I already feel more like I belong here than I ever did back at home. If you can even call where I come from home. Not to mention, I am itching to strike a blow against my former captors, or those who are aligned with them. And unless I am mistaken, you are intending to do just that."

Ell weighed the former slave's response carefully. It seemed sincere, genuine. "Is it really so important to you to get revenge on you former masters?"

"I do not know that I would refer to what I seek as revenge. I would prefer to say that I wish to make a difference. I wish to do all that I can to prevent others, like me, from becoming enslaved. It seems that working with you and your family is the best chance I have of accomplishing that goal." Kalabi kept his gaze trained on Ell's face. There was no denying that the human knew how to keep his composure when he wished to.

Ell stared back at him. "Why should we take you with us, let you become one of us?" It was time for another, different angle to this question. Ell might be bold, and even reckless at times, he might be willing to risk his and his family's safety for the sake of a worthy goal, but he would not risk adding a member to their group without clearly understanding his motives and what that person could contribute.

Arendahl snorted, in the way he always did, when he thought Ell was being ridiculous. Ell turned his head in annoyance and raised his eyebrows waiting for the old elf to elaborate.

The old elf bit, never one to hold back his opinion. "A bit of a stupid question, isn't that, Ell? I mean it's obvious what he brings. He is trained to make things, invent things. He could likely make us more handfire, or even something else. Useful addition in my opinion."

"I agree." Dahranian finally spoke after watching the exchange in silence.

"And I," Dacunda seconded his son. All of the others nodded their heads in agreement. Finally, Ell turned to Miri and saw her smile warmly and nod her head encouragingly to him, as well. Alright, then if everybody wanted it that way.

"Fine," Ell said. "But you keep up and you obey orders. We move fast and we do things a certain way, we function as a unit. If one of us tells you to do something, you do it, no questions asked. Agreed?"

Kalabi put a hand over his heart. "I swear it shall be so."

"Well, if it's suicide you wanted, then you joined the right band of renegades," Ell muttered.

"A little danger goes a long ways towards providing one with a fulfilling life," Kalabi responded with a smile. "Besides, people who *do* things are ever so much more entertaining than people who do not."

"Looks like you've joined the right group then." Ryder clapped him on the shoulder, celebrating his official acceptance into their little family unit.

The human smiled and Ell saw real joy in his expression. What a terrible life he must have endured, for strangers that he had known mere hours to be the people he most wished to spend his time with.

As if thinking the same thoughts as Ell, Miri asked, "What was home like, Kalabi?"

She asked quietly, her voice holding curiosity but hardly loud enough to rise above the noise of Kalabi's welcome. Yet, somehow her question cut through it all. Kalabi paused as if not sure he wanted to answer. But then he did.

"I have spent almost fifteen years on this continent—nearly half of my life. Home was a couple of tents in the midst of a sea of tents, one for sleep, one for work. These luxurious tents had all the objects and items a person could desire. But it was also a place of chains and solitude. And no man should live shackled." He fell silent as if he had revealed more emotion than he had planned.

Miri put a comforting hand on his arm. "Well, if there are any people in this land who understand the importance of freedom, it is us," she reassured him.

"Hear, hear," seconded Rihya.

"To freedom." Dacunda raised the water skin from which he had been about to take a drink. Kalabi inclined his head.

"To freedom," echoed everyone else respectfully, even though most of them didn't have a draught to raise with Dacunda.

"So, did you sail across the Fracture when you came to our land?" Ryder asked, interrupting the somber moment, eager as a little boy for news of something new, something different.

Rihya rolled her eyes and shook her head. Kalabi seemed to agree with

Ell's sister as he looked reproachfully at Ryder. "No one sails across the Fracture. It is impossible." The human spoke flatly, stating an absolute fact. Oddly enough, Ell realized that as he continued to speak, he sounded much akin to Arendahl when the old elf was in full swing as an instructor. Kalabi elaborated on his statement. "The Fracture is impassable. Where there are not giant walls of glaciers, there are smaller, jagged, frozen teeth of ice ready to gut the hull of your ship. As if that were not enough, there are riptides and swirling currents that change continually and are strong enough to pull any ship to its doom upon one of those teeth. No, the Fracture is a death trap. Our ships hug the coast on both sides of the Fracture, Ryder, and my journey to arrive at these shores was normal. I sailed up the coast to the Great Bridge and then was transported down the eastern coast of your continent by a slave ship to reach the camps."

"Oh, right." Ryder frowned.

"Enough pestering of our new companion," Dacunda said. "Today we will take as a full day of rest and then depart tomorrow at first light." He had forgotten again that he was not in charge. Awkwardly, he glanced at Ell, but this time Ell didn't have a desire to contest the decision. It was a smart choice, resting today. Ell simply nodded his agreement, and picked up a flask of water to take a long drink. The midday meal had replenished some of his energy expended while training, but he still felt parched, and no wonder, considering how much sweat had coursed from his skin during the time he spent practicing with his powers. It was a heavy mental strain, especially since he had been practicing something new. That mental strain manifested itself in physical fatigue as well, and he felt like doing nothing so much as basking languorously in the warm afternoon light, letting his body and muscles relax.

He did so, reclining on a long, wide block of stone—possibly the remnants of a fallen wall. The mossy covering softened the rock surface making it a comfortable spot for resting.

Miri hopped up onto the rock, her weak leg only giving her the slightest of hitches as she propelled herself up and onto the stone next to him. She leaned in close for a kiss and then pulled back wrinkling her nose and sniffing pointedly as if to punctuate his earlier thought about how much he had been sweating.

"How long has it been since you bathed, Ell?" Miri asked with a smile twitching at her face. She fought hard to keep her face straight.

Ell rolled his eyes in good humor and smiled. "Too long, no doubt, by the way you are looking at me."

"Not looking at you, smelling you," Miri corrected him, but snuggled herself close to him nonetheless.

"I thought I was stinky?" he teased.

"You are, but I am not going to spend some of our last hours together complaining." Her comment brought reality crashing back in on him.

He sighed. "You know I wouldn't go if it wasn't important. But it is my family, and I have to save them. I will do whatever it takes." Ell didn't realize the steel that had crept into his voice at the end of his statement, but apparently Miri had.

"I understand, love, really I do. But promise me one thing, will you?" Miri said seriously.

"Anything."

"Do not let this quest for your parents make you lose sight of other things in life." She spoke in the way she often did when she was trying to lead Ell to a conclusion.

"You mean, the war?" Ell asked dubiously. Miri rarely talked about the war since it was not her favorite subject.

She made a little vexed sound. "There is more to life than battle, Ell, and do not forget it!"

"Not this old argument again, Miriyah." It was a mark of his frustration that he used her full name. They had debated endlessly about the fruitfulness of war. Miri expounding ideas that were idealistic, fanciful notions that required peace in order to exist. Ell was a realist. He saw the facts for what they were. This battle, this war, existed. It was not going to go away, and anyone who ignored it was likely to end up dead or captured and made into a slave. Miri understood, at least she claimed she did, accepting that the fight was necessary.

"Alright, Ell, we do not have to have this discussion again," she emphasized the word discussion contradicting Ell's assertion that it was an argument. "All I am saying is what I have always said, there is more to life than fighting, and you would do well to remember that." Ell kissed her temple, a silent peace offering, telling her he had heard her point. She snuggled in closer and Ell closed his eyes letting himself drift off.

Ell awoke from their nap, feeling like he was covered in a blanket made of heat. Evening was fast approaching, but it felt like all the hot air in the world had settled down to rest upon him. He felt to his side, but Miri was already awake.

"You must have been tired, you slept for a couple hours." Miri arrived next to him as he sat up, and handed him a flask of water to wash the taste of sleep from his mouth.

Ell shrugged. "Long night, and then a hard practice with Arendahl. I guess my body just needed it."

Miri was staring at him, focusing her gaze on his face as he spoke. Her own visage was one of extreme concentration.

"What are you doing, love?" he asked slowly, not sure what was on her mind. Miri blushed, startled by his question. Maybe she hadn't been aware of the strange look on her face.

"Nothing." She collected herself and brushed his question aside. Ell made a reproving face. "Nothing," Miri said again, slightly guiltily in response to his unspoken pestering. "Oh, fine then. I was trying to see into your mind, you know through the Grafting I did."

Instantly, Ell was on guard. "Well, what did you see?"

"Don't be like that, Elliyar. It cannot be all bad, this Grafting. Besides, I didn't see anything. Nothing happened," Miri finished a bit grumpily. Ell couldn't help but be glad for the fact that she had been denied access into his mind, although he kept the thought to himself. If she couldn't get in, then there were less odds of her experiencing pain in the future when those important and potentially deadly moments happened. Or at least he hoped that was the case.

They both let the matter drop, neither wishing for another argument just now. Instead they spent the evening of unusual rest with the others. Games involving the throwing of knives were the entertainment of the evening, at which Rihya, of course, won nearly every match. Her only loss was to Ell, during a game in which Ell had thrown particularly well.

Rihya tossed her green hair. "I'd have been worried if you couldn't win at least one game against me, little brother. I might begin to wonder if you were fit for combat." She nudged him in the ribs playfully and he accepted her smirking jab at his technique with good grace.

"As for the rest of you," Rihya said, shooting a scathing look at the rest of her family, "you could do with some serious practice."

Dacunda and Dahranian eyed her complacently, not rising to the bait. Ryder however, hefted his moss-covered axe with a strong hand. "Knives are only one tool of war, my little cousin, do not forget the many facets of battle." He stood and twirled his long axe between both hands menacingly.

"Don't call me little," Rihya responded with narrow eyes. She was touchy about nearly everything, not least the fact that she was the smallest of them all in size.

Ryder ignored her. "I tell you what, little Rihya," he grinned as he emphasized the word she had just told him to avoid, enjoying the dangerous look it elicited in his cousin's eyes, "I'll give you three knives. If you can pink me with any of the three throws, I..."

But before he could say what he would bet, Rihya jumped in with a proposition of her own. "...You'll give all your meals to me tomorrow." She said it with a confident flick of her eyebrows.

Ryder puckered up his mouth sourly. "Well..."

"What, not so sure of your skill now, when it has to do with your stomach?" Rihya taunted.

"Fine!" Ryder rose to the bait. "You pink me, you get my food—tomorrow only. If you don't make me bleed from any one of your throws, then you don't criticize or boss anyone around for a week."

"Done!" Rihya agreed.

In a moment, they stood maybe ten long paces apart, Rihya holding in one hand three knives by their blades, ready to throw, while Ryder was limbering up with his axe, stretching and twirling it with a nonchalant twinkle in his eye.

"Bets?" Arendahl asked.

Dacunda and Dahranian staunchly gave their vote of confidence to their immediate relative, Ryder, while Ell and Miri quickly supported Rihya. Arendahl was the last to bet.

"I think I will take the girl, also. She has a mean look in her eyes, and I think she's determined enough to get the job done." He chuckled with delight at the dangerous glint in Rihya's eyes. The old elf had a penchant for enjoying danger, both for himself and others.

"Ready?" Rihya half taunted, half asked her large cousin.

"Born ready, little cousin," Ryder responded taking advantage of his last opportunity to tease her before the contest. Rihya's eyes narrowed.

"Is this a good idea? Surely someone might get gravely injured," Kalabi asked politely but Ell detected a tone of real concern and nervousness in his voice.

Ell put a hand on his shoulder to reassure him. "Don't worry. I am betting on my sister being able to nick him with a blade, but even I don't think she will deliver a seriously dangerous toss. She's good, but so is he. Besides, we have enough Source Water to sort out most injuries that might take place."

Arendahl overheard his comment to Kalabi. "Don't be foolish, Ell, we aren't wasting precious Source Water on injuries from a game. Taking risks is all well and fun, but you have to be able to pay the price for it when it's over," he finished with an excited yet firm gleam of teeth.

Then, it began. Rihya flicked one of the blades from one hand to the other and threw with practiced, violent ease. The other two blades followed suit entering the air almost as soon as the first left her hand. She really was a wonder to behold with those knives, the fastest hands Ell had ever seen without any kind of supernatural aid.

Ryder spun his axe in a blur deflecting the first with the haft, twisting his body slightly to avoid the second knife as it streaked past his arm and buried itself in the tree behind him, then catching the third blade on the flat head of his axe to send it clanging safely out of the way with the ringing of metal.

A satisfied grin spread across his face. "Oh, it is going to be so great to have a week without your constant picking at us," he chortled with glee.

"Don't be so sure of that," Rihya responded with a smirk, indicating he should look at his left arm.

"What?" Ryder asked in confusion. Then he looked down and saw a tiny speck of reddish pink color dotting his sleeve and the smallest of holes in the arm of his tunic. The second blade he had twisted to avoid must have just narrowly nicked him as it flew by.

Rihya smiled with satisfaction of her own now. "And that is how you win a bet."

"No! That's barely a scratch, I could cut myself worse than that on a piece of blade grass!"

"A deal's a deal, Ryder. The bet was whether or not I could pink you and clearly," Rihya strutted forward and dabbed a finger to his arm which came away with a hint of blood, "I did. So, that means double portion of food for me tomorrow."

Everyone collapsed into heaps of laughter at the look on Ryder's face as he realized he wouldn't be eating anything for the entire next day.

Chapter Fourteen

The levity and entertainment of the previous night was gone. In its place, Ryder displayed a sullen, surly silence at being deprived of food. It might still have been funny, Miri thought, if it weren't for the fact that Ryder's bad mood had seemed to permeate the rest of the group. As much as they all tried to fight it, for various reasons, it felt difficult to ignore a foreboding and pervading gloom that seemed to hang over their company as they traveled.

For Ryder, it was his stomach. For Dacunda and Arendahl, it was Ell's continued determination to maintain control of their expedition, even going so far as to decide all the small details, such as when they would leave, where they would stop, and how far they would travel each day. He clung so hard to his role as leader, that sometimes Miri wondered if his desire for control was about more than just keeping the ever present Arendahl and Dacunda at bay from regaining their positions of leadership. Sometimes, Miri thought that perhaps he was actually trying to convince himself that he had made the right decision, that he really did want to lead, and the only way to do so was to demand that every little detail ran through him.

For the entire group—Miri and Ell especially—the appearance of a Pillar on the far southern horizon was cause enough for distaste, as it symbolized their entry into territory that was well and truly under the dominion of the Departed. For Miri, however, and for Ell, it was the first tangible reference to their imminent separation. Miri would leave soon, turn back, go elsewhere, Wherever Arendahl was taking them. They all knew she would slow them down much more than even a human. Not for the first time, Miri's zen-like attitude towards her old injury, the facade she kept in place and convinced herself of, threatened to dissipate. The thought of leaving Ell's side, especially at a time like this, when Ell was in need of emotional support, was almost unbearable. The only real consolation was that due to the Grafting, there was at least the faint possibility of being connected across the distance. Ell might view it as a negative, but Miri knew her strength. She could bear up under suffering.

Any connection at all had to be a good thing, hadn't it? She firmly chose to believe it was so, to believe that connection was always good, no matter what it cost a person. Miri determined to practice, or at least to try and practice the use of her Grafting. She would make use of this talent, this gift—for that was how she chose to view it.

"Come on, Rihya, just hand me a bit of that venison. I'm starving," Ryder begged for some victuals, extending a hand towards his cousin.

Rihya shook her head in annoyance. "A bet is a bet, Ry, don't try and weasel out of it now." Ryder scowled in response, but rescinded his hand, as if realizing she was right. A frustrated pout settled upon his visage.

Miri turned her face upwards as the first rain of early autumn spattered down lightly from the grey sky above. The first rain of the year was always cause for celebration. After a hot summer, the dry earth needed replenishing. It was nature's cycle and should duly be celebrated. Yet, as the falling water intensified from a light sprinkle to a steady rainfall, everyone trudged on in silence without even a smile. It was as if the sky was mirroring the attitude of the company, grey to match the glum atmosphere that surrounded them all.

They walked most of the morning and covered ground at a steady pace until stopping for a midday break and meal under the cover of a dense copse of trees. The roots bulged up from the ground like tangled, writhing snakes, some large, some small, but all seemed to be hoping to catch at the ankles of those who walked and stood among them.

"We are in enemy territory now," Dacunda said.

Dahranian nodded to his father. "We should send out a runner ahead of the group to scout. I can go." Dacunda glanced at Ell who nodded to him before giving a similar nod to his son.

"After you have eaten, Dahranian."

Dahranian stuffed a handful of berries into his mouth and forced a smile at his father. The others ate in relative silence, mouths moving mechanically as if entering lands that had once belonged to the Highest but now were under control of the southern Departed sapped them of their abilities to converse lightly.

Finally, breaking the heavy silence, Arendahl spoke. "Well, I think I've come about as far as I'm going to." Heads swiveled towards him in surprise.

"You're leaving now?" Rihya asked angrily.

Ryder echoed her emotions. "The Pillars are just ahead, and beyond that Dark Harbor itself. We need you now more than ever!"

Arendahl pursed his lips at the reactions of Rihya and Ryder. He did not like to be questioned. Age had made him wise but also intolerant at times.

However, even Dacunda seemed to feel the act of his leaving now as tantamount to desertion. "Must you, Elder?" he asked in the most respectful tone, but Miri had rarely heard him question Arendahl's decisions. It spoke volumes of his worry that he would do so now. Dahranian mirrored his father's concern, vocalizing his support for the old elf to remain with them.

Art looked on in silence, young enough to miss the heart of many conversations. He happily chewed his way through his meat and one of the few grain cakes they had packed back in the spring before leaving Little Vale. A small smile played across his face. Miri felt a rush of affection for him. He alone in the group was like her—not a warrior. One day he might be, but for now he was not. It was a comfort, some days, not to be the only one who did not see fighting as the only objective in life.

Miri turned her head sideways. Ell leaned against a tree next to her, standing, a few faint droplets of water from the canopy of leaves above landing on his face, making it look like he was weeping. Of all his family, he was the only one who did not contest Arendahl's declaration of departure. Perhaps he saw it as inevitable. Perhaps he was glad that the old elf wouldn't be there any longer to wrestle with him in his new role as decision maker. Yet Miri had the sneaking suspicion that he did not protest the old elf's departure because, as much as he despised the need to send her away, he knew that Miri could not stay with them—for her safety, she had to go, and Ell believed that the sooner Arendahl left, the sooner Miri would leave this dangerous region and return north toward safer areas of Andalaya. He never mentioned this, but Miri knew him better than he suspected.

As if to punctuate her thought, Ell finally spoke. "Enough." The finality and decisiveness in his voice was unexpected even to her. Miri saw Dacunda look at him in surprise.

Ell continued. "Arendahl has made his decision. He believes there are matters to which he must attend, and I trust him. Therefore, I am not likely to try to dissuade him. After all, the last time he said something similar, he was heading south to ascertain whether the Unsired really had returned." Ell cast his gaze sternly around the group and people looked away guiltily at his chastisement. Clearly, they felt he spoke reason. Yet, her mate's true intentions were betrayed when his gaze finally fell upon her. Miri saw the small flicker of a guilty conscience in his eyes as he looked at her, and she knew that she had her proof as to the real reason he would not protest Arendahl's departure. He saw the old elf's leaving and Miri's chances of greater safety as intertwined.

Miri didn't reveal his thoughts to the group. Instead, she smiled a bit sadly at him. They had known this day was soon to come, the day of their separation. She only hoped it would not be for too long.

"Will you go now?" Kalabi asked, his darkly toned skin and close-cropped dark beard glistening with a mixture of rainwater and sweat from the walk.

Arendahl flicked a glance at Miri. "Soon as I've had a moment more to rest." Miri knew he said that for her sake. It was true, her leg was aching more than usual. It seemed the day spent resting on the outskirts of Castn Yol had only served to make her leg even more sore for some reason. Perhaps breaking up the rhythm of walking every day had not been beneficial. She reached down and idly massaged her calf while listening to the rest of them discuss a plan of action as they proceeded south.

Ell put his arm on her elbow and guided her a few yards away from the others, under the pretense of sitting her down on a rock and massaging her weak leg. Well, perhaps it wasn't entirely a pretense—he had often done the same thing for her this summer after a long day. But this time she knew it was also an excuse to grab a last moment alone together.

Ell was never one for small talk and cut right to the point. "I am sorry. You know leaving you is the last thing I want."

Miri shook her head and somehow found the will to laugh. "Don't. Just don't, Ell. We have said it all before, and I know that this is the only way." She pulled his face close. "Just kiss me for a short while before we depart each other's company."

Ell obliged. It wasn't the passionate kiss of lovemaking or the affectionate kiss of greeting, but rather the tender, wistful half kisses of a mate who felt guilty for what he was about to do.

Miri disabused him of that guilty notion by pulling him headlong into a deep, rich kiss, in which she tried to convey as much love and emotion as she could. The world spun dizzyingly and for an instant she thought the lack of breath was making her lightheaded. But then she was inside his head and she knew it had happened again. Only this time she couldn't see—no gleaming red eyes gazing at her mercilessly. Why couldn't she see? Then she realized Ell's eyes were closed and she was inside him, and therefore would see nothing more than the inside of his eyelids the way he did as he thoroughly kissed her.

But she felt. Oh, how she felt.

It was like the first time when she had initially Grafted him. She felt a wellspring of emotion at which she was the center. Pain and worry at leadership flickered around the edges of his consciousness, excitement at the quest ahead also was a small and rather suppressed emotion—he would not be Elliyar Wintermoon if a little danger didn't excite him. Anger and bitterness towards the war.

Miri kept kissing him, savoring the sweetness, the closeness of the moment, oblivious to anything other than him. Guilt swirled rather large in his thoughts right now, guilt at having to leave her shredded his insides and made her want to do nothing more than comfort him. Guilt also for a family he had long thought dead, guilt that he had never saved them was also present. Miri could feel Ell's logical response to that emotion—he knew it was not his fault, yet the guilt remained and it drove him to press on in this journey.

Her arms wrapped around him and the fingers of her left hand twined themselves in the back of his mane of blond, wavy hair. His hands pulled her close. Love. Miri felt the core of his emotion and gloried in how central this emotion was to how he viewed her and the world around them. She was the most important thing to him, she felt it like a blazing light that he buried deep within himself.

She kissed him until she felt the sensation lift. The insight into his head, his feelings disappeared and Ell pulled back grinning roguishly at her shortness of breath. However, as she leaned back to rest on the rock, her hands propping her up behind her, he narrowed his eyes as if he suspected something more had happened. He read her nearly as well as she could read him, she admitted to herself.

"What...?" he began, but she interrupted him immediately.

"Stop. Don't ruin it."

Ell's gaze darkened as he seemed to guess what had just happened, but he stayed silent. Miri savored it, remembering the feel of every last little hidden part of him. Just in case...but no, she would not let her mind travel further down that dark and desperate path. No, she convinced herself that she savored it just because it was good, not because who knew when—or if—she would see him again.

Idly, Miri wondered why that kiss had been important enough to bring about the Grafting experience. According to Arendahl, she would only witness moments of importance from the piece of her soul melded within Ell's consciousness.

"It will be agony to leave you." Ell said soberly, almost as if reading her thoughts and answering the question. Yes, agony was usually important, whatever its cause. She smiled fondly at him, even though she could tell from the sour look on his face that he was not glad she had been inside his head again.

And then Arendahl was beside them, saying it was time to go. The moment had arrived. How could it have come so soon? Suddenly flustered, Miri hugged Ell fiercely, feeling the hot warmth of tears upon her cheeks. She kissed him once more, her mate, the one person with whom she felt most alive, most known, most safe, and most comforted all at once. She kissed him and then before any more words could be asked of her—because she was certain words would fail her now—she turned, grabbed her pack and Art's hand, and walked away with Arendahl leaving Elliyar Wintermoon and the rest of his family behind.

Chapter Fifteen

"Where will we go?" Miri asked finally, after hours walking on their new path.

Arendahl had taken it in stride that she wanted silence, and Art could always be counted on to intuit what those around him desired. But the old elf now answered her briskly.

"I have friends to the west of here, friends we need to speak with." His stilted voice was a match for his rugged, grizzled appearance. It made sense. The sun wasn't in the sky, but Miri could see its faint gleam behind the greyness of the sky ahead of them, indicating the direction in which they traveled. The rain had slackened but the clouds remained. They felt appropriate, coupling the strange numbness, which she struggled to throw off after enduring the first real separation from Ell since their Joining this past spring.

"These friends are part of whatever task it is that you need to accomplish? A task more important than going with Ell to keep him safe?" She couldn't help the edge that entered her voice.

Arendahl merely smiled wolfishly at her. "You've got a bite hidden somewhere inside you, don't you?"

"Not that hidden," Miri snapped back, with more venom than she had known she possessed.

"Well, I've certainly not seen it until now. Normally, you're all sunshine and smiles."

Miri tossed her hair angrily as she limped as quickly as she could, matching his stride. "Well, you hadn't abandoned Ell when he needed you most before now."

"Abandoned?" The old elf snorted. "Please. That boy can handle just about anything thrown his way. Rode an Icari he did, and without even using his powers. The nerve!" Arendahl cackled, throwing his head back.

Only slightly mollified, Miri pressed on. "Well, why didn't you stay? Aren't you always saying how he needs to train, to learn, so he can help our people? Who is going to train him now?"

The old elf's laughter ceased and he grunted sourly. "True, that is unfortunate. But know this, I do what I do for our people. No matter what. And right now, what Andalaya needs is for us to go west, then probably back north."

"Why? What is so important? What are we doing?" They were both surprised when Art joined the conversation. However, it appeared his curiosity had won out and made him voice his question.

Arendahl peered shrewdly at the boy for a moment and then responded. "Hope, boy, we are bringing hope."

And with that, the old elf refused to answer any more questions and Miri was forced to confront the maddening quality Arendahl had of not giving more information than he felt was needed—a quality of which Ell had complained to her time and again, but which she had never fully experienced before now. It was beyond frustrating to listen to him walking along in studied silence, only a whistle projecting from his lips every so often in response to her constant queries.

That was how they passed the next few days. Walking at a pace that Miri and Art could maintain, Arendahl pointedly ignoring her constant requests for more information. Miri slipped into a sullen silence that was quite unlike her. On the third day, after another night of failed questioning and subsequently a restless night's sleep where she dreamed of various disasters all night long, Miri resolved to get her answers that day.

"You cannot keep ignoring me old elf. Eventually you will have to speak." Miri put as much insolence in her voice as possible. But Arendahl, of all things, let out a loud guffaw of laughter, startling a bird out of the bushes next to the path on which they walked with the noise of his mirth.

"Resorting to insults now, girl? Well, I've been called much worse than old in my day. You're going to have to do better than that," he chuckled.

"Why won't you just tell me where we are going and what we are doing?" Miri almost stamped her foot. She refrained at the last minute from doing so, thinking it would make her look too childish to be taken seriously.

Arendahl shook his head in disbelief. "You two are a better match than I first thought," he said with a sidelong glance at Miri.

"Why do you say that?" She asked taken aback.

"You should hear yourself, demanding answers, less than twenty name days and you think you own the world and everything in it." The old elf snorted. "Sounds just like the boy. 'Tell me Arendahl, why must I not close my eyes while I train? Why didn't you tell me about my powers earlier rather now? Why? Why? Why?'" Arendahl said, his voice mimicking Ell's questioning voice.

"He does not sound like that," Miri grumbled halfheartedly, "and neither do I."

"No?" Arendahl laughed again.

"Well, have you ever once thought that maybe answers might make him—and me—give you some peace and quiet?" Miri proposed.

"Have you ever thought that maybe your elders know best and that you should trust them?" The grizzled elf fired back in annoyance, a scowl forming on his face. He was clearly growing tired of the argument.

"Talk to me, just explain to me where we are going. Please?" Miri changed tactics. Maybe some sweetness would do the trick.

"Heh, you'll not wheedle anything out of me that I don't desire to tell you," Arendahl chuckled again. Miri was growing tired of being his source of humor. "I tell you what," the old elf volunteered, "if you want to chatter away at me so badly, why don't we talk about something else instead?"

Now it was Miri's turn to growl. "Don't change the subject..." she began hotly, only for Arendahl to halt her words completely with his next sentence.

"How about we talk about that Grafting of yours?"

Miri froze, so surprised that she actually stopped walking for a moment.

Arendahl shrugged at her abrupt standstill and slung the small pack off of his back, set it down on the ground and began digging around for food and drink. "I suppose it's as good a time as any for a midday stop." He handed a flask of water to Art who drank from it readily. The boy was maintaining his usual silence.

"You want to talk about Grafting?" Miri repeated slowly, hardly believing her luck. "Why now? Why will you talk to be now about this, but not our immediate plans?"

The old elf rolled his eyes with a grimace. "I didn't talk to you before because I wanted to avoid a full blow out fight with your mate. Oh, don't make that face at me. I know Elliyar, and the boy has it in his head that this Grafting is wrong. If I had started chatting to you about it, then what tenuous influence I have over him would have disappeared in a heartbeat." Miri opened her mouth to disagree, but upon second consideration she found his logic sound.

"Alright, but why this? Why will you talk to me about this but not our plans?"

"I scarcely feel that I need to share our plans with you, girl," the old elf responded testily. "I have things well in hand, and those decisions don't concern you. However, the Grafting is different. The boy is stubborn, but I am not." Miri wasn't sure she agreed with the second half of that statement, but she didn't interrupt as Arendahl spoke further. "I'm a realist, much more practical. You've done it now, you've Grafted him, and there is no going back, not ever.

And while that boy can be silly, I am not. If you have a talent, or an opportunity or skill, you learn to use it, to control it. And that's what you need to do now Miri."

Control it. Arendahl was offering to help her do the very thing she had been wanting during the weeks since it had happened.

"Alright then," she said, with a calm reasoned voice.

"Oh, so you're all buttercups and honey now, are you girl?" Arendahl said, with a sour twist of his lips, and then muttered something unintelligible about the rashness and impatience of youth. This time it was Miri's turn to laugh at him.

"You are not nearly so fierce as you try to pretend you are. Did you know that?" Miri asked him with a wide grin. Art, who had been watching the altercation, joined in with a giggle of his own as they watched the grimace on Arendahl's face slowly fade to an expression of minor annoyance.

"There are many dark creatures and Departed who would dispute that," Arendahl said, with a dangerous glint in his eye, and Miri was reminded of who she was speaking to—first Water Caller to be born for centuries, maybe millennia. Yes, he was formidable indeed. But the old elf softened his look and, with a wink that told her whatever conflict they'd had was patched up, he pressed onward into new territory of conversation.

"So, I think what you need to do more than anything is practice." The old elf stated baldly.

"Practice?"

He nodded. "Practice. Try and access Ell's mind—or rather that part of your mind that you forged into his. Go ahead. Try."

"Now?" Miri asked, taken aback.

"Do you have a better time in mind, girl?"

Miri didn't have a reason to give him why she shouldn't try to access Ell's consciousness, so she decided to attempt it. Although, what try meant, she wasn't sure. She had never intentionally accessed that part of her mind that resided in Ell's consciousness. Nevertheless, she tried. She scrunched up her forehead and focused on Ell, on his thoughts and emotions. She remembered how it had felt when it happened, like a window had opened into his soul, his emotion. She pushed her mind the way she had done when the initial Grafting had taken place. Nothing.

She opened her eyes. "Nothing happened. I can try again if you think I should." But her mind felt surprisingly tired and she hoped that he would not ask for her to do it again.

"Again?" Now it was the old elf's turn for surprise. "You've been at it for almost an hour. I think you've done enough for now."

"An hour?" Miri exclaimed.

"Yes, it was extremely dull," Art said with a glazed look in his eyes.

Arendahl's eyes narrowed as he gazed at her. "Well, that's something at least."

"What's something?"

"We know something was happening even if you didn't exactly achieve what you wanted." The old elf responded.

"What do you mean?" She asked.

"I mean, you don't lose track of time that way when nothing out of the ordinary is occurring. Simply the fact that you got lost in your own mind shows me that there is potential there. What precisely, I am not sure, but potential for something to be trained and nurtured nonetheless."

Now it was Miri's turn to furrow her brow. "But I thought you said it only happened—that I could only access his consciousness during an extremely vital or important moment. So how am I supposed to do it by choice?"

"I did say that, and it's mostly true, or at least the legends say that it is. But I must admit I am woefully uncertain regarding the details of Grafting." Arendahl pursed his lips in annoyance as if the very fact that there was some part of Highest lore that he was not an expert on was somehow a failure on his part. He continued. "It hasn't happened for a long, long time. Long enough to be mostly forgotten. And even when it was more common, people couldn't claim to fully understand it. So yes, it happens in important moments of Ell's life, but there could be more to it. I believe we are stepping into uncharted territory, girl. Who knows what we might discover!" He said it almost excitedly, as if relishing the chance to watch the Grafting link unfold between Miri and Ell from a firsthand perspective.

Arendahl clapped his hands together. "Right, a daily regimen of practice and training should yield the best results." Her excitement and anticipation of earlier was now slightly overshadowed by the lack of results from the last hour, and by the old elf's brisk statements about rigorous training. Miri supposed, with a sinking feeling, that she was about to experience the rigors of having Arendahl as a teacher. Ell had complained many a night to her, while they were alone in their own private camp, about the difficult methods of having the old elf instruct you in something. She was about to get a firsthand taste of the same training.

"Enough lolling about. We have ground to cover before dark. Hopefully, we'll run into them soon." Arendahl set about preparing to depart from their midday resting point.

"Them?" Miri felt like she was constantly parroting questions back at the grizzled elf, but she supposed that was all a person could do when they were kept relatively in the dark about everything.

"Yes, them. People, living beings, elves. Now, enough babbling, let's be off!" He spoke as briskly as the pace he set, walking out of the little mushroom-dotted clearing that had served as their stopping point.

As usual, Miri could pry no more information loose from Arendahl about whom they were seeking. She decided to leave that matter alone for now. Miri did not wish to press her luck. Arendahl was currently on her side of matters regarding the Grafting. In fact, he was willing to help her practice in any way she could. It might be onerous training, to be sure, but still, if it enabled her to see Ell from afar, to be inside him again, then it was worth it. She definitely was not going to ruin that chance by pestering the old elf with more questions. Miri resolved to be as patient as possible.

* * * *

The terrain around them gradually sloped upward. The oak trees, once spaced distantly, had grown closer together, and more underbrush clogged the sides of the trail. Sycamores, maples, and elms began to reappear as they moved west and slightly north, back towards the Andalayan coast. Two days passed uneventfully. Miri dutifully attempted to practice utilizing her Graft into Ell's mind whenever they stopped, but to no avail. The rest of the time they passed in idle conversation punctuated by long but not uncomfortable periods of silence. Miri had never engaged Arendahl in direct conversation for any long periods of time over the past few months, but alone with only him and the boy, she found that sitting around the fire at night there was naught to do but spend the time listening to his tales of elven lore, and his personal anecdotes from a lengthy and adventurous life. She found him comedic, refreshingly honest, short-tempered at times, but more than anything, wise. It was no wonder that Ell—whether he admitted it or not—valued Arendahl's opinions so greatly.

On the third day of their travel, as twilight beckoned in full night, they finally found what they were looking for. Or rather, it found them.

"I would not move a step further, if I were you." The voice sounded out on the path ahead of Miri, Arendahl, and Art. Three elves stepped out of the shadows and onto the trail, arrows trained on the three of them, strings pulled taut and ready to loose.

"Is that really necessary, Iyonei? I have been looking for you after all. Not polite to welcome an old friend with an arrow." Arendahl responded with a hint of exasperation, directing his comment at the tall female member of the Highest who had spoken.

The elf—Iyonei presumably—was tall for a female and extremely well-muscled. She wore tight fitting clothing of greens and browns that blended in with the forest shadows with a natural ease. She would have been pretty—well she was, Miri supposed, in a rather fierce, brutal way—but for the eye patch covering her left eye that disrupted her striking features. Her right eye, though, gleamed green in the moonlight. The eye patch was covered in moss and the leather thong that bound it to her head made it look as if nature had been melded to her face. Her light brown hair, the same color as was shared by Dacunda's family, was woven to the left in a fat braid that ran down her head and coiled along her neck. A thinner, shorter braid dangled behind the opposite ear.

Iyonei grunted. "Arendahl. I should have known it was you. You're the only greying elf in the whole of Andalaya. I thought you would have died of old age by now. What are you doing this far south?" Miri noted that she didn't sound pleased to see him. However, she did lower her bow and with a nod to her companions, they did the same.

"I could ask the same of you." Arendahl said lightly, with an air of humor.

"As usual, we are looking for a fight," Iyonei answered.

Miri took a closer look at the two other elves—both female—who had lowered their bows. One was nearly as tall as Iyonei, with straight blonde hair woven into similar style of side braids as Iyonei. Blue eyes and fine features were marred by a long scar along her lean jaw. The other elf, also blonde, was a bit smaller than the other two and slightly less muscled. Her hair hung unbound, loose and straight, except for two small, thin braids along the sides of her head. These braids dangled straight down along with the rest of the hair. Her features were diminutive, even charming, but Miri noted a steel in her eyes that belied the pixie appearance.

"This is Miriyah, mate of a close friend, and Artorious, my traveling companion." Arendahl indicated each of them in turn.

Iyonei nodded her head toward the larger scarred female. "This is Satiri. On my left is Briesom, but everyone just calls her Brie," Iyonei said, indicating the smaller of the two. And that was as far as introductions or conversation went at the moment. They turned and melted into the darkness of the trail ahead of them and Miri, Arendahl, and Art had no choice but to follow as quickly as they could. They only walked for less than a mile, but Miri's leg ached viciously, as the group of the female elves set a faster pace than Ell and his family did. Every member of Ell's family understood and accepted Miri's limitations, and when those limitations prevented her from accompanying them, as was the case now, she understood. But she wasn't used to pressing her body to a faster pace such as this.

"We are nearly there." Brie said to Miri, glancing down at Miri's lame left leg as she limped. There was no pity in the gaze, but all the same, for the first time in a long time, Miri found herself embarrassed by her body. Not only was Brie gorgeous, but she moved with the kind of fluidity and grace becoming of an elf, the sort of movement Miri would never attain. It had been a long time since Miri felt like a cripple, but she did in that moment.

Just then, the sounding of a drum rolled towards them faintly out of the blackness of night. A few more minutes and they followed Iyonei's lead off of the beaten trail, through the underbrush, and over mossy stones into a thicket of trees. Starlight sparkled and twinkled through slight gaps in the branches of the canopy. Miri and the others walked until they pushed through a last bit of underbrush and entered a small, protected clearing, glowing orange with firelight.

There were ten or so elves—all female—dancing wildly around the flames. Some of them leapt the fire, while others undulated and twirled to the beat of the drum. Miri couldn't tell if there was a celebration afoot or not, but either way, Satiri and Brie immediately joined the dancers, laughing freely as they did so.

"You are all female." Miri didn't realize she had spoken out loud.

"Not all. We have one male warrior." Iyonei said, pointing to the drummer.

In all her life, Miri had never seen an elf as small as he. He couldn't have been much taller than the boy Art, although he would have tripled him in weight. He was also the darkest and most heavily muscled elf Miri had ever seen, like a tiny war hammer.

Again her mouth voiced her thoughts without allowing her to think them through first. "How does he manage to fight, so small as he is?"

Iyonei, looked at her with a fierce light in her eyes. "You have it all wrong, Miriyah mate-of-Arendahl's-close-friend. He does not suffer in battle. Far from it. In fact, we often send Yendil to spearhead our attacks. He is like a small boulder rolling down the mountain, breaking the knees and crushing the ankles of our foes."

They were standing close enough for Yendil to hear her comment. He looked at them and smiled in response, clearly not offended by Miri's question. Instead, he continued to bang on the small drum in front of him with the wild staccato that sent limbs and braids of the elves twirling in the flickering light of the night fire.

Arendahl leaned in close to Iyonei. "We must speak. Privately first, but then to the group, I think."

Iyonei shrugged off his request. "Later, elder. After the night's entertainment is finished." And with that she leapt away into the fray of dancers, joining in as vigorously—if not more so—as any of the other elves.

Chapter Sixteen

This camp was as different from Ell's and his family's as Miri could imagine. Ell's family made relatively cautious, quiet camps, punctuated sometimes by boisterous laughter, but more often than not kept safe by trained warriors always on guard. Iyonei's band of elves reveled loudly and deep into the night, with dancing and singing and drumming until their legs and lungs could take no more. They did not seem to worry about their noise attracting unwanted visitors. Two elves were patrolling the perimeter and surrounding area, and apparently that was enough.

Well into the night it was when at last people found their way to beds of moss and under blankets woven from long grass and leaves. Morning came too quickly for Miri, who was not accustomed to staying up so late and then rising early. People were stirring all about the camp, flasks of water being held to lips, pieces of grain cakes exchanging hands. Smiles and laughter still filled the air, but it was nothing like the night before.

Miri made her way towards the small campfire that was still smoldering from the night before and held her hands out in front of her. The crisp morning air reminded her that autumn was nearly here, if it wasn't already. The warmth of the fire was welcome, as the cold morning rays of sun slid through the trees to illuminate the camp with their dappled light. Miri thought to wake Art, but instead decided to let him sleep and saved him a few pieces of food for when he finally awoke. The boy deserved some rest.

Miri observed the camp as she sat strategically near to Arendahl and Iyonei, near enough to overhear their conversation. Brie was sharpening a knife in between handfuls of berries. The scarred Satiri was washing the grit from her eyes with a flask of water. The tiny, but thick, Yendil was one of the few still sleeping, sprawled out as wide as his small frame would let him near the fire.

"How goes the struggle?" The old elf inquired seriously, his attention all towards the female seated on the ground next to him.

Iyonei grimaced. "There are few of us fighting and the gains are correspondingly small. People have forgotten from where they come, from the long lineage of warriors who preceded us in Andalaya. Too many simply hide and run. Blood has grown weaker."

"Not the blood, I think, in fact I believe the blood may be stronger than ever." Miri knew Arendahl must have been thinking of Ell and his powers as a Water Caller. "No, it is despair, despondency, and hopelessness clinging to every root, tree, and rock of this land that saps our strength as a people."

Iyonei grunted in a non-committal way. She held her silence and Miri watched as Arendahl probed a bit further with his talk and questions. Was this part of the reason they were here? What was the old elf after?

"Have you paid attention to events these past months?" Arendahl was asking Iyonei obliquely.

Iyonei snorted derisively. "You mean the wild fancies of delusional hopefuls?" She responded with a nodded affirmative. "I have heard tell of some fable of a battle far to the north that supposedly took place. But you know, as well as I, that nothing of the sort really happened."

"On the contrary, I was there," the old elf said quietly, staring intently at the female who was clearly the leader of this roguish band of elves.

"Do not jest, old one," Iyonei said almost angrily. "I would have thought better of you than to further the cause of these pointless tales of triumph and magic. Those fanciful hopes are the rope by which fools hang themselves."

Arendahl shook his head. "It is no tale, Iyonei, save a true one. I was there. The battle happened, and other events occurred, as well."

The one-eyed elf narrowed her good eye as she strung a bow with a fresh string. Almost cautiously she proceeded, as if she could not dare to let herself believe. "The Traitor?"

"Is dead." Arendahl answered decisively. Iyonei let out a sigh and closed her eye, almost as if she had been holding her breath these last twenty years since Silverfist's betrayal.

"Do not lie to me, Elder," she said in a much more respectful voice. "Can this really be true? The stories coming down from the north sound like nothing more than wild imaginings. There were reports of a small army of slavers, but even a defeated army would leave signs of its retreat and no such signs were found. Besides, there has not been an army in Andalaya large enough to defeat a foe in years. Not to mention there were murmurings...."

"The army was mostly destroyed not leaving behind enough of our enemies to leave a trail, and as for the rest, what murmurings did you hear?" Arendahl had opted to abandon his usual short, stilted manner of speech for the role of a silky questioner, leading his conversant down the path towards understanding.

"Rumors of magic, like the powers in our ancient lore, abound, Arendahl. But I thought them nothing but tales." She paused and glanced sidelong at the grizzled elf, but when he did not laugh at her she continued in almost a whisper. "They say there was a boy hardly of age who slew the army singlehandedly. They say he was the spirit of our ancestors from the First Days returned."

Now Arendahl did smile. "Well, the facts are not all correct but the core of the matter is true. Power has reawakened in Andalaya, such as has not been seen since the First Days. The boy exists, and he is not singular in his possession of these powers, he is simply the most... impressive. The time for solitary bands of the Highest is passed." His eyes flicked around her camp, as if indicating what he meant.

"What would you have of me, Arendahl?" Iyonei asked warily apparently recognizing the same as Miri that Arendahl was building towards something. "You know that I respect you, Elder, but you do not command me. Ask what you will, but I will make my own decision."

Patience gone, Arendahl snapped back into his usual testy self. "Girl, don't be an idiot! The time to stand alone is gone. Andalaya must band together again."

"Andalaya hardly exists," Iyonei spat bitterly. "Do not speak to me of fighting. You whittle your days away fighting a forgotten war in the north while the south and the east destroy us. Or do you forget where you were when Verdantihya fell to the human and Departed coalition? When has the south ever concerned you?"

Arendahl stood suddenly and loomed over the still-seated Iyonei. Silence fell immediately across the camp as every elf's eye watched what had become a loud altercation.

"Mock me if you like, Iyonei, but do not make the mistake of ignoring what you so foolishly call a 'forgotten war in the north'. That battle is every bit as real as the cause for which you fight here in the Lower Forest. Or have you spent so long here in the southern reaches, that you have not seen the increase of Ghouls and Ogres plaguing us once again. Icari fly by night and ravage the countryside." Miri had never seen Arendahl so frightening. However, Iyonei was braver than Miri and she stood to face off with the grey haired elf, although her visage was slightly less angry and aggressive than it had been a moment before.

"The south and the north are aligned now. They are unified. There is only one battle now." Arendahl spoke the last bit with a special emphasis. Miri, privy to information, knew that Arendahl meant that the Unsired had returned, and this time they were being transformed from the ranks of southern elves, the Departed.

Even Iyonei faltered a bit at that statement. "You cannot mean what I think you mean, Elder."

"I do!" Arendahl stated aggressively, pressing the advantage he now possessed. He turned his head and spoke to all, not just their leader. "The Unsired have returned and the First Days are back upon us. The time for raiding and ambushes is over. We must gather and unite or we will die, hunted down in pitiful ragged bands of our people." Silence greeted him, but Miri could tell it was the quiet of thought and pondering.

Yendil had awoken at some point and his squat frame squared off with Arendahl, he spoke respectfully, but he still questioned. "How do we know that any of this is true, Elder? You are just one elf. Could you not be wrong? How can we know that the powers and dangers that you speak of really exist?"

Iyonei latched on to that argument immediately. "Yes, how do we know what you say is real? Can you prove any of this to us? Can you prove not only your warnings but also the hopes you monger? Prove that this magic, this ancient power from the first days has returned to our people."

Arendahl stared at her solemnly. "If I prove it, will you listen to me and do as I say?"

Iyonei stared back for a moment. Finally, she spoke. "If you truly can prove it, then yes, my strength and the strength of all who I command will be yours. I would not be one of the Highest if I promised anything less. But," she held up a finger, "if you cannot prove it, then you and your friends will depart from us, and spread your fanciful tales elsewhere."

Arendahl grinned wolfishly, tying his lank grey hair back. "Done. There are around a dozen of you, yes? Pick your ten best. If you can defeat me then we will leave. But when I defeat you, you will apologize for questioning the sound advice of an elder."

Iyonei looked at Arendahl incredulously. "I do not wish to see you get hurt, old one. Certainly ten is too many?"

Arendahl laughed ruthlessly. "It is you who are more likely to be injured, whelp. That is why I left two free from the fight to care for any who are injured. Remember, you asked for this."

Iyonei looked uncertain now. An old grey elf challenging her and nine of her best to a fight and clearly expecting to win was not what she had expected.

Looking like she had swallowed something sour, Iyonei began rattling off names. Satiri, Briesom, and Yendil were among the nine that she selected along with herself. Miri watched with a certain amount of trepidation as the warriors arrayed themselves in a circle around Arendahl. Miri had no doubt as to who would win this encounter. She had seen Ell fight while tapping his powers as a Water Caller and ten elves were nowhere near enough to stop him.

The old elf stripped off his shirt exposing an extremely lean but well-toned torso. Age had not softened him. He was a piece of granite from the northern mountains, a rock broken off by storms to impact the canyon floor, chipping, but not destroying him, making him sharp enough to kill.

"Last chance to yield, Iyonei." A dangerous look glittered behind his slate grey eyes as he stood within the circle.

Iyonei opened her mouth, but it seemed that pride more than any common sense clicked her jaws back together. Miri could tell by the short time she had spent with her, that the leader of this band of elves was not one to back down from a fight or a challenge.

Arendahl smiled faintly at Iyonei's inability to back down. Then, crouching down to one knee, he closed his eyes and placed his palms against the dry soil beneath him. Miri had never seen Ell do this and so she wasn't sure whether it was necessary or just an affectation that the old elf had developed to dramatize the effect of accessing his powers. However, when he arose, Miri noticed the similarly foggy look to his eyes, the same way her own mate's eyes clouded over when he tapped into his supernatural abilities. However, no mist formed around him the way it did with Ell. Strange. She would have to ask him why that was.

Tension clogged the air and there were more fighters than bystanders. Miri made sure that she and Art were off to the side with the two female elves who were not to take part in this contest of arms.

"Will you yield when blood is drawn?" Iyonei asked Arendahl seriously. He didn't answer, he just tilted his head and crooked a finger mockingly at her. Her gaze flattened to an anvil. And without further ado, Iyonei charged.

Nine other figures closed with her, swooping in on the old elf. They were all lightning-fast, Iyonei even more than the rest, her lack of one eye seemingly no detriment to her fighting capacity.

But Arendahl was a reed in the wind, a snake in the grass. He swayed slightly in an almost lazy fashion, barely moving, but precisely enough to dodge a blow or shift his stance to deliver one himself. And then, in a sudden movement, he would strike like a viper. The ten elves attacked him with blades of all sizes, Iyonei wielded a sword that was beautiful to behold, glistening silver with a milky green agate pressed into the hilt, etchings of thorns wreathed the hilt and grew upwards along the blade itself. Yet, she could not strike a blow to the old elf.

Grizzled features and grey hair shifting in the breeze, gnarled fingers and hands delivering open fisted strikes along with those of a closed fist, he fought. Miri found she was holding her breath, as he reminded her of nothing so much as an avalanche—swift and relentless, powerful, and wrought from the mountains.

Elves dropped in quick succession and soon there were only five left in the fight, all limping slightly from bruises along their bodies. Three charged Arendahl together and, almost defying gravity and the laws of nature, he leapt at the last possible moment to avoid their strikes, rising twenty feet into the air with a back flip to land some feet away.

Everyone's jaws dropped in stunned silence. Arendahl motioned with his hands for the remaining five to attack again. He was focused entirely now, not because he required it to survive, but rather, Miri was sure, because he wished to end this farce of a contest. Miri knew he relished the battles he fought, but she knew that he did not want to hurt his own people.

The five elves attacked. Briesom, in the front with two hand-axes, cut and slashed. Arendahl ducked and her blade stuck into a tree. As he rose, the old elf lashed out with a vicious kick of his heel to send her tumbling across the clearing.

Satiri and Yendil advanced together, but they could not strike a blow either, and finally Arendahl was left facing Iyonei one-on-one. She continued the fight because she had entered the contest and had honor, but Miri knew from the look in her eyes that she knew she was already defeated.

Arendahl avoided her as the remaining lone combatant with embarrassing ease until finally he chose to dispossess her of her sword with a disarming blow to her elbow that caused her to release the sword and stagger back. Without hesitation, Arendahl snatched the sword and snaked it up to kiss her throat.

Dead silence followed the minutes of combat that had felt like hours. Nobody spoke, wondering what Arendahl would do. And then, surprisingly, he laughed. The old elf threw back his head and laughed wildly.

"Good fight," was all he said as he flipped the blade around deftly and handed it back to Iyonei hilt first, the flat of the sword lying along his forearm.

The old elf walked over to the crowd of spectators and grabbed a flask of water. He poured the drink in his mouth and then swallowed gratefully. The sound of groans drew his attention. Arendahl began making the rounds, checking limbs, looking at cuts. Luckily no one was seriously injured, he had controlled his attack enough to maximize his ability to disable them from the immediate fight while limiting any real damage.

"Heh, nothing a few sips of Source Water can't fix," he said as he examined the worst of the wounds he had inflicted—an inch long cut on the cheek of Yendil. Accordingly, the tiny ball of muscle drank from a flagon of Source Water, and Miri watched as the cut closed, then pinked into a scar, and then, because it was a minor wound, the scar disappeared altogether.

Finally, when the wounded had been tended and the groaning stopped, the old elf turned to look at the leader of the group, Iyonei. "Well?"

Iyonei grimaced, more out of dislike for losing the contest than any real anger. "It appears you have won the contest. I—we all—are yours to command. For now," she added, with a hint of her prior fire. "And, it appears that not only have I misjudged your capabilities as a fighter, but also the nature of those abilities." She shook her head in wonder. "I have never seen an elf move so quickly and with such force. That leap, it was incredible." Iyonei trailed off as if she did not know what else to say.

"Good," Arendahl said gruffly. "Glad that's settled." He leaned in and spoke to Iyonei a little more quietly. Quiet enough that only Miri, standing close by, could hear. "And if you think I am impressive, you should see the boy—the one who slew Silverfist. He is quite remarkable."

"If you say it is so, then I can only imagine." Iyonei responded, all traces of antagonism gone from her voice.

"I do say so, and it is behind him that we will rally Andalaya."

Miri was stunned, so this was what his pressing matter was—the rousing of Andalaya behind the standard of Elliyar Wintermoon. Miri felt a mixture of emotions, pride clashed with worry at what it might entail for Ell, as well as uncertainty at how her mate would take to learning about this information. But most of all, she felt trepidation for what was to come. A war was well and truly on the way.

Chapter Seventeen

"So where is this…other one, this boy like you?" Iyonei directed her question to Arendahl as she tore into a piece of dried meat.

"Water Caller." The old elf prompted.

"Fine, Water Caller. Where is this remarkable boy?"

Arendahl smiled faintly. "He is to the south attending to a personal matter in Dor Khabor. Accompanied by his uncle, Dacunda."

Miri observed Iyonei, curious as to what her response would be to that information. The one-eyed female grinned widely.

"Ha! The boy must be everything you claim him to be, or brash beyond all measure to venture there. Have any of our kind entered Dark Harbor and returned freely other than traitors? Either way, I like it. He will be a good emboldening influence on Dacunda."

Miri was surprised to hear that Iyonei knew Dacunda. Although, in hindsight, she supposed they were about the same age so it stood to reason that their paths might have crossed at one time or another. Especially considering they both were occupied with the violent defense of their homeland.

"You know Dacunda?" Miri asked tentatively, curiosity driving her to fish for more information.

Iyonei turned an eye on Miri. "You related to him?" She grunted, sensing Miri's probing question.

"She is." Arendahl supplied the information. "Related by ceremony after Joining with his nephew."

Iyonei nodded her head. Answering Miri's question, she said, "Dacunda and my paths have crossed on more than one occasion in recent years. And in our youth, we were in the same company along the walls of Verdantihya. He was by my side during the fall of our great city, when I lost this," she pointed to the empty eye socket behind her mossy eye patch, gesturing with the piece of dried venison in her hands. "We were close then." Iyonei trailed off as if lost in thought.

"But you are not close now?" Miri asked, fascinated by information about Dacunda's younger years, however minor that information was.

Iyonei shrugged. "Paths do not always stay as one. You have been amongst our woods. Two trails will converge and run as one for a time and then split off to go separate ways again. It is the way of the world."

As if deciding that philosophy and treading along the walkway of old memories was not ideal, Iyonei changed the subject.

"Well, it sounds like this boy—your mate I presume—" Iyonei inclined her head knowingly at Miri, having deduced the connection, "will balance out Dacunda some. I respect Dacunda, but he is overly cautious for my taste." Iyonei laughed loudly. "Dacunda would hide from a flock of birds just to make certain he has enough arrows before he attacks."

Although Miri sensed the joke in the statement, she rose to the bait slightly. "I have seen my uncle make decisions that would prove that statement false," she said hotly, with a snap in her voice. Dacunda had followed Ell's journey south and had been waiting to fight and help rescue her after Ell had liberated Miri from enslavement on the Pillar last spring. Her uncle had also traveled north to warn the people of Little Vale, then stayed with his family to defend her home against overwhelming odds. Miri did not take kindly to the notion of someone insinuating he was cowardly.

"Ha!" Iyonei laughed with apparent glee. "You have more fire than it looks like, girl. Especially for a cripple. I like that!"

Miri's eyes narrowed to see if she was insulting her or being serious. In the end, she decided the one-eyed female was being honest. Her way was to be blunt, outspoken. Abrasive, much like Arendahl could be, but there was also a value to people who would always speak their mind.

Arendahl watched the interaction with a faint smile on his lips and an interested expression on his face as he watched Miri defend her new family.

"I did not mean offense, Miri," Iyonei continued. It was not an apology; it was simply the clarification of the prior statement. "I know how brave Dac can be, but he is also cautious beyond anyone I know. He will plan and strategize until the time for fighting is past. Sometimes the action required is spontaneous, impulsive." Iyonei grasped the hilt of her sword leaning against the log on which all three of them sat. A feverish light entered her single eye, and Miri could tell that this was an elf who desired action above all else.

Arendahl interjected. "Yes, yes. He is overly cautious and you, Iyonei, are reckless. We all have our faults, but in the end we fight for the same cause—the freedom of our people."

"Freedom is about more than escaping slavery and staying alive, old one." Miri didn't think she had ever heard someone speak so irreverently to Arendahl and she kind of liked it. Even when Ell was furious with the old elf, there was a certain respect for his person that Ell maintained. Every time Miri heard Iyonei call Arendahl 'old one' she felt the urge to laugh.

Iyonei was not finished. "Freedom is as much about living free from fear as anything else. Why do you think we drum and dance into the night, without regard for noise or the worry of attracting our enemies to us?" Miri had to admit, she could not have imagined Dacunda allowing such raucous revelry this close to enemy territory.

"There is more than one way to be free of fear, and boldness and caution are not mutually exclusive," the grizzled old elf replied sagely.

The one-eyed elf shook her head slightly. "That may be true, but for us," she extended her hand in a gesture to the rest of her company that was attending to the daily details of life, "fearlessness means being ready to fight and die at any time and accepting that. Some might call us reckless and rash, some might look at the fact that we rarely retreat and never avoid a fight no matter the odds, as foolish. But for us it is how we assert our freedom from our oppressors." Iyonei finished fiercely.

Miri respected what she was saying. There was truth to the need to assert one's freedom, yet Miri couldn't help but think that fighting and dying was not the only way to do so. Could one not declare one's own freedom by finding joy in every moment, no matter how big or small? Could the recognition of how precious life was, of the inescapable beauty of existence not function as a way of asserting one's freedom, as well? Miri wondered, but did not speak. It was the age-old debate she'd had with Ell on many occasions—whether fighting was really the answer, and if it was, to what extent was it important? Miri saw the need for violence, but she clung fiercely to the opinion that there was more to life than battle, more ways to show defiance of oppression than to lash out with violent strength of arms.

"Enough," Iyonei said with a slashing motion of her hand. "Back to more important matters. You say this boy, this Water Caller, is in Dark Harbor?"

"Elliyar Wintermoon is on his way there," Arendahl agreed.

"Wintermoon, the son of Adan the Green." Iyonei mused thoughtfully.

Arendahl waited silently for her to continue. "But if he is to the south then how are we to rally people to his name?"

"The cause is all our cause, not just his. The elves of Andalaya will understand the importance for all." The old elf replied complacently, not seeming to be worried at all about Ell's distance from Andalaya.

"Besides," Miri volunteered, "word of him has spread. You heard of his exploits even if you did not believe at first. There will be others who will have heard the same stories, passed from mouth to mouth across the land." Miri wasn't sure why she was latching on to the old elf's purpose and supporting it. She wasn't sure Ell would be at all happy to return and find himself the figurehead of an army. But then again, she was not sure. Ell had certainly desired leadership on this current expedition, so perhaps he would adjust well to another step up.

Arendahl seemed pleased she was helping him champion his cause and nodded approvingly.

"The girl is correct. Word of Ell's exploits have already flown across the land. Rumor begets rumor and not all will be true. But enough of them are real, that I can verify them and inspire people to flock to us when the time is right." Arendahl finished with a piercing gaze at Iyonei.

The female elf stared back thoughtfully. "I suppose you may be correct, old one. But I am not so confident in the courage of our people as I once was, and as you still seem to be. Too many of us cower and cringe before the wrath of our foes instead of standing tall and facing it with weapon in hand."

"They lack hope, Iyonei," Arendahl said instructively in his crisp voice. "Without hope, people's vision for the future perishes and they will not have the courage to stand up for themselves and for what is right."

"We are going to return that hope to them, reignite it." Miri finished his thought musingly.

"Yes, Miriyah, we are—and Ell will be the manner in which we reignite that fire."

"Well then, let us hope he does not die in Dark Harbor like every other member of the Highest who has ever set foot there." Iyonei muttered fatalistically, a grimace on her face.

Miri swallowed at the mention of Ell dying. It was a cold, bitter thought to ponder.

"Tomorrow it begins. We set out north to begin our task of rousing Andalaya from the ashes of its funeral pyre." Arendahl said to Iyonei. She grunted her assent. She had lost the contest and subsequently must follow his orders as she had agreed to do. But that did not mean she was happy to receive commands.

"And don't be so pessimistic, Iyonei, not every Northerner has perished upon entry to Dor Khabor." The old elf spoke with a roguish smirk.

Iyonei raised her eyebrow skeptically. "And who might have survived such a harrowing and dangerous journey and returned to our fair land to tell of it? I have certainly never heard such a tale, and I would have if it were true."

"Come now, girl," Arendahl spread his hands and shrugged his shoulders with a pleased and knowing smile on his face, indicating he could only mean himself. Miri was glad it was not just her he referred to as 'girl'. The old elf would refer to anyone younger than him as 'girl or boy' without remorse.

Then with a wink at Iyonei's surprise he finished his thought. "I don't tell every single story of my many and varied exploits. After all, modesty is a virtue."

Chapter Eighteen

Ell thought the nights would be worst. Being separated from Miri was horrible, but his prior expectations about which part of their separation would be the hardest were wrong. He had thought he would miss her most at nights when the air was cool and the smell of wood smoke saturated the air. Ell expected to miss the warmth of her body next to him in the dirt, or on a mossy bed, and he did. To be sure, it was difficult. But the worst part of Miri being gone was the daytime. All the stolen glances and hidden smiles she saved just for him. The half laughs and the witty quips as they talked and ran, or the snatches of conversation about the deeper topics of the world as they sat on a rock and ate their midday meal. Some days had passed since they had taken leave of one another, and each day was as hard as the one before it.

The night air was chilly. Even this far south, autumn had arrived in force. Daylight kept the temperature high, but at night the fingers of fall twined themselves through the land. Ell sat under the stars, listening to the breathing of his family as they slept. He had first watch.

It was difficult, but this was the easiest time because soon he would wake his sister for the second watch and sleep and dream of his love. It was one thing to leave for the day on a hunt knowing he would return to Miri's company come twilight, as he had often done in the summer. He had missed her then. Yet it was quite something else to be separated for days at a time, weeks, months maybe, not knowing when or if they would ever return to each other's embrace. Ell held no illusions. He was a realist. They were seeking to enter Dark Harbor, the Departed stronghold and capital. It was bound to be a perilous journey. He wished he had told Miri he loved her once more.

Ell kept his eyes open, peeled toward the edges of the campsite, ears straining to catch any unexpected or odd sound that might signal danger nearby. Yet, as he heightened his senses, he let his mind drift. He thought of her. Ell remembered summer days spent swimming in the many rivers and lakes of Andalaya. The cool water running across her skin, and the heat of the sun baking them dry as they lay out under the blue skies. Ell missed the scent of her clean sweat in the high heat after bathing, the shape of her nose, just too wide to ever be called elegant. He missed looking into her eyes, eyes so knowing that he could lose himself in the truth that she alone knew him completely in a way that no other soul could.

And owl hooted and Ell swore as the sound startled him. So much for maintaining his focus. You're a fool! He berated himself for the waking dream in which he had been indulging. The only way to make sure he finished this journey alive and returned to Miri was to pay attention to his surroundings. Ell made sure to not let his mind drift for the rest of the watch. When the time came to end his period of vigilance, Ell walked quietly to where his sister was sleeping, her dyed green hair splayed out on the ground around her head, the moonlight glancing off it in just the right way to make it reflect the light.

He shook her slightly, and as he did, her eyes flew open and a hand went to her belt knife before she realized it was just Ell waking her for her time on night duty.

"Lucky I did not mark you with my blade, shaking me awake like that," she mumbled groggily.

Ell smiled in amusement. "How else was I supposed to wake you? Shout your name for all the night to hear and wake the others? Little good that would do, sister."

Rihya grunted sourly, but her mind seemed to be clearing. "Well, I suppose. Anything unusual on your watch?" She changed the subject to matters of importance.

"Nothing. All quiet, except for the night birds."

Rihya nodded. "Get yourself to sleep, my little leader. You could use the rest."

Ell didn't mind when Rihya teased him, not even about his decision to assume control of the mission. With others he might still be touchy about that subject, but it was hard to feel annoyed with her for a little lighthearted banter. Besides, she was the one person who he could count on, other than himself, to see this mission through. It was for her parents too, after all. She was always there for him, his sister, always fiery, sometimes frustrating, but always lending her support.

Ell surprised even himself with a rare show of emotion as he pulled her head close and kissed her on the forehead. She crinkled her brow and looked at him quizzically.

"Don't," Ell forestalled her with a yawn and a raised palm. "It's late, and I'm tired. I don't know what has gotten into me."

Rihya smiled. "Good, I would hate to think you were going soft on me."

He laughed softly. "Never that."

"Get some sleep." Rihya melted off into the shadows to stand watch over her slumbering family members.

Ell lay down with his head on his pack and was asleep almost immediately. The night seemed to pass swiftly, and when the grey dawn of morning arrived Ell felt rested enough, but he still could have used a few more hours to sleep. However, that was not possible. Everyone ate a quiet breakfast and then gathered what few things they had and set off south.

They were truly in enemy territory now. What had once been the southern edge of the kingdom of Andalaya now lay squarely under the control of the Departed. Pillars dotted the horizons, but Ell and his family gave those table-top fortresses a wide berth, not wishing to pass too near to the strongholds that functioned as holding pens for slavers trafficking their captives south, or as unassailable fortresses which even a full enemy army would have difficulty penetrating.

Well, they were nearly unassailable. Last spring Miri had been captured by slavers and taken to the northern most Pillar. Ell, wild with fear and grief, had done the unthinkable and attacked the Pillar and its combatants singlehandedly. Pillars were built with a cylindrical base, moving upwards to a flat tabletop platform, fortified as any fortress was. It was unable to be scaled or climbed due to its shape, and the inside of the cylindrical base was a series of single ladders, pulleys, and narrow stairways which a few elves could hold against an entire army. In short, the Pillars had been deemed impregnable. Yet, Ell had found a solution. He had scaled the north crag, hitched a ride by force upon the back of an Icari, and flown south to rescue his love.

Ell had instinctively tapped into his powers and fought his way clear out of the Pillar with Miri, the boy Art, and a few other captive elves who'd perished as the Departed pursued them. Luckily, Dacunda and his family had followed him south and stood ready to help with their escape.

Ell shook his head from memories and focused on the landscape around him as they ran on. Instead of reliving the past, Ell focused on an issue that had begun plaguing him as soon as they entered the Pillar region. It was as if entering the heart of enemy territory drove home the reality that before long, Dark Harbor would darken the horizon. Ell needed a plan, a manner of entering the southern port and ascertaining the whereabouts of his father and mother, or whether they were even alive. Up until now, such a plan had eluded him, and Ell felt his anxiety building. His family's lives were in his hands. He was responsible for them in a way he had never been before. He was asking them to risk their lives in pursuit of what might very likely be a dead dream. Ell needed a viable plan, one that maximized his ability to keep them as safe as possible.

He had no such plan yet, and the pressure—and the guilt of that fact—weighed on him.

As the days passed and they traveled south through sparsely wooded land, Ell pulled away slightly from the others. He drew within himself as he searched for an answer. But no answer came.

One day as they were running through this arid, sparse forest, so different from the lush, green of Legendwood or Andalaya proper, Dahranian came running lightly back towards them along the path.

"There is something you should see." Dahranian directed this toward the air in between Ell and Dacunda. Ell noticed the somber expression on his cousin's face, an expression even tinged with uncertainty. That was unlike Dahranian, and enough to fully get Ell's attention.

Turning to Rihya and Ryder and Kalabi, Ell spoke. "You three make camp in that dense thicket of trees over there. It's the only real cover around." He motioned with his hand off to the right of the trail.

"Might as well, it is nearly evening, almost time for dinner." Ryder mused as he anticipated the meal to come.

"I want a dark campsite, no fire." Ell said to Rihya. She nodded her agreement and the three of them loped off the path towards the copse of trees.

"Lead on, son," Dacunda indicated to Dahranian.

Ell, Dacunda, and Dahranian ran lightly for a short way until they reached a rise. As they neared the top of the ridgeline they approached the last few feet on their bellies, the dry brown grass of this southern most region of the Lower Forest scratching at them.

Ridges were a great vantage point for reconnaissance, but they also provided danger if a person wasn't careful. If you stood at the top of the rise, the light behind you could highlight your shadowy silhouette to anyone with a keen eye for attention, betraying your location to the enemy. If Ell had learned anything from Dacunda it was to temper his passion and aggression with caution, and so they squirmed their way up to the top of the rise.

The scene beyond was an odd one, foreboding and sinister. A Departed stood face to face with one of the Icari. The winged beast hovered with steady beats from its massive, ashy-grey, feathered wings. Icari, among the most terrifying of all the dark creatures Ell had confronted, were two or three times the size of an adult elf, with the torso and legs of an elf, talons like an eagle in place of feet, and great wings instead of arms. It had a humanoid or elvish face, but with rows of sharp fangs in its mouth and eyes that glowed a fiery orange-red. They were muscled and bursting with power, intelligent, and very deadly.

Ell had flown on an Icari before, and he had also fought them and knew the Icari to be ruthless predators. To observe it engaging in a peaceful interaction with this Departed could only mean one thing—it was not one of the Departed at all, but rather an Unsired.

The two beings shared a few more moments of interaction before the Icari flapped its powerful grey wings and rose up into the air and began moving rapidly north. Ell and his uncle and cousin flattened themselves against the brown of the hillside praying the predator's raptor gaze would pass them by. It did, and it was gone from sight in no time at all. Ell was glad he had chosen a dark site for the camp. The Icari's eyes were keen, and a fire, no matter how small, would have been a beacon to it.

They rolled back onto their stomachs and watched what they now knew to be an Unsired survey the scene and watch the departing Icari. It had a sickly look to its face, and the hands and arms sticking out of its black leather vest had a diseased cast to them. The blank gaze that Ell remembered from some of his close quarter combat with the Unsired was there, and Ell felt himself shudder. There was something unnerving about the Unsired.

"Should we kill it?" Dahranian was already reaching over his shoulder for his bow, but Ell stayed his hand.

"No." Ell said.

Dacunda seemed surprised but pleased by Ell's reaction. "Why is that, nephew?" he asked in an appraising tone.

"The Unsired was clearly on a task. He will no doubt be missed if we kill him, and vanquishing just one of our ancient foes is not worth the risk it will cause. Better for us if we can slip behind enemy lines without alerting them of our presence." Ell explained briefly. He did not want to waste any more time convincing his uncle that he knew what he was about.

Dacunda made no comment, but there was an approving look in his eye. As they ran quickly back to camp they broached the unsettling subject of what they had just witnessed.

Dahranian was the first to break the strained silence. "It looked like it was… conversing with the Icari." He spoke almost tentatively.

"He was." Ell confirmed in a curt voice.

"This does not bode well. The development of communication between the dark creatures and the Unsired can only bring harm to our cause." Dacunda was clearly worried as well.

Ell understood their concerns, but for some reason he wasn't as surprised. They needed to pull themselves together and move past their fear.

"What did you expect? Arendahl told us that the Unsired were the Lords of Darkness during the First Days. The Unsired controlled the dark creatures, commanding and marshaling them in battle against the Highest. You should not be surprised." Ell finished a bit harshly, but neither Dacunda nor Dahranian seemed offended, if anything, they saw that Ell spoke sense.

"Besides," Ell continued, "when I rode the Icari, I spoke to it and it understood. It also spoke a word back to me, so I know that not only can they communicate, but they can do so in our language."

Dacunda was nodding to himself as they turned off the path and made a straight line for the dark patch of trees where they knew their camp awaited them. "Yes, in this, Nephew you have more experience than us."

Dahranian swallowed. Ell was not accustomed to seeing his oldest cousin show fear. Perhaps the sight of a dark creature receiving orders from one of their ancient foes—the overlords of the evil that plagued the land—was enough to unsettle even one of the most stoic elves Ell knew.

They reached the camp and relayed what they had seen. Kalabi did not seem to grasp the full extent of their news since he did not know the full story of their history with the Unsired, but nevertheless, he and Ryder both looked concerned by the news. Rihya, though, was unfazed as she often was, able to process the information and move beyond it. She was braver than most.

Talk around the night's camp deliberately moved on to lighter matters. It was a common tactic of warriors. Never spend too much time agonizing over things you could not change. The Unsired had returned and clearly they were beginning to exert their old control over the dark creatures. There was no preventing that fact. Better for morale to joke and laugh and tell a few tales at night rather than discuss suppositions and conjecture about what lay ahead. When a person faced death regularly they had to learn to grab hold of the little moments of peace and enjoyment.

However, Ell found it more difficult than he ever had before to engage with the laughter. Weighed by the burden of leadership, with the knowledge that he may be leading his family to what might prove to be their deaths, and wrestling to conjure a plan of how to avoid such an outcome, he just stared moodily at the starlit sky, praying that the answer for how to get his family in and then back out of Dark Harbor safely would come to him.

"You are quiet this night, Nephew." Dacunda had come to sit next to him.

Ell nodded without speaking. He did not feel inclined to chatter. But it appeared that Dacunda was not interested in idle conversation either.

"Unburden yourself, Elliyar. When you command, you must be able to speak your mind at times, to release the stress. Tell me, what is it that troubles you?"

What could it hurt? Ell thought. His uncle had led for many years and kept them safe.

"I do not have a plan." It was harder to admit than Ell had thought it would be, especially to the elf who he had forcibly supplanted as leader on this expedition.

Surprisingly, the usually somber Dacunda chuckled quietly. "Was that so difficult to say?" He looked at Ell inquiringly. When Ell didn't answer and instead shot a flat gaze at him through the dim light of the moon, he smiled and continued.

"Nephew, you are mistaken if you think I always had a plan at the ready. Sometimes, the necessary actions come to you in the moment before battle."

"But you never led us on a mission as dangerous or foolhardy as this, Uncle."

Dacunda inclined his head in admission. "True, but there is always danger in what we do. We live a life of battle, Elliyar. It was never likely that each and every one of us would live to see a ripe old age."

Ell was startled by the bluntness with which his uncle spoke of the possibility of some of them dying. It was a new side of him.

"Do not misunderstand me. I do everything I can to protect us. Have I not counseled caution all these years? But neither have I advised fear. We are bold and we attack bravely. I was opposed to this mission out of duty to your father, for the promise I made to him long ago to do my best to protect you. But we are committed now, and as much as it pains me to admit it, perhaps you were partially correct to bring us south. Finding my brother, your father, and any of your relatives still alive and rescuing them would be a buoyant moment, and strike a small but significant blow to the enemy. It will show them that we will not accede to their every plan to dominate our people. Elliyar, I am not fully in agreement with this mission, but I do see some of its merits, and whether you believe it or not, I do have full faith in you. The answers will come."

His long monologue finished, Dacunda didn't wait for a response but instead stood quickly and made his way back closer to the others and the quiet laughter of the camp. His admissions and support were startling and comforting. Knowing that his uncle didn't bear him any ill will for grabbing control of this mission made him feel better than he had in days.

Ell sat quietly watching the stars, but it was a different silence than before. The brooding mood had left him and he grabbed the instant of peace as it provided itself to him. He listened to the quiet laughter as Kalabi told a funny tale from the human lands. The answers would come. When he lay down to sleep that night, the thought was still rolling in his head, comfortingly, giving him relief from the strain of leading.

* * * *

The following weeks passed quickly as they made their way ever onwards towards their destination. They crossed the North Tributary—a smaller offshoot river from the Mayn River, which ran the length of the continent from north to south—and made steady progress. Kalabi became leaner as they traveled. Keeping pace with northern elves after a life of privileged slavery as an inventor in the tents was bound to yield results. He hardened slightly, and the pockets of excess fat around his middle and at the cheeks in his face disappeared. He would never quite look the part of warrior, he was still too clean for that—he managed to keep the lines of his beard straight and tidy and the beard itself trimmed and groomed—but he did not look so out of place as he once had, especially once they dyed his white linen clothes with brown substances found along the way so that he blended in with them and the land around them.

One day, Ell was running ahead as a scout when the woods around him ended from one step to the next. A giant swath of land was completely devoid of trees. The stumps could still be seen jutting up like the bones of those long dead. The clear cut was massive and on the far horizon Ell could see a fringe of mountains.

The Hillforts.

The small coastal mountain range surrounded in a ring the harbor in which sat the southern capital—Ell had looked at maps of the south lands as a child, dreaming of travel long before he had understood the war and conflict that raged all around him. It had been the yearning of youth to see the far corners of a distant land. He was about to see them now, but in a much different capacity.

At each small pass between the peaks sat a well-fortified fort. They were known as the Hillforts and protected the landed gateway into Dark Harbor.

They had reached their destination.

Chapter Nineteen

Ell made his way quickly back to his family. Ushering them off into a denser thicket of bushes and trees, he told them what was ahead. Relief at completing the first half of their journey was tinged with trepidation at what lay before them. The truly dangerous part of their mission was now about to begin.

"So, do we storm the gates?" Ryder asked, half-jokingly, but Ell heard a hint of eagerness in his voice at the prospect. Ell's cousin was not dim, but he was also never one to back down from a fight.

Ell forced a smile through his seriousness. "No, Ry, we most definitely do not storm anything. That will only get us killed. And I aim to make sure that does not happen!" He finished with more vehemence than he had expected, and felt a rush of gratitude at Dacunda's approving gaze.

"What we need right now is a place to lay low and figure out a plan." Ell spoke to the whole group, inviting ideas.

"We cannot hole up here," Dahranian stated the obvious. "These woods are not thick enough and do not provide adequate cover."

Rihya jumped in. "And if what you say is true, then the clear cut lies ahead and it will provide even less cover than here. So where does that leave us?"

"The mountains ahead. They are small but they are bound to have a few nooks and crannies in which we can hide ourselves," Ryder volunteered.

"It will be right under the enemy's nose," mused Ell.

"So close to them that they will not think to look closely there. Besides when was the last time Dark Harbor suffered an attack? They must have lowered their guard somewhat." Rihya grinned at the prospect of thumbing her nose at the Departed by hiding so close under their watch.

"Do not underestimate our foes, Rihya. Time has not dulled their watchfulness. Yet, I do believe we might be able to find a place for us to be safe while we plan the next step." Dacunda cautioned all of them with a firm look, even though his statement had been directed at Rihya.

They all stared somberly back at him. Smile they might, but none of them were unaware of the peril in which they now stood. Ell waited a moment more for Kalabi to speak his piece but he stayed silent.

Decisively, Ell spoke. "Done then. Evening is fast approaching. We shall wait here until nightfall to cross the clear cut and then find a place somewhere in the coastal range." Nods of agreement met his decision. Again, Dacunda gave him an approving look. His uncle's approval bolstered his confidence. Perhaps Ell was learning how to become a leader after all.

They passed the next few hours in tense silence. The thicket in which they hid was not the best cover, and more than once Ell thought he heard a noise approaching on the nearby path, expecting to have to burst out in ambush to secure their anonymity in this foreign land. Yet both times it proved to be nothing but the wind, and Ell was forced to come to terms with the realization that he was more nervous than he had ever been. Every time in the past when he had undertaken a wild, impossible task—scaling the north crag, fighting and riding the Icari, pursuing Silverfist and defeating him—it had been on his own. Ell was accustomed to danger, to placing himself in harm's way, yet somehow being responsible for leading the rest of his family into similar circumstances left him jumpier than he had ever been before. Ell breathed slowly and deeply to clear his thoughts and steady his heart. It would do nobody any good if he could not stay calm and focused.

Night came and without speaking, everyone followed Ell's lead as he stood up in the twinkling starlight and made his way south. Idly, he glanced upwards and thought it odd that this foreign kingdom, this land of his foes, would be graced by the same starlit presence in the nightly heavens as his northern home, Andalaya.

They made their way swiftly, surefootedly, as only the elves of the northern haunts could do. All except for Kalabi, who often placed his feet wrong, snapping twigs and displacing stones with a clatter of pebbles every now and then. There was nothing to do, but to press on. The human was not used to moving silently and there was no time to teach him. Ell simply prayed it would not cost them this night.

Before long, the clear cut area opened up around them. Stumps dotted the landscape for miles in all directions. The moon in the sky was full, filling the open area with a brightness that was detrimental to their task. Yet the silvery light shone down and highlighted worrying features of the land they traversed. Even at a fast run, Ell could make out the strange look of the land around him. Black fungi grew and encroached all over the clear cut, speckling the stumps and dirt of the region. In some places, dark swaths of what almost appeared to be black tar pooled, caught by the glancing moonlight to create a sinister sheen.

It reminded Ell of the strangely diseased look that many of the Departed bore when they became Unsired. Ell did not understand the process by which a Departed became one of those ancient foes, nor did he know the significance of the sickly look they bore, but he recognized it for what it was—a disease upon them, upon their minds, inflicted by the path of darkness they had chosen. The land surrounding Dark Harbor bore the same affliction and it was an ominous sign that speckled the landscape with its sickly appearance. Never had Ell felt the need to end this southern threat more pressingly. He could not abide by his continent falling prey to the darkness. Andalaya must survive this plague of evil at its southern border.

Without speaking, they ran hard through the night, crossing the clear-cut territory at a near sprint. By the time they reached the rise of land signaling their approach to the small range in front of them, Kalabi was gasping for air.

"We had better stop, Cousin, otherwise our clever friend here will alert every Departed within five miles of our presence with his incessant avalanche of wheezing." Ryder smirked as he teased the former slave.

Kalabi tried to laugh, but could not manage through his gasps for breath. Instead, he just put a hand on Ryder's shoulder and balanced himself as he heaved over and retched in the dim light of the night. Ell supposed it had been a fast pace even for elves, and for a relatively unfit human it would have been difficult indeed. In fact, it was impressive and displayed fortitude that the ex-slave had managed to keep up at all.

"Fine, then. Five minutes and then we move on. We are exposed here and must find a decent shelter before sunrise." Ell said.

Everyone sat, making the most of the break, but they all kept their eyes peeled for any sign of danger. In no time at all, they were up and moving again, and climbing into the foothills of the coastal range that surrounded the huge bay in which the island city of Dark Harbor was located.

It took hours of searching, but they finally found a decent cover. It was a cave with an extremely small entryway, only wide enough for one person to fit through at once.

"Good, defensible position," Dahranian murmured thoughtfully as they squeezed one by one into the dark interior of the crevice. The cave opened up a little bit as they entered, but it was still a tight squeeze for six people to fit into at once. The cave was dark and they dared not light a flame for fear it would flicker out into the darkness beyond the mouth of the cave and betray their location. They sat down on the hard packed earth of the cave floor. It was not wet, but the earth was cool from lack of sunlight in a way only caverns can manage to be.

"We rest, eat, and come up with a plan now." Ell stated, even though it was obvious what was needed.

Ryder grunted his approval as he dug his hand into one of the pouches of food they carried with them on the journey. Ell watched his sister sigh in relief and lean her head back against the rocky wall of the cave and close her eyes. All the day and most of the night running without sleep took a toll on a body. She was not the only one with a thankful look on their face as they closed their eyes and rested. The tension Ell had felt earlier appeared to have not been a concern of his alone. Ell saw the same anxiety on their faces and in the tension of their bodies slowly melt away into sleep. It would, no doubt, return with their waking, but for now, the peaceful oblivion of sleep could help them forget that they were in the heart of the enemy's world.

Dacunda shared a look with Ell, as they were the last two with their eyes open.

"I will take the first watch," his uncle whispered, and shifted his body nearer to the mouth of the cave.

Ell opened his mouth to argue, but decided against it as a wave of exhaustion broke over him. It would be nice to close his eyes and maybe to dream of Miri. He did so, and drifted into the murk of sleep.

* * * *

"I could go, turn myself in as a runaway slave." Kalabi volunteered.

Rihya shook her head in disgust. "But how would you get back out? It would be for nothing if you could not tell us the information you gain by entering the city."

Kalabi responded with a stubborn expression. "I have escaped captivity once. I can do it again."

Ell shook his head. They had been going around and around in circles, rotating their ideas all morning long. A few hours of solid sleep had done a world of good for their bodies, but it did not seem to have sharpened their wits at all.

"We must be wise in our choices from here on out. No risks that we do not need to take. My niece is right, Kalabi, we cannot send you back into slavery on the hopes that you glean useful information." Of them all, Dacunda was the only one not to have slept since they arrived in the cave. Ell could see the dark shadows under his eyes, the fatigue in his face. But he knew his uncle had gone longer than this without sleep before, and Dacunda knew his limits. He was never one to push beyond his capabilities. When it was time for him to sleep, he would do so without complaint.

"We could capture a sentry from one of the Hillforts." Ryder shrugged as he proposed the option.

His brother put an end to that idea. "It would only alert the enemy to our presence in these hills. There is no guarantee that a lowly guard would have the information we seek."

"He most certainly would not," Ell agreed with Dahranian. "We seek to find my family amongst the slaves. Thousands of them must have passed through the gates of this city in the last two decades. He could not know what we need. What we need is to get close to the slave barracks—wherever that is. Someone must infiltrate Dark Harbor."

"You think it should be you, Nephew?"

Ell inclined his head in response. "How many times have you used me for reconnaissance in the past, Uncle? This is no different."

"You were not the leader those times, Elliyar. A leader does not often take part in high risk scouting expeditions."

Ell felt a twinge of annoyance that his uncle attempted to use Ell's leadership to bar Ell from entering the city. First he protested Ell's decision to command this venture, and now he twisted it and used it against Ell. Not this time.

"I will be the one to enter. Not only am I the most equipped to do so, but I have the right, it is my family within." Ell stared almost belligerently at his uncle.

"It is my family too, Ell, do not forget that." Rihya narrowed her eyes as she spoke. Ell quelled her anger with an apologetic motion of his hand, as if to say that of course he agreed.

"So you will gain entry under cover of darkness." Dahranian stated. It was not a question, a fact that was obvious to them all. Ell nodded.

"You want someone along to guard your back?" Ryder asked, hefting his moss-encrusted axe.

Ell shook his head. "No, the more bodies, the more chance of being noticed. It will be safer if I go alone. It will be difficult enough for me to blend in, even at night, so I must do everything I can to tip the scales in my favor."

"What if you could blend in?" A human voice interjected in a slow, pondering fashion. Ell could see an idea brewing just beneath the surface of Kalabi's face.

"Speak." Dacunda encouraged the ex-slave.

"Well, there are free Northerners in the Departed's ranks, are there not?" Kalabi tilted his head and raised his eyebrows as he proposed an idea none of them had thought of until now.

146

"You'll never catch me posturing as a traitor!" Ryder spat, not in anger at Kalabi, but in general disgust at the prospect of sullying himself with the ruse.

Rihya however had no such qualms. Keen and cunning, she liked the idea immediately. "Yes, then a few of us could enter unnoticed, nothing out of the ordinary."

"No." Ell said. Rihya turned to him in surprise.

"Brother, do not be foolish. Posing as a traitor is the best idea we have had yet." She nodded her head at the human to give credit where credit was due.

"No," Ell said again. "I am not saying the idea is faulty. It is indeed the best we have had yet. But it will still be me who enters alone."

Rihya opened her mouth to object, as well as his uncle, but Ell overrode them. "Hear me out!" He held up his hands for continued silence. "One pretend traitor could possibly slip in unnoticed, but too many new faces, especially irregular faces such as the northern traitors, will stand out in Dark Harbor. More than one of us will attract too much attention.

"I will enter alone. Young males are the most common to betray us, and therefore I fit the stereotype much more than you do, sister. I think a green haired female traitor from the north would attract far too many eyes." He winked to soften his decision to leave her out. She put on a sour expression, clearly showing her dislike for his decision. Yet she saw the sense in it and kept her mouth closed.

"There is just one little detail," Dahranian said.

"Which is?" Dacunda always paid close heed to his eldest son.

"The small matter of the distinguishing mark upon the faces of the traitors. I am speaking, of course, of the Traitor's Tears." Dahranian spoke of the small red tear shaped tattoos pioneered and brought into fashion by Silverfist who had adopted them as the first traitor. They were mandatory now for all those northerners who wished to join the service of the southern elves.

Ell felt his first apprehension. "I will not brand myself a traitor for life..." His voice trailed off as he spoke.

Kalabi shook his head and motioned with his hand that there was no need to worry. "It is not a problem, Elliyar. I will delicately stain you skin, with red dye in the shape of tears. It will last some weeks but will fade with time. There are berries here in the southern half of the continent that are very good for such purposes."

Ell breathed a sigh of relief, but Dacunda wasn't so certain. "Are you sure the false tattoos will look enough like the real ones?"

Kalabi shrugged. "There is only one way to find out. We can make the final decision about how to proceed after we have tested the dye."

"So," Rihya said, "one more day of waiting, then tonight we gather the berries and make the dye, then make a mess of my brother's pretty face."

"And the following day, I enter." Ell finished her thought with a flash of a smile for her. "It is a good plan. Assuming the dyed tears will look authentic enough to pass for a traitor, this will provide me with an excellent cover. I will be a new traitor, just arrived from the north, and it will make sense if I have more questions to ask than most."

Dacunda grunted his assent. He was clearly worried about Ell entering the city alone, but what else was there to do?

With everything more or less decided, the next course of action was to sit and wait again. They would need to procure the necessary berries under cover of night so as not to be sighted by any scouts or sentries defending the Hillforts surrounding Dark Harbor.

The day passed slowly, but dusk eventually arrived. Ell watched the sun slowly sink, looking out through the crack in the mountainside as the light faded to the dark purple of evening and then into the true darkness of night.

"Ready?" Dahranian asked Kalabi. The human nodded and the two of them slipped out into the gloom. Like the excursion into Dark Harbor, the fewer the people, the safer they would likely be since it would be easier to avoid notice. One person to fight—Dahranian—could keep Kalabi safe as he searched, by the pale light of the moon, for the necessary berries to render the juice into dye.

Again, they waited. Ell was an elf of action, and waiting was harder than just about anything. He fantasized about a summer day with Miri. Weeks had now passed since they had seen each other but the scent of her lips, sweet from the lily water she drank, was still fresh in his memory. Her smile, just a tiny bit lopsided and mischievous, was what he missed more than anything. Ell occupied the next few hours of waiting with thoughts of Miri and it made the time pass more quickly. Soon enough, Dahranian and Kalabi returned carrying with them pouches of berries collected from the hillsides of this coastal range.

"It should be enough to make dye, at least enough for a tattoo—it is not like we are dyeing an entire set of clothing, after all." Kalabi set about doing what needed to be done to create the dye from the liquid.

"Are you sure about this?" Dacunda asked him quietly.

"It's not like it will hurt to simply see how well the dye sets, Uncle. We can make a final decision after we see how convincing the false tattoos look." Ell's response seemed to appease his uncle's worry, at least for now, and Ell sat down next to his sister.

Rihya was in a foul mood. All the waiting had been even more difficult for her than it was for Ell. She was impatient and bored, and had no excursion the next day to look forward to the way Ell did.

"The dullness of this mission will kill me, little brother," she grumbled, squatting next to him and switching the dirt floor of the cave with a long piece of grass she had collected at some point along the journey.

Ell did not want to endure any more of her whining. He had been forced to listen to it for hours while they waited for Kalabi and Dahranian to return.

"Rihya, I am so sorry to inconvenience you with the tediousness of searching for our parents," he said in his most sarcastic voice.

The comment mollified her somewhat, and she even had the decency to look a little bit embarrassed, but her grumblings continued, although she at least kept them quiet and to herself now. Ell leaned back against the uncomfortable, uneven wall of rock behind him. He put a hand on his sister's shoulder, and tried to convey his apology for snapping at her, even if she had deserved it. She forced a smile for him and all was well between them. Of course, she was jealous that he was the one entering Dark Harbor. Rihya always wanted to be in the thick of things where the danger was hottest and hated feeling on the outside. But she realized that this was the best plan. They all had, even Dacunda, who clearly did not wish this to be the plan, had acknowledged that he could think of no better option.

"Good enough, I think," Kalabi said, after mixing the berries in a small bowl. They had chanced a very tiny fire so that the ex-slave could boil the berries down into juice and then crush and stir them to the right consistency.

Ell came close and Kalabi set to work, staining Ell's cheeks with the right pattern to match those of the traitors who had abandoned Andalaya. Fortunately, having lived his life in the human camps, Kalabi had seen enough of the northern traitors come and go over the years so he knew how to recreate the Traitor's Tears on Ell's cheeks. Kalabi delicately brushed on the berries that resembled more of a paste now. He had Ell lie on his back so the paste would sit on his face and not run off.

"Stay like this for at least an hour," Kalabi commanded with an authority his voice gained only when he was doing or explaining things in which he was experienced. "It will take some time for the juices to stain your skin. We shall wipe it off later and see how well your fair skin has taken to the dye."

Ell lay on his back for what seemed an eternity. Rihya's impatience was nothing compared to the way he felt now that events were in motion. He wanted to get up and leave immediately, but he forced himself to wait.

One hour passed. They were creeping halfway through the second hour when Kalabi took a close look at Ell's cheek and deemed that the paste was

149

ready to be removed. The human did so with the corner of his tunic and in no time the berry paste was gone.

Ell could not see his own face, there was no liquid to use as a mirror, but the disgust in his family's face was a clear indicator that the experiment had worked.

"Vile. That look is absolutely disgusting on you Ell," Rihya said with a shudder. Ryder also gave a shiver as if the sight of Ell looking like a traitor was too sinister to imagine.

"It does seem to have worked...impressively well," Dacunda said slowly, and with an unease from which Ell could tell that he too, did not like the look of the red tears upon Ell's cheeks, fake though they were.

"Now, we wait again." Kalabi once more told them all what was to happen. "In the dimness the false tattoos seem to have taken well to you skin. But we cannot be sure until it is light out. At dawn we can check once more, and also test for water resistance. If they are adequate, you can be on your way."

"Wait, what about his teeth?" Ryder asked with surprising insight. Ell cocked his head in question.

"Ah yes," Kalabi responded, "many of the traitors adopt the southern fashion of filing their top row of teeth into fanged tips."

"But not all," Ell said quickly.

"Not all, but most." Kalabi said.

"Silverfist did not file his," Ell declared.

"True, but he was in many ways...exceptional," Kalabi said delicately, understanding that Silverfist was a sore topic with Andalayans. "He was the first, and by far the most dangerous of the traitors, and he was also cunning and in a place of real power. So he could get away with starting some customs and eschewing others."

"No," Ell said firmly. "I will not disfigure myself permanently with something that is not an absolute necessity."

"Very well, but prepare for some questions, if you walk into Dark Harbor without your top teeth filed." Kalabi's warning was for Ell's benefit, he knew, but it still rankled him that the human thought he should file his teeth. It was too permanent. The dye would fade eventually, but Ell could not imagine living the rest of his life looking like one of the vicious Departed.

With the need for the fire gone, they snuffed it out quickly and waited in darkness, their eyes not having yet adjusted to the increased shadows left by the absence of the fire.

"Get some rest," Dahranian advised Ell.

Reluctant though he was—his mind was racing with adrenaline and excitement at the thought of finally entering the port city to look for his family—Ell knew it would be wise to get a few solid hours of sleep before dawn's grey light crept into the cave through its crevice.

Sleep was difficult to come by and when it came it was fitful. Ell awoke barely feeling refreshed, with a grittiness in his eyes that made him wish for a cool forest pool to bathe in instead of this hot southern climate that made him sticky even in autumn. Nevertheless, he rose and freshened his mouth with a sip of tepid water from a flask. Today was the day. He might actually see his father for the first time. Unlikely as it was that he would see him or even recognize him on the first day upon arriving in the city—it was still possible, and that possibility filled Ell with an unusual adrenaline.

Today, he would finally enter the menacing home of the infamous Half-Mask and the darkly fabled King of the South. Today, he would gain entrance to Dark Harbor.

Chapter Twenty

"Do not be alarmed if I am not back by nightfall. It could look suspicious if I leave the same day I arrived, so I will likely stay the night in Dark Harbor." Ell was addressing his family regarding the final details of his reconnaissance trip into the city.

"If you must," agreed Dacunda soberly. "Remember, do not share much about yourself. The less you reveal to those within the walls, the less chance you have of being discovered as false. But do not be too close-mouthed either. You must offer enough of yourself to satisfy those who might have questions and quell any suspicion." It was a mark of Dacunda's nerves that he was yet again repeating the instructions that he had been telling Ell every hour since the final decision had been made for Ell to attempt to infiltrate the city.

Ell nodded along as patiently as possible. The truth was, he was eager to be off. The incessant warnings and instructions from his uncle were wearing on him. However, Ell bore it as best he could. His uncle loved him and was worried for him in what he clearly believed to be a dangerous mission. For some reason, Ell wasn't anxious. Perhaps it was the adrenaline that accompanied undertaking an endeavor that was slightly rash and reckless, or maybe it was simple excitement at seeing something new—a new city, a new place—but Ell felt good about the venture that lay ahead.

"Careful, little brother." His sister clapped him on the shoulder harder than usual, still disappointed to not be accompanying him into the city.

Kalabi had never been to Dark Harbor, having lived his life in the human encampments, but the human alliance with the Departed had afforded him more opportunity to observe some of their kind outside of battle. Ell had never seen a Departed that he was not trying to kill. Kalabi's advice was ominous, but vital.

"Do not hesitate to act with force, Elliyar. I have seen them interact amongst their own during their visits to the camps. Violence settles many disputes among your southern cousins, and those who hesitate to do so, often are the first to die. You will not draw attention to yourself by fighting, in fact, to be too passive is much more dangerous for you." Ell filed Kalabi's advice away and thanked him with a hand grasping his forearm.

"Kill someone for me, Ell," Ryder grunted through a mouthful of nuts, which was all the farewell he received from his cousin.

It was Dahranian who had the most poignant and unsettling advice for him just before he departed from their small crevice of a cave. "Cousin, you are bound to see many of our people enslaved within the confines of the city. You must be wise and not react. You cannot save them all. You must focus on the task at hand, which is finding your family."

"I will try, Dahranian."

"You must be careful," Dacunda agreed with his son. "You have always been impulsive, Nephew, one misstep, one wrong word or a fit of rage, and this will all be for nothing and our danger will be increased tenfold."

Ell understood the direness of their warnings. He filed the information away, but still could not shake the bubble of excitement that threatened to burst free from his throat. If he laughed now, they would think he was ignoring them. Ell held his composure and kept a straight face.

"I will see you tomorrow then," he addressed the entire group, and without another word, he ducked out the cave entrance and into the dim light of early morning. Subconsciously, he checked his weapons as he walked, reassuring himself of their presence. Two long dueling daggers, the length of his forearm, were strapped to the outsides of both thighs. A belt knife at his hip, and his bow with a quiver of arrows was at his back.

The trek to the nearest gate—the northernmost Hillfort—was shorter than he had expected. His family really was concealed right under the nose of the enemy. As he approached the gate, Ell began to feel his first apprehension. He did not know if there was any sort of ceremony or formality one needed to say or do to gain entrance to the Hillfort. Ell opted for the boldest course of action as he felt it would be the best given his lack of information. He simply walked decisively up to the gate as if it were perfectly natural for him to do so. Acting like one belonged somewhere was often all that was needed to convince people that one actually did belong.

There was a brief hesitation as he reached the gate and Ell heard a muttered conversation from high above him on the wall, then a shout loud enough to be heard for miles, and then a small sally port in the wall opened, large enough for a single person to fit through at once. Ell walked forward, again as if this were completely normal, and entered the fortress.

The Hillfort was essentially a one-walled fortress. One massive wall—thick and wide—split the gap between the two peaks on either side of it, plugging the pass. The defensive side of the fortress was unenclosed with southern elf warriors manning the stone ramparts and standing at the ready. It was guarded by enough enemy soldiers that it almost appeared as if the Departed expected an attack at any time. That could only mean they were protecting themselves against a human invasion since Andalaya had not had an army since the fall of Verdantihya.

Departed warriors with their swarthy skin, pointed ears, and thickly muscled bodies were everywhere. Ell's senses and instincts screamed at him to attack, but he forced himself to stride nonchalantly as he walked through the defensive side of the fortress, still unchallenged.

Many of the southern elves had their top teeth filed to points, like the fangs of a predatory wolf or feline, and the long, shiny black hair on their heads was shaved at the temples. The tails of hair were held in braids or with thongs and looked like the manes of wild horses. They wore dark leather clothing and lightweight armor. All elves liked to move quickly and fight with mobility. None of them were as heavily armored as the human soldiers often were.

Finally, someone approached Ell as he walked. Apparently, a runner had been sent to someone in charge and while Ell had not been stopped at the gate, clearly someone wanted to speak with him. An imposing warrior, with a battle-scarred face and a wicked scimitar strapped to his hip, came striding up to Ell after having left a building nearby.

"What news of the north?" The Departed soldier asked without preamble.

"Nothing new to report." Ell responded, not wishing to get entangled in a longer discussion of his dying homeland.

The Departed grunted. He must be some type of commander. He looked to be about Dacunda's age.

"We hear strange mutterings from the lands of our northern cousins, traitor." The commander was still fishing for information, grasping for any new news.

Ell clenched his teeth at being called traitor, but did not retort. From the way he said it, using the term 'traitor' might be some sort of identification or title that was a common occurrence.

"You should not pay such attention to rumors, Warrior. Those are for the children." Ell tried to put some disdain in his voice. He didn't want to hint at the outrageous events of last spring. He was not sure what information about the death of Silverfist, about himself and Arendahl, had reached this far south.

Ell feared he had put too much insult in his response, as the Departed commander snarled silently, revealing a mouth full of sharpened top teeth, some chipped from what could only have been biting through tough substances—maybe sinew and bone. Not for the first time, Ell wondered if the rumors were true that the Departed bit their enemies in battle. He had never witnessed it, but he believed the rumors.

The commander eyed him as if thinking to draw steel and respond to Ell's insult. Ell remembered Kalabi's warning and placed a hand on the hilt of one of his dueling daggers. Something in his eyes must have unsettled the Departed and stilled his desire to attack, because a wary look replaced the sneer and the Departed retreated within a stony, masklike expression.

"Be about your business then," the commander said, and abruptly turned away from him and back to the command outpost building from which he had come.

Ell was surprised at the ease with which he had entered the fortress and the lack of questions put to him. He supposed that traitors must not be uncommon in Dark Harbor and the surrounding region. Ell also suspected that they had never had a false traitor before. When something had never happened—in this case the incidence of a northern impostor—sometimes people began to think it impossible. It worked to Ell's benefit that he was the first of the Highest to try and pose as a traitor to gain access to the Dark Harbor. It would make his task easier.

As he walked purposefully, Ell observed what surrounded him. The giant wall was behind him, and the two peaks on either side served as the sidewalls of the fortress. The back opened onto a road leading down towards the great bay in which Dark Harbor was situated. All around him, the elements of war were apparent. Forges to make the cruel scimitars and wicked half-moon axes. Fletchers crafting arrows. Soldiers in training yards practicing their craft. As Ell walked, a sinking feeling grew in his stomach. There were many warriors. This was only one of many Hillforts, how would the Highest ever hope to match the numbers of their enemies? Ell forced that grim thought away in brutal fashion and picked up his pace to a light run as he moved south towards the bay.

His path dipped down into a small depression and then rose back up onto the cusp of a steep descent. This was the final and long descent down to the shore from the coastal range. As Ell topped the rise, a grandiose view assailed him. He could see the coastline for miles and even out to sea where small islands were visible—the Enclaves as they were known, ran far out into the western ocean and up the coast, as well—and the bay lay beneath him. It was massive, big enough for thousands of ships to fit in it comfortably. Although Ell was not sure if there were that many or not. From this high above the bay, the ships looked too small to count. Causeways ran from the smaller settlements along the shore of the bay out to the island city in the center of the harbor. Ferries also, carried elves to and fro the mainland and the island. Dark ocean water filled the bay and Ell recognized the city's true namesake. Maybe it was the thunderhead clouds that were building overhead purpling the sky that darkened the water beneath in the absence of sun, or perhaps the water itself had different properties here, lending to its dark hue—Ell was not sure. But what he did know was that Dark Harbor was aptly named.

Ships clustered in about the wharfs, everything from small skiffs to warrior-carrying long ships. Even a few heavy-laden human scows—slaver ships no doubt—labored their way in and out of the bay.

The journey down took a few hours. The path had numerous switchbacks and Ell did not want to appear too rushed. It would seem odd if he were to be moving so much faster than the people around him. What appeared to be merchants or small-time ware hawkers moved in both directions. Dark elves carted food, such as dried or steamed fish, and strange, shelled creatures, up from the port to sell at the fortress, while warriors on leave traveled down to the city to enjoy their days off. People walked, a few ran lightly, and Ell forced himself to move no faster than them. He already stood out as a Northerner, as proven by the looks and glances that flew in his direction from every passerby, but he refused to draw extra attention to himself by seeming rushed.

Some of the looks were curious, others were glares. In both cases, a shift of his hand to one of the hilts on his body was enough to curtail any altercations. Barely. It appeared that Kalabi was right. Much of the Departed culture centered around violence and strength of arm. Those who could win their fights won what they desired. Many fought amongst themselves, despite the fact that they served the same master. Yet, something in Ell's countenance or his appearance was enough to quell these looks before they brewed into something far more dangerous. Although, Ell could hardly doubt that before long—certainly before he was finished in the city—he would likely become embroiled in a physical altercation. He could feel the atmosphere of fear, and aggression, anger, resentment, and bloodlust boiling under the surface of this culture.

As he travelled, Ell kept a keen eye out for any signs of Unsired. There were a few soldiers who held the glazed look in their eyes and had the pocked and sickly looking skin on parts of their body. There were even a few civilians who bore the same appearance. But over all, there were less Departed who had seemed to transform into Unsired than Ell had expected. He pondered this. Perhaps most of those who underwent the change—whatever that transformation might be—were sent immediately out on duty to the war zones. It was the best and the only theory Ell could think of, so he pushed it from his mind, and simply kept his guard up as he walked. It would not do to lower his focus for even an instant.

He finally reached the settlements along the shoreline of the bay. Ell could see there were many of them around the edge of the body of water, and larger clusters near the various roads that led down from the mountains and linked the Hillforts to the harbor.

Ell followed the elves walking towards the city until he reached a throng of warriors and a few merchants clustered around a wooden pier at which a rickety ferry was docked.

"Three rakkas for passage," screeched a female southern elf who was in charge of the ferry, extolling the amount of coin it would take to cross. Ell realized she was the first female Departed that he had ever seen up close. Departed warriors were almost all male, and even along the road from the Hillfort there had not been many females to see, or perhaps he had just not paid close attention.

Either way, Ell stared curiously at her. She was swarthy like her male counterparts, but thinner, like a northerner, not as thick as many of the southern elves were. She had raven black hair than hung down her back—it looked like it might have once been lustrous, and still could be if she were to bathe. But her appearance was unclean, the grime of what looked like many days covered her hands and face. She wore billowy black pants and a sleeveless tunic like many of the males. Her dark brown eyes stared piercingly at the crowd of would be passengers. No one would enter her ferry without the required money.

Money.

It was the one thing that had slipped all of their minds as they talked last night and early this morning. With a reproachful thought, Ell felt that Kalabi or uncle should have remembered that things functioned differently in the south than in Andalaya. After the fall of Verdantihya and the ensuing war, Ell's people, the Highest, had become nomadic, staying on the move to avoid capture and death. Their civilization and society had shifted. Barter had replaced coins and Ell and all the elves of his age in Andalaya were as unfamiliar with coin money as they were with populated cities.

Ell watched as the people clustered around the ferry, clamored for their money to be taken and granted passage, handing dull metal coins to her, which she stuffed in a money purse. He had no money, so for now he would continue to walk. Ell followed the rest of the people who walked upon the causeway towards the city of Dark Harbor.

The causeway led out from the port settlement—a settlement comprised mostly of buildings made of log. The ancient-looking causeway, built from rough-hewn stone, rose up and created enough distance from the water to allow ships to pass. Ell ascended the steps with the many other dark elves who were heading towards the island city and followed the growing mass of people using the causeway for transit. Ell kept an eye out for money collectors but it appeared that the stone causeway required no fare to be walked. Ell walked, surrounded by his people's enemies, the blackish ocean water frothing at the pillars of stone that supported the causeway. The bay's dark water was capped with small flecks of white from the choppy, but small, waves that rolled incessantly along its surface. Ships of all kinds cut through those waves, prows sinking then rising slightly with each meeting with a whitecap. Shouts rang out from the water and from the walkway. Sailors cursed as they followed their captains' bellowed orders and near Ell, vendors hawked wares—everything from fishnets to fileting knives and black leather vests. Food was being sold. Fish like the merchants had carried up the mountain, but also spicy-smelling stews garnished with bright red peppers that stood out against the overall grim and dark appearance of everything near Dark Harbor.

Ell watched fights break out over everything from theft, to the groping and fondling of body parts, by both male and female. There were very few female warriors in the armies of the Departed, but that did not seem to prevent the female southern elves from taking part in their fair share of tussles. Lustrous black haired heads rolled on the ground with shorter haired counterparts. Male warriors of the Departed wore their hair in long tails with the sides of their heads shaven, as did many of the non-military elves. In Andalaya, almost every elf had long hair, no major affections involved—Rihya was one of the few exceptions to that with her dyed-green, short hair. However, Ell saw a number of civilian Southerners with shaved heads who looked like fishermen and others with ear-length or shoulder-length hair hanging freely. Dark Harbor was a medley of styles and customs. They were, however, unified by the black or dark brown clothing and the look of grim determination bordering on desperation that every elf wore. The only elves who did not share this look were some of the Departed warriors.

The walk along the causeway took some time. He had to weave his way through throngs of people and the distance was great. It was farther from the shoreline to the island city than Ell had previously thought. From high above on the mountain slopes where he had viewed the area early this morning, the distances had not seemed as long. But here, now, walking the causeway, Ell determined it must be miles from the shore to the city. Small defensible walled gates dotted the causeway as an extra line of defense of the city should the Hillforts fall to an invading force. Stone gargoyles dotted the walls of these gates and the openings were small and defensible, causing traffic to pile up around every one of these gated openings in the sporadic walls. Striding along the causeway surveying the crowds of elves, and stationed at each gate, grim faced warriors hefted axes and scimitars, spears and swords. Ell checked his weapons almost continuously, tense from being surrounded by foes and unable to fight. He forced himself to breathe calmly and release his hold on the hilts of his blades. He was an outsider here, but his disguise—the red tears tattooed on his cheeks—gave him a pass, made him belong as much as any Northerner could. Oh, certainly, dirty untrusting looks were shot his way, but nothing out of hand occurred.

When finally he reached the city proper, fat raindrops had begun falling from the cloud-laden sky. The rain soaked the stones, darkening them from a grey to a charcoal color with wetness. The causeway slanted down gradually until it gave way to rough stone steps. Ell had reached Dark Harbor and the island on which it sat.

Cobblestone streets were bursting at the seams with people. Many of the cobblestones had gone missing over time and dirt and grime had filled in those empty spaces. The rain muddied the streets and Ell felt his soft leather boots tread on firm ground one moment and soft mud the next. He grimaced at the smell of refuse and waste as it wafted from dark alleys and the scent of dead fish drifting up from the wharf and off the harbor. The causeway ended in a small square area with a stone statue of what looked like a water dragon climbing a pole. The serpentine creature had many fins and scaly skin and twined itself about the stone pillar until its rocky fanged face reached the top, the mouth open, as if to send forth gouts of flame. It was delicately carved, almost beautiful in construction, and provided a strange contrast to the rundown look to the streets, buildings, and causeways. Perhaps it had been recently carved.

Ell walked slowly, getting his bearings of Dark Harbor. Looking for his father immediately would be pointless, as would trying to find any information about a specific slave. The city was too big, and there were too many thousands of slaves who had been taken from Andalaya over the past decades for Ell to have any hope of stumbling upon his father the moment he set foot in the city. If his father was still alive. A small voice in the back of his head cautioned him that the likelihood of his father's survival was probably equal to the likelihood he was already dead.

Instead, Ell decided it would be better to simply wander for a time, learn something about the city, find out what Dark Harbor was like by observing it. After reconnaissance, he could begin asking questions. Pubs and taverns where grog and mead and ale flowed freely were bound to have people who were willing to talk. As soon as he was relatively comfortable in his surroundings, he would begin trying to ascertain the general location of the slave barracks, where slaves did their work, and any other pertinent information regarding slave life that might aid in the discovery of his father and the rest of his family.

Ell weaved his way through the crowded streets and, when necessary, crossed on footbridges over the muddy canals that ran throughout the city. He decided not to strike into the heart of the city right away—getting lost didn't seem the best plan—instead, he began following the wharf circling around the edge of the city, moving south as he went, keeping his sense of direction and recognizing the straight line back to where he had entered the city should he wish to return or retrace his steps. When he grew comfortable and picked out a few landmarks, he struck inwards, doing his best to remember which streets were which in the warren of the city.

Ell had never been in a city—at least not a city alive and filled with people. He had spent many days in Verdantihya over the years when his family returned to refill their flasks with Source Water, but Verdantihya was a ruined and deserted city, a colossus of creation blending architecture and nature, half wild it had returned to nature, and in many ways, certain parts had never been separated from nature at all. Dark Harbor was completely different. Nature was gone. Ell had never felt so cut off from the land around him. Salty air reached his nostrils, but that was the only hint of Creation that he could sense. Stone streets and stone or lumber buildings were piled up on top of one another almost haphazardly. As he walked inwards towards the heart of the island city, he walked along streets that were mostly dark, lit by torchlight. It was not nighttime, but the dimness of the stormy day coupled with the fact that the buildings piled upon each other in such a way that the structures tended to overhang the street, obstructed much of the day's weak light. It was as if the island had long ago run out of room for its inhabitants to expand, but the population had continued to grow. Without being able to expand outward, reaching its limits at the sea, Dark Harbor had instead grown upwards, piling up on top of itself in a gnarled and twisted fashion. It almost resembled the roots of an old oak tree that twisted and turned over on themselves so much, it was difficult to see where one part ended and the other began.

Windows were shuttered tightly, whether against the storm or against unfriendly faces, Ell was not sure. People abounded, but they engaged in business or violent altercations without many friendly conversations to be heard. The grim, foreboding atmosphere Ell had sensed earlier only grew stronger the deeper within the city he went.

Ell wandered up crooked hills and down sloping streets, feeling a sick fascination for this city, this nightmare out of legend that his people had feared for so long. The dirty log buildings around the outskirts of the city gave way to older stone buildings as they lay closer to the heart of the city. However, the tops of many of those stone buildings had new additions recently added, hanging over the streets below. The new additions to these buildings were mostly made of wood, showing a strange contrast of new and old all combined into one building. The muddy streets near the harbor gave way to fully stoned streets toward the center. Ell could see the spires and towers of a grim palace thrusting upwards from the center of the city of Dark Harbor like the biggest, longest legs of some filthy spider sticking out from the rest of its tangled body.

The palaces and fortresses of Verdantihya were ruined, yet they were still beautiful, twined with ivy and covered in moss, they were masterful constructions of masonry and architecture. Verdantihya was gorgeous in so many ways. In contrast, the palaces of Dark Harbor were darkly artistic. Gargoyles adorned gateways and parapets, towers protruded from the sides of their walls and climbed skyward as if yearning to be free of the stinking city below. Ell could imagine a time in the city's younger years when it had once been beautiful. Maybe. The construction of the buildings reminded him of the beauty of a bat in flight—perhaps not the most elegant or respectable of creatures, but beautiful in the sense that it was doing what it had been created to do. Dark Harbor was impressive in such a way, as if it was not trying to be anything it was not—it was not straining for the elegance or artistry of Verdantihya—adhering instead to its cluttered streets and walkways. The city and the people inside of it, while ominous, were nothing more or less than authentic and adapting to whatever age it was in which they existed. Yet, the city itself bore a weathered look as if efforts to sufficiently repair the damage of countless sea storms ravaging its walls had not been successful. Pocks and marks of age abounded, dirty sections that had not been cleaned for centuries stood out, and—for a split second—he was reminded of the bodies of some of the Unsired who were slightly diseased looking, causing Ell to consider that Dark Harbor resembled nothing so much as one of the Departed who had once been normal once and even good, perhaps, but had morphed into a hulking, brooding beast of evil.

After wandering the streets of Dark Harbor accompanied by the emptiness that only a loud storm could create, Ell decided to head back towards more familiar surroundings. The wind and rain had been beating down for hours now and he was soaked to the bone. But he had been cold before and he would survive. Perhaps a tavern would be a good place to begin sifting through information. It was time to finally speak with the inhabitants of this city.

In Andalaya, everyone hunted and gathered and generally contributed to the overall welfare of their family or whichever group of people with whom they resided. Ell had spent his whole life fighting and raiding with his family and matters other than survival and subsistence had been trivial when compared with the ring of steel or the flash of blood spray in the sunlight. His family fought together and lived together, sharing everything. What one hunted and killed the others could eat without any reservation. The idea of buying and selling was strange to Ell. He had heard his uncle speak of such things during the days before the fall of Verdantihya, when Andalaya had been a closer kin to their southern cousins, the Departed. But Ell had never used coin money in his life. A barter of goods or services made much more sense to him in terms of how to secure the things you could not obtain for yourself. Yet, here in the midst of a teeming sea of people—more elves than Ell had ever imagined could exist in one place—he began to see the value of having a set monetary item to trade for the things you needed. It was strange, but he could see the value, or at least the ease in it.

The problem was Ell had no money and he was famished. Not bringing food had been an oversight. He had never been a thief, but it was time to become one. Someone had to have a purse at their hip. Ell began scouring the hips and belts of the hardy souls like himself who were still out in the storm like he was. His blond hair damp and bedraggled, even beneath his pulled up hood—the rain had soaked through the cloth—Ell finally noted the passing of a Departed on his left. Walking fast and away from Ell. The Departed was in a hurry and looked to be affluent, much cleaner and well-dressed than the rest of the unkempt bodies near the wharf. If he was going to steal, he might as well steal from the rich.

Ell crept up behind the rich looking southern elf and with an ease that surprised even himself, Ell freed his belt knife and sliced through the fabric of the purse, separating it from the belt at which it hung, without even disturbing the folds of the rich Departed's robes. Was he a wealthy merchant? Or a noble of some kind? Dacunda had spoken of how there were nobles in Andalaya long ago, how royalty had existed. Did it still exist here in Dark Harbor? Ell decided not to stick around to find out. Money purse in his hand and the robed Departed none the wiser, Ell melted off into the crowd in the direction of the docks. It was time to find a tavern and buy a hot meal and a hardy drink with his newfound coin. Ell peered inside the purse. There weren't too many coins, but they looked to be sufficient for his needs.

There had been a stormy darkness all day, but even what weak light there was began to fade with the approach of night. Ell shouldered his way through a particularly dense knot of people clogging the street. A mean looking group of sailors spat curses as he forced his way through, and he heard one of them mutter a curse about filthy northern traitors. Ell's lip curled in disgust and anger, but he held himself in check. It was not the time for fighting. Yet.

Setting his sights on a seedy-looking tavern right near the waterfront only a few buildings away from the causeway upon which he had entered the city, Ell pressed on. He opened the door of the tavern and stepped inside.

* * * *

The common room was not full, but neither was it empty. A handful of dark elves sat at tables scattered randomly around the room. A roaring fire crackled in one corner and the smell of some kind of meat roasting wafted out of what had to be the kitchen. Ell pushed back his hood without thinking, wishing only to let his hair dry some in the warm air near the fire.

The steady bubble of conversation stopped the instant his blond hair and blue eyes were revealed. Hard, wary stares focused on him and reflexively Ell placed his hand on the hilt of his belt knife just in case. Forcibly, he made himself release the grip on his knife to assume the most natural and relaxed appearance he could muster.

"Arrogant bastard!" a Departed spat venomously, loudly enough that he clearly intended Ell to hear. The southern elf who had spoken was a warrior, no doubt. His hair hung in a long tethered mane down his back, and the sides of his head were shaven. Dark eyes stared out of a scarred, hardened face. He fondled the haft of a hand axe at his belt—a small yet wicked looking version of a half-moon blade.

Ell turned the full weight of his gaze on the off duty warrior and ignored the rest of the tavern, which was deadly silent as if waiting for violence to erupt. Remembering Kalabi's warning that he might need to be violent to assert himself in this city, Ell swaggered forward as arrogantly as he could until he was within a few hands lengths of the Departed who had ridiculed him. He might as well live up to the insult. Ell grabbed the tankard of ale from the Departed's hands and took a large swig, to the surprise of the warrior and everyone else in the tavern, as well. Red blood darkened the elf's already swarthy face as he watched Ell finish his drink in anger.

It was a fiery ale, spicy and hot in a way that Ell had never tasted. Honey mead was the common drink of Andalaya with a much sweeter taste than this spicy southern brew. Ell smacked his lips deliberately and handed the empty tankard back to the elf.

"You were saying something?" he said, as insolently as possible to the dark elf.

The Departed's lip curled into an angry snarl and he tightened his fist to strike. Ell tensed his body and readied himself to fight. The warrior took a massive swing with the hand holding the clay tankard, hoping to smash the mug across Ell's face. Ell was far too quick. The drunken soldier's attempt to strike him was no match for reflexes sharpened by years of ambushes. Ell didn't even need to tap into his ability as a Water Caller. He simply ducked the blow and then smashed his fist into the face of the Departed, sending the elf crumpled to the dirty floor in a heap of limbs. Unconscious, the elf did not rise.

Ell turned to face the rest of the tavern full of spectators. Hard eyes and angry faces stared at him still, but a respect was there. They could see he knew how to handle himself in a fight.

"Anyone else care to insult me?" Ell asked casually, but with a steely undertone.

Eyes followed his every move as he walked slowly to a table, but nobody volunteered to speak. Apparently his show of strength had been enough. For now. A barmaid approached, lank black hair damp with sweat from working in a hot kitchen.

"What do you want?" she asked in an unfriendly voice, eyeing the unconscious elf on the floor as if it was nothing out of the ordinary.

"Do you have any honey mead?" Ell asked politely.

"No."

"None?"

"What did I just say? You would do better to leave your past behind you and adapt to the present. Here we drink fire ale and grog. Barley draught is strong and also fairly popular, as well as some wines." She stared at him with a flat look as if daring him to question her again. She had nerve to speak so in a tavern full of elves who looked darker and more dangerous than many Ell had seen.

"Barley draught," Ell said picking something that sounded like it could have been brewed closer to his home. The fire ale he had tasted had been interesting, but he was not sure he had enjoyed it. The southern elf maid nodded and walked lithely back to the kitchen to get him his drink.

Ell surveyed the crowd as he waited for his drink and saw that most of the people in the tavern were still casting glances his way—some hiding them, but others not trying very hard at all to conceal their interest or disdain for his being there.

The bar maid returned holding a tray with a small glass full of brown liquid. She set it on the table and held out a palm, her thin fingers elegantly belying her trade as a kitchen wench. Ell stared in confusion for a moment. She snapped her fingers impatiently and he realized she wanted money. The concept was still foreign to him, but he covered his mistake by quickly reaching for the stolen purse. He poured a few coins out onto his hand, wishing he had observed a transaction outside so that he could be sure of the worth of the different coins. He picked up a couple dull coppery looking coins and placed then in her palm. She gazed at him for a moment, and Ell wondered if it was insufficient, but then she pocketed them and was away again, without a word.

Ell resumed his perusal of the common room and lifted the small glass of liquid to his nose to sniff. It was much smaller than he expected, not more than a gulp of liquid, and it smelled pungently of some sort of oaky smoky flavor.

He put the glass to his lips and poured it down his throat, swallowing the barley draught in one mouthful. Ell nearly spit it up in surprise but forced it down despite the uncomfortable way it burned his throat. He coughed once, but suppressed any more coughs as he saw a few smirking gazes drawn his way by the coughing sound. Slightly embarrassed, heat rushed to his face and he put on his stoniest look possible. He gazed around the room, meeting eyes wherever he looked.

A few minutes passed, during which time Ell listened to the chatter of the room swell back to the normal level at which it had been before he entered. Conversations resumed and Ell spent his time willing his ears to catch any hint of information that might pass idly from mouth to mouth, hoping to overhear information about slaves or where they might live.

Ell was nearly ready to reach out and buy someone a drink, hoping for a chance and an excuse to chat and ask a few questions, when the biggest Departed in the room rose from his chair in a dark corner of the common room and walked over to Ell's table. The massive dark elf was broad shouldered and powerful looking, with a scimitar strapped to his hip. He sat down unceremoniously at Ell's table. A few people glanced their way, but conversation didn't stop the way it had when Ell had faced off with the first elf. Apparently, two seated elves were not nearly so interesting as two standing elves preparing to fight.

The dark elf raised his hand imperiously and snapped his fingers, summoning the barmaid. The kitchen servant hurried over, her flowing black pants and black vest spotted with grease and stains from the kitchen. She looked harassed but seemed to know better than to ignore the big elf's summons.

"Vandi. Stew and two more barley draughts." The big elf's voice was deep and rough, dangerous sounding. "One for me and one for my... friend." The way the Departed called Ell his friend made Ell certain he was no such thing. Nevertheless, this saved Ell the effort of having to seek out company, perhaps he could glean the information he needed from the huge southern warrior. It was only a matter of moments before the serving girl—Vandi—was back with bowls of fishy stew and two more small glasses of the deep brown liquid that Ell had just tried. She set the drinks on the grainy wooden table and collected the few coins the dark elf paid her, and then disappeared from their vicinity.

They stared at each other not speaking for a few moments and Ell watched the large elf's shrewd dark eyes and scarred face. His hands were big knuckled and callused from fighting. Finally, after what seemed like an eternity of staring, the big elf lifted his drink and indicated that Ell should do the same. Ell picked up the glass of dark brown liquid.

"To the Prince of Darkness," the Departed warrior toasted Half-Mask with a raised glass. Ell inclined his head as graciously as he could despite the bitter bile he tasted in the back of his throat at having to toast his people's dire enemy.

They tossed the brown barley draughts back and then swallowed simultaneously. Ell managed to avoid coughing this time around, although he still felt like the liquor was burning a hole in the back of his throat.

"Thank you," Ell said, hoping to break the ice with polite conversation. The large elf ignored his grateful platitude, staring with a stony face at Ell.

"Why have you not filed your teeth like the rest of the traitors?" The dark elf asked in his harsh voice. It was not an angry tone exactly but it brooked no nonsense and demanded an answer.

"I have the tattoos," Ell responded carefully, feeling the burn of whatever brew he had just consumed mixing with the tankard of fire ale in his belly, warming him from the inside out. The Departed grunted at his response and changed angles.

"What news do you carry from the north? There have been rumors of a battle. A battle is said to have taken place in some nameless valley along the Westrill."

"None, I have no news." Ell dodged the question as best he could.

"You tell me, Traitor, you tell me what you know. Now." The dark elf's voice heated slightly. "They say two Northerners massacred nearly a thousand of us without blinking. What do you know of this... power?" His voice was demanding, requiring an answer.

Sweat broke out on his brow. Ell couldn't reveal any hint of the Water Calling abilities that he and Arendahl possessed. It was vital that their powers remain as secret as possible, a hidden weapon to fight the enemy. Ell realized this interaction was another test. First he had proved himself to the crowd by his willingness to resort to violence, silencing his earlier critic with a fist. Now this elf was challenging him to see whether he could assert dominance over Ell, bully him for information, or just for the pleasure of making a northern traitor follow his orders.

Ell wasn't sure if it was the fiery sensation in his belly coupled with the looseness of his emotions after having three drinks in quick succession, or whether it was his normal impulsive nature, but in an instant he decided upon a course of action. He would maintain his arrogant attitude, even with this extremely large and dangerous looking dark elf.

The steady hum of the common room continued as Ell lashed back with his response. "If a power like that existed—for two elves to kill that many Southerners—do you think I would be here with you?" Ell scoffed at the dark warrior seated across the table from him.

Ell continued, "And for your information, I joined the winning side, not the side I respect," he finished rashly, indicating the red tattoos beneath his eyes, and then flashing an insolent grin to show the unfiled teeth. The dark elf curled his lip in a snarl and revealed the top row of teeth filed to points like a wolf.

"Careful boy, you are all alone in this city. It would be well for you to show me some respect." The Departed's voice was angry, but it still carried a hint of caution towards Ell at his willingness to start a fight with the biggest, meanest looking elf in the room. Ell could tell that while his decision to maintain his blatant arrogance might yet result in a fight, it had still been the correct response. The Departed's grudging respect was proof enough of that.

Ell stared back as coolly as possible, readying himself to fight if the moment arose. But the large dark elf across from him seemed to feel that Ell had received his warning and relaxed enough to resume their conversation. They talked carefully of travel conditions on the road from the north between mouthfuls of stew, of battle tactics and ambushes, of enemies killed and females. Ell could sense that the Departed was probing Ell for information of any kind, carefully, just as Ell did. Ell asked questions about the city, questions that appeared random and unimportant, the likes of which a new traitor would ask after relocating to the southern capital. Ell discovered that there were a number of slave barracks, in different portions of Dark Harbor. It would likely take days of searching to find them, and to learn whether his family was in one of the barracks or if they ever had been.

The dark warrior never told Ell his name, and Ell did not volunteer his own, but by the end of a few hours and many drinks of barley draught, Ell felt surprised at how much he had discovered of the elf at his table and about the Departed as a people, in general. Kalabi had been right, violence was seen as a solution to almost everything, but it was not a matter of cruelty with the common folk, but more a measure of strength. Almost like in nature's order, in which the strongest survive and the weak fail. Dark Harbor was a brutal place from what Ell had seen and from what he had gleaned from the warrior, yet it had a strange appropriateness to it, as well. The way the calm and the storm both belong in the world. Ell was firmly convinced that he would rather live in the midst of a calm tranquility.

Slightly unsteady on his feet from the drinks, and uncomfortable with his lack of balance should a fight arise, Ell decided it was time to retire for the night. The tavern was next door to an inn. Ell took his leave of the dark warrior and crossed the few rainy yards between tavern and inn. With his stolen money, he paid for a small room in the back corner of the inn's upper story—a room which leaked with the rain and rattled with the heavy winds—and hunkered down on the bed until morning arrived and he could make his way back to his family in the cave to report on what he had found.

Chapter Twenty-One

It was strange to be waking up in a bed. The only times Ell had slept in a bed of any kind was during the infrequent stays in Verdantihya—some of the ruins and palaces still had usable beds left for travelers who searched thoroughly enough. This particular mattress was lumpy and little more than a stuffed pallet placed on a wooden frame. Ell had slept on beds of moss that were infinitely more comfortable. Yet he could not deny that the pallet mattress was still more comfortable than the rocky soil he had often been forced to sleep upon when he and his family raided far from the comforts of the lush Legendwood.

The walls and ceiling were also anomalous. Ell was used to sleeping under open sky or a canopy of branches, not these planked and shuttered buildings. The room was rickety and seemed in disrepair with small holes in the window frame and wooden squeaks of distress every time he moved. Yet, he could not deny that this tiny room at the back upper corner of the inn had kept him safe and dry from the tremendous gale that had swirled raucously through Dark Harbor last night. With his head spinning from drink, the thunderous storm rain had ushered him to sleep, and the spattering of rain on wood and the screams of wind were his nighttime companions.

When he arose and looked out the window, Ell saw that the purple skies of the previous day and night had cleared, leaving a fresh greyness that hinted at cleanliness—a cleanliness that he doubted Dark Harbor often experienced. It seemed to be a city steeped in discourse and darkness.

Ell had slept fully clothed, boots and all, so there was no need to dress. He walked downstairs, fully armed, in his wrinkled clothing and doled a few more coins to the innkeeper—the fattest elf he had ever seen—in order to secure his room for another night. Business taken care of, Ell strode out the door. He would be back tonight, Ell was loath to let any chance to search for his estranged family escape him, but now he must return to his family hidden in the cave outside the northern Hillfort. They would be edgy, so close to their ancient foes, and without knowing if he was alright, their anxiety would only increase. Best to relay what information he had to them, convene on a plan of sorts, and then return to the port city to continue his search.

Ell walked in the early morning light. Dawn was not far gone and the streets were surprisingly empty. Ell doubted it would be long before street hawkers and merchants began to step lightly and quickly about their work. Not long from now, the servants and slaves that Ell had seen all over the city yesterday would step out on their many errands and tasks for their masters. Ell made his way along the wharf and to the causeway leading back to shore. It was a strange stillness in which he walked. In Andalaya, even when one was alone, there was always noise—the sound of a river running, wind in the trees, birds calling and animals scampering through the underbrush. But here, Dark Harbor lay frozen in this early morning emptiness with a silence more profound than anything to which Ell was accustomed. It was a quiet that spoke of the lack of life and nature, in the city. Without elves bustling about, this place was just a dead city made of crumbling dirty stone and dead trees cut to lumber. The only sound of life was the steady lapping of waves against the pier. No, Dark Harbor and its society had a very different feel than its northern cousin, Andalaya.

Ell made his way quickly across the causeway, covering ground much better than when he had traveled this course yesterday morning through throngs of people milling this way and that. He reached the shore and set his course up the steep road to reach the Hillfort. It was an uneventful journey and he reached the forted area in what felt like a much shorter time than he had experienced yesterday. The lull of the city was not apparent at the single-walled fort. The businesslike morning trainings of soldiers was already underway, as well as the many other various tasks that kept a fortress running—servants carrying water, runners with messages, guards and sentinels watching all directions. These Hillforts were not to be taken lightly. They were well fortified and well-guarded. They might not be the impregnable structures of the Pillars in the Lower Forest, but they would repel most any attack. With steep peaks at the shoulders of the wall, an army would find it difficult to breach a wall of such height and breadth. Ell left the fortress by the small gate where he had entered upon his arrival the previous day, murmuring an excuse of wishing to hunt. The guard let him through without question, and again Ell was astounded with their lack of suspicion regarding a Northerner such as he. But then again, traitors that left Andalaya renounced their very identities and had no place left to go. Betraying their new allegiance was unlikely as they would never be welcomed back to the north. They were stuck with their southern lot and the Departed realized this. For that reason, they must allow the traitors an element of trust. Besides, it was not uncommon for a Northerner to wish to hunt. Ell shouldered his bow and ran lithely away from the fort and across the clear cut into the forest. He would double back and return to the cave on the hillside, but he would try and do so outside of eyeshot of the Hillfort's walls.

By the time Ell reached the cave entrance, it was mid-morning. He was pleased to have discovered what a relatively painless process it was to leave the city and reach his family in the cave.

His entrance into the crevice was met without surprise. Dahranian had been standing watch and must have spotted him coming from some way off and had given warning. His cousin clasped his hand in quiet greeting and steadfastly continued to eye the landscape around the entrance to the cave.

"Well, did you have fun larking about Dark Harbor while we were all penned in this dank grotto in the mountain?" Rihya asked acerbically, clearly having been bored and feeling useless.

"I missed you too, sister," Ell replied as cheerfully as possible, with a hint of jest and mockery in his voice. He quirked a smile at her. "Have you had a good time in my absence?"

"It was odiously tedious, Ell. I cannot stand it much longer."

"It was not so bad as you say," Dacunda reproached her. "Did you find out anything useful in your first day in Dark Harbor?" he asked.

"Useful? Much. But nothing specific to where my family might be or if they are even there," Ell was forced to admit.

Ryder propped himself up on an elbow as he lay on the ground where he had been napping in the dim light of the cave.

Ryder tried to encourage him. "We'll keep looking then. Don't give up just because we did not find anything specific immediately."

"We?" Rihya asked sourly. "*We* didn't do anything other than sit in this stupid cave all day and night."

"You know what I meant," Ryder said dismissively.

"My son is correct, do not give up yet." Dacunda always managed to sound serious.

Ell smiled back at them, appreciating the encouragement. "I was not planning on it. But I am glad to hear you are not growing impatient with me." He winked at his sister to tweak her nose just a bit. She grimaced.

"Well, what have you discovered?" Kalabi spoke up from the darkness at the back of the cave. He stepped closer, into the clearer light near the entrance.

"I spent much of the day in observation. As you said, Kalabi, violence rules in Dark Harbor. It creates disputes and also settles them. I engaged a few Departed in conversation last night in the tavern, and from them, I gleaned what little I could. The best I can say now, in regards to our mission, is that there are many different barracks that house slaves. I was planning on returning tonight to the city and starting the search again tomorrow, by visiting some of those slave quarters." Ell told them, outlining his basic plan.

"Perhaps another of us should falsify the tattoos and join you as a traitor in the city? Many hands make light work." Dahranian volunteered from the cave entrance, without looking their way, his eyes maintaining their steady perusal of the clear cut and the sloping mountainsides surrounding their cave shelter.

"I will go!" Rihya volunteered immediately.

Dacunda shook his head. "I have never heard of a female traitor. You would draw too much attention. It must be a male."

Rihya muttered a few curses to herself as her proposal was disregarded immediately. But she did not argue, she knew it was too risky for a female to pose as a traitor. Choosing instead to declare, "Yes, we females have much more inner fortitude, that is why you have never seen us running away to join the enemy." She spoke with a lofty, yet cutting, annoyance, but there was an undertone of jest to her statement.

"Yes, well, that may be, Valerihya, and I am sure it will bring you much consolation when you sit here while another of us joins Elliyar in the city," Dacunda said. It was the closest Ell had heard Dacunda come to a joke in some time, and Ell couldn't help but let out a small chuckle. Ryder smirked at Rihya also. She only grimaced again and tossed her hair.

Ell recovered from his mirth and contradicted his uncle. "Dacunda, I think it best if I go back alone again. As we discussed before, too many fresh faces entering the gates at the Hillfort will draw attention. It will be easiest if it is only me that I must worry about. And sneaking in is not an option, the coastal range will not permit it." This coastal range of mountains were small, but they were very steep. The Hillforts were built at the only safe passes. It was part of the reason why Dark Harbor was so well protected. The mountains and fortresses around its bay were a wall of defense to repel any army.

Dacunda appraised him for a moment before nodding. "As you wish, Nephew. Yet, at some point, we will all likely need to enter the city. Freeing slaves will necessitate violence, I think, and it would be best for you not to undertake such a venture alone."

"That may be," Ell agreed, "but we will cross that bridge when it comes. For now, stay here while I do what needs to be done in Dark Harbor."

"Do you have any orders for us as we remain here?" Dacunda asked, with a completely straight face. Ell almost choked on the water he was drinking when he heard his uncle ask him for orders. Accepting Ell's leadership on this one mission had been a reluctant concession by his uncle in order to gain admittance on this venture. Ell had not expected him to embrace it any further. Perhaps he was only being polite.

Ell took a moment to gather his thoughts before responding. "Come dark, scout the surrounding area—the woods beyond the clear cut, the coastal range, the Hillforts. Who knows when we will be here again? It may be advantageous to have knowledge of this region."

Dacunda nodded approvingly at him and even with a hint of surprise. Ell had clearly chosen the course of action that Dacunda himself would have recommended had he been in charge of this expedition. Ell felt a strange surge of pleasure at having his uncle's approval of his decision-making.

"It will be done, Nephew."

The rest of the day was spent in discussion and debate about Dark Harbor. Ell relayed all he had observed and the information he had gathered. He spoke of the oppressive gloom that hung over the city, the dirt and grime, the violence, the tension. Ell conveyed the cramped existence away from nature in the middle of a dense city. They chatted idly about what different aspects of his information might mean.

As dusk began to descend, causing lengthening shadows to fall across the mouth of the crevice, Ell took his leave. He did not know if the Hillfort allowed entry after dark and he did not wish to miss the opportunity to reach the city tonight so he could have an early start to the day tomorrow. He said brief goodbyes to his family, clasping forearms with everyone and a quick kiss on the cheek for Rihya, and then he was out of the cave and back on his feet heading towards the northernmost Hillfort. As he went, he formulated his story. If anyone at the fort asked, he would claim to have cooked his kill and eaten it already, which would be plausible since most of the game in these parts were scraggly rabbits and other small vermin. The tale would suffice. Thoughts of food however, sent his stomach rumbling towards thoughts of that strange spicy stew he'd eaten the day before. There was at least one thing to be said for the south—even though its government was his enemy—the food was decent.

* * * *

The city was buzzing with life when Ell stepped off the causeway. It was night, but it seemed that Dark Harbor was equally as busy as it was during the day, if not more so. Street vendors still lined the streets and propped their carts and wagons against buildings, creating narrow passages that forced Ell to zigzag his way through the maze of protruding cart handles and people. The sound of axels squeaking and wheels trundling over cobblestones and dirt punctuated the cacophony as a few less than hardy souls gave up selling their wares to go home for the night. But new faces appeared in the crowd. Ell paid particularly close attention to anything he saw, however small, because he did not know which detail might make the difference between success and failure—

any moment might provide the information or inspiration that allowed him to find his family and devise a plan to rescue them.

As such, his attention was keen and he noticed the wealth of bodies slinking throughout the crowded streets, slipping fingers into pockets and knifing purses from belts with a silken ease. Ell was glad he had placed his meager pouch of coins inside a hidden pocket within his hooded tunic. He supposed he could always pick another purse but why go to the trouble when he had his own handy? Ladies of the night also began to appear, selling more than just their bodies. Vials with pungent scents were opened and those smells wafted through the air, creating a lusty, delicate balance to the tang of the sea and the grimy refuse piled in the alleys and gutters. Although he could not ascertain the ingredients, they invoked a desire in him that he was unfamiliar with while all alone. It caused his thoughts to wobble from their keen appraisal of the city and to drift in and out of memories of his time spent with Miri. All the while he strode towards the nearby inn where he had his small room reserved.

Where was his mate now? Was she safely in the north, or had Arendahl taken her on some mad quest of his own? Ell could not help but remember the old elf taking Ell to the Barren Maze not long after they had met. Just the two of them, Arendahl had led them into the heart of Ghoul territory just in the hopes of finding a fight that would force Ell to tap instinctually into his Water Calling powers. They had found Ghouls, and more than they bargained for, when a Stone Ogre had awoken and nearly killed them. Ell hoped the grizzled old elf was not placing Miri in needless danger.

He reached the inn standing next to the tavern that he had visited the previous night. Ell had been so focused on getting out of the rain and into bed when he left the tavern the first night, that he had not noticed the tavern's name. "The Sea Witch" it was called, and the tavern bore the likeness of a creature that appeared part elf and part something else, with kelpy, seaweed-like hair stringing down around its shoulders and its naked body striated with discolorations and stripes like a camouflage to blend in with some underwater environment. The painting was on a flat board just above the entrance to the tavern and it was roughly painted, matching its seedy waterfront surroundings.

Ell opened the door to the inn and stepped inside, leaving the noise of The Sea Witch and entering the squeaky stillness of the inn. He had paid to reserve his room, so he ignored the innkeeper's suspicious look and climbed the stairs to his small upper room. Strangely, the room felt homey, like some sort of familiar hidden haven in the midst of a terrifyingly new and dangerous world. He had navigated the shoals of Dark Harbor so far, but something told Ell that things were only going to get more difficult the longer he stayed. Urgency built within him as he tried to fall asleep, and when he finally did, it was to the sound of ships creaking and clunking in the nearby harbor, and the squawk of sea birds roosting along the waterfront. It was the sound of the birds more than anything that helped him relax. It was the first real reminder that there was a natural element to Dark Harbor, however insignificant that element might be in the midst of a teeming mass of elves and stone, steel and danger.

Ell awoke the next morning with a sense of purpose. He would begin searching for clues of his family's whereabouts near the actual slave barracks. The air outside was hot and muggy. It appeared that autumn this far south resembled something more akin to midsummer in the north, albeit with the exception of a few raging thunderstorms every now and again. The sun didn't continuously pierce the dull grey overhang in the sky, but it seemed that the heat was infused into every aspect of the world around Ell. Hot air, sticky sweat, warm cobblestones all radiating the heat back onto the people. Ell almost expected the harbor to be at a fine simmer when he looked out onto the water, but it was not, and Ell was forced to conclude that he was simply not accustomed to the ever-present, permeating humidity of the south. He longed for a crisp autumn day in Andalaya, clear air, the scent of pines, and the smell of Miri's wildflower hair. But that was not to be. Yet. He must instead focus on the here and now, on the task of finding out anything he could about his enslaved family's whereabouts.

Ell walked south around the outskirts of the island, listening to conversations and watching the elves at their tasks, until he reached the location of a certain slave barracks he had heard about in conversation the other day. When he reached it, Ell loitered in the shadow of a darkened alley, watching the activity of people entering and leaving the building. It was mostly people leaving. At this time of morning, slaves were filing their way out in lines, connected to one another by chain manacles or rope nooses. It appeared there was little trust for the northern slaves. Perhaps they would be let off their leashes to work once they reached their destination, but they walked shackled together. Ell watched as slave masters cracked whips and barked orders, ushering the dejected slaves whichever way they pleased. Ell had never seen such a dispirited mass of elves. It set his blood boiling and suddenly Ell realized that he had instinctively tapped into his ability as a Water Caller. Poised for action, Ell realized just how foolish it would be to attack the slave master and try to free these slaves. They were on an island with no means of escape, surrounded by enemies. He could surely kill many of the Departed with his powers before he was overwhelmed, but in the end he would likely die and the slaves would simply be recaptured. There was nothing to be done for them. Ell clenched his teeth and watched. He held his power, not releasing his ability as a Water Caller, feeling the strength pulse through him like a radiating light, but he only held it. Ell held it until the gang of slaves was gone, far out of sight.

With a deep breath, he released his power and calmed himself. It was right of his family to have warned him to keep his cool while in the city. He must not act rashly. Right now, he had to ascertain his parents' whereabouts—if they were even here. Ell continued to survey the slave barracks.

The building was squat and wide, with no windows and a narrow doorway. Other chained groups of slaves filed out led by slave masters, but Ell recognized no one, although he acknowledged that he had no way to recognize his family whom he had never met. How would he know his parents or sister if he saw them? It was a question he shoved aside for now. Angry at the situation forced upon his enslaved people, he surveyed the waterfront region around the slave barracks, watching his enemies as well as the slaves that frequently filed out of the building.

There were a large number of Unsired striding about the masses of Departed near the docks. Warriors with slightly glazed expressions, unusually dark eyes, and a sickly tinge to some of their bodies, walked purposefully through the crowds. Ell noticed that those of the Departed who had not yet become Unsired gave them a wide berth and averted their gazes. It was interesting to note that not all of the Unsired walking freely about the city were soldiers. Certainly most of them were, but there were some who were merchants, sailors, street vendors and nobles alike who had the same visage and behavior as the Unsired. Not all of the Departed were Unsired, that was clear, but their numbers were obviously swelling. How rapidly, Ell did not know, and he hoped to never have to find out. However, he knew that hope to be false, to be a petty desire for this conflict to cease even though it would not end any time soon. Not without a fight at least.

Ell left the slave barracks and walked to the location of the next one of which he had learned. It was also near a wharf, this time on the south side of the island. He observed it from a distance, same as the other one, but there were no elves emerging from this one. Likely they were already gone, having left to their daily work with the crack of whips sounding over their heads. Ell impulsively decided to grab a quick drink at a tavern nearby. It was hot in this midmorning heat and he wanted a wet throat more than anything right now.

Stepping into a tavern, known as The Maelstrom, with a giant whirlpool painted above its door, Ell enjoyed reprieve from the sweltering heat outside. It never failed to amaze him that this late in the year it could be this hot. Did winter even exist in Dark Harbor?

He sat and a server with long, unshaven hair covering his pointed ears took his order for a honey mead. Ell briefly considered that this might be an odd order this far south, but he was a northern traitor after all, and as a Northerner, it probably wouldn't blow his cover to order a northern beverage. In exchange for some of his dwindling supply of coins, he was brought the worst honey mead Ell had ever tasted—clearly the brewing practices of honey mead this far south were lacking—yet it tasted better than anything Ell had ever drank. The weak honey flavor was spring on his tongue and the lukewarm liquid soothed his hot throat and belly better than any fire ale ever could. Ell smacked his lips after a long pull from the tankard.

He surveyed the room. It was full of sailors and soldiers, just as The Sea Witch had been. Conversation was at a slow buzz and Ell tried to listen to see if he could pick up anything interesting or useful. Before too long, Ell noticed a completely shaven elf sitting in a dim corner of the tavern, as far away from any windows as possible. What struck Ell's interest was how this shaven headed elf seemed to be the only elf in the room other than Ell who did not look comfortable being there. Shifty eyes flicked back and forth across the room as the elf sipped what looked to be a small glass of the strong barley draught Ell had sampled the other night. The unsettled elf had gold and silver piercings in his ears, nose, and on his eyebrows and lips. It was strange to see such a sight. His pointed ears and tanned skin were worn, with a hint of a weathered look about them, as if he had spent much time under the hot sunny skies of open water. A sailor then, if Ell was not mistaken.

Impulsively Ell rose and strode over to his table. "Care if I join you?"

The elf appraised Ell a moment and then grunted his assent, kicking a chair out for Ell to take a seat, his bare foot callused and worn from walking a deck. They drank their separate drinks in silence for a few minutes. Ell wasn't sure how to proceed after initiating the contact and the sailor elf seemed to be perfectly fine with not talking, his eyes flicking nervously about the room even more than Ell's did. Ell finished his drink and was just gathering words to speak when the Departed beat him to it.

"Piripeos."

"I beg your pardon?" Ell wasn't sure what the Departed meant.

"Piripeos. That's my name." The southern elf spoke with a gravelly voice.

"Elliyar." Ell indicated himself, giving his real name without thinking any better of it. He would have to be more careful in the future. The elf nodded.

They sat again in silence for a minute until the serving elf came to clear their mugs. Ell ordered another of both and gave the serving elf coins to pay for two more drinks. Piripeos nodded his head gratefully, while maintaining a keen eye on Ell. Clearly he did not trust Ell any more than he trusted the rest of the room. Ell had seen fearful elves all over the city of Dark Harbor, but Piripeos was different. Something about his manner carried more of an edginess, a careful wariness, than real fear. It was not like the terrified, subdued expressions that many of the lower class elves wore in Dark Harbor.

"Been here long?" Ell decided to feel the southern elf out with some small chatter as they waited for their new drinks.

"A time," Piripeos said noncommittally. "Longer than the last time, that's for sure." The southern elf spat, and again Ell felt a surge of confidence that this elf had no love for Dark Harbor. He didn't know how he knew it, but he could intuitively tell that there might be a useful contact with this Departed.

"Sailor?" Ell asked another superficial question, as their drinks arrived.

Piripeos sipped his barley draught as if it was hardly stronger than water before responding. "Captain. Traitor?" Something in the way the southern elf spoke, the few words he used, reminded Ell of Arendahl, and the grizzled old elf's stilted way of speaking.

Ell swallowed and forced himself to nod. Yes, for now he was a traitor. But not forever.

"New to the city, eh?" Captain Piripeos said knowingly.

Ell nodded again as he sipped his honey mead. "I am just down from Andalaya, and am familiarizing myself with everything. It is larger than I expected." Ell spoke truthfully, feeling like the closer he stuck to the truth the easier his ruse would be to maintain.

"I can tell. You're still green, in more ways than one." Piripeos grunted a laugh at Ell, and even though he wasn't a traitor for real, Ell felt a flush of anger at the comment. Strangely he felt the need to defend himself.

"I am not so green as you think, Captain." Ell said stiffly.

"Don't go all northern pride on me now, traitor. It wasn't a criticism, just an observation. You're still green—literally." He pointed to the forest green, hooded tunic Ell still wore, and the green breeches. "Most of us Southerners wear black, of sorts," he indicated his black vest and voluminous dark brown trousers. "Eventually the traitors all adjust to the style—sticking out in Dark Harbor isn't a good idea, and you stick out like a sore thumb, all blond hair, blue eyes, and green clothes. Plus, you're still drinking honey mead. Sure sign you're freshly recruited. Give it a few weeks and you'll see, it's better to go unnoticed and that means blending in."

Ell wasn't planning on being here forever, but he played along, acting his part as a new traitor as best he could. "I will remember your advice. Tell me, is there anything else I should know?"

"Like what?" Captain Piripeos asked.

Ell did his best to make his voice sound nonchalant. "Oh, I don't know. Important customs, places to avoid, how slaves are kept…" He trailed off as if he was idly listing random things.

Piripeos wasn't fooled. His eyes narrowed shrewdly. "You'll do well to avoid the slaves. Your job is capturing them, not associating with them once they're here. Many a traitor has found himself in a load of trouble by getting to near the slaves. Besides, the slaves don't take kindly to you lot." Piripeos didn't elaborate on what sort of trouble, but Ell could hear the truth in his words. He inclined his head.

"I will remember that also. Tell me," he changed the subject before the Southerner could grow suspicious, "why do you look so different than the rest of the Departed?" The shaved head and piercings stuck out, and Piripeos was also shorter than many of the Departed.

"I'm from the Outer Rim," Piripeos said as he swigged back another small glassful of the barley draught and signaled the serving elf that he wanted another. "We Rimmers aren't like the rest of the Southerners. We're our own kind. Just been absorbed into the southern kingdom."

Ell racked his brain to remember what he knew of the Outer Rim. As far as he could remember it was a ring of islands way out into the western sea, far beyond the Enclaves. It was populated by mostly fishers.

"You are your own kind?" What had he meant by that?

Piripeos nodded forcefully. "We are!" A passion filled his voice. "Fishers mostly. We provide the kingdom with a large portion of the fish that are consumed. We can sail anything from deep-sea vessels to lighter shore craft. Practically born upon the water, we are." The captain spoke with pride about his people, his gravelly voice swelling forcefully.

"So why did you join the Departed, if you are so different?" Ell asked cautiously.

"Why did you?" Piripeos grunted rhetorically. "Because it's useless to resist. They're too strong. My kind were absorbed into the kingdom centuries ago, just like your people will be eventually. You traitors are just the first. Only, my kind get to serve and live relatively normally, you Northerners will most likely be slaves." He grimaced apologetically. Piripeos was an odd elf. Blunt, he spoke his mind, but without any real joy derived from the idea of the enslavement of the Highest.

"So you are loyal to the kingdom then?" Ell was emboldened to ask the dangerous question by the Rimmer's matter of fact attitude.

Piripeos looked at him as if he was insane. "What are you playing at, traitor? Asking those type of questions…Of course I'm loyal, I'm not an idiot, Northerner! You don't rebel against someone as vicious as Half-Mask." Piripeos paused and gained a sly look. "However, that doesn't mean that a few rules can't be bent here and there."

Criminal. So that's what he was. It suddenly became clear. Captain

Piripeos might not be a revolutionary, but his shifty gaze and lurking attitude screamed criminal clear as day. He was probably a smuggler.

Ell dropped the dangerous line of questioning and resumed safer topics. They spoke of customs in the north and out west in the Outer Rim. Of drinks and foods, of weapons and storms. Ell was surprised to find that he actually enjoyed the Southerner's—or should he think of him as a 'westerner'—company. In fact, Captain Piripeos was probably the first elf who was not a member of the Highest that Ell had ever spoken to that Ell didn't completely view as the enemy. Piripeos' people had been conquered centuries ago. In some ways, they were not so different from the Highest.

After a few hours of conversation, Ell eventually took his leave. He bid the captain a genuine farewell, and left the dusky interior of The Maelstrom. The sky was grey but the heat was still sweltering. He wandered for a bit before striking towards the heart of Dark Harbor. He decided it might be time to observe one of the slave quarters near the interior of the city. Eventually, Ell found another barracks—it was squat and low like all the others. They almost seemed to have a uniform shape. He waited as the afternoon wore on, figuring he would wait until dusk when the slaves would perhaps return from a day's work.

When the slaves began arriving, chained into gangs like they had been at the other barracks, Ell watched eagerly, hoping for some clue as to his family's location. At the very least he hoped to glean some new information about the habits of the slave masters as they deposited their possessions back into the slave quarters. However, nothing new arose—no extra piece of information, no hint as to where or how to find his family.

Discouraged, but not willing to give up on the day just yet, Ell walked towards a nearby tavern in the twilight. He found humor in the fact that he was spending more time drinking in the last few days than he had in nearly all his life. However, he knew it was the best way to strike up conversations and glean information. His encounter with Piripeos had been proof of that. Ell had learned valuable information about the customs of the Departed, about the small fissures within the southern society. These were all pieces he would put together to help him figure out a way to rescue his family.

Ell opened the door to the tavern and stepped inside.

Chapter Twenty-Two

Ell immediately realized he was in a fancier drinking establishment with rich clientele. Tapestries hung on the walls and there were as many hands holding wine goblets as tankards of ale. All sound trailed off as he entered until a moment of silence hung, long and heavy and awkward. Stares followed him as he walked up to the bar and indicated that he wished to order a drink. The eyes that followed him silently were not the hard, suspicious gazes of the downtrodden and the worn warriors that Ell encountered while near the harbor front. No, these eyes were haughty and scornful, shooting daggers of hatred and disdain towards him. Ell had never felt so out of place or unwanted in all his time in Dark Harbor, and that was saying a lot since he was a foreigner in every part of the city.

Noble Departed were seated at tables or stood near the bar with ermine robes of sable or scarlet draped over their shoulders. Swords were encrusted with jewels and circlets of beaten metal adorned the foreheads of many of the southern elves. All head hair was worn in the fashion of the warrior, with the sides of heads shaven and long black hair tailing down the back of heads in braids or loosely bound. Pointed ears and filed upper teeth were upon every head. Ell took a deep breath and kept his composure. It would not do to appear frightened. The violence of this city and the brutal nature of many of its inhabitants was apparent. Some instinct told Ell that the biggest mistake in Dark Harbor and especially here near the noble heart of the city, was to show fear. There was also a small part of him that refused to show his nerves simply for the sake of pride.

Ell ordered a barley draught and paid for the drink with coins from a second purse he had cut earlier in the day. Stealing was becoming second nature here in Dark Harbor. He turned around from facing the bar and surveyed the room, only to see a circle of stony-faced elves close in around him.

"Are you lost?" one mean looking warrior asked, a luxurious midnight cloak covering a thin sheet of finely wrought chain mail. It was strange, Ell had never seen any of the Departed fight with armor. Perhaps it was just an affectation of the nobility.

"You are not wanted here, Northerner," another noble said, fingering the hilt of a sheathed sword with a black marbled ruby set in the hilt.

Another approached and this one had the cold, dead eyes of the Unsired, staring at him in an almost vacant expression. "Who are you?" It asked with a slow curious tone, and Ell's skin prickled as the ambiguous nature of the Unsired's question. What was it asking? What did it know? It tilted its head as it looked at him again, and Ell saw the sickly, diseased skin on the side of its neck and up towards the Unsired's cheek become exposed as the collar of its robe shifted.

Not knowing who to answer first, he simply addressed the three of them and any other Southerners close enough hear him. "I am new to the city. My name is Mantiriol."

The lie of name sprang to his lips this time without thinking. Better to let them believe he was some random Northerner named for a great hero from legend than take the chance that one of them might have heard the name Elliyar Wintermoon. Ell was fairly certain he could pass on his own name near the waterfront where the poor and needy rubbed shoulders with the beaten down warriors at harbor taverns. But here, in the presence of what seemed to be Dark Harbor nobility, he thought it might be likely that some of these elves might be important enough to have read specific reports sent down from the north. It would be disastrous if someone recognized him by his name before he had even had a chance to learn more about his family.

A fourth Departed spoke in a more commanding voice than the others. "New or not, you should not have come here. You filth might be useful in the north, but here in the city, you traitors must be taught your place. A lesson in humility is needed, I think."

"Humility?" Ell asked indignantly and with an edge of worry. He could defend himself with his powers but that would ruin his cover as a traitor. Ell wasn't sure he could effectively defend himself against them all without his Water Calling abilities. "What have I done to offend?"

"Other than appear where you are not welcome…" The fourth noble trailed off as if that was enough reason by itself. The noble waited with a quiet smile before seeming to make up another excuse. The noble reached a powerful yet slender hand with the nails lacquered in black paint. He grasped one of the black, Dreampine arrows from Ell's quiver between two of his fingers.

"I quite think that carrying these arrows merits the label of arrogance." The noble turned to his fellow Dark Harbor inhabitants and directed his next question at them. "Don't you think?" The murmurs and rumblings of assent made Ell's muscles tense. He had been around violence long enough to know when a fight was brewing.

Nevertheless, Ell took the bait and asked through gritted teeth. "And what is so wrong with my arrows?"

The fourth, commanding noble with elegantly filed teeth spoke as if his reasoning was common knowledge—which Ell supposed it might indeed be, here in the south. "Those black arrows, made of Dreampine wood from the far northern reaches of Andalaya," he spat the name of Ell's broken kingdom as if it tasted bad in his mouth, "are a favored arrow of the raiders who harry our slavers. The arrows are not common and are a symbol of the pretentious resistance of the few who stand against us. After all, whoever does not bow to the Prince of Darkness deserves to be punished. No?"

Ell stared him straight in the eyes and the noble's face darkened at Ell's insolent gaze. Ell's hand crept towards his belt knife.

The noble narrowed his eyes dangerously. "I am Vragar, acquaintance and confidant to the most revered Prince of Darkness, and you would do well to show me respect, Northerner." He spoke quietly, calmly, but Ell heard the silk of death in his falsely soft tone.

Ell still didn't answer. And suddenly the noble seemed to grow bored with the altercation. The noble snapped his lacquered fingers and what looked like three bodyguards materialized around him almost instantly. They were hulking shapes, some of the largest Departed Ell had ever seen.

"Take him outside and teach him some manners. I care not whether he survives the lesson." The noble directed his command to his three guards.

And with that the noble turned away, completely ignoring Ell to engage the elves around him in conversation again. Haughty glares and smirking laughs followed him, as Ell allowed himself to be dragged from the establishment by the three body guards. Better to fight them outside in the dark than to reveal his skills as a fighter in such a crowd of people. If Ell was forced to tap into his abilities he wanted as few witnesses as possible.

The guards cast him onto the cobblestone street and Ell fell with a roll, surging lithely to his feet immediately, dueling daggers drawn in both hands. The guards advanced with the stoic, blank faces of mindless servants, and for a fleeting instant Ell realized how similar their servile expressions were to the thoughtless blank gazes of the Departed. Was that what the Departed were—blank minded slaves to the darkness?

The guards strode towards him, loosing swords from sheaths and Ell prepared himself to fight. Gambling, he decided to tap into his abilities. No one was watching the fight, it was an empty quiet street. Ell reached out his senses quickly, feeling the salty wet air. He drew strength from the moist sea air, from the incessant crashing of the waves on the docks and piers. Ell reached out his consciousness and tapped into the slowly building, ever-present power of the ocean—the surges of the deep swells and grand currents. Power flooded him like it always did when he managed to reach his power. He felt the pooling sensation of power in his chest the wealth of potential and possibility as if anything he wished were possible. The guards were almost upon him and they had no idea what they were about to face. They had no clue they were outnumbered—only three of them about to attack a Water Caller, fabled ancient lineage of the Highest. Ell grinned in the darkness.

The fight was brief and brutal.

Ell ducked their blows with ease the way he would a child. He hamstrung one and disemboweled another. The third, he kicked so hard, he was sent flying into a stone building across the street.

He decided not to finish them off, allowing the groans of the injured to pierce the silence of the night. Well, one might die, he supposed clinically. It was difficult to recover from disembowelment. The other two would likely survive with proper care. Ell loped off into the night, deciding it was high time he returned to the comparatively friendly region of the waterfront. He had learned much today. Not only had his discussion with Captain Piripeos been useful, but his interaction with these nobles had shed more light on Dark Harbor. Traitors were apparently second-class citizens, something that made him grin with delight. Ell would have hated the thought of his traitor kin receiving places of importance and lavish roles within the southern society. He had also learned that the nobility were as much or more likely to lash out with violence to solve their issues as the commoners. Ell would have to use extra caution during any further excursions into the heart of the city.

Ell wove his way back toward the Sea Witch and the neighboring inn on the northern side of the city. The city was a warren of streets and alleys with seemingly no rhyme or reason, but eventually he made it. Blood still rushing in his head and veins, Ell felt the flush of excitement. Despite his cover, he had finally had the satisfaction of drawing enemy blood. Ell hadn't realized how much his body had been aching to lash out and fight his enemies until he had given it such release. He grinned. He might be only a solitary Highest, but he was the most dangerous of his kind. Dark Harbor was not aware that there was a wolf raging it its midst.

Chapter Twenty-Three

Miri did not know what she was doing exactly, but as she lay under the stars waiting for sleep, she stretched her consciousness out. She imagined it traveling south until it reached Ell. She imagined that part of her mind that was nestled within Ell's consciousness was active and able to tell her what he was thinking, what he was feeling. For an instant she felt a thrill of fierce excitement but it was gone more quickly than a spark dies after it leaves the heat of a crackling fire. She must have imagined that flush of excitement the same way she had been imagining her mind, her soul traveling south. It had felt so real, like she was connected to Ell for a moment in time, but the experience had been fleeting.

Miri gave up and rolled onto her side, curling her knees up under her. Time for sleep, time to stop trying to practice something that she had no idea how to practice—a talent that for all his knowledge and encouragement, Arendahl had been unable to shed any helpful light upon. The piece of her mind that was Grafted into Ell's was a conduit between them, a one way conduit for her to see and experience his emotions and thoughts, but it was a medium that seemed only to work whenever Ell experienced something deeply enough on an instinctual level. Miri had seen little success in the past weeks since they had joined Iyonei and her band in activating the Graft between her and Ell. It was frustrating. She missed Ell desperately and if only she could tap into this link she had forged then she could feel a little closer to him, or at least be informed about what was happening to the south. Anything had to be better than this void in her heart. The gulf between them felt enormous on nights such as this.

She let her eyes droop shut and her breathing slow until it joined the rhythmic breaths of the rest of the sleepers. But sleep would not come. Briesom and Satiri slept near to Miri, while Iyonei and Yendil were curled up opposite her. Arendahl was nowhere to be seen. Perhaps he was on watch.

Miri rose silently and wrapped her arms around herself, pausing briefly to crouch down and warm her hands by the coals of the burnt out fire. After receiving warmth from the glowing embers, she straightened and peered out into the night, finally sighting the old elf where he leaned against a maple tree surveying the darkness with wolf-like eyes.

"Can't sleep, eh?" The old elf said without preamble.

Miri shook her head as she folded her legs underneath her and sat down next to Arendahl. "I was trying to practice, like you told me to, but nothing was happening—well I thought I felt something, but it must have been just my imagination. It was too fleeting to have been real, not like the concentrated merging of consciousness that I experienced the other times."

"Keep practicing. It will be useful," was the only response the old elf gave her. She had long since grown used to his stilted way of communicating.

Miri figured that since they were both awake that she might as well try and dig some more information out of him—hopefully more useful information this time.

"What is it like to tap into your abilities as a Water Caller—you know, for you and Ell? I was thinking that maybe if I understood that a bit more then maybe it could help me tap into my Grafting skills."

Arendahl turned his shrewd gaze upon her for a moment then went back to surveying the night. "I doubt it will be of much help, you see, because they are very different experiences."

"But they both are utilizing your mind, your consciousness—stretching it out." She had heard the old elf teaching Ell during some of his previous lessons and some of what Arendahl said to Ell sounded similar to what he told her now.

"Not exactly, Miriyah. It's like pushing and pulling. Both actions require the use of the arms and the motions themselves are not so dissimilar. But what they accomplish are very different—opposite you might say. One pushes something away, the other holds it close. Water Calling is like pulling, yes, we stretch our consciousness out but then we tap into our oneness with Creation, with the power of the land, the water around us, and we pull that strength into us somehow. It is hard to describe. But accessing your Graft is like pushing. You also stretch your consciousness out, but you do not pull anything into yourself, instead you push. You push your active mind and try to slip it into that pocket of yourself that you have already pushed—forged—into Ell's consciousness. Do you see the difference? Similar motions, but singularly different aims and results."

Miri thought she understood. So far, it seemed that she could only access the Graft when Ell experienced something powerful enough to instinctively activate it. Usually, that was fear or pain. She feared what might happen in Dark Harbor for that to happen again.

"You should get some rest," Arendahl said curtly.

Miri ignored the advice. She hadn't had a minute alone with Arendahl for days and she might as well get some answers out of him while she had his focus. Or at least, whatever focus he wasn't giving to the dark woods around them.

"What are we doing, Arendahl?"

"Hmm?" The old feigned misunderstanding.

Miri sighed. "Why are we doing what we are doing? Why now? You have practically been telling every member of the Highest that we come across to sharpen his spears and prepare for war. Why now?"

"Because of Ell," the old elf murmured softly. "The time has come to gather again. Our people have been running and hiding for two decades. The time is soon upon us to either fight back or perish completely. I believe Elliyar can be the one we unite behind. Especially when people see what he is capable of."

"You mean his powers." Miri stated flatly. For some reason, Arendahl's calculated response to her inquiry bothered her.

Arendahl nodded his grey head. "His abilities certainly give him an edge, but he has accomplished great things even without his powers. He is unique, don't you think?" He ended with a question. Of course she thought her mate was special, but she wasn't sure it was for the same reason as the old elf.

"Why not you? You could lead," she said.

The old elf sighed. "I am strong, but brittle. I wouldn't inspire the same confidence that Ell would. Youth and vitality triumph over age when inspiring people to fight.

"If you think he is so qualified to be leader one day—someday soon—why did you put up such a fight about him leading the mission south?" Miri asked, curiosity burning within her. Arendahl was not usually so open and she decided to make the most of it while it lasted.

The old elf quirked a satisfied smile, as if he had secretly accomplished something he desired. "I wasn't as opposed to it as I may have led you all to believe."

Miri cocked her head to listen to what he had to say. Arendahl continued, the ghost of half a smile still on his face.

"The mission south was bound to be dangerous. I may not have supported the idea at first, but once Ell seemed set on doing it, I continued my opposition more to test his resolve. I believe Ell can accomplish nearly anything once he puts his mind to the task, but any expedition infiltrating Dor Khabor was going to require exceptional commitment and the willingness to put not only himself, but those he loves in danger. Ell has never done that before, not as a leader, and I wished to see how committed he was to such a notion." Arendahl paused, then spoke further. "In fact, this will be a good way for him to cut his teeth on leadership."

Miri wasn't sure of the truth of what the old elf was saying. Certainly he seemed to be telling the truth, or a truth he now believed, but she could vividly remember he and Dacunda advising Ell not to undertake this mission. Perhaps hindsight had done much to change his position, and now the old elf was simply rationalizing his actions to himself. Either way, she chose not to point that out.

"So why have you kept me along?" she asked somewhat tentatively.

"I promised the boy I'd keep an eye on you," Arendahl said brusquely, but then he winked at her to show he was partly joking. "Besides, as soon as you figure out this Grafting, you'll be quite useful—more than just another mouth to feed."

Miri smiled. Arendahl thought she might be useful. It had been some time since she'd felt useful at all. It would be wonderful to be able to contribute something necessary, rather than holding back her family. She just had to figure out the link she had forged with Ell's consciousness. The brief surge of gladness she had felt at the prospect of being useful dissipated as she was faced with the impossible task before her—the puzzle of working out a talent, a connection, that had already been rare and mysterious centuries ago, let alone now.

The grizzled elf seemed to read her mind. He patted her shoulder with a knobby hand, all knuckles and joints.

"You'll figure it out, girl."

Miri appreciated the encouragement, but responded by switching the conversation back to the previous subject.

"You should have told him your plan, Arendahl—the plan to make him a figurehead. Ell would have wanted to know. He deserves that much consideration, doesn't he?"

The old elf's eyes took on a faraway look. "We don't always get what we want, girl."

Chapter Twenty-Four

Nothing was happening the way Ell had wanted. He had been here for weeks now. In and out of the city, from Dark Harbor to the cave, to report on his failings to his family and then back again. Their impatience was growing. Rihya was not the only one lacking the desire to continue waiting. Ell imagined it must be harder for them, cooped up in the cave by day, scouting the area by night. He on the other hand might be in dangerous waters, posing as something he was not while in the midst of the enemy, but at least he was doing something. Even though he had found no trace of his family, it was still better to be taking action than having to sit outside the city and wait for someone else to find them. He'd grown more accustomed to, but no more comfortable with, the enemy city.

Ell spent his mornings observing the early exodus of slaves from one barracks or another as they left to go to their places of work, chained or tied together like animals. He had looked at most of the slave quarters now, with no luck. There were only a few barracks left that he had not yet been able to check for his family. He had begun asking questions as well, questions about his family. Asking for slaves by name, however, had yielded no fruit. At best, his questions were met with confusion as to why a traitor would be looking for a particular slave by name, and at worst with hard, uncompromising stares of suspicion. He quickly learned not to ask those questions. Ell was left to hope he would catch a glimpse of someone he recognized. Dacunda had mentioned his resemblance to his father enough times over the years that Ell could only hope it was true, and that he would see someone that looked like himself. It was a thin strand of hope to cling to, but Ell was not ready to give up yet. To be so close to where his father and mother might be, after all those years of thinking them dead, only to give up and leave without exhausting all possibilities was not an option for Ell. If he finally did leave Dark Harbor, he would need to do so knowing something definitive Finding them or learning they were dead were his only options.

And so he searched. Morning and evening he waited by barracks. Day and night Ell plied more sailors and soldiers with ale and wine to loosen tongues, stealing purses to feed their appetites, but to no avail. In his small upper room at night he practiced his craft. His general Water Calling abilities came to him more often than not now, and he wondered if Arendahl had been right about his earlier anger at his elders getting in the way of tapping into his powers. That anger had abated. Whatever the reason, it was easier than it had ever been, and this encouraged Ell. He also began to practice focusing his power like the old elf had begun to teach him, which would allow him to do specific things with his abilities—like heal wounds—but so far he had struggled with that side of his ability. Often as not, he was unable to do anything other than tap his general abilities. Ell would have never thought that feeling the swell of power within himself would be frustrating—it was not long ago that simply accessing his supernatural abilities as a Water Caller would have been a significant victory—but now that he could tap those general abilities more easily, he craved the satisfaction of progress, of moving forward in his powers. He wished, rather ruefully, that Arendahl was there to train him. And that surprised him. The old elf was a stern taskmaster and Ell had spent countless hours wishing the exact opposite, that he could have a break from him. But now, over a month after parting ways, Ell realized how much credit he had to give the old elf in aiding his growth as a Water Caller. It was much harder to progress alone. And so he sat on his bed at nights or stood on the rickety, creaking floor of his room while both sleep and the ability to focus his powers evaded him.

The rest of his time, Ell spent trying to concoct a plan on how to remove slaves from Dark Harbor should his luck change and he find his enslaved family members. But as of yet, he was just as stuck as he had been before. He saw no way to not only free slaves but also get them out of the city and especially out through a Hillfort without raising alarm.

It was early morning and Ell had left the inn as dawn's grey light was just creeping over the city. Dark Harbor was still mired in the serene stillness that overhangs a city just before it awakens. In the empty morning streets, Ell could almost imagine that it was a city like any other, that it wasn't the bane of his people's existence. The scent of baking breads floated out of windows as elves began their morning food preparations. Soon enough however, Dark Harbor sprang to life. Ell was wandering into the center of the city, deep into its heart to observe the morning comings and goings of a particular slave quarters, which he had not seen yet. As he walked, people began emerging from houses, and the streets were soon clogged. It reminded him of a time when he had seen an anthill wake and the insects boil out of its many holes in the dirt, such were the inhabitants of Dark Harbor now.

The last bit of darkness of the night was banished by the time he reached the inner heart of the city, yet the overhanging nature of Dark Harbor and its vertical and ramshackle construction ensured that shadows remained everywhere. The streets were fully cobbled here, and the buildings began to look bright and burnished as he moved further inward. There was a statuesque feel to the heart of Dark Harbor, a menacing presence as if a sleeping monster was about to wake. Ell couldn't say why he felt that way exactly but perhaps it was because he had spent too much time now in the city to see it in a completely one dimensional light. Spend enough time in the waterfront district and any fool could see that people were hurting. Elves fell sick and died regularly, many were thinner and leaner than they should be. Ell had been forced to admit that not every person in this city was his enemy, not every southern elf was to be feared and hated as he once had thought. In fact, many of these elves could be quite pitiable. Yet, here in the center of the city—where nobles lived in luxury, where palaces abounded and Half-Mask reigned from his throne—the beating heart of Dark Harbor was apparent. It was from here that the darkness infecting his land took root and spread.

Ell remembered his encounter with the noble and his body guards in his early days in the island city and he strode carefully, keeping his eyes open and his wits about him. The streets rose as the city swelled onto a hill and Ell felt the familiar comforting sensation of a slight added resistance to his walking as he climbed. It was the warmth of his muscles loosening with minor exertion after a night's sleep on a cramped bed.

As he moved deeper into wealthier territory, gargoyles began adorning small palaces, hanging over gates and doors or monitoring the corners of rooftops in stony silence. The carvings had many forms. Stone sea monsters and flying beasts were common. Ell even saw a few stone Icari and shuddered compulsively at the sight of even a statue of the winged demons that plagued the north.

He was almost to the slave barracks when he slowed his gait, searching for a good vantage point from which to observe the slaves leaving for their morning work. Hood already pulled up to obscure as much of his fair-skinned face as possible, he slunk into a shadowy corner, under an overhanging building. It was not long before a troop of slaves shambled out of the squat windowless building, chained together. No one in the group looked familiar in any way. They walked slowly but steadily away, the clinking of their metal shackles sending a chilling note into the morning air. There would be a few more bands of slaves from this barracks—there were usually at least three or four chain gangs per building. Ell waited while the second and the third proceeded out of the barracks and off in one direction or another to find the location of their work.

The fourth group of slaves was tied together by rough ropes around the neck. They shuffled out slowly obeying the crack of the slaver's whip giving them unspoken directions. Strangely, the slaver seemed to have forgotten something inside and he ducked back through the darkened doorway into the murky interior of the slave quarters. He did not reappear immediately but the slaves stood perfectly still anyway, trained not to disobey their new masters. Heads hung low and eyes trailed the ground, but despite the apparent lack of confidence, not all the slaves had succumbed to submission. A few flickering glances of fiery pride and resolve still existed on some of the faces of his downtrodden people, yet they kept their emotions in check.

One of the male elves with a hint of fire still left in his face raised his head. Ell stepped forward out of the shadows and pulled the hood off his own head subconsciously so as to see better. The fiery elf, caught Ell's movement out of the corner of his eye and instinctively surveyed the scene with the remnants of a warrior's mentality, despite the chains holding him in place. Ell took a few more steps forward and their eyes met.

It was an instant of absolute recognition. Ell had never seen this elf before but it was as if he was looking in a mirror that added a few decades. Dacunda had not been lying. He was the spitting image of his father, for there was no possible explanation for such physical similarity. Sapphire eyes, wavy blond hair, facial features elegant and beautiful like Ell's, if slightly more gaunt and worn from his captivity.

Ell could see the recognition in his father's face also. Adan's shocked expression spoke louder than words and attested to his father's recognition of Ell as his son. All the moments of pain as a child, all the bitter anger and fighting he had endured since, all the time spent scouring this city while his family sat impatiently in a cave evaporated, and Ell felt a wholeness he had not known he was missing seep into his soul. This was his father. His father! Ell savored the sweetness of the moment.

Their eyes still locked across the few yards of space separating them. Only a few seconds had passed since their mutual recognition but it had felt an eternity. Ell opened his mouth to speak, a smile forming, but the words froze in his mouth. Recovering from his shock, Ell's father, Adan, shot Ell a look filled with such disgust and loathing that Ell physically recoiled. Ell felt himself shrink, perhaps not physically but in every other sense of the word. Nothing could have prepared Ell for the pain he felt in that instant. Adan looked at him with scathing revulsion for a moment longer and then turned his face away and resolutely ignored him.

The slave master returned from inside the building and soon after the clinking of manacles sounded as the slaves began their shuffling march away from the barracks. Ell stood in a new kind of shock, the sun playing a false warmth on his skin, a warmth that could do nothing to match the icy shame clutching his gut. If he had eaten breakfast this morning Ell might have vomited up the meal, so sickened was he by the sight of his father's disgust. His stomach turned in upon itself.

What could make his father react that way? Ell wracked his brain, but nothing stood out. That he had recognized him, that they had recognized each other even after decades of separation, was clear by the shock on their faces. His father's disdain especially signified his recognition that Ell was his son. One could only feel that level of revulsion for something in which one was emotionally invested somehow.

Ell stood in the stillness of the morning, the world, the city seemed to have frozen around him in the minutes since his father's departure. Perhaps it was just a quiet moment in Dark Harbor, or maybe Ell simply lost all sense and ability to perceive the environment around him. Either way, Ell stumbled numbly back towards the waterfront, the sights and sounds of the city lost to him. Shame piled upon him as he walked. It might have taken him an hour or a minute to return to the wharf, so lost was he in his painful detachment.

When finally he reached the inn, he strode inside, climbed the stairs and sequestered himself in his rickety little room. The relief of tears finally released and Ell felt the wetness running down his face, thawing the numbness in which he was mired.

It had all been for nothing. He had finally found his father, after all these years, and so many desperate days searching. Ell had finally found his father.

And his father hated him.

Chapter Twenty-Five

Ell wasn't certain how long he sat on the wooden floor, arms curled around his knees. It might have been only a few minutes, or a lifetime. The moment, the pain of his father's rejections seemed all encompassing, so much more important than simple definitions of time.

When finally he felt the pain ebb, just slightly, it was like a fog lifted. Ell began thinking, really thinking for the first time since he had witnessed his father shuffle away in chains. Questions began to arise once more. Why had his father reacted that way? What possible reason could there be for such a betrayal? Ell stood and felt the anger brewing in his chest, enough rage to quench the painful numbness that he had been feeling. Ell struck out violently, his fists finding the wall. The timbers of the rundown, waterfront inn shivered and creaked beneath his wrath. Ell almost drew upon his Water Calling abilities but at the last moment he stopped short, knowing that if he gave in and lost himself in the power he possessed that the room was likely to wind up shredded beyond repair. That kind of attention would only be bad for him, an impostor and someone who was better suited to avoiding notice.

Ell looked at a few bloody scrapes on his knuckles from striking the wall. He walked over to the washbasin, which was still filled with tepid water, left over from the morning's wash. Ell stared down blankly for a moment, almost giving in to the terrible numbing pain again, hands poised just above the water waiting for the plunge. But then something caught his eye. Red tears tattooed upon his cheeks surprised him out of his pain. He had almost forgotten his disguise as a traitor.

Realization crashed down on him and everything made sense allowing a weight to lift off his heart and chest. Ell could have leapt and danced for joy, but instead he just smiled and stuck his hands into the water as he began to wash them clean, even whistling an old Andalayan melody.

It was clear now why his father had responded in such a manner to the sight of his grown son. What respectable member of the Highest wouldn't feel shame at the sight of their flesh and blood appearing as a traitor—especially an elf who was enslaved and persecuted by them. Ell's father, Adan, had surely recognized Ell as his kin, but he had no way of knowing that the tattoos on Ell's cheeks were not only a ruse, but in fact a subterfuge with the specific purpose of bringing about his freedom. Ell felt the urge to laugh. All he had to do was explain himself. Tell his father the truth and all would be well, he knew it would be so. It had to be.

Ell looked out the window and saw that it was early afternoon. Another few hours and the work gang would be brought back to the slave quarters. He could try and make contact again with his father then. But perhaps it would be better to wait and follow him to his work site tomorrow. It might be easier to catch a solitary moment there. At the very least, a little bit of reconnaissance wouldn't hurt. Tomorrow it was. Tomorrow, Ell would reach out to his father and this time he would explain himself. He would make his father see the truth.

Mind made up that tomorrow would be the day, Ell decided it was time to eat. He hadn't put a single thing into his stomach all day and he realized that he felt famished. He stepped lightly down the rickety stairs to the common room on the ground floor and ordered a plate of food from the kitchen. He handed over a few coins, enough for a leg of bird—some fowl they called a chicken— and a small bowl of fishy stew. Ell ate it more quickly than he would have imagined, spooning piping hot mouthfuls down his throat as if his life depended on it. Finished eating, he decided it might be a good idea to continue gathering information. No place was better for that than the tavern next door—The Sea Witch.

Ell thanked the swarthy serving girl for his meal, even though her face was as sour and untrusting as any in Dark Harbor when confronted with a northern elf. He stood and exited the inn and walked lightly over to the tavern. People had become accustomed to seeing him in The Sea Witch over the last few weeks. Ell bought himself a fiery ale and enjoyed the cooling prickle of sweat that the drink brought to his forehead. It was autumn, and the weather was gradually cooling, but it was still much hotter than to what he was accustomed. He had learned that spicy foods were a staple in the south for just that reason— they elicited sweat and cooled the person down who was eating. Spicy drinks were no different.

Ell sat at a corner table, his back to the wall so he could keep an eye on the entire room. He might be slightly more comfortable here in The Sea Witch than other places in Dark Harbor, but old habits died hard. It was best to keep your enemies in full view.

He took another swallow of the ale and allowed the fiery sensation to slip down his gullet.

"Northerner!" It was the first greeting Ell had heard in Dark Harbor that he could even remotely classify as friendly. His eyes followed the sound to its source.

"Rimmer," Ell lifted his mug of ale in greeting, inclining his head to Captain Piripeos, the elf captain who hailed from the Outer Rim. Piripeos waved him over to his table, and Ell graciously accepted.

"I did not know you frequented these parts," the captain said. He was one of the shorter elves Ell had ever seen, his fully shaven head and piercings also making him stand out from the warrior caste in the tavern.

Ell almost smiled. "There is much we do not know of one another," he answered.

"True." The Rimmer finished his tankard of ale with one long pull and then waved over the serving girl to order a round of barley draughts for the both of them. Ell sipped his ale as they waited for the draughts to arrive. When the drinks came, he raised the small glass filled with smoky brown liquid and held eye contact with Piripeos.

"To the ficklest of all ladies, the sea!" The captain toasted, and Ell murmured his agreement, swallowing the pull of liquor and feeling its warmth burning down into his belly in familiar fashion. He had expected a toast to Half-Mask, or the King of the South. Piripeos' toast to the sea, to the wild of nature was a surprisingly pleasant way to celebrate the shared drink. Perhaps Ell could make Piripeos more than an acquaintance. Not a friend no, that was unlikely, but perhaps an ally. A plan began to form. Today seemed a day for realizations.

For a time, they spoke, of trivial topics, the heat of the autumn, the sound of the sea rocking ships against stony quays, the spring in the Outer Rim and of summer in the north. Ell told tales of Ghouls and of long gone hunts. Piripeos informed Ell of the nature of ships and the ways to predict a storm in the morning. There was an ease to their discussion, unfamiliar to Ell from his time in Dark Harbor. It almost felt like he was speaking to one of his cousins. Yet, he could never fully let down his guard. He forced himself to remember that this elf was a Departed, and for all the history of his people's subjugation to Dark Harbor, the Rimmer had still proclaimed himself loyal to the southern crown. Although, in hindsight, what else was he to have done—declaring anything else while within the confines of the city was tantamount to suicide.

As they spoke, Ell noticed the captain's eyes flicker about the tavern. He was boisterous at times and more full of laughter than most southern elves, but there remained a tense wariness to his manner. He started occasionally at sudden movements in the shadows. His surveillance was more that of a fugitive on the run than a trained warrior.

The conversation trailed off, having spent hours in discussion of many things, and Piripeos turned a keen eye upon Ell.

"You will forgive me for saying this, but you seem to be an elf with a secret." The captain spoke carefully as if he was feeling Ell out about some unknown topic.

Ell narrowed his eyes as he fired back. "If you don't mind me saying, you look like someone who is in fear for his life, half ready to leave town at a moment's notice."

Piripeos smiled crookedly. "So do you."

"I might be," Ell conceded, unsure if the admission was wise or not. But if he was to ally himself with the captain and take advantage of this contact, then he would have to take a risk at some point.

Piripeos paused and they both regarded each other for a minute or two. Ell needed to find a way out of the city. He had finally found his father, but how was he to free him and sneak him out through the heavily guarded Hillfort? It was near impossible to imagine. But liberating his father and then escaping via a faster mode of travel—perhaps by sea—could be just the plan they needed.

It was as if silent communication passed between Ell and the captain, a quiet where they both regarded the other, weighing the costs and benefits of trusting a relative stranger. Trust was a hard commodity to come by, especially in Dark Harbor. Ell could tell that Piripeos knew that and was wondering if Ell could be trusted.

The captain took a moment longer to study Ell's face before speaking again. Piripeos still spoke cryptically but Ell could hear, could feel, the weight and implication behind his words.

"I am awaiting a certain legal decision that I am likely to find unfavorable." The captain paused again, gauging Ell's response. Satisfied, he volunteered the next piece of information. Almost tentatively he spoke, slowly, as if testing the waters of their uncertain companionship. "I have a ship but no crew."

"I have a crew but no ship," Ell said with a half smile, neglecting to mention that none of his family had ever spent time as sailors.

Ell continued. "And unless my instincts are mistaken, we both have need of leaving this city in a hurry."

The captain's knowing smirk was all the answer Ell needed, despite the Rimmer's silence.

"Well?" Ell prodded.

"You see to the heart of matters, I think, Northerner. Perhaps we could be of use to one another." Their conversation was still cautious but it was growing in confidence.

"Indeed, perhaps." Ell said. They ordered more ale and spoke quietly, divulging tidbits carefully as they went until they both had a semi-clear picture of what was at stake.

Of course, Ell did not specifically say that he was a false traitor, that revelation might be too much. Yet he spoke to the captain with as much honesty as possible, telling him the basic facts: he needed to secret an elf out of the city without attracting notice, he had a crew, albeit a relatively inexperienced one, which Piripeos claimed was not a problem since he was a good enough captain to teach them the foundations of sailing without too much difficulty.

For his part, Piripeos was also honest, at least Ell believed he was. The captain was a smuggler and had run afoul of the law. He had a ship, but the cargo had been confiscated and his crew reassigned to other vessels while he awaited trial and the almost-certain sentencing. No crew would sail with Piripeos, branded a lawbreaker for all to see, so he was in need of hands to handle a ship, which was where Ell and his family came in. It was a mutually beneficial arrangement. Ell would be able to rescue his father—and possibly his mother and sister if he could find their location—and spirit him away from Dark Harbor without running into the many guards between the city and the Hillforts and beyond, while Piripeos made good an escape, leaving the city and his legal problems behind him as he embraced the life of a renegade. Apparently pirate coves and small settlements were not so unheard of the further one sailed west. Piripeos was convinced he could find some measure of safety once he was able to escape Dark Harbor.

They conversed for some time longer until they both decided that if they were to be collaborating in such a venture, then it might be best to not be seen in each other's company for hours and hours at a time. Ell took his leave of Piripeos, agreeing to meet again the following evening—albeit at a different tavern, in order to avoid the unwanted notice of consistent affiliation, given their situations. Ell left The Sea Witch and returned to the inn for another small bite of food. It was the same stew of fish and seafood that he had consumed earlier but it was still tasty.

As he ate in the silence of the near empty common room, Ell pondered how to get his uncle, cousins, and sister into the city to crew the ship for Piripeos. They could not all pose as traitors—it would be too problematic—but that didn't mean they couldn't be disguised. It would be risky, dangerous without a doubt, and much could go wrong, but Ell felt the beginnings of a plan forming. They could pose as slaves, captured Andalayans. Who in the Hillfort would say no to a new bunch of slaves being brought into the city? Maybe one more of his family could pose as a traitor—after all they only had to enter once and then make clean their escape soon after. If the sight of two traitors together set off questions in the guard's heads, at least they would be done using the Hillfort as an entry and exit point. It might work. Perhaps, Dahranian—traitors were often younger. That meant Rihya, Ryder, Dacunda, and Kalabi would have to pose as captured slaves. If something went wrong, they might actually end up in captivity. Ell felt a chill when he thought of the risk, but then he thought of his father, twenty years a slave, and he knew his family would not hesitate to take the risk.

So a plan formed to bring them in. The last part of the plan to figure out was how to free his father once he made contact. Ell wasn't sure how it would be best to make contact with him, and no immediate ideas came to mind. Without really realizing what he was doing, he found his feet leaving the inn and striking towards the interior of Dark Harbor. He passed a few canals filled with dirty water, but soon left the waterways behind as the terrain lifted and cobblestone streets carried him up hills towards the heart of the city.

Before Ell knew it, he was near his father's barracks. Dusk had come and soon the slaves would be filed back into their quarters—Ell had witnessed the routine at the many different barracks he had observed while hoping for a glimpse of his enslaved family members. The twilight deepened to purple and shadows lengthened until the light was nearly gone. Finally, the weary line of slaves shuffled into sight.

Ell was smart. He would not make contact tonight. He would wait, follow tomorrow, and make certain he got as much information as possible before initiating contact again to finalize his plans. Tonight he simply watched. He saw the dirty golden mane of his father's hair falling about the elf's weary shoulders. The shackles hampered the slave's walk and when one tripped they all nearly tumbled to the ground. The slave master swore and cracked his whip, drawing blood on the fallen slave's back. Ell watched his father reach down and help the slave to his feet. Whether it was an act of kindness or simply self-preservation in making sure he would not trip on the fallen slave and be the next to fall and be whipped, Ell wasn't sure. There was a despair in his father's face that had not been there this morning. Ell couldn't wait to contradict what he knew his father believed—that Ell was a traitor. Ell imagined what it would be like to replace that look of tired, washed out dignity with real hope and belief.

Ell watched as they entered the building, his father disappearing from sight. He prayed a good night's sleep and peace for his father and then whisked back into the night at a quick run, lithely making his way back to his temporary home at the waterfront inn.

Chapter Twenty-Six

It was a simple matter of waiting near the slave quarters the following morning until the slaves began to exit to the sound of harshly barked commands and whips cracking. In the dawn light, Ell stayed some distance back and carefully followed the slow gait of the chain gang. He stayed in the shadows and followed, keeping far enough behind so that a wandering eye would not necessarily connect him with the slaves. Ell followed through the cleaner, well-constructed streets of the city center out to the southern side of Dark Harbor. The pace was so slow it was vexing, but eventually he watched as the slaves reached their work site.

Along the south wharf was where his father and a number of other slave gangs worked. It was an excavation site, something had been knocked down and uprooted completely—a row of taverns and inns perhaps, maybe rundown housing, Ell couldn't tell since it was gone. In its place foundations were being dug for something big. Maybe a newer and larger warehouse for storing the goods of a wealthy noble or merchant prince? It didn't really matter, Ell told himself. What was important was making contact with his father.

Ell observed the slaves at their tasks. They had been unchained to work, since there was nowhere they could go without being under the supervision of slave masters, unlike within the streets of the shadowed city. Some slaves were hauling away rubble in slings on their backs or roughly made sledges. Other slaves were digging foundations or cracking through large stones that happened to be in the way of excavations. Ell scanned the mass of slaves working in the hundreds, and finally found his father. Luckily, his father was swinging a pickaxe in the corner of the site nearest to one of the streets. It should be possible for Ell to 'stroll' by and have a brief conversation since at that section of the site, the slaves working—in this case his father—were within touching distance of the cobblestoned street.

With the cries of gulls in the air and the rhythmic lapping of small harbor-waves against ship hulls and the nearby piers, Ell made his way along the street, walking idly as if he had no care or direction leading him. He sidled up along the excavation site some way away from his father, and began studying it curiously. To the glancing eye, he would appear nothing more than a curious spectator. He strode a few more steps and stopped again, studying the site. A few slaves glanced at him, but their faces hardened when they saw his tattooed cheeks. One spat in disgust and Ell strolled further along, not wanting to create a scene before he 'happened' to come close enough to exchange words with his father.

Finally, he was close enough to speak with his father. Adan Wintermoon was swinging an axe with determined despair, breaking stones in front of him wearily but without any real desire to do so quickly or efficiently. It was clear he was doing enough to avoid notice from the slave master, but not much else. Adan wore a sleeveless smock that was given to all the slaves, with a belt around the waist as it hung down over formless, brown breeches. The muscles of his arms were hard and lean, and Ell could tell his father had the type of body one acquires from years of hard toil without much food to pad your body with flesh. Every ounce of fat had been stripped away until only sinew and muscle and tendon remained. Ell inhaled and the scent of unwashed body assailed his nostrils. Whether it was his father or not, he did not know, but he doubted any of these slaves had been given water to wash for quite some time—their grimy hands and faces attested to this.

Ell watched him for a moment more, unsure of how to start, until he realized his window of time was closing as a chance spectator and he needed to make the most of it. Now or never, it was time to speak. Finally he would talk to the father he had never known.

"Adan?" Ell's voice sounded more tentative than he had intended. He kept his voice low and spoke again, this time willing more strength to his question. "Adan?"

The elf swinging the pickaxe froze for a moment, and then followed through on his swing with unusual force, splitting the stone into many pieces.

Adan turned his head and looked at Ell out of the corner of his eye. "I have nothing to say to you, traitor. Go away from here. Leave this place and me to my work." The bitterness in his father's voice sent bile threatening to surge up Ell's throat, but he forced it down. An explanation would solve this misunderstanding.

"Father," he entreated with a softer voice. "All is not what you think. Let me explain. Please."

Adan Wintermoon froze, as if hearing himself called father after decades of having left that part of himself behind was enough to stall the angry retort on his lips. Adan nodded his head jerkily that Ell could and should explain himself, while he maintained a steady swing of his tool.

Already feeling a loosening in his chest, Ell sighed with relief. He had been granted a chance to explain. The first and most important battle was over. It would be simple from here on out. Well, as simple as freeing a slave could be.

Ell gathered his words to speak and when he did, emotion colored his voice, tinged it with passion and force. "I am not a traitor, this is all a ruse," were the first words out of his mouth.

Adan's shoulders loosened and his back straightened subconsciously at that good news. But he did not seem willing to trust Ell completely yet. "You bear the tears," he questioned softly, glancing at the red Traitor's Tears stained onto Ell's cheeks."

Ell responded, voice thick with relief and the need to remain hushed. "Fake, just like the rest of this deception. I needed to walk the streets of Dark Harbor unquestioned, and this was the only way to do so. They are temporary, the tattoos will fade with time, and so, I hope, will your shame for your son."

Adan stayed silent, but Ell could see his countenance softening. It was not soft, no elf could manage that after surviving two decades of slavery, but it was not the hard mask his father had worn at first.

"Why?" His father got straight to the point. "If all this is true, you must not spend too much time near me. It will draw suspicion on you and a painful punishment for me."

"It is all for you, Father. I came for you, to get you out, to rescue you. And for Mother and my sister, if they are still among the living."

As Adan swung the axe, Ell watched as a mingled look of fierce pride and sorrow and fear skittered across his father's face.

Adan spoke softly but forcefully. "You should not have come. It was brave of you, undoubtedly, I do not doubt your courage. But it was foolhardy to come here. Leave now while you still can!" His father's urgings carried a hint of desperation.

"No," Ell responded resolutely, unconsciously grasping the hilt of one of his dueling daggers in a reflex born of a fighter's existence. In the face of fear and terrible odds a warrior had to dig deep and resist, trusting upon his strength of will and strength of arms to carry him. Ell's daggers had carried him for many years.

"You should not have come!" Adan Wintermoon barked again in frustration. "My brother should never have told you of my fate." Adan turned a pleading look on Ell. "Please, Son, I could not bear it if you were caught and suffered what I have suffered all these years. Go now, Elliyar, while you still can."

It was the first time Ell had ever been called son, and it resulted in the opposite effect his father had hoped. Adan's desperate imploring of Ell to abandon him and save himself was brushed aside by the fierce love Ell suddenly felt rushing into his body. There was absolutely no question of leaving his father behind. None whatsoever. He would rescue his father or die. It was as simple as that.

His face must have mirrored his internal emotions as he saw his father's head fall and Adan shake his head with weariness and fear.

"I will not leave you. Believe me, I am capable of much more than you think. I have been here for weeks now and no one is the wiser of my status as an impostor."

"Dacunda gave me his oath that if I were ever captured he would tell you I was dead. He should have kept that promise." Adan mumbled.

Ell felt a sudden surge of empathy for what he had put his uncle through these past months. All the anger he had felt towards Dacunda evaporated. His uncle had only been following through on a final promise made to his elder brother. He could not fault him for that loyalty.

"He didn't tell me," Ell said compassionately. "Dacunda kept his promise, he never betrayed your trust."

"How did you find out?" Adan asked dully, seemingly in some mixture of shock and still weighted down by the fear that Ell's being in Dark Harbor would lead to his son's demise.

"Silverfist."

Adan's eyes blazed at that name with a ferocity Ell had not seen since meeting him. The old warrior, the guardian of the walls of Verdantihya, was apparent for a moment.

"That traitorous bastard!" Adan spat, the pickaxe coming down harder on the word.

Ell murmured his agreement, then waited for his father to speak again.

Adan collected himself from his anger, swung his pickaxe, and seemed to regroup and recover from some of the shock and fear at Ell's presence in his curiosity to hear the full story of how Ell had arrived in Dark Harbor.

"Why would Silverfist tell you of my fate? Why were you speaking with him?" His father's voice hardened with accusation as he spoke his second question.

"He used information about you, about my family, as a bargaining chip while he was pleading for his life," Ell stated matter-of-factly.

"He is dead, then, Silverfist?" The eagerness in Adan's voice made Ell glad to be able to convey the next piece of information.

"Yes," Ell answered.

"Who did it?" Adan asked curiously.

"I did." The flat tone Ell used startled Adan. There was no pride nor joy in Ell's voice, only the calm, cold resolution of a Water Caller protecting and defending his people.

"You..." Adan murmured wonderingly. Then Ell's father snapped out of his surprise. "You should not have faced him, he could have killed you. Silverfist was ever wily and beyond dangerous even before betraying us, and only more so after."

Ell smiled at his father's concern. It was strange to experience it after so many years. "It was a close fight, Father, but I am stronger than you think. Much stronger." Ell emphasized the last bit and Adan glanced at him curiously, but Ell did not venture anything further.

"So it seems, so it seems," Adan Wintermoon said, a hint of wonder once again in his voice. Adan seemed lost for a moment in thought, as he swung his pickaxe, the tool rising and falling with a slow but steady rhythm.

Ell allowed his father a moment of quiet contemplation before finally asking the question that had been burning in his mind for some time now.

"Father," he began tentatively, "what of my... mother? And my sister?" It still felt strange to speak of people he had never known as if they were familiar.

Sorrow flashed across his father's face and stayed there, a mask of pain born from the horrors of this evil city and its terrible practices. Adan shook his head.

Grief flooded through Ell. Pain that he had not expected to experience. It was as if finding his father had birthed a hope in him for something greater something even more spectacular than he had ever dared hope for—his family whole and together again. It was not to be so, it seemed. Ell controlled his emotions and focused on being grateful his father was still alive. One parent returned from the dead was more than anyone could hope for.

"I see," was all Ell could muster in response. He wanted to console his father, as he watched a deep grief play across his face, but Ell could not find the words. They stood in silence for a moment until Adan jerked his head up slightly in alarm. Ell followed his gaze and saw that a slave master was watching them with suspicion.

"We have spoken too long," Adan said. "You must strike me now. Hard."

Ell shook his head. He did not want to harm his father.

"You must!" Adan declared with an authority Ell obeyed compulsively. "Interactions between slaves and traitors are not friendly. We despise them and they us. You must strike me, as if I said something offensive and you are punishing me for it. If you do not, then you will be looked upon with suspicion and I will be punished much worse for speaking when I should be working."

Ell gathered his strength and struck Adan Wintermoon across the jaw with as much force as he could make himself use. He did not tap his powers to do so, he did not want to injure his father, but neither did Ell hold back. He did not want his father punished worse for speaking with him.

The blow rocked Adan and sent him to his knees painfully. Adan had a slightly glazed look in his eyes.

"Never speak to me in such a tone again, you filthy mongrel!" Ell shouted violently, and the slave master smirked at the interaction. The ruse seemed to have worked as the slave master cracked his whip at another slave and his attention went to other matters.

Whispering Ell spoke to his father in parting. "I must go. You were right, I have tarried too long in conversation with you. Look for me in the coming days. Hold on to hope, I will free you, Father!" And with that Ell strode away resolutely, willing himself not to look back to make sure that his father had risen from his knees to return to his work. Ell trusted his father's strength. Twenty years a slave meant he must have plenty of spirit to have survived that long. A blow from Ell would not be enough to keep him down for long.

Ell vanished away from the prying eyes of slave masters and slaves at the worksite, making his way north through the rabbit warren of streets and muddy canals of the city. He needed to get to the north causeway and out to the cave to tell his family of these most recent developments. His plans were finally coming together. It would not be long before the final phase of the escape began.

* * * *

It was only a couple hours of hard running to cross the city and then proceed across the causeway, up the range and out through the Hillfort gate. Ell reached the cave just after midday, and although he was eager to report his news, especially to his sister, he knew it would have to be a short visit. Ell had made plans yesterday to meet again with Piripeos this evening at The Sea Witch and it would not be good to miss such an appointment.

Once again, his family was not surprised to find him at their entrance, today's lookout—Rihya—had given fair warning from the tiny crevice opening. There was the usual clapping of shoulders, clasping of forearms, and inquiries about each other's health. Ell did his best to be polite but he was bursting with desire to speak his news.

"I found him," he stated plainly, without preamble, after finally wading through the niceties of seeing his family for the first time in days.

"Adan?" Dacunda asked, dumbfounded, as though he had never really dared to hope that his older brother could really be alive after all these years.

Ell nodded his affirmation. He noticed a brief look of jealousy flicker across his sister's face, but it was quickly suppressed. It would have been hard for her to wait so long and patiently outside the city and away from the action.

"Was he… well?" Dacunda queried, a half wistful face of regret now replacing his surprise.

"As well as can be expected after decades of enslavement," Ell responded, a little more harshly than he had intended, and Dacunda recoiled slightly under the words. Ell softened his tone. "He was angry with you for allowing me to come, Uncle. You did right all those years in keeping me away, keeping it secret. At least, in his mind you did."

Ell saw the expression of relief flood his uncle's face and it was almost pitiable. A tear rolled down Dacunda's cheek.

"My brother always was brave. He would have rather bore any torture than have you enslaved on his behalf. We must make sure this escape goes off without a hitch, else I fear my brother may never forgive me."

"We will, Uncle. Do not fear." Ell flashed a confident grin at Dacunda. Everything was going to be fine, he felt it deep down in his bones. It had to be. After all this time, it would be too cruel to come this far and find his father, only for events to transpire that denied his freedom and theirs at the last.

Dacunda nodded his agreement and wiped away the tear, a smile replacing his worry. His brother was alive.

"What of Mother? And Delle, our sister?" Rihya asked quietly. Ell had forgotten that being a few years his elder, she might have memories of them. Ell had been but a babe when they were killed—taken. Rihya, on the other hand, perhaps, still bore some fleeting remembrance of their love and care, immortalized in her memory.

Ell shook his head sadly. "Be glad we can get our father back, Rihya. It is almost beyond believable that even this much is within the realm of possibility."

Rihya smiled wanly. "It would have been nice to hear her voice, or…" She trailed off in a small voice, sounding unusually vulnerable. "But I suppose…" She did not finish her sentence. Ell felt a wave of protectiveness for his strong, fiery sister.

"We'll rescue him and become a family again—well even more of a family than we already are," Ell amended, with a familiar and grateful smile towards his uncle and cousins.

"Yes, of course. It will be amazing to see Father after all these years." Rihya's voice gained confidence and strength and a glad smile played upon her lips. "You had best not try to hog all the glory for this rescue, little brother. You should know I was always his favorite and I won't have that changing." She winked playfully and jabbed an elbow in his ribs. She had recovered from the old, but newly recognized grief at having lost the women of her family all over again.

"Ha!" Ell jested back. "We shall see about that."

"I am happy for you, Elliyar, and you, Valerihya. It is a joyous occasion to be reunited with family. After so long, it will soon be upon you." Kalabi volunteered his quiet congratulations after hanging in the background for much of the discussion. Ell clasped his forearm warmly in thanks.

Everyone began clamoring with plan of escape, asking for information about the city and overlapping each other, getting louder and louder. "I cannot stay long. I have a contact in the city with whom I must meet who is integral to our escape plan," Ell declared.

The others perked up even more, eager for more information and Ell relayed to them his plan to sneak them into the city posing as slaves and then loose them from their bonds under the cover of darkness. Then the next evening, they would free his father somehow—he hadn't sorted out the details completely yet—that would come more as he spoke again with Piripeos and also with his father—but once free they would strike out for the captain's ship and sail out of the harbor with no one the wiser. What was one more ship leaving the port compared to the magnitude of vessels coming and going every day?

Everyone agreed with the legitimacy of his basic plan, although his uncle questioned the trustworthiness of Captain Piripeos. Ell trusted the captain more than he could anyone else in the city, and Dacunda was forced to agree that trying to escape back out through the Hillfort with slaves was out of the question. Ell decided that they would sneak his family into the city in three days' time. They would be entering as slaves, and unable to bear arms. Sailing out of the city meant they would not be stopping by this cave again. That meant that Ell would need to make a number of trips to the cave and back to the city in the following three days to be able to carry in a few extra weapons each time and stash them in his room without notice. What was one or two extra weapons on his back to be noticed when compared with the bow, arrows, and assortment of knives and daggers that he already bore? Weapons in place, he would sneak his family in and rearm them in time to help free his father and commandeer Piripeos' ship.

Kalabi further calmed Ell by informing him that they had been using their time well out here on the mountain. By night they had been scouting and surveying the area and helping Kalabi gather the ingredients to make more handfire. Ell was thrilled to know that they had a small sack full of the deadly weapons at their disposal should they need them. He thanked the industrious ex-slave with a firm grin. Things were definitely looking up.

It had been a short but happy few hours with his family, relaying the exciting news and celebrating the survival of his father. However, it was not long before Ell knew he must strike out once more. He bid his farewells and left for the city and for his meeting with Captain Piripeos. Ryder's axe, a knife of Rihya's, and the sack of Kalabi's handfire were not heavy enough to weigh down his good spirits. He ran lightly, almost effortlessly despite the added weight, and reached the city as evening was falling, just in time to collaborate once more with the slick and furtive Captain Piripeos.

Chapter Twenty-Seven

Ell dropped off the excess weapons in his room at the inn and then met Piripeos in a tavern on the eastern side of the island. It was a brief meeting, in which Ell gave him a few details of the plan. They both wanted out of the city, but Ell was not about to leave immediately. It would take a few days to move all of the weapons, and eventually his family, into the city unnoticed. He told Piripeos to be patient, and with some reluctance, the captain agreed to wait the few days Ell needed to complete his plan for leaving Dark Harbor.

They took leave of one another with a rather friendly clasp of the forearm and set up one final meeting to take place three nights from now, as a last moment to finalize any details of their escape plan. Piripeos was his usual self as he left the tavern ahead of Ell, casting frequent glances at his surroundings and over his shoulder. Ell had never pressed him on what Piripeos had originally referred to as a legal decision, but he believed the captain when Piripeos stated dolefully that if he wasn't out of the city soon then he was likely to never leave at all. Ell promised him that they would be gone just as soon as everything was in place.

They departed from the tavern, separating into the jagged, moon-shadowed streets of Dark Harbor. Ell slipped quickly and quietly back across the active night streets of the city until he reached the inn on the north side and his small room within. A good night's sleep was just what he needed.

Ell awoke the following morning and made his way to the work site on the southern side of the city where Adan toiled. He arrived early and was waiting some minutes before the prisoners shuffled in, chained together, and then were loosed to begin their excavation and foundation work. Ell ambled idly up to the portion of the site that abutted the street and spoke in a whisper, barely audible over the ringing of picks and shovels against stone and earth.

Ell told his father to be ready to move in three days' time. They would come at night, break into his slave barracks, and then flee on the Piripeos' ship. Much could go wrong, but it was the best plan they had. Adan agreed and promised he would be ready. Ell didn't want to linger long, not wanting to draw suspicion soon before their plan would commence, so he took his leave of his father quickly, leaving him to the drudgery of his slave labor. Yet Ell found solace in the gleam of hope that was suddenly to be seen in his father's eyes as Ell took his leave. Ell understood. Twenty years a slave would rob anyone of hope. Despair was the only natural response. It was a wonder his father had even survived the soul crushing desperation of waking up every day under the power of your enemy. Soon, it would be done. Soon, Ell would gather his father and bring Adan home to the north, to Andalaya, where he belonged. The thought gave him more satisfaction and anticipation than he could ever have imagined.

The next few days were restless and Ell's impatience nearly wore out, thin as it already was. He made a trip each day, through the Hillfort and to the cave, returning with a few extra weapons each time, but not enough to attract the notice of the fortress guards, and soon his little upper room at the inn was littered with steel and blades. The only thing missing now was his family on the outer slopes of the coastal range. They would follow soon. It was only a matter of sneaking them in as slaves this evening with the cover of darkness.

At midday of the second to last day, Ell met with Piripeos again. This time they found a table in The Sea Witch.

"Everything ready?" Captain Piripeos asked gruffly, shrewd, narrow eyes gauging his newfound partner in crime.

"So far, all is well," Ell responded comfortably. "This evening, I'll collect my crew, and we'll take our leave just before dawn tomorrow. Will you be ready at the south wharf?" Piripeos had given Ell directions to the wharf and the ship they would be taking to depart.

The captain nodded. All was well. Everything was about to come off without a hitch. As that positive thought formed in Ell's mind, a flicker of movement darted out the front door of the tavern and Ell's gaze was drawn to the body leaving. At the last moment, the departing elf glanced back, as if to reassure himself of what he had seen and Ell locked eyes with the traitor for a moment.

Ell was shocked, stunned even, to see the traitor Borian frozen in the doorway sharing his gaze. Why Ell should be surprised to see the elf from Little Vale—the traitor who had betrayed Miri and all their village to Silverfist last spring—he was not sure. Borian was a traitor now—the sides of his head shaven, the tears of blood tattooed on his cheeks, even his upper teeth filed—of course he would have free run of the city, the same as Ell had experienced these few weeks spent searching for his father in Dark Harbor. Yet, it was a shock nonetheless. He felt a hatred for the traitor that surpassed almost any he had felt since killing Silverfist. Ell and Borian had come to blows before, with the now-traitor receiving the wrong end of Ell's supernaturally enhanced fists. There was certainly no love lost between them, and especially none since they were now on opposing sides of the war. Once a traitor, always a traitor—there was no going back for Borian now.

As if seeing the hatred etched in every line and curve of Ell's face was enough to restart his prior movement, Borian seemed to be shaken from the frozen moment created by their locked gaze. In a flash he was out the door and gone. Disappearing with the whirl of a black cloak.

"Never mind what I just said, Piripeos. We leave as soon as possible. Can you be ready by this evening and waiting at the ship?" Ell asked the captain hurriedly.

Piripeos bit his lip, pondering. "Is it best to leave while there is still light? Our plan was to secret away in the dark of early morning with none the wiser."

"I don't have time to explain, but I fear I may have been recognized." Ell had never fully explained his situation as an impostor, and Piripeos' eyes narrowed in worry and confusion accordingly.

Ell continued, "You must trust me. If you wish to use me and my people to crew your ship, then I advise we leave as soon as possible. If the elf I just saw carries word of me to the wrong ears we may not last through the night."

"Fine," the short Rimmer muttered. "I'm risking my neck for your safety, though, and don't you forget it."

"And I for yours!" Ell fired back in frustration, chafing at the time this was taking. "You need me and mine as much as we need you." The captain grumbled some sort of non-committal agreement.

"The ship. Early evening, before twilight truly falls." Ell confirmed with a full confident voice.

"I'll be there." Captain Piripeos said.

With that settled, Ell dashed to the door of the tavern, hoping for a glimpse of Borian's retreating form, but it was a hopeless wish to spot one particular elf amidst the sea of hooded black cloaks. He would like to find and silence the traitor, but that did not appear to be possible. Ell felt a keen sense of worry. Who would Borian tell? What would this mean for the mission?

Ell had to move his timetable up, sneaking his family in at night wouldn't work now, they would have to pose as slaves by day entrance. It could still work. Ell reworked the plan in his head. There wasn't time to wait until the dark stillness of early morning to free his father from the barracks. They would have to free him from the site at evening, a much more dangerous endeavor, but necessary due to Borian's arrival and his recognition of Ell. Adan would need to be warned, to be prepared for what was about to happen. But should Ell first warn him or first smuggle his family into Dark Harbor as slaves?

Settling on warning his father of the changes first, Ell set off at a near sprint, covering the distance to the south side of the port in record time, and reaching the work site breathing hard. Ell found his father and with less subterfuge than usual made his way near to Adan's position.

"What are you doing here?" Adan asked sharply.

"Plans have changed Father, be ready to fight your way clear this evening."

"Are you mad, Elliyar? We cannot hope to escape notice if we fight our way to freedom if the fading light of day still illuminates our actions."

Ell shook his head in frustration. Not at his father's disagreement, but at the truth of it. If this was what leadership really was—making split decisions on a moment's notice whenever something went awry—then he was not sure he enjoyed it. He knew the original plan was better. Leaving at night meant less chance of being noticed. Yet, something in his gut told him that even a few hours delay would mean his escape plans would be thwarted. Ell had always trusted his instincts.

"There is no time to waste, Father. It must be soon. Be ready." Without waiting for any more disputation, Ell left, leaving his father in the dusty air of the work site. Ell prayed everything would work, that the new and improvised plan was not too ludicrous to employ. A part of him worried that it was. Fighting their way out of Dark Harbor did sound insane, but fortunately the site of Adan's labor was near the wharf where Piripeos' ship was, so it would be a short trip from one to the other. Hopefully, they could free Ell's father and, in the chaos of the moment, slip into the crowded streets and make their way to the ship without anyone the wiser. Ell grimaced. It was a far from a perfect plan now. It was fraught with ifs and hopeful desires, imprudently lax of planning and certainty. Ell cursed his luck and fate, for bringing Borian across his path at the worst possible moment.

Ell ran north through the tangled warren of Dark Harbor, crossing a few dirty, smelly canals until he entered the cleaner heart of the city. Although to call the interior of Dark Harbor clean was a bit inaccurate. Aesthetically, it was more pleasing and less grimy than the waterfront districts, but there was a sinister feel to the heart of Dark Harbor, as if it were the ugly heart of some giant spidery beast. Ell ran on, entertaining his dark thoughts and worries.

Ell rounded a corner and skidded to a halt. His luck had gone from bad to worse. The face he dreaded seeing was at the end of the alley into which he had just entered. Borian's face was lit with a vengeful glee, and Ell almost charged him to begin the fight until he saw the forms of a shadowy troupe behind the traitor. Ell paused, pondering his options for the moment. Running would likely not accomplish anything—they had already seen him and he was unlikely to shake their pursuit in time to accomplish all that he needed. Fight, then. That was the only option left to him. Ell tensed his muscled, coiling in upon himself like a snake waiting to strike. He surged his mind, pushed his consciousness out, and felt the depth of the moisture in this humid southern air and the powerful and incessant lapping of the waves and the swells in the harbor surrounding him. Ell tapped into the land, to Creation, as only a Water Caller could do. Ell accessed his powers and felt the familiar well of energy of power within his chest. He felt strength radiate from his core out through his limbs and fingers and into every muscle and tendon of his body. A cloudiness entered his eyes and his vision, making it harder to see, yet everything was clearer. Mist dewed up along his drawn blades and clung to the air around him. He was a Water Caller and he was about to teach this traitor and this pack of enemy dogs a lesson.

* * * *

Ell was about to close the distance and attack when he realized with the stirrings of anxiety that Borian was not in charge. A dark cloaked shape almost seemed to glide to the front from within the pack of enemy warriors. The shape stepped to the fore and then walked a few yards towards Ell in the alley before stopping. Whoever it was stood arrogantly and unafraid. Ell felt his instincts kick in. Without a shadow of a doubt, he knew that this person was to be feared—perhaps more than anyone else in the world. How Ell knew, he wasn't sure, but something made him certain it was so. A pungent whiff of the Bonewinds swirling through the alley set his nerves on edge even more. An Unsired? But Ell had faced the Unsired before and not felt this dread.

Ell made himself take a few steps forward as well, to appear unafraid. Predators could sense fear and every nerve in his body was screaming to him that the dark figure ahead was a predator indeed. Ell relaxed his body and made himself continue walking. The hooded figure did the same and they reached the center point of the shadowy alley, the light of day mostly obscured by the overhanging structures of Dark Harbor.

Stopping a safe distance from the dangerous foe, Ell readied himself for whatever would come next. The hooded figure pulled down his hood and Ell saw a Departed by all regards—shaven sided head, loose war braid down the back, swarthy skin, and packed muscles. The only difference was the sleek, black, form-fitting mask crafted to cover the left side of his face from forehead to jaw. Until he smiled, then more differences became apparent. The Departed's mouth was grotesque. The upper and lower teeth had been filed far beyond what the average southern elf underwent. The teeth were filed to needle points like some ghoulish fish from the deep, and when the cloaked figure smiled his dark eyes lit with a sinister gleam that was complimented by the ghastly mouth beneath.

"Who are you?" Ell found himself asking, almost compulsively.

The dark figure maintained his satisfied, confident smile. "I am Half-Mask."

Of course. Everything clicked into place in Ell's mind. This elf was an Unsired—or possibly something more, something worse? The small voice in Ell's mind murmured the question, as the sense of dread Ell felt was only growing.

"And you are Wintermoon, Elliyar Wintermoon, the boy from the north who slew Silverfist." Half-Mask practically purred, as if savoring the taste of his words.

"How did you know that?" Ell asked, then instantly regretted the stupid question. Borian was there, of course he knew Ell's name.

"Word of your...exploits has traveled." Half-Mask conceded indulgently, the way a relative would to a child hungry for praise. "Your adventures are but scratching at the surface of what some of us are capable of." Half-Mask left no doubt in Ell's mind as to who the Prince meant by 'some of us'. Half-Mask was clearly alluding to whatever sinister abilities he possessed. Ell was now more convinced than ever that the leader of Dark Harbor was indeed something more than an Unsired.

Half-Mask continued as he strolled a leisurely circle around Ell, as if for all the world Ell was nothing more than a curiosity, not something of which to be wary. "However, your small gains have nevertheless been a trial to me—to my plans. The much lamented Silverfist was... necessary to a few of my undertakings." His tone was edged now, silk tempered with hot, angry steel.

Ell retorted with as much insolence as possible. "Glad to hear that. Especially since I haven't gone out of my way to thwart any of your plans. Imagine what I could accomplish if I actually put my mind to it and tried."

Ell watched a flicker of anger betray Half-Mask, but then the calm, indulgent expression was back.

"You are little more than a boy, a nuisance. Nothing more. Hardly something to be feared," Half-Mask said softly, still appraising him as he circled. It was just the two of them in the alley now, apparently the soldiers of the Prince of Darkness knew better than to get in his way.

"Oh, I believe I am much more than that." The bravado in Ell's voice was only half faked. He was nervous, frightened even, but beneath that fear simmered the anger at his people's condition, and the strength and power the abilities of a Water Caller availed him.

Ell spoke on in a cool detached tone that sometimes accompanied the accessing of his powers. "Why don't we see who should really be feared."

"Yes, why don't we?" Half-Mask agreed almost, breathless with a dark excitement. Anticipation gleamed in the dark elf's eyes and Ell tensed himself, readying for the fight he knew was about to come.

Half-Mask shrugged off his cloak with a nonchalant ease and Ell started at the sudden movement. The Prince smirked at Ell's twitch and lazily drew a silvery sword from a sheath at his hip. Half-Mask twirled the sword idly as the two of them circled, ready to fight.

"Well...?" Half-Mask finally asked, after a few long moments of tense silence, each waiting for the other to make the first move.

Ell bit at the bait and lunged. He moved swiftly with all the coiled speed of a viper, a Water Caller in full force. Ell's body closed the distance and his blades arched together as he dodged in close, hoping to inflict an early wound.

He was not prepared for the swiftness with which Half-Mask countered. With ease, the Prince moved out of the way. Half-Mask blocked Ell's blades with a sweeping parry of his silvery sword and then moved forward into the attack. They tested each other, their speed creating a sparking ball of clashing blades and tempered, controlled fury. Neither giving more than an inch when possible, or a few feet whenever was necessary. Ell fought as he had never fought before, he felt his senses hone to an edge, saw the flick of water droplets descend from his slashing dueling daggers, which quivered with restrained energy in their owner's hands. Ell could feel the swell of power within him, enough to overwhelm many foes at once.

And yet, it was not enough. It was barely enough to defend himself. Half-Mask was a black ball of death, whirling in and coming close to delivering a killing blow multiple times. As it was, Ell picked up a nick on his cheek, just below his right eye. The Prince also inflicted a shallow gash on Ell's ribs and another nick to the shoulder. Try as he might, Ell only managed the tiniest of wounds on his opponent's forearm. Ell swept in close, in a flurry of blades, and managed to land a blow—somewhat luckily he had to admit—to the forearm of Half-Mask's sword arm. Half-Mask hissed in annoyance and Ell watched a thick, black blood—the blood of tainted evil, of an Unsired or worse—bead along the shallow wound.

Ell might have marked his foe, but Half-Mask recovered from his surprise and grasped Ell's own forearm and wrist in a vice-like grip. Ell immediately felt the most peculiar sensation begin to overtake his arm. Ell spun away and broke the grip, creating space and a moment to glance down at what Half-Mask had done to him. Welts had risen along the wrist, and skin was already sloughing off. It looked like the diseased skin of the bodies of the Unsired that

Ell had seen before. Ell felt with fear, the growing, pulsing, stretching of the diseased flesh as it morphed and stretched up his arm.

Half-Mask laughed, and then spoke the first words to break the ringing, deadly sound of their fight.

"It will soon be over now, Wintermoon. Your death is already upon you."

Ell indeed could feel the pulsating, sickly doom that was already spreading along his flesh. If ever there was a moment to focus, now was the time. Ell tried to remember every word spoken to him in the last training session with Arendahl. Ell focused, he focused on his power, honed his general abilities to a knife's edge, as he tried to bring about the will and power to heal. It was do or die.

Ell focused his power, willed the healing power of the land and the Source Water that was ever-present in the miniscule droplets that permeated Creation from their supernatural origin, but which only Water Callers could recognize, and embraced it. He focused his power and fought the burning of death as it tried to overwhelm his system with a plague of sorts. As Ell fought and won, he felt the healing power of a Water Caller purging the disease from his body, his flesh, saw the diseased appearance of his skin shrink and then disappear as he burned away the last of the inflicted illness. Healthy and whole, he stood ready to fight again.

Rage mottled Half-Mask's face. He snarled and his hideous mouthful of teeth looked like nothing so much as a demon ready to rend flesh. But Ell was ready, he was stronger, more capable than he knew. Had he not just demonstrated his abilities by finally succeeding in focusing his powers to heal?

Ell smirked at his foe as best he could, taking the moment's pause in the fight to catch a much needed lungful of air.

"Enough!" Half-Mask shrieked, the calm and composed individual who had started the duel seeming to have disappeared when his attempt to wither Ell's very flesh had been thwarted.

Half-Mask lunged forward to attack, his rage giving him a reckless strength. Normally, Ell would have been confident that the battle was his, an out of control enemy was a defeated enemy almost every time. Yet, somehow that was not the case here. Calm Half-Mask had been Ell's equal—perhaps even slightly his better—in combat. Their mutual powers seemed to balance each other out. But the wild and volatile Prince of Darkness that Ell now faced was fearsome to behold. Wispy smoke seemed to trail from his fingertips mingling with the misty air around Ell. Once or twice, Half-Mask flickered into a smoky insubstantial form as he fought, and his rage drove Ell back from the fiercely attacking silver sword. Ell tried to withstand the tempestuous Half-Mask, but he had just barely been the prince's equal before, it was now all Ell could do to fend for his life when faced with the ferocious attack.

Ell blocked a sweeping strike on his blades and spun away hoping the speed and agility that was his as a Water Caller could enable him to beat his foe, but Half-Mask reacted with equal swiftness. The dark elf fought with a permanent snarl on his face and a dark gleam of victory in his eyes. Ell was not the only one who could feel the tide of the fight turning. As he blocked and parried, he felt his strength begin to ebb. And then it happened.

Ell fell for a feint and with a lightning, fluid speed, Half-Mask struck. Like an adder striking its prey, Half-Mask won. His silvery sword snuck in elegantly and viciously, pinning Ell to the rough wall of the alley. Ell struggled for a moment or two but felt the life and the strength flow from him with surprising speed. The silver sword protruded from his right breast, and as Half-Mask let go of his sword in pleasure and stood back to appraise the scene, Ell pitifully attempted to grasp the hilt and pull the weapon out of his body.

Half-Mask chuckled. "Look at you, boy, scrambling and scrabbling still. Do you not see it is over?" The rage was gone, replaced again by the smug, smirking satisfaction he had possessed earlier. "Do you not see that you are no match for me?"

Ell grimaced at the taunt, but could do nothing to free himself, and his pride wouldn't let him disagree. Any retort would be a lie. Half-Mask was telling the truth. He had beaten Ell—dominated him—and there was nothing Ell could do to deny it.

Half-Mask reached forward and casually plucked the sword from his chest, the way one would pull the thorn from a palm. Ell fell forward on his face in the cobblestone street. Half-Mask rolled him over with the toe of one black leather boot.

The smirk was still there. "You are nothing," the Prince of Darkness purred, and his followers, guards perhaps, and Borian now closed in around Ell and congratulated their lord like the sycophants they were. However, Half-Mask only had eyes for Ell, his vanquished foe.

"Tsk, tsk. You should know better than to challenge your betters, boy." A glint of something in the eyes of the dark elf lord frightened Ell—terrified him even more than the death that was swiftly approaching. Half-Mask continued. "I have an idea. A splendid notion, indeed."

Half-Mask pulled a vial of something from his hip and held it up to his mouth. The dark prince took a small, delighted swig of the dark liquid and exhaled in ecstasy at the taste.

"I had thought to kill you, Wintermoon. But now, having seen you and how pitifully weak you really are, I think this will be ever so much more fun." Dark glee tempered the prince's face. Instead of stoppering the vial, Half-Mask crouched down and loomed over Ell, holding the tiny flask in his hand. He hovered over Ell, pouring a few drops of the dark liquid into Ell's various wounds. A few drops in the nick below Ell's eye, another few along the shallow gash on his ribs, and then a larger amount into the bleeding hole in Ell's chest.

Life was seeping out of his body, and on the cusp of death, Ell felt a fiery burning as the dark liquid penetrated his body. He screamed. He screamed for what felt like an eternity. All he could think about in despair was how he wished he would just die! The pain ate him alive.

And then it was gone. Just like that. Ell wasn't sure if it had been moments or minutes or hours. But the pain was gone and not only that, his wounds were healing. He could feel the burning sensation turn to a warm closing feeling as his flesh sealed itself together again. He still felt weak, too weak to move. Ell lay there in a healing heap on the street.

"What are you doing to me?" Ell groaned.

"You are an artist," Half-Mask began, but Ell wasn't sure what he meant. Was he referring to Ell's power as a Water Caller as an art form? The Prince of Darkness continued. "But I am also an artist—of a darker aspect. A Spectralist. Your art can heal, but then you are hardly in possession of your full talents, are you?" Half-Mask's tone was dismissive of Ell. "I, on the other hand, have had a lifetime to hone my craft. My art can also be used to mend rents in the flesh—albeit more painfully. I will enjoy watching and knowing that you will squirm for the rest of your life as you try to ignore what will live inside of you from this point forward. The burning need you will feel to kill, the sweet release of death. You will try to resist. And you will fail." Half-Mask's voice was exultant, more pleased than it had been during their entire interaction and then duel.

Ell felt the seeds of terror sprout. What was Half-Mask talking about? What would he live with, what was inside him now?

"What do you mean?" Ell asked, as he propped himself against the stone wall of the alley.

Half-Mask tilted his head as he gazed at Ell, penetrating eyes staring into Ell's as if the blackness of his soul could swallow Ell whole.

"I have begun the process to making you into one of my servants—what you call the Unsired. I have started the process and now it is just a matter of waiting for that process to complete itself. You will become mine, body, mind, and heart. Just like they all become mine. Eventually." Half-Mask's tone took on a hard edge as he promised Ell's future subservience.

It couldn't be true. It was not possible. The horror of what Ell had just heard was too much to believe. Yet, he glanced down at his wounds and saw them healed, but in their place ugly black scars occupied his flesh instead of the fresh pink of a normal scar. A hint of the former heat of the dark black liquid still remained in the wounds as if a memory of the painful healing.

Reality—or at least a reality fully erected and influenced by fear and Ell's current weakened state of body and mind—saw his resolve crumple.

"Don't do this to me!" he half shrieked the plea at Half-Mask. Shame instantly filled him as he realized what he had just done—begged the greatest enemy of his people for something, like a wounded animal.

Half-Mask chuckled darkly. "It is already done. There is no going back now." And with that, he turned and began to stride away, surrounded by his followers and Borian—who looked decidedly sickened and unnerved by the whole event, although also a bit vengefully satisfied.

"Wait," Ell cried out, desperate for more information, for anything that might put this nightmare into perspective. "You're just leaving? You're letting me go?"

Half-Mask paused and looked back. "I told you, not a day ago I would have ordered your execution. In fact, I had already given commands for it. But now, having seen you," Half-Mask sneered scornfully, and the disdain on his face was almost more than Ell could bear, "I can see you aren't worth the trouble. No, knowing that you will fight the darkness, the urges I have seeded within you, will be ever so much more enjoyable."

"So I am free?" Ell asked, trying to make sense of it all.

"I think we both know you are hardly free," the Prince of Darkness answered ominously. "We will see each other again, and when we do, it will be an entirely different encounter." And with that Half-Mask picked up his discarded clothing, cloaked himself, pulled up his hood, and vanished with his coterie around a corner, leaving Ell in miserable silence.

Ell sat for a time in the shadows of the alley, terror, horror, shame, and anxiety all boiling in his gut in varying amounts. Was he really to become a monster? Was that his fate? Had some queer twist of destiny made it so? The terror he felt at the idea of becoming an Unsired and slave to whatever greater, darker power Half-Mask possessed was almost too much for Ell to contemplate and still cling to his sanity. What had Half-Mask called himself? Through the dredges of pain and worry he tried to recall what he could of the dark elf's words. A Spectralist? Had that been it? Ell let the thoughts go for now. For the moment he had to simply survive, move on.

He forced himself to go a little numb. He shoved the pain, the fear aside, pushing it down to a low more manageable simmer. Half-Mask, whether in confidence or arrogance, had left him. That meant Ell still had a mission to complete. He dragged himself to his feet, balancing as best he could on wobbly legs. He still had a father to rescue. That much was still within his power.

Fighting off the dreadful fear that threatened to overwhelm him, he made his way north through the city. He had a family to smuggle in as slaves. All he could do now was be about his business as best he could. Only time would truly tell whether Half-Mask had been telling the truth about what he had done to him.

Chapter Twenty-Eight

The knife clattered weakly off the tree trunk. Most of the time, that was what happened. Occasionally, Miri was able to get it to stick, but even then, it was usually merely quivering in the tree by its point, having barely pierced the bark. It was more difficult than it looked. After spending so much time with Ell and his family, whose prowess with arms was unrivaled by her standards, Miri had grown somewhat complacent. She had begun to assume that perhaps blade work wasn't as challenging as it seemed—especially when watching Rihya who had by far the quickest hands and the deftest touch when throwing knives. In reality, it was so much harder than it looked! There was a flick of the wrist needed to get just the right trajectory of the knife that Miri just could not seem to master.

"Practice, Miri. Learn the craft, Miri. Do the work, Miri. Learn to protect yourself, Miri," everyone said. But everyone else had not spent their entire lives trying to avoid violence. Miri had never wanted to learn to use weapons—even for hunting. If she could, she would just quit the whole learning process right now. She had been perfectly happy before she had ever tried to throw a knife. Miri stumped over to the tree and lifted her knife from where it lay on the mossy ground. Andalaya was in full autumn now and that meant rains were more common, and the morning dew took longer to dissipate—if it did at all. The knife was moist, and even a bit muddy from a bit of wet dirt it had collected from its fall to the ground. Miri wiped it on her breeches and walked a few paces back to try again.

She threw the knife with all her force to vent some of her frustration, and the blade sailed wildly past the tree and into the lush foliage behind. She wanted to scream with annoyance, but settled for a small, vexed sound as she waded her way into the greenery behind the tree and practically soaked herself on all the wet underbrush.

It was Arendahl's fault that she was soaked to the bone now. He was the one who had decided she needed to learn to defend herself, often pairing her with the young Art to practice. Some weeks back, when their trainings surrounding the Grafting had been yielding no result, he had decided it was time for a different approach to her tutelage. Miri gritted her teeth as she searched for the fallen knife. Where was it? Her annoyance with Arendahl boiled over and she kicked out at a bush. Her bad leg caved as it sometimes did when used as the plant leg and she tumbled to her back onto the wet ground.

Miri lay there not knowing whether to laugh or cry. Where had all her tranquility gone? She had always prided herself on her composure, on her unwillingness to give in to self-pity and frustration at her body's limitations. That peace had transcended her old injury and she had learned to apply it to all areas of her life. But these days she seemed to have lost that calmness completely. It was Arendahl's fault! she thought again, somewhat bitterly. He was the one insisting that she learn to defend herself. Miri recognized her thoughts as somewhat petulant, but indulged in them all the same.

"There is a war coming, girl," he would say. "You cannot expect others to defend you all your life. Pacifism only works in times of peace, and peace is won with the sword." Arendahl practically recited that litany to her every time she complained.

Hadn't she taken care of herself just fine all these years? Steel had never been necessary then. She lay on the wet ground and felt the water soaking into her back. She should rise. She should find the knife and keep practicing, or perhaps try her hand at the bow again—she was incrementally better with the bow. But she stayed on the ground instead, indulging in her frustrations. She had always looked after herself. She didn't need a grizzled old elf's instructions. She didn't need people to protect her.

A small voice in the back of her head whispered she was wrong. Where would she be now if Ell hadn't protected her, hadn't rescued her from the Pillar last spring? She would probably be the plaything of some dark elf slaveholder, that's where. The truth was a bitter draught to swallow sometimes, but Miri was strong enough to make herself do it. She wasn't sure if she agreed entirely with Arendahl—peace was not always won on the edge of a sword—but she could concede when she allowed herself to be honest, that it wouldn't hurt to learn a bit of self-defense.

Rolling onto her knees she finally saw the knife. She picked it up and then walked back to the small clearing where she practiced alone. Sometimes she and Art would practice together—he was the only elf in the band who did not completely embarrass her with their skills with weapons—but today, she was alone.

Thinking these thoughts, of last spring and the Pillar, her captivity, always made her wonder about her mate. They had been separated for over a month—

was it close to two now?—since they had parted in the Lower Forest, just before she and Arendahl and Art had joined with Iyonei's band of raiders. It seemed like longer. Miri ached for him, to see his smile, hold his hand.

She tossed the knife almost nonchalantly, and wonder of wonders, the blade buried itself in the trunk almost effortlessly. Miri stared at it in surprise. Perhaps the key to all this was not over thinking it. Miri allowed her thoughts to return to Ell as she practiced her knife throwing. For all the training she had attempted on her Grafting, she had made almost no headway. She had imagined she might have felt something a few times, but the only real time when she was sure Ell had experienced something powerful enough to activate the Graft was some days ago now. She had been sitting in camp, tending to a few menial details—mending her tunic, sealing a drinking gourd—when a sudden rush of shame had filled her, then a strange numbness. There had been no visual image to accompany the Graft this time, not like when he had been attacked by the Tree Ogre, yet the emotions had been very strong. Not long after the feeling of humiliation had faded and been replaced by an unbridled joy. It was odd to have those two emotions sandwiched together, such differing emotions, but Miri was happy to have felt some of Ell's gladness. She could only assume that such joy meant a success of some kind. Perhaps he had met one or all of his family and rescued them. Hopefully, he would return soon.

Miri threw a few more times then decided to take a break. Since her back was already wet from the fall in the undergrowth, she decided to give in and just lie down for a moment or two on the damp ground. She stretched out, feeling the simple pleasure of being connected to the land as all Highest were. How terrible it must be to be one of the Departed, having cut off that direct link to Creation and the land that birthed them. Miri's thoughts flickered to her connections. She thought of Ell and of home—Little Vale. Most elves in Andalaya were nomadic, but she was one of the few who had grown up in a permanent residence. It had turned out to be a foolish decision. The battle for Little Vale had demonstrated the dangers of settling in one location.

A leaf drifted down lazily in the breeze from the limb of a spreading maple. Miri followed the path of its fall, her eyes following its dance back and forth as it drifted in the air. Its languid movements made her feel more peaceful than she had in weeks. She had missed this feeling. Miri let herself lie there, doing nothing, enjoying the few blissful minutes of rest and nothingness. A pleased smile crept onto her face as she rested.

The tranquility of the moment was shattered utterly and completely.

Miri screamed in shock. She was suddenly in a dark alley, daggers in hand, dancing a deadly dance of blades with an opponent wearing a dark mask. Or was Ell? No, she was there. Miri felt the stones beneath her feet, saw the shadows of overhanging buildings, buildings so dense that they blocked out most of the sky. She felt the silvery blade of her foe nick her cheek. The dance continued with her, but she remained in the meadow too. She was in the forest, not a city. Confusion reigned for a moment until some part of Miri realized it was the Graft again—although more powerful than she had ever felt it before. This event was momentous. Ell was fighting for his life, and not only was she witnessing it from his perspective, but Miri felt almost as if she *were* Ell. As if she were both herself and him simultaneously.

Miri tried to keep herself distinct from Ell, but couldn't keep the distance. She gave in and let the moment consume her, let herself be both him and herself at once. Miri lay on the green, dewy grass. Miri fought in the dark, sinister shadows. Miri felt her heart in her throat as she watched her lover fight for his life a thousand miles away. Miri lunged and slashed with deadly accuracy, skill born of endless hours with a blade in her hands. She was separate from him, yet one.

The fight raged on, whether it was minutes or hours she did not know. And then, suddenly, it was over. The silver sword pierced her chest and pinned her painfully to the wall behind her, pinned her the way a sliver of wood is used by a sadist to pin a bug to the forest floor. She wriggled and squirmed but it was no use. She was dying.

It was as if that realization, that she was dying, snapped everything back into focus. She still felt and saw everything through Ell's eyes, his body. But she was more clearly herself than before. She saw it all from up close, but was aware of the fact that she was also far away. Miri had become more Miri than Ell again. However, it was almost worse this way. In him, she could at least feel like she had some way of taking action as his actions felt like hers and gave her the illusion of doing something. Now it was worse. From a thousand miles away, she watched and felt her mate dying. The sword wrenched from his chest and allowed him to sink to the street. Tears poured from Miri's eyes and her gut and heart felt like they were sick with some kind of terrible illness. He was dying. It was almost too much to bear, too much to believe.

Dully, thoughts pounded around her consciousness as she watched the death of Ell from afar. Why didn't he cry from the pain? It was excruciating. She had felt it, could still feel the ghost of that agony. Why wasn't he afraid? He was dying, why was he not scared? Why was she almost certain that the only thing he felt was regret. Miri's mouth hung open in silent sobs.

And then it came, the surprise. More pain, endless pain, and Miri screamed as Ell screamed and their consciousness merged completely again. Then they were separate and Miri watched from afar again as Ell gazed up at the masked face of the dark elf who had defeated him. It could not get worse—what could be worse than this? Miri finally understood why Ell had been so worried about the merge. She didn't want to see this, didn't want to witness this. She closed her eyes to shut it out, but of course that did nothing to prevent her from seeing with her mind.

And then the worst came.

When the terror arrived, it was nearly blinding. Fear shot through every fiber of her being. Horror, endless waves of bludgeoning dread and panic washed over her, consumed her. What could possibly frighten Ell more than death? Miri didn't want to know. She forced herself to stop wondering about it. It was better to not know she told herself.

And just as suddenly as it began, it was over. She was alone again, only herself again, in the meadow, in Andalaya. She was far from Dark Harbor, but she wished she were there, right by his side. She wished she was in Dark Harbor, but she wasn't. Instead, she was gasping for air, for breath, for a tranquility that was no longer possible. She lay alone in the meadow, half stunned by what she had witnessed and experienced. It was too much. He was dead. The thought echoed dully in her mind. The pain was barely significant through the numbing cloud of shock. But was he dead? The terror had come after the added pain, the extra agony after death had seemed final.

What had happened, really? Was Ell alive or was he dead? Miri realized, as she lay there, that the one thing she was certain of was that she did not know what had just happened.

She lay until the sun gained height overhead and then shifted even more, signaling midday had passed. The greyness of the sky attempting to hide the sun created a bright sheen of whiteness above that was hard to look at. Miri stared at it until it felt like her eyes would burn. Going blind would be better than seeing all that she had just seen.

Chapter Twenty-Nine

When her nerves calmed finally, Miri got up and walked the short distance back to camp on shaky, unsteady legs. It was a rest day. They had been wandering the countryside looking for any of the Highest they could find for Arendahl to attempt convincing them of the coming need to join together and fight back once more. It seemed ironic to Miri that the actions Arendahl was advocating were in such opposition to the counsel Dacunda had given to the people of Little Vale last spring—ridiculing them for building a village and living together as a group in the small valley along the Westrill. But, she supposed, they had not known then what they knew now. The Unsired had returned, dire times were upon them, and in those times sometimes all you could do was stop running. Arendahl had used himself, and Ell especially, as a means to inspire hope and courage into the hearts of the Highest who they encountered. Hearing that not one, but two of the ancient figures of elven myth were come again made many elves swear that he or she would join the fight when it commenced once more. Arendahl sent many of those elves to other parts of Andalaya to recruit more support as they were doing as well.

Miri wobbled over to a stump near Arendahl and sat down. Immediately, the old elf recognized that something was amiss. Apparently, Miri had not recovered her peace as much as she had hoped while lying in that meadow.

Arendahl reached a gnarled knuckle up to her cheek and wiped away the beginnings of a tear. Miri could not help but begin to break down again as she recalled what she had just witnessed.

"What is it, girl?" Arendahl spoke without his usual garrulous tone, and his stilted speech was softened as he saw her pain.

Miri put her head on his shoulder and let the tears fall. Surprisingly, the old elf did not dig for information and details the way he normally would. Instead, Arendahl let her cry herself out, her head slipping down off his shoulder to his chest as he hugged her close to him. The camp bustled around them with activity, elves attending to chores that were necessary on their day of rest from travel, but everything seemed to fade away except for the old elf's chest, the rhythmic pounding of his heart, and her tears.

When she had finally cried herself out for the time being, he pulled her head off his chest and looked keenly into her eyes. "Are you ready to speak now?"

Miri nodded reluctantly, but knew she must tell him. Despite her reluctance to relive the event, what had happened was too important to keep from Arendahl. And so she did. She described it all—the duel, the wounding, Ell lying there dying on the ground, then the terrible pain, and finally the animal terror Ell had experienced just before the Graft linking them stopped.

When she was done explaining, Miri practically wailed, "And I don't even know if he is alive." The tears came afresh.

"I believe he is, girl. You would know with certainty were he dead—that is one of the few things from Grafting lore that I know to be true. If he were truly dead, you would not be left wondering."

The statement calmed Miri somewhat, but it did little to completely dispel her anxiety and pain after the torturous ordeal.

"I wish I had never linked with him, never Grafted him, the way I did." Miri spoke the words harshly.

Arendahl's shrewd stare was still soft as he looked at her, but it hardened slightly with insight. "Don't be silly, girl." His stilted, gruff manner was returning. "I know you better than that. You've a heart bigger than most, and are capable of more than you give yourself credit for. You can withstand a bit of pain. Deep down, I know you're glad of the link between the two of you."

Miri swallowed. "It was all so horrible. You may be right, Arendahl, but I finally understand why Ell was so concerned when it first occurred. He knew something like this might happen."

"He cannot protect you from everything, Miriyah."

The old elf's kind but firm chastisement sent a shiver of truth through her soul. It was true. She had to learn to protect herself—at least as best she could. Silently, she vowed to redouble her efforts with the knife and bow. She would not be weak any longer.

"I know," she responded quietly to the old elf.

"I am sorry to say this, but I must admit that I am glad that you two are linked in such a manner. This might have been a terrible ordeal, but it has given me vital information." Arendahl spoke to her like an equal, rather than someone who he must look after. The shift in tone and manner had been subtle but different during than the past weeks of travel.

It dawned on Miri that she was useful now. She provided Arendahl with not only her sunny disposition and cheerful company, but also with knowledge.

The old elf continued.

"I know now, for certain, that he is alive—I am not spreading tales to Andalaya about a dead Water Caller." Arendahl waved a hand vaguely at the landscape around him, to indicate the people spread throughout the shattered kingdom of the northern elves. "I know this because you would have felt his death shake you to the very core. I also know that he has faced Half-Mask and survived—however that may have taken place—and while the circumstances of that survival give me pause to worry," he said with a real pause as his eyes narrowed in pondering, "he has survived nonetheless, and few if any can say they fought Half-Mask and lived."

"Is that who that was?" Miri asked with a sort of dull curiosity, not wishing to relive the event, but strangely craving details to understand better.

"From your description of his foe's appearance, and the way the elf fought, I can only assume that Ell squared off in a duel with the most dangerous elf in the southern kingdom—well, excepting the King of the South, perhaps." Arendahl stated this plainly, calmly. He spoke of Ell's near-demise at the hand of the southern prince as if it was a normal or routine event. Miri felt a strange bitterness that her Ell would live a life that required such actions and circumstances that Arendahl would simply take it as a matter of fact that he had dueled the most dangerous elf in the world as if it were nothing significant.

Only a weariness about the old elf's eyes belied his calm demeanor, giving Miri cause to pause and doubt whether he was as complacent about the events of Miri's Graft vision as he seemed. In fact, upon regarding him further, he seemed more worried than she had given him credit for.

Was he worried about the same thing as her? Miri couldn't help but remember the abject fright Ell had felt at the end of the linking. What could he possibly fear more than his own death? It was an ominous line of contemplation and Miri could not help but believe that it portended nothing good—for him and for them all.

Arendahl broke the weary silence between them. Putting a hand on her shoulder he asked, "How goes your practice?" Despite their bitter discussion, he even managed to slip a wink in her direction, knowing how vexing she found her weapons training.

Miri couldn't help but muster a wan smile at the mischievous twinkle in his eye. "As well as can be expected, I suppose," she responded noncommittally.

"I doubt that, girl. We can always expect more of ourselves, so it is unlikely that any of us often meet those standards." Arendahl was serious once again. "You must practice, Miri, to the best of your ability. You may never be called upon to stand on the front lines of battle, but that does not mean the war will not find you in some other capacity. War has a way of becoming pervasive."

Miri nodded her agreement solemnly. She understood. Miri took her leave of the ancient Water Caller and wandered over to the cook fire where a midday meal had been prepared.

Briesom handed Miri a meal of spit-roasted fowl, grain cakes, and a few berries, all served on the smooth underside of a large piece of bark. The bark served as a practical and easily disposable dish for someone who was frequently traveling.

"Alright, Miri?" the pixie-ish blonde elf asked with a concerned look on her face.

"Fine, thanks," Miri lied, and took the food gratefully. "Just a bad dream during a lazy midday nap." As soon as she said it, she knew the lie sounded pitiful. It clearly fell short as the diminutive elf stared knowingly at her for a moment. Brie however, chose not to question the statement.

"Nothing a good meal can't fix, eh?" Brie grinned.

Miri smiled. "Too true." She couldn't help but think that the Brie and Ryder would greatly enjoy each other's company. They both jested more than they were serious, both looked forward to a fight more than just about anyone she knew, and they were both some of the best company to be around when you were having a bad day. They would either tell a joke to make you laugh or regale you with a humorous anecdote. And if that didn't work, they would sit in silence with you—the comfortable kind of silence, the kind that made you feel closer to someone rather than farther away.

Brie glanced edgewise at Miri as they shared their meal, and Miri could tell the warrior girl was gauging how best to pick up her spirits. Finally, it appeared the little elf settled upon talking over silence, since she opened her mouth and began to speak. Brie told a number of her funniest stories, and even a few details of her more humorous moments regarding various amorous trysts. Miri couldn't help but laugh, and by the time they had finished eating and talking, they were giggling like little girls. Miri was surprised to find how much she had missed this sort of thing. She and Rihya were close and in the weeks since Miri and Arendahl had left with Art, she had not felt this sort of kinship with their new companions. Perhaps it was finally forming. It was a pleasant addition to what had been an altogether horrible morning.

"Like I said, there is no mood too foul that a good meal can't shake off." Brie reminded her with a friendly grin.

"And good company," Miri said, and found herself blushing almost shyly as she paid the compliment. She wasn't sure why she felt this way. Maybe it was the voracity with which these female warriors fought that only pointed out the glaring differences between what they were capable of and what Miri could not do. It had shaken her self-confidence much more than she could ever have anticipated.

Brie ignored her shyness and threw an arm about Miri's shoulders. "You're one of us now—or we're one of you..." she said in mock confusion. "I guess I'm not entirely certain of who joined whose band, and who is in charge." Brie grinned at Miri with a roguish expression. "But either way, we're in it—whatever it is—together."

"I'm glad of it." Miri responded with an answering smile of friendship.

Brie hopped to her feet with a bustle of energy. "Come on, then. I couldn't help but overhear the old nag bothering you to practice your weaponry every time you talk to him." The pixie elf warrior was delightfully irreverent, especially when she spoke to or about Arendahl. It was as if the very fact that his age and stature deserved respect that made her find joy in poking fun at him.

Miri cocked her head in an unspoken question of confusion at the topic's relevance.

Brie shook her head in mock exasperation. "Well, I'll teach you silly. I'm the best at casting knives that you've ever seen," she boasted. "If I can't teach you to hit your mark, no one can."

Miri grinned at her new friend's confidence, even arrogance, and she couldn't help but think that if Rihya ever met Brie and overheard the diminutive warrior say that, that Rihya might just take cause to disagree.

Chapter Thirty

Stopping at the inn only long enough to procure a needle and thread to swiftly mend the rents in his hooded tunic from Half-Mask's sword, Ell was soon on his way over the causeway and out of Dark Harbor once more. Uncertain as to why he didn't want his family to see his blackened scars inflicted by the duel with Half-Mask and the vicious healing afterward, Ell wanted to make sure his clothing was patched and able to conceal them. He would tell them about the fight sooner or later, just preferably later, when they were safely aboard the ship and away from this wretched place.

Ell was exhausted, and something told him his fatigue was more than it should be after a bout with weapons. Well, he did almost die. Perhaps that explained it. Whenever he was healed by Source Water, it sealed up the wounds as much as possible in relation to the quantity drunk, but it often did not completely dispel the post-wound tiredness that accompanied normal recovery. Whatever Half-Mask had done to him seemed no different. It was a chore just to get across the causeway at the pace he was going, let alone climb the shore-side slope of the coastal range to reach the Hillfort.

Eventually, he did reach the fortress in the pass, and they let him exit with hardly a question, although for some reason they did gaze at him more strangely than usual. He thought maybe it was the unusual fatigue he knew he was exhibiting. All elves had stamina to embarrass any human, but the northern elves especially were noted for their litheness of movement and their ability to run for days without faltering—whereas the dark elves of the south were thicker and slightly more muscled, more at home on one of their raiding longships than a trail. The gate guards at the Hillfort must be surprised to see him lagging in his movements such as he was. It was nothing more than that, he managed to convince himself. Nothing else could go wrong now. For some reason the Prince of Darkness had let him live and disaster had been averted for the moment, but Ell didn't think that his now-rushed, half-cocked plan could weather any more misfortune.

He ran raggedly along the mountain face until he reached the narrow opening in the rock wall. The cave was dim inside after the brightness of day and Ell's eyes took a moment adjusting to the dark.

He opened his mouth to begin giving hurried orders, but the worried expressions on their faces made his words freeze in his mouth.

"What happened, Elliyar?" Dacunda asked solemnly, with more authority than he had ventured on this mission in weeks.

"What do you mean, Uncle?" Ell tried to dodge the question, unsure why he was uncomfortable talking about what had happened. "There's no time to chat. Borian—the traitor from Little Vale—recognized me in the city and the plan has been moved ahead. We go in now, and break my father out as dusk approaches."

Dacunda, however, wasn't to be swayed from his line of interrogation, and the others also clamored for details, voicing worry at his having been recognized or excitement from finally being moved to action.

"Make time, Nephew. You will tell me what happened. Why you have that blackened wound under your eye." The worry in his uncle's voice was palpable.

The wound on his cheek. In his hurry to conceal the injuries to his ribs and chest, he had forgotten about the minor nick on his cheek. It would be a blackened scar just as the strange liquid had made his other wounds.

Ell glanced away with a sudden rush of shame at having to relive the humiliation of his defeat as he recounted the story to them.

"It was Half-Mask," he mumbled quietly to Dacunda. The voices hushed immediately in stunned silence. The leader of Dark Harbor was used as a monster myth to fright little children all across Andalaya. And truth be told, even the adults feared him like they feared no other living elf.

"What!" Dacunda exclaimed, grasping Ell by the shoulders. "But you are alive. How?" he asked in stunned disbelief. If the rumors were true, nobody fought the Prince of Darkness and survived. Not even he—not even a Water Caller could defeat Half-Mask. He'd only survived because that bastard let him live, just to toy with him. The humiliation colored his cheeks red.

Ell told them the tale as briefly as possible. He told them of Borian seeing him in the tavern, his rush to find his father to warn him that the escape would take place this day. Ell told them of the misfortune of his path crossing Borian's again as he cut through the heart of the city, only this time the traitor was accompanied by Half-Mask—who the traitor must have alerted somehow to Ell's presence since Half-Mask had certainly known Ell's name.

Ell spoke of the duel, how he had fought with his powers and still lost, how Half-Mask had wounded him near to death and then healed him somehow just to taunt Ell by showing him how little Ell worried the prince.

Here, Ell somehow found himself altering the story ever so slightly. He made no mention of the prince's desire to transform Ell into the Unsired. Instead, Ell emphasized the prince's arrogance and disdain, and even though his family had disbelief for the whole encounter in their eyes, they seemed to swallow the story whole. His uncle did seem to have questions in his eyes, but Ell looked away and tried to force the conversation onwards from the tale. He wasn't sure why but he was reluctant to tell them the full truth. Maybe it was shame, possibly fear. He could wrestle with the reasoning of it later, but for now, he shoved his lies into a darkened corner of his mind and steered the group away from the story and back on track.

"So he healed me to spite me and told me how pitiful I was," Ell said bitterly. "His arrogance will cost him." Ell made the last statement into a promise, sealing it in his heart.

They all nodded, again seeming to find no fault in his words, for what reason did they have to think he was withholding anything from them? Ell continued, "There is no time to waste. We must be gone from here and make our way to the city as quickly as possible. It's time to see if our ruse will work."

Kalabi spoke up. "We have been preparing. As we discussed, one more of us will pose as a traitor. I found more berries and stained Dahranian to look the part."

Ell glanced at his eldest cousin and realized with a start that in the midst of telling his tale he had not even noticed his cousin had the traitor's red tears tattooed upon his cheeks. With distaste, Ell realized also, that in part, his inability to notice the tears on his cousin might stem from how accustomed Ell had grown to seeing them on his own face whenever he caught his reflection in a mirror or a washbowl. The sooner the filthy things faded from his cheeks the better. They only had to last one more day. Only now, Ell had a blackened scar on his cheek as a reminder of Dark Harbor. Ell felt a bitterness towards the scar as if its dark ugliness defiled his face somehow. He had never felt this way about a scar before. But then again, he'd never been healed with liquid used to create Unsired either. New experiences led to knew emotions.

Dacunda, the only one not seeming to fully buy into Ell's tale, forced a long swig of Source Water they had been able to carry with them onto Ell, and Ell drank some. Part of him knew he was as healed as he was going to be from whatever fiery process Half-Mask had induced, but the other part of him thought it couldn't hurt to use a bit of his own people's healing. Desperately, he thought that maybe the Source Water could undo some or all of what Half-Mask had said he had done to Ell. When that thought flickered through his mind, Ell drank greedily, a little too much, out of fear and hope. Dacunda pulled the flask away from Ell's lips.

"Enough, Nephew. We have little Source Water and you seem fine to me. Just a swallow or two is all you need."

Ell nodded his head in agreement, but licked the few droplets left on his lips with a silent wish for it to set his body right.

"Come now. We must go. There is no time to waste. My presence is known now in Dark Harbor, and while I was allowed to leave Half-Mask's presence this time, who knows what his fickle nature will decide in the future. We must act now if we are to save Adan." Ell remembered too well the crazed shift in attitude that Half-Mask had presented, going from calm to enraged and then back to silky smooth gloating in barely any time.

They agreed, and soon enough they left the cave and began making their way back towards the Hillfort. Rihya walked next to Ell.

"Do you hurt?" she asked in a sisterly tone of voice.

"More tired than hurting at this point, but yes, there is still some pain." Ell answered.

Rihya's tone changed on a needle-point sharp turn. "Good!" she exclaimed. "That's what you get for letting yourself get skewered by some southern noble. Don't let it happen again, or I may become moderately displeased with you." Her scowl covered up her face. Noble. Ell laughed to himself. Of course Rihya would have the audacity to refer to the Prince of Darkness as just another noble.

"I love you too, big sister," he replied with a tired grin. Her anger—real or fake—had provided him with just enough levity to regain his mood from the dark meanderings it took whenever he dwelled too long on what had been done to him earlier that day.

However, his regained lightness of attitude was quickly soured by his uncle's curiosity.

"Remind me again how Half-Mask healed you?" Dacunda asked, whether out of genuine curiosity or some more sinister and well-merited worry, Ell was not sure.

"I did not really say, Uncle. I was nearly unconscious and I am not certain how it was accomplished." Half-truth. Ell had been fading fast, but he knew what had been done, what had been poured into his wounds and what must now be flowing through his veins.

Dacunda nodded as if he understood and they all continued to run lightly. Soon after leaving the cave, they formed into the shape that their disguise would take. Ell took the lead, followed by all but Dahranian, who formed the tail of the small column. The rest of them had their hoods up and their wrists bound and tied to the person beside them, forming a line of prisoners like many

235

of the slaves Ell had seen traveling from their quarters to their work sites and then back to the barracks again. It would be a good disguise. It had to be. Otherwise they had no hope of getting through the fortress gates. Leastwise, it was the best plan they could devise. Nothing was ever gained without taking some risks. Especially in war, and there was no doubt in Ell's mind about whether or not this was war. This might be a small-scale battle—the freeing of a solitary slave prisoner—but it would be a heartfelt victory nonetheless if Ell and his family could accomplish the endeavor.

As they went, Ell studied his family one more time, making sure they looked the part of slaves—as much as possible at least. They wore their normal clothes, but Ell had instructed his family to fray them and tear them in places as if they had become slightly ragged during a violent capture. Before leaving the cave, everyone but Ell and Dahranian—who were posing as traitors—smudged a bit of extra dirt on their hands and faces as if they had been traveling hard and without the option to bathe for many weeks, which was not far from the truth. Ell had the only flask of Source Water at his hip, the rest of the water having been smuggled into the inn with the other items he'd brought, so his pretend slaves had nothing with which to occupy their hands other than their bindings.

"It's chafing quite a bit, O fearless leader," Ryder said. He was the first slave in the line and right behind Ell. Ryder lifted his bound hands and wiggled them at Ell to prove his point, wincing slightly as he did so.

"Good," Ell said, with a ghost of a smile on his face, "that will make it look more realistic for when we pass through the Hillfort."

Dacunda raised his voice. "Is there anything else you recommend to us that will make our guises appear more realistic?"

Ell studied his company. The guise was as good as it could be on short notice with the lack of options or supplies. There was only one thing to add.

"Only if you all could assume a look of dejection and despair. Slaves in Dark Harbor have a broken, beaten look to them, and all of you just have too dignified an air about you still. Try to empathize and get into character. Maybe hang your head a bit."

"Good idea. I can attest to the fact that none of your faces bear the marks of true slavery," Kalabi agreed with Ell.

"So what do we do exactly?" Ryder asked.

"Simply pretend that the most precious thing in the world has been taken from you and there is nothing or no one who will or can give it back to you." The ex-slave spoke somberly and from personal experience.

"And that is?" Rihya tossed her green hair with a flourish completely unbecoming of a slave. Ell couldn't help but laugh at her flair, but he also knew she needed to subdue that same verve before they reached the gates of the fortress in the coastal pass.

"Freedom," Kalabi responded.

They ran lightly onward, everyone silent now, attempting to connect their emotions and thoughts with the disguise. The distance evaporated quickly, and before long, Ell saw the looming form of the one-walled Hillfort ahead of them. He slowed them down to a walk.

"Remember, look like you're wallowing in despair," he reminded them one last time. A few grunts of response met his reminder and then there was silence again. They approached the gates of the Hillfort and without much ado, the small sally port entrance was opened for them.

The Departed warrior who manned the single entry gate had a glazed look to his dark eyes that Ell had come to recognize as one who was becoming, or had already transformed, into one of the Unsired. A chill shot down his spine as he realized that if Half-Mask had been truthful, then he too might have that vacant eyed expression in his own future. Ell shoved the thought aside.

"Prisoners," was all he said gruffly to the guard. The Warrior narrowed his eyes for a minute, but apparently their appearance satisfied him. He jerked his head inwards towards Ell, beckoning them to enter.

The small gate closed behind them and the afternoon light fell across their faces and the faces of those around them, highlighting many sharp and unfriendly eyes upon them. Warriors looked at them—some with distaste or disdain, others with a dangerous glint in their eyes signaling repressed violence hovering just beneath the surface, and still others gazed upon their small party with a look of pleasant satisfaction that more Northerners were caught and forced into servitude.

Ell nodded to a few warriors that he recognized from his time passing in and out of these gates. Apparently Ell had been seen here enough by now that he was not an uncommon enough sight to warrant much attention, even with a small troupe of slaves at his back.

They left the giant wall behind them and made their way out through the open aired interior of the fort and towards the road leading down to the city. A lesser commander strode over to meet them but it was nothing more than a formality.

"Prisoner transport," Ell said in his most bored tone.

The Departed commander answered him in an equally disinterested tone. "How many?"

"Four."

The Departed made a written note of the information for some sort of fortress record, then the warrior cuffed Ryder along the side of his head viciously.

"Do not eyeball me, slave. Know your place."

Ryder's face went red, but he had the good sense to drop his gaze and feign submission. Ell let out a sigh of relief as the lesser commander stared in satisfaction at Ryder for a moment and then resumed his bored expression.

"Take them to the city and have them allocated. Quickly, the afternoon is fading." Then the Departed turned and walked away leaving them free to continue on their path.

They walked in silence still, Ell leading the way and Dahranian bringing up the rear until they reached the road and were out of sight of the Hillfort. They descended over the crest of the pass and began to move downwards, picking up their pace as they went. Adan and the rest of his slave companions were transported back from the site to the barracks at twilight, which was not many hours off. Ell and his family needed to get to the inn, arm themselves, and then arrive at the excavation site in time to ambush the slave masters and free his father. That did not leave them a lot of time for error. They broke into a run at Ell's urging and the downward slope of the road coupled with their fast pace ate up the miles between the pass and the causeway.

Ell's family had never been inside the protection of the Hillforts and the coastal range so their eyes danced interestedly back and forth, sucking in the sights almost eagerly. They passed through the smaller shore settlement at the coast side of the causeway and then across the causeway itself. Their party drew some eyes, but fresh slaves were common enough in Dark Harbor that nobody glanced twice at them. They fought their way through the crowded throngs of people and at one point along the causeway, as Ell attempted to clear a path through a particularly knotted pack of elves, he nearly screamed in fury and frustration. Time was winding down and their window to reach his father and rescue him was closing. The dim light of dusk was creeping across the city.

They finally reached the end of the causeway, stepped down the stairs leading to the muddy, grimy streets and set foot in Dark Harbor proper. Ell led them into a particularly empty and dark alley before loosing their bonds.

"Put your hoods up and keep your heads down so that people won't look at you closely. Keep your hands in your pockets until its dark so that your fair skin won't draw too much attention. Dahranian and I are fine because of the tears on our cheeks but the rest of you are in grave danger as long as we remain in the city." Ell gave the directions tersely, eager to be done with the mission and out of the city. For a moment, he really appreciated and understood of the risks his family members were taking and he was proud for their courage. Posing as an impostor traitor was one thing, but sneaking in as a slave without the protection of the Traitor's Tears required exceptional bravery.

There were nods of agreement and hoods went up and hands were stuffed into pockets or concealed as best as possible by long sleeves. Ell guided them quickly to the inn, which had functioned as his home for weeks now. Leading them in through a back entrance, they climbed the stairs and piled into his tiny upper room. It was far too many people for that tight of a space, but it was only a matter of redistributing the weapons Ell had carried into the city little by little to stash there. Then they were back outside in the fading light, shadows creeping across the streets and buildings with a speed that made Ell nervous about being able to reach his father before the slaves were settled in their quarters for the night.

Ell led them on a swift race across the city. It would take some time to travel from the north wharf to the south harbor, but he hoped it would not prove to be so long that it derailed their plans. Twilight encroached and the shadows of the tangled maze of buildings lengthened. The streets of Dark Harbor were becoming more familiar to Ell, but he frequently saw his family members casting wondering looks at their surroundings. Like him, they had never before spent time in a living city, having spent their days in the wilds of Legendwood and the Lower Forest. Their few forays away from nature had been to peruse the streets of ruined cities in the north. Ell could see a wildness about his family member's eyes. Of all of them, only Dacunda had experienced such a bustle of people and crowded spaces. Dacunda had been not much older than Ell was now when Verdantihya had fallen. Before the great northern capital had been sacked, Dacunda had lived there and had experienced life in a huge city. Granted, it was a different sort of city than Dark Harbor, having been a living, breathing blend of creation and elf, natural beauty and architecture. In contrast, Dark Harbor reminded Ell of a fat old spider, its body heaped upon itself and its sprawling tangle of streets and alleys the spindly legs and the web it had spun. It was perhaps a fanciful imagination of what the city was, but Ell could not shake the feeling that Dark Harbor was a sinister, brooding beast, waiting to spring a trap upon its unwary visitors. His family seemed to feel the same way as their eyes darted about, searching, waiting for an attack that never came.

Their path cut through streets clogged with evening vendors and mobs of people buying food from street carts or other wares being sold on the street. Ell ducked into darkened alleys, followed by his family, and sprinted through squares centered with ominous statues of ancient southern nobility or gargoyles or monsters of southern myth. Fantastical carved sea beasts filled a square here and there but Ell could take no time to study them since he led his family at as fast a pace as the bustle of the city allowed.

When finally they reached the work site near the south harbor, Ell slowed their pace and lined them up in the shadow of a wall in a side street. Their hoods were still pulled low, obscuring their faces, and their hands clutched white-knuckled to the hilts and hafts of weapons they were ready to use on a moment's notice.

"There, do you see him?" Ell spoke in a low voice and pointed his father out of the many slaves finishing up their duties for the day.

"How could I miss him, he looks just like you—or you, him, I should say—and exactly how I remember him," Dacunda breathed in wonder as if the sight of his brother lost these twenty years was almost enough to overwhelm him.

Rihya bore a slightly stunned expression as well, but she did not yet speak. Ell started issuing directions briskly.

"As soon as the sun sets properly, the slave masters chain them up and lead them back to their quarters," Ell began, his eyes training across the numerous slave masters working the site, and holding cudgels and whips to keep the slaves in line. "Kalabi, you're not a fighter, not properly anyway, and I want you to stay close to us, but hang back and let us take care of the combat. We hit swiftly and deliberately, right when the masters are about to chain them up. Adan is the only target." Ell paused and looked at each of the people he was leading in this venture. "I know this is hard to see, it sets my blood boiling also—seeing our kinfolk enslaved like this—but we cannot save them all. Our priority is my father. We strike hard, liberate him, and then follow me. I'll lead us to our getaway vessel which is not far from where we are now." Ell finished his explanation succinctly. It had been a mouthful, but he was fairly certain the important points had been covered.

"Do you really suppose we can escape without a fight after drawing such notice to ourselves?" Kalabi asked doubtfully.

Ell grimaced. "It is a long shot, but what other options do we have? We cannot leave my father here, not now after all we have been through. And we do not have time to plan further, my presence is now known in the city." Ell looked at the human with a friendly but serious gaze. "I will not hold it against you if you wish to back out now, Kalabi. You owe no debt to us or to my father, and if you leave now it will perhaps be possible to find some other way out of the city."

The ex-slave shook his head.

It was settled. They would follow through with the plan, risky as it was. It was no surprise really; Ell had expected nothing less than pure boldness from his family. Dacunda had led them on too many raids and guided them out of too many skirmishes where they faced long odds for anything less than hardened mettle to form their core. This would be no different. They were in the heart of the enemy's territory, surrounded by foes and about to attack a group of heavily armed slavers who outnumbered them greatly. But it was this or nothing, and

Ell was not about to leave here empty-handed.

The slave masters began corralling their charges, and Ell turned to his family.

"On my order, we attack," he said. "When it's done, follow me."

They watched for a moment longer as the slaves were herded to the gated entrance of the site, right across the cobblestoned avenue from where Ell and his family waited. The slaves were divided into groups of twenty or thirty and tied together or chained together with manacles and then led off towards their respective barracks. Luckily, Ell's father was in one of the latter groups, so few of the slavers had left, leaving long odds still, but a better ratio than before.

Adan's group was up next and just as the slave train in front of Adan's group left and began shuffling along a side street leading away from the site, Ell motioned preparedness. The goal was to hit hard, hit fast, right before his father was chained, and in the fury and the confusion spirit him away. At least that was the plan.

Turning to his family for one last word, Ell flashed a grin of excitement that was met with answering grins by Rihya and Ryder, as well as sober, resolved expressions by his other companions.

"Ready?" Ell asked. "Nobody lives forever. I'll see you soon or in the next Reality," he murmured the old warrior's saying of the Highest and was met with a grim chuckle and a few nodded heads.

"Now!" Ell urged, and they burst into the open, twilight-darkening street from the shadows in which they had been hiding.

* * * *

The southern stars appearing in the sky were foreign to Ell, not the ones he had grown up watching in the nightly heavens of the north. But fighting was as natural and normal to Ell as the stars were strange. Still running, Ell tapped his ability as a Water Caller, feeling the power swell inside of him effortlessly. Ell said a silent thank you to Arendahl for teaching him to access his abilities with eyes open and in mid-action in a way that even the old elf himself could not do—Arendahl having learned alone, roughly, and without a teacher, making him pick up bad habits.

Full to blazing with strength of many, Ell led the charge and clattered into the mass of slavers surrounding the slaves waiting to be chained and taken away. He didn't look to see if his family was behind him, but he didn't have to—he knew they were. The surprised looks on the faces of the Departed warriors were pleasing to Ell and he killed three of them in swift succession before any of them were fully aware they were under attack.

Shouts of alarm eventually sounded, and the crowded streets of the southern wharf district became a seething mass of fear and worry as noncombatants attempted to get away from the fighting. Ell and his family faced up with the slavers who left—and enough enemies were still there to pose serious threat to his family's safety. Ell was grateful for his ability as a Water Caller in this moment, because it enabled them to equal the scales. Without his powers, they would have been simply a handful of reckless Northerners attacking half a hundred Departed soldiers and slavers. What would have been a suicide mission became an even fight—if not one that was slightly tipped in Ell's favor.

His family engaged the enemy. Ryder's long axe swung sharply and decisively keeping enemy warriors at long range. Rihya's knives flew thick and fast, piercing arms and slicing muscle and tendon as she flitted in between her foes like some kind of fairy of death—green hair flashing queerly in the twilight sparkle. Dacunda and Dahranian, as usual, fought in unison, their swords unsheathed from their backs, hewing through flesh the way one would chop wood for a fire. They fought almost mechanically, yet beautifully too, with form and power and a bracing surety of movement that could only be called graceful.

Yet for all his family's prowess in battle, it was Ell on whom the enemy focused the majority of their attention. Spearheading the attack, Ell clattered into the midst of the enemy first and drew their immediate attention. Bodies swarmed about him, threatening to overwhelm him, but he was used to it. If there was one thing he had learned to do as a Water Caller, it was to fight against large numbers of elves at one time.

His dueling daggers whirled brilliantly in the growing light of the moon and stars, severing hands from bodies, disemboweling foes, and hamstringing opponents like it was nothing more than a training exercise. Departed—or Unsired, in the haze of battle he wasn't sure—screamed and fell before his wrath. A black desire to kill and maim his enemies bloomed inside of him and he fell upon his enemies like a tempest raging in off the western sea. Before he knew it, twenty or so soldiers were down or dying, and still they attacked, his family mopping up the stragglers and chopping through the chains and ropes that bound the remaining slaves. Ell heard his uncle yelling for the slaves to run, but out of the fog of battle, Ell barely noticed that only a few seemed to follow his uncle's instructions, the rest seemed too confused or beaten down to take advantage of this opportunity to slip away and possibly escape.

Ell focused on the fight, on the remaining enemies that surrounded him. He had done this before, slain masses of the enemy all at once. On the Pillar, and then at the battle for Little Vale, Ell had led the charge against a veritable army of the enemy and broke their lines with his enhanced physical abilities. As then so it was now, and the enemy could not withstand him. Warriors fell, and still he fought on, an anger stewing deep inside him, threatening to escape. For a moment, Ell nearly gave in to the blackness, nearly dropped his weapons to begin clawing and slashing with his fingers and nails. Ell felt the urge to rip hearts from chests with his bare hands like some kind of wild beast. He felt the urge like a burning desire, but he fought it down, suppressed the urge as best he could, and continued to fight methodically and practically, incapacitating enemies, but not mangling them with any more brutality than was necessary. The screams of pain were sweet to his ears and for the first time, he feared his own prowess—that his savagery could elicit in him this kind of dark delight at inflicting pain.

He fought on a moment longer, his supernaturally enhanced speed, agility, reflexes, and power finally vanquishing any enemies that remained. And then it was over. Ell spun around and realized he was damp from the mist that often clouded around him as he fought as a Water Caller. Facing his family, he saw awed looks on their faces. They might have seen him fight with his powers before, but it was still a sight to see. He also noticed hope in their eyes, as if the fact that he could do what he did lifted their spirits, made them feel like the war was not over yet. He could see himself in their eyes, a rallying point for his kind.

Ell glanced at his father and saw a look of stunned disbelief. Of course, his father hadn't seen him fight, didn't know what Ell was, that he was a Water Caller.

"What are you, Son?" Adan Wintermoon asked wonderingly, a look of fierce pride in his worn features so similar to Ell's own. The question should have elicited pride for Ell, but instead it touched a nerve. What was Ell now? Was he a Water Caller of the Highest? Or was he something else, transforming even as they spoke into one of the Unsired—the very things he hated and despised? The brutal enjoyment he had felt while fighting, the wish to tear into his enemies' flesh with his hands and even his teeth with increased savagery and bestiality sent warning bells ringing in Ell's mind. Was that savagery a side effect of his transformation?

The thought was too much to bear and Ell shoved it away. No, he was just angry, and venting pent up frustration and rage at losing to Half-Mask and at the plight of his kinfolk and father.

Ell wiped the spatter of blood off his face with the back of his hand as best he could before looking his father in the eyes. "There will be time for answers later. Right now, we must be away. We should have already been away." Ell avoided answering his father, not wishing to dwell upon the painful and worried meanderings of his mind just now.

Adan had questions in his eyes, but he was a warrior first—despite his years a slave—and he knew when to take orders and focus on a job at hand. They left the scene as quickly as they could. Kalabi joined them from where he had been hanging back. There were some minor wounds, but nothing a few mouthfuls of Source Water couldn't heal once they were safely aboard Piripeos' ship. Ell and his family dodged quickly into a side alley, hoods pulled up again. They left the slaves behind who had not slipped away on their own already. They could not come aboard the vessel with Ell and his family, there was neither room nor supplies according to the captain, and besides, the ones who stayed at the worksite had more vacant expressions than even the Unsired possessed—theirs was a numbness of despair and the desecration of their spirits after years of hardship rather than the supernatural transformation of their bodies and minds into something else, something not quite elven.

They raced away at a fast pace. The pier where Piripeos had his ship docked was nearby, and Ell wanted to be away and on the seas before the moon rose any further. The battle at the site had sent the streets into chaos. Elves were running in fear and anxiety and so a few extra bodies into the confusion went unnoticed. In the darkness of the torch lit streets, no one paid enough attention to see that Ell and his family had clothes darkened and dirty with fresh blood. The shadows were their friends, and though the sound of boots tramping on stones sounded from behind them, Ell and his companions were already away from the site by the time reinforcements arrived and it appeared as if their plan was going accordingly. Now all they had to do was reach Piripeos and sail away into the night—a clean, good escape—and then Ell could leave not only this city behind but perhaps the fearful promises of Half-Mask's taunts, as well. He hoped. Ell hoped with all his heart that he could leave everything about this place behind.

The pier became visible as they rounded a bend in the street and between the wooden plank buildings and waterfront taverns and inns, Ell saw the small ship that Piripeos had described to him. A small merchant rigger, not a war vessel built to carry armies or a longship meant for raiding parties. The ship was built for trading and for cutting through waves with a cargo full of a few precious goods. A smuggler's ship no doubt, it had a blackened hull and two darkened masts and sails to blend in better for night sailing and slipping past patrols.

Ell saw his accomplice and led his family towards the captain. Piripeos grasped Ell's forearm in an amiable greeting, but Ell saw his eyes flashing all around, the wariness he always possessed was even more focused on the night of their departure. His eyes widened as he saw Ell's companions and he swore vociferously into the growing night.

"Why did you not tell me!" Piripeos practically yelled at Ell.

"Because you would not have agreed to join me in this venture," Ell responded calmly, while his family looked on in confusion.

"You should have told me," the captain hissed venomously. "I had a right to know that I wasn't just breaking the law, but committing treason!"

"What is the difference, Piripeos? I have heard you speak, I know that you bear no real loyalty to the Prince of Darkness and his rule. Why worry about that now?"

The captain looked away, scouring the pier in anxiety. "It's not a matter of loyalty," he grumbled, "but there are other factors to consider."

"Like what?" Ell asked, his patience wearing thing.

Adan answered the question for the Rimmer. "Like the repercussions. Law breaking might be punishable by death, but treason draws a far worse fate— days of torture until you beg for the merciful release of death." The captain eyed Ell's father in a shared understanding. They alone were truly familiar with Dark Harbor and the southern ways.

"All the more reason for us to go then, rather than sit around and wait to be caught. You have no crew and need to escape. Here we are. As promised, I have brought you your crew, now let us climb aboard your vessel and depart." Ell urged the captain with an authority in his voice, an authority gained from giving orders during command of the mission.

Piripeos seemed convinced and agreed it was time to leave, regardless of the circumstances surrounding his loyalty, but he hesitated a moment longer as they looked down the pier toward where the ship was docked.

"What is it?" Ell asked, sensing there was something the captain wasn't saying.

"Well, I may not have been completely truthful to you either." Piripeos had the dignity to look slightly embarrassed, especially after his own prior outburst at Ell's failed disclosure.

Ell stared flatly at the Rimmer until the sea elf answered.

"You see, that *is* my ship there, the *Water Wasp*—named such because its small and quick, and hard to catch. It's all mine. Just not exactly mine right now, leastwise not until after the legal decision is reached, the decision I don't plan on waiting around for."

"We have to steal it." Ell supplied the information stonily, annoyed also at the captain's lack of forthcoming conversation in the build up to this moment and the days of their meetings and planning.

Piripeos nodded. "I didn't think you'd agree to the plan if you knew what you were signing up for." He managed a wry laugh as he heard the similarity of his excuse to Ell's. The captain continued. "However, seeing what you are willing to risk by freeing living property, I don't suppose theft will be much of an issue."

Ell was annoyed, stealing a ship meant that their departure would be noticed, and likely followed. He had wanted to slip away unnoticed, as quietly as possible, but right now the priority was actually slipping away, the manner in which that was accomplished was of secondary importance. They would deal with the repercussion of this twist of fate when they had to.

Forcing himself to suppress his momentary vexation with the captain he clapped him on the shoulder. This elf was the first decent person he'd met in Dark Harbor—an ally among enemies—and he did not want to ruin that now. A genuine smile formed on his lips and he gave a rueful shake of his head.

"Alright, Captain, let's go steal ourselves a ship."

Chapter Thirty-One

The sentries guarding the *Water Wasp* were not warriors per se, and looked rather like uncouth sailors who spent the majority of their time in taverns when not at sea. These particular sailors were barefoot, with loose breeches hanging to mid-calf, and many of them were bare-chested. They did not have the sides of their heads shaven and manes of black down their backs in the manner of the southern warriors. Instead, most of them had fully shaved heads, their pointed ears framing grimy faces. Some however, wore their hair uncut, and those who did looked like they had not washed their hair for days. They were likely guarding a ship for some extra coin—a ship deemed 'unfit to sail' until its captain had received trial and decision.

Ell and his companions moved quietly closer to the ship. Two options. Slip around the side of the hull and clamber aboard along the large mooring lines that fastened the ship to the quay, or they storm the boarding plank in plain view of the sailors guarding the ship. Impatience made Ell consider a front assault on the gangplank, but that would cause a ruckus. Caution and Dacunda's years of mentoring had instilled a desire for silence whenever it was possible, though they were unable to do so with their attack at the work site, but when stealth could be achieved, it was preferable.

Ell whispered the commands for what was to take place as they drew closer to the mooring lines. The guards were not warriors and they did not have the vigilant manner of sentries who were employed by a true military presence.

"Rihya, Ryder, and Captain Piripeos—you three go up the lines and clear the deck for us. Don't kill if you don't have to," Ell added as an afterthought.

Ryder and Rihya gave Ell surprised looks at his last statement. Ell clarified their confusion.

"Not every single person in this city is our enemy. These are not warriors, they're sailors. There's a difference."

247

Dacunda pondered his words and cast a thoughtful glance in his direction. "There was a time, not long ago, when you would not have thought it so."

"That time is not now," Ell responded sharply. He wanted this to come off without a hitch, and sitting there wasting time and answering questions was not the way to ensure their success. Dacunda nodded in acquiescence. Not all those in Dark Harbor were their enemies. Ell had seen enough destitute and impoverished elves—none of whom were Unsired—to know that not everyone in the southern capital had evil interests at heart. Many were merely clinging to survival.

Rihya, Ryder, and the captain slipped carefully up the mooring lines, slick with seaweed. The captain went first. He might not be the best fighter, but Ell wanted someone with knowledge of a ship and its workings on the team of his people who went about clearing the ship of Departed.

Ell and the others held their breath in anxious silence.

"Are you sure three is enough?" Kalabi asked.

"It is if we want this to stay silent," Ell answered, hoping that his words proved true.

A few muffled grunts and one brief shout were heard, but in no time, Rihya was darting down the boarding plank, beckoning for them to hurry aboard.

"Help us with the bodies." Rihya spoke peremptorily as she pointed to the handful of sailors lying in a crumpled heap where she, Ryder, and Piripeos had dropped them on the deck of the ship. Ell motioned for them to do as she said, grabbing hold of the feet of one sailor while Adan grasped the sailor's limp shoulders. Hurriedly, the sentries were deposited on the wharf and then Ell and his companions were back on the ship and Piripeos was issuing quiet, but commanding orders.

None of them had sailed before, but Captain Piripeos was good as his word—he could teach anyone the details of being a sailor, even in a short amount of time. It helped that the vessel was one of the smallest merchant ships in the south harbor. Two-masted, it had a few large sails to unfurl—which they did at Piripeos' direction—mooring lines to untie, and then they were slowly ghosting away from the quay and disappearing from the harbor into the dimly lit night, propelled by the wind. The moon was hiding behind the clouds as they left the torches of the harbor behind, and Ell was forced to trust Piripeos and his eyes as the Captain stood behind the tiller setting their course through the midnight waters. The front sail of the vessel was angular and cut down towards the prow. It sliced through the dark air like a fish through water as they gained speed and a breeze filled their sails, propelling them further away from the nightmarish city of Dark Harbor.

The vessel's disappearance would be discovered, and when it was, there would be pursuit. Half-Mask had released Ell, but he did not know his plans. Something as mundane as the legal matter of a ship's disappearance would be dealt with by lower ranking city officials without the Prince of Darkness ever being notified. They would be pursued, and Ell had to hope that by the time pursuit began, he and his companions would be far enough away for it to be irrelevant to their escape, for the prince's scornful arrogance would no longer offer him protection.

Now, out in open waters and away from the shelter of the bay behind them, the need for utter silence had passed. Piripeos barked commands, orders, and instructions in an incessant string of words. His demands for action were punctuated by colorful language that the Rimmer seemed to feel was a necessity upon the deck of a ship on the open sea. Ell and his companions were not accustomed to the acts of sailing a ship, but the sea was calm and the captain explained what he needed of them in simple terms without resorting to sea jargon until he was certain they would understand. Captain Piripeos didn't seem frustrated with their slowness to act upon his direction or the need for his instruction. In fact, the Rimmer seemed in extremely high spirits, feeling his escape from the city that would likely have spelled his doom, was now almost complete.

Ell tied off a line that needed securing and glanced sideways at his father, who was working nearby. The years of servitude and physical labor had given Adan Wintermoon a ropey, sinewy strength. It almost reminded Ell of the way Arendahl looked, a strength that did not appear solely fast and lithe, but was almost the opposite. It was a strength whose power was based in resilience and determination as much as any kind of skill. Adan did not, in any way, look as old as the ancient elf who mentored Ell, but he did appear older than Dacunda, who was only a few years his junior. The years of slavery had aged him faster than the decades his younger brother had spent raiding.

"I am sorry, Father." Ell found himself saying without even realizing what he was doing. He knotted off the rope and turned to face Adan.

Adan finished his task quickly, with assured hands, and Ell wondered if perhaps he had served part of his time on a ship or working on the docks, for his father appeared more assured on the deck of the ship than the others. Ell and his family were yearning for green-leafed woods and crisp mountain air, rather than the salty tang of the sea breeze wafting by.

"What could you possibly be sorry for, Elliyar?"

Ell swallowed. "I am sorry we weren't in time to rescue mother and my sister also. Tell me, how did they die?" Ell was torn between wishing for truth and the bliss of ignorant denial. Easier to imagine they had died long ago, before they ever reached that evil city—much like he had thought for most of his life—than hear how they had suffered and eventually perished.

Adan looked confused for an instant. "What do you mean, Son?" Hearing him call him son, sent a strange thrill of pleasure through Ell.

"I mean, you said they were dead—when I asked you in the city, before we rescued you, and you told me we could not rescue them also."

Understanding lit in Adan's face, illuminated by the pale moonlight as the white orb poked out from around an inky cloud.

"I fear you have misunderstood me."

Ell felt fear clamp his heart. They couldn't have left the city without the rest of his family, could they? His father, Adan the Green, famous for his defense of the walls of Verdantihya, recognized for his bravery—he could not have wished so much for his own freedom that he would direct Ell to rescue just him and leave the others behind. Could he? Ell voiced this worried question with fear in his voice.

The hurt in his father's face that Ell could have thought that of him was almost palpable, and Ell felt a moment of anguish for thinking poorly of his father. However, he defended himself mentally—they really knew almost nothing of each other. They would have to forgive each other certain instances of misconception.

"Look at me, Son, I would never leave you mother and sister to their deaths in that wretched city. I would fight to the death to save them."

"But..." Ell stretched the question.

"But they were taken, many, many years ago."

Ell felt a new anguish, the anguish of a son without a mother and a mate who could do nothing for the sundering of his family.

"Where?" Ell asked, finding it easier to speak in monosyllabic words.

Adan shook his head in despair, an ancient pain, a despair steeped in years and years of morning. "Across the Fracture. They were shipped to the human lands, to Etheros, over a decade ago now."

Ell swallowed again, oddly fighting the urge to cry, willing the burning in his eyes to cease. He nodded to his father, a nonverbal indication that it was not his fault and Ell knew that. Adan placed a comforting hand on Ell's shoulder and for a brief moment, it nearly had the opposite effect of lending strength. For a moment, Ell nearly collapsed into something he'd never truly had, the comforting arms of a father. But he willed himself to be strong and tightened his core and his resolve.

Adan left his hand on Ell's shoulder for a minute longer before removing it. Silence between them stretched, but it was a shared silence. The tasks of the company seemed completed for now, and Piripeos had ceased barking his orders. The lull was pleasant, silence stretched on the ship and seemed to match the gentle swelling of the calm sea.

"Elliyar."

Ell turned his gaze away from the moonlit water and looked at his father in questioned wait.

"Elliyar, I would... I would like to spend a moment alone with my daughter—your sister. Valerihya."

Ell felt a fool. Not that there had been time to waste since the skirmish at the site and the taking of the ship, but Ell should have made sure that his sister was given a chance to speak to and be alone with their long-estranged father. Instead, here Ell was dominating his father's time, having already had a number of occasions to speak with him in private during his weeks in the city.

"Of course, Father, you know where to find her. She's the one with the green hair and fiery disposition." He could not help but grin as he looked with pride at his sister.

"Yes, I do. She looks much like her mother."

Ell pointed Adan in the direction of his sister, and watched from afar as his father approached Rihya. They shared a long embrace, tears were shed, and then Rihya led her father into one of the aft cabins for a chance to talk privately. Ell smiled to himself. Not only was he regaining a father, but so was his sister Rihya. He couldn't think of anybody who more deserved to have a family member returned to them after being deprived their presence for so many years. As Ell thought longer, he amended that thought. He could think of one person he knew who deserved to experience that as much as his sister and that was Miri. Without thinking any further, he climbed the ladder steps to the Captain's deck where Piripeos stood calmly, holding the tiller and setting their course.

Piripeos nodded to Ell with a roguish grin. He winked at Ell.

"Looks like we've given Dark Harbor the old grand escape, after all. Fortune brought us together and it has seen us safely away."

Ell clasped the captain's forearm in shared celebration, but he had other things on his mind.

"What course are you setting for us?" Ell asked the captain.

Piripeos, no stranger to twists of fate, narrowed his eyes. Ell imagined he could practically see the mechanisms of Ell's mind whirling with impossible thoughts.

"What have you got in mind, Northerner?" Piripeos asked, cautiously.

"Just answer the question, Rimmer, what course are you setting?"

In the privacy of the elevated captain's deck Piripeos and Ell exchanged a long shared look, then Piripeos caved and spoke.

251

"West for now. There are smuggler's coves that I know of scattered all throughout the Enclaves. We sail west for a time, find the nearest of those coves and make port, hidden from the watchful eyes of the southern kingdom. Then, when the time is right, I add a few more crewmembers, and we sail north, jumping from hidden cove to cove until finally we make the break across open water and up the northern coast. I assume you wish to return to Andalaya— based on your antics, it appears you are not really a traitor to your kind?"

Ell nodded reluctantly. What harm could it do to add this final piece of information to what the captain already knew? After all, he knew they had liberated a slave from the custody of its slave owners. Ell pressed on further.

"And then, Captain Piripeos?"

"After that, I leave you in your homeland and strike for the Outer Rim with my newly acquired crew. Simple as that, Northerner."

Ell thought for a moment, the gears of his mind spinning. Impossible had never really stopped him before. Had he not taken many actions within the last year that were deemed impossible? He had reached into the feared Dark Harbor and plucked a slave and a criminal right from under the nose of the authorities. He had survived a duel with the Prince of Darkness himself. It behooved Ell in his current line of thought to ignore the fact that he had done so only by the arrogance and derision of Half-Mask. But Ell was too far gone dreaming to let that detail set him off course.

"What is it, Northerner? You have a gleam in your eye that I do not like." Piripeos nervously drew Ell's attention back to himself.

Ell flicked a blazing grin towards the Rimmer as he set his heart on what now lay ahead. Boldness filled him and Ell felt a reckless fulfillment. Not just Rihya deserved such a reunion.

"Change course, Captain. We shall not sail a league farther west."

Piripeos stared at him in disbelief. "What madness is this, Northerner? You hatched this plan and I agreed to it in order to save my life, not lose it in a suicide mission. This is my ship and I choose where it is steered. No safety lies to the south. Our only hope for our continued freedom is to chart our course west."

"South," Ell said again, calmly resolutely. His tone brooked no nonsense, no debate. Ell said that one word and let his voice resound with as much authority as he could muster.

"No!" Piripeos objected again, fear and frustration filling his voice. "Where do you plan to go, and why? I hardly know you, Northerner, and I'll not risk my life for nothing. I've worked too hard these many years protecting the skin on my back."

Ell stared ahead burdened with a burning purpose. "I am Elliyar Wintermoon, and we sail south so that we may then sail east." The captain looked at him as if he really had gone insane this time. Ell answered the unspoken shock on the captain's face.

"I mean to sail across the Fracture."

Chapter Thirty-Two

"Madness!" Piripeos shouted loudly over the clamor of Ell's family. "It is sheer madness to think we could sail across the Fracture. No ship has ever entered its deadly waters and returned."

"He is right, Son," Adan said, having emerged from the cabin where he and Rihya had been visiting. Ell's father still bore a slightly haggard appearance, but his face seemed visibly lighter after having been reunited with his daughter "I spent enough time in Dark Harbor to learn that not even the Departed venture to cross the Fracture—and their longships and merchant vessels sail the seas fearlessly. It says much that they do not dare to attempt such a crossing."

Piripeos volunteered yet more information, his loud voice tinged with a faint frantic note. "Ice Mountains float throughout the core of the entire length of the Fracture, not to mention smaller icebergs, sharp enough to gut the hull of your ship without a second's notice. And if that wasn't bad enough by itself, there are riptides and small whirlpools, even bigger maelstroms in spots that will drag your vessel under, or dash it to pieces against the frozen and jagged ice walls." The captain ended, huffing slightly, as if his vehement opposition to the idea had left him searching for air.

Rihya, ever-fearless Rihya, looked calmly towards Ell. "Why don't you explain this sudden desire to sail across the Fracture to the human lands, little brother."

Ell nodded complacently, a strange calmness washing over him. This was happening. If he had anything to say about it, it was. "My mother and sister are there, across the Fracture and I mean to see them freed." He stated it matter-of-factly, as if it was not momentous news.

Piripeos swore, and Kalabi's face paled slightly at the prospect of returning to the land from whence he came, the land where his imprisonment had begun. Dacunda and his sons seemed thoughtful, casting lingering looks between themselves without responding. Rihya's eyes lit up at this new prospect. It was as if seeing her father for the first time in living memory was enough to make her believe anything was possible.

"I am with you, Ell," she stated stoutly, forcefully, and Ell allowed himself a small smile of satisfaction. They stuck together. He loved her for that loyalty.

It was Adan's response that was the most unexpected. Ell had thought perhaps his father would be excited by the prospect of rescuing his long estranged wife and daughter. Or, if he was unsure, then it would be a minor reluctance, and easy to persuade him otherwise.

Ell had been completely unprepared for his father's angry outburst. So far, Ell's father had exhibited most of the characteristics one would expect from somebody enslaved for twenty years. He was quick to work, slow to speak, and he thought through his answers thoroughly before responding. Adan often drifted to outskirts of a conversation waiting to see what the result was before volunteering an opinion. But not this time.

Ell saw his father's face harden as Ell told them what he planned to do. Adan turned a steely gaze on Dacunda and for a minute all seemed to cease as the two brothers faced off.

"Foolishness!" Adan declared. "This venture is suicide, it is absolutely out of the question!" His voice practically crackled with authority. For a moment, Ell imagined how he must have spoken when he led the defense of the walls of Verdantihya so many years ago. Dacunda shrunk slightly under his brother's angry gaze.

"What were you thinking, Dac? Allowing them to come south like this, to risk everything, just on the off chance that they might rescue me. Did you not promise me that you would keep my plight secret, that you would tell my children I was dead? Now look what they have set their minds to! It will be the death of them."

Dacunda had withered with each sentence, as if his brother was raining blows down on him. "I didn't tell them, and I certainly did not allow this venture. But you have no idea how... determined your son can be." Ell's uncle sounded odd excusing himself in such a manner. Dacunda did not excuse himself to anyone. Ell was also certain that the word 'determined' was not the word Dacunda would have chosen. He more likely wished to use a word such as stubborn, or rash, or even foolhardy.

The argument raged on. Adan was in full force now. "Sailing across the Fracture is suicide. I will not have my children die to achieve the fancy of a long dead dream. My wife is gone. My daughter is gone. There is nothing to be done about it."

"That's what they told Ell about you, Father, after he learned of your survival from the mouth of Silverfist, right before he slew him." Rihya spoke quietly, yet her willingness to contradict Adan quieted down the others. "They said rescuing you was a suicide mission, and look, we have freed you."

"We are not fully clear yet, their longships prowl the seas like wolves on the hunt." Adan grumbled, but his eyes narrowed in thought, and his tone mollified ever so slightly.

Rihya pressed her advantage. "You do not know what my brother is capable of. If he wants to cross the Fracture and believes we can accomplish it, then I believe him, because he must have reason to think so." Her staunch support of Ell, without even knowing if he had a plan worked out or not, warmed him.

Adan cast an interested gaze at Ell, as if not entirely sure why Ell was the one in charge. In fact, Ell himself wasn't sure of that. The initial mission was over, his father rescued. Dacunda had sworn to obey him no longer than the mission. However, if maintaining control was the only way to set their course to the east and rescue his mother and sister, then Ell was determined to keep hold of command.

Ell's father turned his attention back to Dacunda. He spoke more softly but he was still frustrated with his brother. "You should not have let them come for me. This is bound to end badly if we do not escape while we can. I love my family, and would rescue them if it was possible, but I know my wife. She would not want us, especially not her children, to die needlessly, in a vain attempt to save what cannot be saved."

"I know, Brother," Dacunda said, anguish written plainly on his face. "I did not choose this either. I fought tooth and nail not to come, but Elliyar can be persuasive and when he is not persuasive he is still forceful and often manages to achieve his goals. Besides," Dacunda paused as if not sure how to proceed, "Elliyar has done the impossible before. Maybe he can do it again." The hope and belief in his uncle's voice was enough to melt any of Ell's residual anger from the lies Dacunda had told him about his family. And now, seeing how angry his father had become, Ell understood why Dacunda had kept his promise.

"It is happening, Father. We are rescuing mother like we did you." Ell still maintained his calm despite the fevered argument that had taken place.

"We do not even know if she is alive." Adan murmured worriedly.

"We did not know if you were alive, but look how it turned out. You must have faith. And we must try to find and rescue them." Rihya said.

And with that, it seemed settled. Somehow, miraculously, Ell was still the one in charge—not Dacunda, not his father, not even the Captain. It was surprising that they all accepted his leadership almost without question now. Ell wondered when exactly that shift had happened. Those closer to his own age, namely Rihya and Ryder, had seemed fine following his decisions nearly from the outset, but Dacunda and even Dahranian had struggled much more with the change in leadership. When had that changed? Had it been when Ell survived a duel with Half-Mask? Or when they found out that his father was truly alive? Or had it, at the last, been when they saw that he had actually accomplished the impossible, yet again, in successfully freeing his father with their support? Either way, Ell was glad of it. It would make things that much easier.

The only one still set against it was Piripeos, and he vocalized his dissent vigorously, naming all the reasons why this venture was insane, foolish, a bad idea, and finally, simply unfair—unfair that he would be forced to accompany them. But they needed a captain and he needed land or ship in order to survive and he would not get either without them. Ell felt a small amount of regret that he must force this on Piripeos, but they had no choice. He was the only true sailor among them and they would need him, especially when the ocean ended this unusual bout of calm weather and began surging and raging around them. Ell promised himself that he would try to win the captain over so that it wasn't a venture forced upon him but something he willingly accepted. However, the words he would need to accomplish that feat eluded him.

The rest of the night passed uneventfully. Everyone went about their tasks as directed by Captain Piripeos, and the ship glided smoothly up gentle walls of waves, over the crests, and then down their slopes. The endless repetition made walking awkward at first, but the agility of the Highest helped Ell and his family compensate for not having sea legs. Gradually, they adjusted and if they were not so nimble as Piripeos on the deck, at least none of them lost their footing.

At one point, Ell overheard a conversation between his father and his uncle as his two elders worked side by side. There was a brief apology on both their parts for any perceived grievance by the other, a heartfelt embrace, and the entire argument between the two seemed forgotten in the joy of once again being reunited. However, rather quickly, Adan transitioned back to a serious topic. Ell learned that his father, while not entirely opposed to mirth, was not an elf given to avoid serious topics in favor of light or frivolous ones.

"There is something afoot in the south, a different sort of enmity brewing against the Highest. I have felt it growing stronger and more powerful with each passing year," Adan Wintermoon was saying. "It is a transformation of sorts. In secret, those not yet afflicted call it the Blackness." Ell thought the nickname was a fitting one, seeing as the transformation to Unsired turned a person's blood black, not to mention the strange darkness to be found in the Unsireds' eyes.

Dacunda looked somberly at his brother without answering. "You already know of this." Adan surmised from Dacunda's expression. It was a statement, not a question. "Tell me what you know of it."

Dacunda sighed. "It is the gravest of news, Brother. Our ancient enemy has returned."

Adan's faced paled slightly in the moonlight. "No, it cannot be."

"It is. Arendahl has confirmed it. In fact, it was he who first divulged the information to me."

"And you believe him?" Adan asked, his voice carrying a desperate hopefulness, as if he could somehow wish the existence of the Unsired away.

Dacunda looked at Adan in disbelief. "When Arendahl tells you something with absolute certainty, news as dire as the return of the Unsired, you know it to be true. Arendahl does not lie, and he is rarely ever wrong."

Adan's face fell. "Of course, it was foolish of me to question his word. I was merely hoping it would not be true. This information would explain much—how the power of Dark Harbor and the southern kingdom is growing despite the dominating presence of the humans on our eastern borders." Ell's father had a musing tone to his voice, and for a moment it was as if the last two decades of servitude had fallen away and Ell was seeing the commander he had been, shrewdly assessing the plans and strategies of his enemies. But then the glimpse of the past was gone, and Adan wilted slightly, as if this information was a blow to him personally.

"If the Unsired are truly returned, then what can it mean for our people other than the grimmest of consequences?" There was a hopelessness in his voice, that Ell could only imagine was born from twenty years as a slave. He could never imagine a battle commander speaking in such a voice. Adan showed flashes of his previous penchant for leadership, but it was clearly not in his nature at the moment. Maybe with time he would regain what he had lost.

Dacunda flicked a glance at Ell before answering his brother, and Ell hurriedly did his best to pretend that he had not been eavesdropping. "All is not lost, brother, there are still reasons to be hopeful." Dacunda spoke softly as if his reassurance was meant for his elder brother's ears only. Adan caught Dacunda's gaze returning from Ell's to his own, and a look of curiosity and bewilderment showed. Adan did not know what Ell was—or Arendahl for that matter—and sooner or later Ell would have to explain it. He just felt the strange urge to avoid that discussion for as long as possible. Fear still wormed in his belly at the memory of Half-Mask's taunts. Ell turned away from his father and uncle and set himself back to his task.

The night passed smoothly, and they slept in shifts, sleeping lightly, should any event arise that required the attention of everyone at once. Awaking from his brief sleep on a cabin hammock, Ell climbed the ladder steps to the captain's deck. Piripeos was still behind the tiller, not having moved all night long, trusting no one other than himself to steer the ship—at some point he would have to teach them to do so, but he had not deigned to do so yet.

"We are friends, are we not?" Ell broached the subject delicately.

"Friends don't force each other onto suicide missions." The Rimmer shot Ell a flat angry look.

"Fair enough. Accomplices, then."

Piripeos grunted his assent. "An apt name for what we are."

Ell gathered his thoughts. He needed a willing captain. They would not survive this sea voyage without a competent and willing captain at the helm. "You have no cause to love the Prince of Darkness."

His comment earned Ell a look of annoyance and confusion from the captain. "What in the name of the tempests of the sea does that have to do with anything? You have us sailing to lands never seen before by free elves, lands far from the control of old Half-Mask."

"But it is connected, it is all connected. The south has alliance with the east—the humans—and any blow we strike at one we strike at the other."

Captain Piripeos snorted disdainfully. "We aren't traveling to strike such a blow, we are throwing our lives away to save you mother and sister—family members, who I might add, we have no way of knowing whether they are actually alive. You forget, Northerner, that thousands have lost more than you have ever had claim to. Asking others to risk what they have for you is selfish."

Ell forced the grimace from his face. The Rimmer was right. Ell's logic was faulty. How to convince an unwilling participant of a venture that was based almost solely in blind faith and resolute determination. He searched for the words.

"Your people were absorbed into the southern kingdom, do you want that to happen to my kind also?" Ell changed his tactic slightly.

"No, I don't." The Rimmer answered bluntly, honestly. "But my people's assimilation was a long time ago, and there's no going back. Why fight against the inevitable?"

"Don't you believe things can change."

"That is wishful thinking, Elliyar, and you know it."

"Wishful thinking freed my father." Ell stated keenly, truthfully.

That statement gave Captain Piripeos pause. Ell had a knack for doing the impossible, and against the odds he seemed to infect those around him with the same indomitable belief in the ability for the impossible to become possible. Ell could practically see those same thoughts whirring in Piripeos' mind.

Finally, the captain spoke, his hand holding the tiller almost negligently, so comfortable was he upon the waves and his deck. "You still haven't told me how dying trying to save a couple of slaves will strike a blow at the powers that be." Ell could practically hear the interest, the slight change of tone in the Rimmer's voice.

"Every war begins with small battles. These are small victories, but significant ones. Never before has a slave been liberated from Dark Harbor, never before has an elven—or any—ship sailed across the Fracture, but we will be the first. He imbued his voice with all the confidence and belief that he felt. And he did believe it, Ell knew it was true. Ell could see Piripeos' anger and commitment to antipathy wavering under the onslaught of Ell's passion and desire.

Piripeos nodded, as if finally, really thinking about what Ell wanted to do. "Still, it has to be more than a rescue. Nothing will change in Dark Harbor, even though your father has escaped. Dark Harbor will function the same. If we travel all the way to the human lands, we must not leave with only a few slaves in tow. It has to be about more than a rescue attempt."

"Who is speaking insanely now?" Ell joked, quirking a wry smile at the captain.

"I am mad. I must be to even be having this discussion. I am not one for futile acts of revolution. Yet..." Piripeos trailed off with a grin and somehow Ell found himself clasping arms with a new ally—a friend perhaps—without really being aware of how it had happened. Somehow, Ell's determination had won the captain over. Not only that, the captain had given Ell something else to ponder, something vital. As Ell departed the captain's deck the words 'it has to be about more than a rescue attempt' seemed to ring in his ears. Ell could not help but feel that Piripeos was right. The reluctant revolutionary had shown Ell the flaw in his plan—its lack of ambition, and Ell couldn't miss the irony in that.

As Ell's soft leather boots hit the top run of the ladder steps Piripeos spoke once more. "There's one more thing we'll need." Ell turned back.

"What is that?"

"A crew—a proper, full crew. We are not enough for a voyage of this magnitude."

"What do you propose?" Ell asked.

"I know of a place, where a crew can be found for even the most ludicrous of adventures—for the right price."

"We have no coin to pay," Ell said grimly.

Piripeos smiled dangerously. "I did not say coin was the price. Some will crew a ship for the promise of many things, from loot and spoils, to even the promise of adventure…or the chance to do the impossible."

"Will it be possible to find such sailors? I cannot imagine many would be inclined—"

"—Inclined to what, be as bold as you?" Piripeos asked, with a wry smile. "Besides, I did not say they would be sane. But then again, sometimes the best of those who sail the sea have a touch of insanity about them." The captain tossed his head back and laughed wildly as if to prove the point—after all he had agreed to join Ell and his family as well now, of his own accord.

"So where do we go to find this crew?"

"I know a place," the captain answered, with a dangerous glint in his eye.

Chapter Thirty-Three

Valdor smoothed the straight blond hair off his forehead and back with his free hand, giving his face a chance to feel the warm sunlit air. Any kind of work was hard at his age. Oh, his strength still sustained him and would do so right up until the moment it wouldn't—right up to the point of physical collapse. That was the way of his kind, the Highest. Valdor pondered the different manner of aging between his elven species and his human captors. Humans aged gradually, visibly, and were ushered into their elder years with rather little left for them to do. At least the lucky ones were. He had seen enough of Lu Fang in his twenty years as a slave to the city to know that not all humans lived a life of luxury, not all humans were cruel and indolent. Just some. The human slaves he had labored beside for two decades were proof of that. But elves aged differently. Elves maintained a semblance of their vigor and strength right up until the moment their bodies gave out and creation called them into the next reality—the Third Reality. Valdor knew his time was soon. One day he would likely pick up a child as he had for years now to provide comfort or solace and his body would collapse, that last child being the final straw. He only hoped he wouldn't be holding one of the smaller, younger ones. That would be a terrible way to go—injuring one of his charges as he left this world.

"Sifra, Sifra." One of the little children tugged on his free hand, shouting the region of Lu Fang's local term for 'Grandfather' to get his attention.

Valdor smiled patiently and indulgently. "Yes, child?" He shifted the tiny elf he was holding on his hip to assure his grip. The elf on his hip buried its face in his side.

"Watch me run!" the little human girl shouted when she saw that she had Valdor's undivided attention. And the child ran.

Valdor put down the elf he was holding and clapped his hands enthusiastically. "Well done, well done," he celebrated the little girl. He had long ago realized that the years from their birth to their fifth name day would be the happiest of his young charges' lives. From age five onwards, they would

262

work in a full capacity. But until their fifth name day, the young ones were Valdor's, free to play and laugh within the confines of their barracks or the outdoor enclosure in which they now were. Valdor had determined long ago to make sure that those five years were as filled with light and love as possible before they left him and endured a lifetime of slavery.

The city of Lu Fang was built on a bay and divided into three hilled peninsulas. There was a slave barrack on each peninsula. The north peninsula housed elves, filling as they arrived from their fallen land. The south peninsula was occupied by humans alone. The middle peninsula however, had a slave barrack that was populated by a mixture of the two races of slaves.

Strange, Valdor thought, that he had spent the last twenty years on a single strip of land after having roamed the forests and glades of Andalaya for so much of his early life. He had not been young when he was captured and transported across the Great Bridge to the human continent. Valdor still remembered what it felt like to hold a bow and loose a shaft. He could still recall the green and stone walls and buildings of his ancestral mountain home. Verdantihya was a place, an image that was impossible to forget.

He watched the child run and run. He wished for the same opportunity himself.

"Sifra," an older voice said, pulling Valdor's attention away from his charges. It was the head of the guard set to watch Valdor and the children's quarters. There was a guard set in every room and corridor, every entrance and exit. Valdor couldn't remember the last time he'd been outside the sight of an armed human.

The man looked at him with genuine respect, an emotion that was hardly afforded to anyone who wore the collar. As if thinking about it caused the action, Valdor's hand subconsciously trailed upwards to touch the copper collar welded around his neck in an unbroken band. The accursed collar marked him a slave of the lowest rank. Not that anyone would mistake Valdor for anything else. Elves in this continent could be nothing but slaves. His elegantly tipped ears marked him as much as the collar.

Valdor raised his eyebrows questioningly and looked the guard in the face. "Yes, Guardsman Engan?"

"A shipment of excess dried and candied fruits arrived from a merchant party for us yesterday. We've eaten some, but there is plenty left. Would you and the children like some?"

It was leftover, but the guard was hardly required to share. The children would love the candied fruit, regardless of their race. Valdor—or Sifra, as he often thought of himself, after having been called that by child and adult, human and elf, captor and slave, alike, for decades now—smiled gratefully and opened his mouth to thank Engan, when a child scampered through the hole in the fence laughing gleefully.

"My apologies Guardsman!" Valdor exclaimed, and rushed to peer through the crack in the fence of the outdoor enclosure. It wasn't vital to reach the child immediately, there were guardsman patrolling the outskirts as well as the interior of the barrack, but on principle, Valdor could be whipped even beaten to death for allowing one of his charges to leave the confines of the barracks.

Valdor saw the child staring with awe at the city around him. The child stood atop a hill on the middle peninsula and could see for miles. It was likely the best view he had ever seen.

"Mishtin! Come back!" Valdor cajoled, without any real desperation. He knew Engan. Guardsman Engan had watched over Valdor and his charges for the better part of a decade now, and they were old acquaintances. Not friends. Surely not that. But there was respect. The child closed its open jawed stare at the sound of Valdor's voice and reluctantly clambered back through the hole at his watcher's request.

Valdor guided the child back to the others. "Remember, young ones, we do not go outside." He said the catechism and the children repeated it back to him by rote. "And why is that?" he asked them in his most instructor-like voice.

"Because outside is dangerous," they repeated again, in a bored but complying tone.

Dangerous didn't really cover it. He and they could be killed if there was a breach in the guardsmen's security and little elves escaped. Any breach of the law was punishable by death after all—a slave had no rights. But the hole in the fence had been there for years and Engan knew Valdor could coax strays back inside the fold without too much difficulty.

"Sorry, Guardsman," Valdor said again, after every little head was accounted for.

"Not a problem," Engan said, in an almost friendly voice. "Now about the sweets, where would you like me to put them?"

Chapter Thirty-Four

The Southern Refuge was a perfectly hidden port. The mouth of the small bay was concealed from the outside ocean. The two arms of land were cliff faces, wrapping around the bay and overlapping at the mouth to create an S-shaped entry point. Only those who knew of the Refuge could find it. All others sailing the seas around the island would only see a flat face of cliffs with no apparent entrance.

Piripeos had angled their course south and west until they reached the Southern Refuge, a day of sailing enough for them to reach the cove. As their small, stolen vessel wound its way carefully through the curved mouth of the bay, Ell felt a flutter of apprehension. He knew next to nothing about this place other than it was a port where Piripeos hoped to find sailors wild enough to crew a ship set to depart for the human continent and sail across the Fracture—a feat never before accomplished.

The winding mouth of the hidden harbor slid by, rocky cliff walls of grey speckled with hanging ferns and a few palm frond plants strong enough to cling to the cliff walls punctuating the stone façade. Ell watched the clear blue water slip by beneath the hull of the ship from the captain's deck while standing next to Piripeos.

"Why do they call it the Refuge?" Ell asked, his curiosity getting the best of him.

"The Southern Refuge," Piripeos corrected absentmindedly as he focused on guiding the vessel through the narrow, winding channel.

"Okay, why do they call it the Southern Refuge?" Ell amended in a tone tinged with slight exasperation, punctuated by a roll of his eyes.

As they cleared the channel, the water opened up around them into a protected cove. This hidden port would surely be ideal for smugglers and evaders of the law such as Piripeos. Ell noticed that on the far end of the small bay there was a port—harbor, docks, the whole works. There were buildings running into the lush vegetation behind, and up the sloping hill.

Having finished the dangerous navigation, Captain Piripeos turned his full attention to Ell.

"It's known as the Southern Refuge for a rather simple reason. It's the last port to the south that is hidden from the crown and a safe haven for those of my kind."

"Your kind?"

Piripeos smirked. "You know, flouters of the law, elves of fortune and opportunity." The Rimmer flourished his hand idly as if the name given wasn't really that important.

Ell stared at him incredulously for a moment. "You're a pirate?"

Piripeos pursed his lips as if the term was somewhat unpleasant. "Well, that's a bit of an unimaginative way of describing me, but in the broadest sense of the word—yes."

"And you've taken us to a pirate cove?" Ell's incredulity was growing by the moment.

"Where did you think we were going to find a crew crazy enough to sail the Fracture?" The Rimmer shot Ell a confused look, as if he had assumed their destination had been completely obvious.

"What is to stop one of them from selling us out, from sending word to the authorities of where we are?" Ell asked, his worry and fear mounting.

"Use your head, Northerner," Piripeos said in annoyance, "these elves are all either wanted criminals or known rabble, suspected of being unlawful and disloyal to the crown, they wouldn't bring the authorities down on this safe haven of theirs."

Ell was forced to accede to his logic.

Piripeos continued. "However, word will eventually filter out that we were somewhere to the south, rumors have a way of spreading, there's no way around that, but by then we should be long gone. Hopefully." His last, muttered word didn't inspire as much confidence in Ell as his previous statements.

"So, what is the plan?" Ell asked, as their ship coasted gracefully across the completely still, tropical blue waters of the cove.

The Rimmer gave Ell a fierce look. "You let me handle this. I do the talking. I want most of you to stay aboard the ship, as even a couple Northerners will be hard enough to explain. I don't want to have to explain why I'm captaining an entire ship full of them. Got it?"

Ell nodded complacently. His family had sat patiently waiting in a cave for weeks. They could handle a day or two in the ship's cabins if necessary. He, on the other hand, would not. Ell was going to hold Piripeos to that 'most of you' statement. Ell was determined to be one of the few to be allowed off the ship. After all, how often in life did you get a chance to wander and explore a pirate's cove? A small bubble of excitement formed.

The ship slid carefully through the water to dock at the wooden pier next to a number of other vessels bristling with masts. None of them were the giant merchant vessels Ell had seen in Dark Harbor. Rather, most of the ships were like the one upon which Ell and his family sailed—moderate in size, sleeker, quicker, and with a much smaller cargo space. Ell assumed such ships were better for smuggling and running from the law. It stood to reason that Piripeos would have captained a ship that was optimum to his illicit purposes.

After they had tied off and Piripeos was done bellowing orders, the Rimmer turned again to Ell. "Remember, stay aboard the ship for now, the less questions the better. If you have to go ashore," the knowing look he shot Ell, made Ell certain the Rimmer knew Ell had plans to explore, "wait and do so when night falls. It will be easier to avoid notice then, with the darkness to shield your pale features. Besides, everyone will be drunker then," he finished with a grin.

Ell acquiesced to the captain's request and went into the cabins with the rest of the group, while Piripeos set out along the pier towards the rickety, ramshackle buildings of the port to conduct the business of finding a crew.

* * * *

They passed the day in the sweltering confines of the cabins, waiting for twilight to arrive. When the sun finally set, Ell and his family ventured on deck to breathe fresh air and stretch their legs. With hoods up, they would look much like any other southern elf—at least from a distance.

Piripeos had been gone since the minute they made port, and he didn't return when evening struck, not that Ell had expected him to do so. Ell's family members were unhappy to be cooped up, but they understood the captain's motives. As night fell completely, Ell and Dahranian—the only two with the fake tears tattooed on their cheeks—slipped off the ship and onto the wooden dock. They were likely to stand out if their pale features were recognized beneath their hoods, but at least the Traitor's Tears gave them an excuse to be this far south. Ell would have gone alone, but his family insisted on his taking someone with him to watch his back. They didn't remember that he had spent weeks alone in Dark Harbor looking after himself. He could watch his own back. He understood the southern culture better than any of them.

Ell forced down the odd annoyance he felt and told himself to be glad for their concern. It would be good to have his cousin by his side. In a fight, one could hardly ask for a better companion than Dahranian. As soon as Ell made peace with the plan for Dahranian to accompany him, he felt lighter, and a strangely buoyant sensation replaced it. They were about to explore new territory, and if there was one thing Ell could be said to have enjoyed during his stay in Dark Harbor, it was the times he had spent just meandering around the city observing its quirks and idiosyncrasies. It would be fun to explore the Southern Refuge also.

Together, he and Dahranian walked away from their family members. Ell was glad of the growing expanse of dock between his back and Rihya's jealous glares. She, of course, had been vexed to the extreme that once again she was to be confined in some small compartment—this time a cabin instead of a cave—while her little brother was off having adventures.

"What are you laughing at, Cousin?" Dahranian asked curiously.

Ell hadn't realized that he was laughing, but responded anyway. "My sister. I always enjoy tweaking her nose just a bit, and being left behind yet again will do just that."

Dahranian allowed himself a small smile. "It will be good for her. She must learn patience." Dahranian would, of course, find the lesson in this. He could find a lesson to be learned in just about any situation. It could grow wearisome at times.

The two of them entered the port settlement, hoods drawn up, and made their way to a drinking establishment. Ell had been in the south long enough to know that this was the best place to glean information. One didn't even have to engage in conversation. The voices of the drunken elves were often loud enough for a silent observer to sit unnoticed in a corner and learn much.

Dahranian was clearly unsure of himself as they entered the tavern—Ell's cousin was unfamiliar with cities and buildings in much the same way that Ell had been upon his arrival to Dark Harbor. So Ell took it upon himself to order two drinks for them, fire ales, to blend in with the crowd. Nobody noticed another two hooded strangers ordering drinks because the raucousness of the common room was enough to allow nearly anyone to slip in unnoticed.

"What now?" Dahranian asked quietly.

"Now we sit. We drink and we listen."

Dahranian nodded and followed Ell to a table in the darkened corner of the room, away from torchlight. They sat for a time, drinking in silence, listening to the many coarse and varied conversations around them. After a time, Dahranian's curiosity got the best of him again.

"What exactly are we listening for, Cousin? Is there some particular piece of information you hope to glean?"

Ell smiled at his cousin. "No, Dahranian, not really. I just wanted off that ship for a time and I figured that if I said I was looking for information it would be the best excuse."

Dahranian's eyes narrowed and he took on a disapproving look.

"Oh come on, Dahranian," Ell said in annoyance, a bit of the former resentment rearing its head. "You cannot tell me truthfully that you would rather be cooped up in that cabin still. It's better to be out seeing things, doing things, rather than just sitting."

Ell's cousin relaxed and allowed himself another small smile. "I guess I cannot argue with that. Besides, we might as well get some benefit from having these grotesque tattoos." Dahranian's look of distaste as he mentioned the Traitor's Tears mirrored Ell's own emotions. It was good to get some bonus from having to wear these false tattoos. If it meant that they got a bit of extra leash to roam away from the ship while the others were confined, then Ell felt that it was only what he and his cousin deserved.

They drank in silence for a time, listening to the boisterous common room around them. They sipped their fire ale and watched pirate elves get drunk and sing songs, argue and have fights, and pass out in pools of spilt ale or, in some cases, even a bit of vomit. It was rougher than most taverns Ell had been in— even in Dark Harbor, the taverns had maintained a bit more decorum than this. But for all the yelling and singing and loud conversations, there was nothing of interest to learn. Ell and Dahranian made small conversation, talking of home and of Miri, the weather and the past, and simply enjoyed being away from the ship for a while.

Ell observed the crowd around them as they stood up to leave the tavern and return to the vessel. Rimmers populated the tavern tables with their fully shaved heads, their piercings and shorter stature. But there were also Departed warriors, the sides of their heads shaved and long manes of hair trailing in braids or loosely down the back of their heads and necks, top rows of teeth filed to points. There were normal southern elves with the look of sailors from the southern capital and the nearby Enclaves as well—not Rimmer-short, unshaven heads, naturally blunt teeth. The scent of unwashed bodies and stale sweat was the one thing everyone had in common.

Ell and Dahranian left the tavern with their anonymity intact, their hoods having stayed up all evening. Stars speckled the southern sky and Ell and Dahranian walked in silence back to the ship. A few palm trees protruded along the sides of the streets and large brown nuts with thick husks, the size of a child's head, dotted the ground beneath the trees.

They returned to the ship to find that Piripeos was still out and had not returned. The rest of their company was sleeping, Dacunda holding watch. Ell's uncle watched them approach and simply nodded his greeting, turning his eyes immediately back to the darkness surrounding the ship. His uncle was ever watchful. Ell and his cousin made their way into a cabin and clambered into two of the hammocks that were still free of sleeping bodies. Ell lay, swaying gently back and forth, the hammock still moving from the motion of his climbing into it, waiting for sleep. It came quickly and Ell slept until he was wakened in the hours just before dawn by the barefoot captain swearing as he stubbed his toe trying to find his hammock bed.

"Did you get what we need?" Ell asked, trying to keep his voice quiet so as not to wake the rest of the cabin.

The captain mumbled something drunkenly unintelligible.

"What?" Ell asked crossly for clarification.

"I said, it will take a bit more time," Piripeos slurred as he dozed off immediately.

Ell forced himself back to sleep, forced himself not to worry. He had to trust that the captain knew what he was doing, even if he did stumble in drunk in the wee hours of the morning. Sleep found Ell again and it was a restful sleep. Dreamless, Ell floated in the dark void of sleep and when he woke, it was full morning and he felt more refreshed than he had felt in quite some time. He was one of the last to rise, leaving the captain sleeping in the cabin hammocks.

Ell swung himself gracefully out of the swaying bed and left the room quietly, his hood up as he entered the grey dawn on the deck. Birds trilled in the morning air, and a few insects buzzed and hummed to create an altogether harmony of background noise. The air was warm and sticky, even this early in the day. The tropics were a humid place, Ell realized as he already found himself beginning to exude beads of sweat on his forehead in the early morning heat. He was the only one on deck. His family had obeyed the captain's demands. Ell stooped to leave the deck and enter the belly of the ship. He heard noise from the direction of the galley and followed the sounds of conversation until he reached a room full of his family members breaking their fast on what food was left. In this case, it was hardened biscuits that were lacking in flavor but full of nutrients. His family members ate with no real sense of enjoyment, and Rihya, in particular, had a look of displeasure as she ate her way mechanically through one of them.

"We need more food, Elliyar." Dacunda was the first to speak to him.

"Better food," Rihya added, with a look that said everything. She tossed her half-finished biscuit back onto a plate.

"I will tell Piripeos when he wakes," Ell promised.

"He's too drunk to wake any time soon," Rihya muttered.

Ell laughed. She had spent no time in Dark Harbor, none of them had. They didn't understand that business in the waterfront taverns was done over ale, copious amounts of ale, barely draughts, and occasionally cheap wine. One didn't conduct business without getting at least somewhat drunk. That the captain had tottered in to the cabin in the wee hours of the morning full of drink was a good sign, Ell thought. It meant he had likely been up all night searching for a crew, talking to sailors who he thought might be willing to join their venture. At least, Ell hoped that was what it meant. There was always the off chance that Piripeos had simply been off getting drunk for the sake of getting drunk. Ell chose to believe that wasn't the case.

Rihya turned her nose up haughtily at his laugh and grin, and sniffed. Apparently, she didn't approve of drunkards. Ell couldn't blame her. Drinking was a warrior's worst enemy, the downfall of even the best warrior could occur if he or she was too plied with wine to stand straight. But Ell also realized there was a time to relax and drink for the sake of drinking, as well. His time in Dark Harbor had taught him that lesson. He would have despaired long before finding his father if he hadn't found a method to release some of the pent up stress of searching fruitlessly. A good fight was the best release of energy, but when an elf wanted to remain relatively unnoticed and out of the attention of the authorities, then a few drinks was often the best remedy.

A few hours passed, and midday approached. They stayed indoors, not venturing up to the ship's deck for fear of drawing attention with their pale faces. However, there was a stillness to the Southern Refuge that suggested that the mornings and even middle of the days were times for rest and sleep. This port of pirates came alive at night and that meant most elves slept during the day.

Eventually, the Rimmer captain groggily made his way to the galley and joined the rest of them. He downed a mug of water and then another, wiping his eyes blearily between his efforts to rehydrate.

"So tell me, what progress have you made in finding a crew?" Ell asked.

Piripeos winced. "Not so loud, Northerner, you don't have to yell."

Ell smirked at the captain's morning after illness and headache. "Rough night?"

"You have no idea," the captain moaned. "I haven't seen some of these elves for years and everyone wanted to buy me a drink, especially after I told them how I slipped the noose in Dark Harbor."

"*You* slipped the noose?" Ell asked pointedly.

"We did," Piripeos muttered, with a wave of his hand to signal that details were not important. "Of course, it was we. But they don't need to know that."

Ell pressed for more information again. "So did you even ask any of your acquaintances if they were looking for an impossible adventure." He kept his voice purposefully light, almost self-mocking. Ell knew they were searching for a crew who would be willing to take part in what was an insanely dangerous mission.

"I made a few overtures to certain sailors that I am acquainted with. I sent out my feelers," Piripeos answered.

"And?"

The short Rimmer grimaced in annoyance. "And I'll likely hear nothing definitive until tonight or maybe tomorrow when I'm having more ale poured liberally down my gullet again."

"Oh, you poor thing! How terrible it is to have drinks thrown at you," Ell mocked the Rimmer good-naturedly.

Piripeos put a hand to his head. "You'd be singing a different tune if you were inside my head right now." The captain grabbed a biscuit and began gnawing on it.

Ell laughed. "Very well, that may be the case. What's the plan now?"

"The plan? The plan is that I'm going to finish this horrible biscuit, go back to sleep for a few hours, and regain my strength. Then I'm going to use the last of my coin to purchase us provisions so we don't have to eat these forsaken hard cakes all voyage. After that, I'll go get drunk again and try to find us a crew!"

Ell shook his head. "You really are a bit of a complainer aren't you, Piripeos?"

"I'm a sailor," the Rimmer responded, as if that said it all. And with that, the captain wobbled back out of the galley heading in the direction of the cabin and a hammock.

Ell turned back towards his family and saw their worried gazes on his.

"Is he to be trusted?" Dahranian asked, worry coloring his voice.

"Do you really believe that his scampering off to get drunk is going to help us find a crew?" Dacunda voiced his frustration, as well.

"Do we even need a crew? We learn quickly and can crew the ship ourselves." Rihya spoke with her usual confidence bordering on arrogance.

Ell shook his head at them and answered their questions. "Yes, we can trust him—I think. Yes, his getting drunk is all part of the process. And no, we cannot crew the ship ourselves, are you crazy, Rihya! None of us knows the first thing about sailing. What happens when we hit rough water? Winter is soon upon us, even this far south, and autumn storms are nothing to laugh at. We'll die at sea before we even attempt to cross the Fracture if we do not find a crew. Of that, I am certain."

Rihya had the good sense to look embarrassed after her ridiculous assumption that they could crew the ship themselves on a long voyage, but Dacunda and Dahranian didn't appear convinced by his answers to their questions. Yet they accepted his response for now.

The day was spent in the interior heat of the galley or the cabins. They ate hard biscuits, played knife games to occupy their time, or took muggy naps on the hammocks until night fell again.

Piripeos had left in the late afternoon to secure provisions, and the food stores he purchased were delivered as twilight was just beginning to creep across the sky once more. Ell and his family waited for the southern elves to leave before loading the provisions from the dock onto the ship. The night had cooled the air slightly, but not enough to be significant, and the sweat slicked their bodies after a day of not bathing. Ell longed to leap over the side of the ship into the blue waters, but that would attract unwanted notice, a fair skinned body swimming in the harbor wasn't normal. Instead, they hauled up buckets of seawater and sluiced the sweat from their skin, only to replace it with the sticky, salty sensation of dried seawater. But it was a small step forward.

When full dark arrived and the moon was full, Ell made his way with Dahranian again up the dock and into Southern Refuge. They wandered through the dirt streets and between the wooden huts and lumber buildings. The whole port town had a ramshackle appearance to it, as if a strong wind might blow down even the biggest of the buildings. But protected in this hidden cove as it was, with the cliffs encircling it, the Southern Refuge was not likely to feel the full wrath of any winds or storm.

They walked further into the port and were about to step into a tavern for another night spent away from being pent up on the ship, when a few of the Refuge's inhabitants stepped out of the darkness in front of them.

"What are you doing here?" a bare-chested sailor asked Ell.

"Yah, we don't want your kind around, Traitor." A second elf—a short Rimmer—spoke, and then spat in the dirt at Ell's feet.

"Go home, or back to your new home in Dark Harbor, Traitor. If you even have a home anymore." The third southern elf looked like a disgraced Departed warrior, the sides of his head shaven and teeth filed to fangs.

A moment of silence followed and the menacing looks grew as neither Ell nor his cousin responded. Ell was surprised to find that he wanted them to attack. Ell wanted to fight. He felt a black desire welling up inside him, hoping for a chance to inflict pain. It was a foreign thought as if not his own, yet at the same time it felt familiar as if it had been his thought all along, only lost some time in the distant past, but reclaimed now. Ell fought within himself, fought a desire to kill that was stronger than he had ever experienced, stronger, and with less reason than ever before.

"I think we should teach them a lesson, don't you?" the warrior said to his companions, misconstruing Ell and Dahranian's silence for weakness.

In a flash, the three southern elves had drawn swords—strangely curved cutlasses—and were leaping into the attack. Dahranian smoothly drew his long sword off his back and engaged the warrior one on one, trusting Ell could handle the other two.

Ell reached out his consciousness to access his power as a Water Caller and felt the power flood him, the strength and agility fill his body down to the marrow of his bones. But this time, with it came something else, something extra.

A blackness crept in with his Water Calling abilities, and there was power in the blackness. Ell had no time to think however, as he drew his dueling daggers to engage the two pirates. He slashed and fought instinctively with the power of a Water Caller, but there was a darker aspect to his duel this night. Ell felt the urge to slay bursting within him. He opened the gut of one of his assailants with incredible ease, moving faster than the elf could manage to react. The short Rimmer launched himself furiously at Ell to avenge his fallen comrade, but Ell sidestepped, dodged, and opened a gash on the Rimmer's face with a whip of his blade. Ell then swung his fist forward as it gripped the hilt of his dueling dagger. As his knuckles collided with the Rimmer's face, the elf went down in a heap, the punch felling him as quickly as a hammer blow would. A surge of power flowed from his fist, into his body, as he connected with the elf. Ell felt a thrill of joy at defeating his opponent, and then the rational side of him, the part fighting for control of his own mind, felt a jolt of fear and concern as he saw the fallen Rimmer's face was now sickly looking, the flesh diseased. Ell swallowed and turned to his cousin's aid, forcing himself to forget it for the moment, and focus on the fight. But there was no need to worry for Dahranian, since Ell's eldest cousin had just dispatched his own assailant with ease, as well.

"All well?" Dahranian asked Ell, and cast a glance at Ell's two fallen opponents.

Ell felt the overwhelming urge for his cousin not to see the diseased face of his fallen attacker. He couldn't say why, but he wanted to sort it out himself, wanted it to remain his knowledge, his secret for now. To pull his cousin's attention away from the fallen elves, Ell grabbed Dahranian's arm.

"We should get back to the ship. I do not know what sort of authorities they have here, or even if they have them, but we don't want to run the risk of being caught with these three dead."

Dahranian nodded his agreement and they ran lightly and quietly through the night and back to the docks. Ell imagined he could still hear the brief ring of steel on steel from their recent scuffle sounding into the night and attracting attention. But it was not so. They reached the ship without issue or alarm and as they boarded Dahranian looked searchingly into Ell's eyes.

"Are you sure you are alright, Cousin? You seem…not your usual self."

Ell shook off the worried question with a forced grin and a murmured platitude that he was perfectly fine before excusing himself and finding a quiet corner of the deck to think.

Ell was in a near panic now that he was back in his right mind. That Rimmer's face had not been diseased before he struck it, had it? Ell was almost certain it had not. But that could only mean one thing, and he was desperate to avoid that conclusion. It was possible, it had to be possible, that he was mistaken. Ell sat in huddled fear, in miserable silence through the night in his out of the way corner of the ship until he heard the captain's drunken feet pattering onto the deck from the boarding plank.

Ell shook himself from the misery of his thoughts and forced himself to focus on his task, on his duties as leader of this expedition.

"And what of tonight? Any headway on finding us a crew?" he asked Piripeos as the captain approached through the darkness.

The captain gave him one startled glance as if he had not been aware that someone was there before answering. "Got us a crew, leastwise, most of one. But with you lot already onboard it should be enough." Piripeos belched loudly, and then immediately hustled to the rail and vomited over the side. "Cost me my belly and liver to get that crew, though," he muttered in drunken complaint before wandering toward the cabin.

"Well? Where are they?" Ell asked, steering the drunk captain towards his bed.

"Be here tomorrow sometime." The Rimmer belched again. "We should be able to set sail by afternoon. Or maybe, make that evening," the captain said as he vomited again, this time onto the cabin floor, and then crawled into the hammock and commenced snoring.

* * * *

Piripeos was as good as his drunken word. By mid-afternoon, a haphazard assortment of sailors had accumulated on the ship's deck. By the evening tide, Piripeos was standing haggardly at the tiller, steering the ship back out of the cove, through the winding, cliff-walled mouth of the bay, to leave the Southern Refuge behind.

They made it to open sea as the stars began to light up the sky. All the while, the captain's bellowed orders were carried out by a crew of sailors who actually knew what they were doing. It might have been Ell's imagination, but the ship actually seemed to move faster, more smoothly, with a crew of real sailors tending to its knots and sails. Either way, Ell was glad to leave not only the Refuge behind, but the dark glimpse inside himself that had been revealed to him in its dangerous alleys.

Chapter Thirty-Five

The *Water Wasp* journeyed south at a smooth and steady pace. They encountered a few days of rough weather after leaving the Southern Refuge, but in general, their days were spent climbing and descending the gently sloped, rolling waves of the seas south of Dark Harbor and the Enclaves.

Ell watched the crew attend to their duties with practiced efficiency and he felt comfort in knowing that the ship was in good hands. From the outset, the crew mingled with his family members. Ell had expected there to be a dislike and disregard, or at the very least a hesitancy, for the southern elves to interact with their northern cousins, but he was surprised by the relative good cheer that awaited them on deck each day. Piripeos didn't elaborate much on how he had managed to convince a crew of sailors to undertake a near impossible voyage, but during his interactions with the new crewmembers, Ell gleaned enough information to piece together bits of clues as to why the various Departed sailors had decided to join with him and his family.

The first thing Ell realized was that not one of the sailors felt any allegiance to the southern crown. They were free spirits—pirates, if you will— and they had loyalty only to themselves and their own desires. That explained why they would ally with members of the Highest. But it didn't explain their personal reasons, the deeper reasons, for why they would choose to accompany him and his family on a journey across the Fracture.

Ell strolled along the deck, watching the crew attend to their duties. A few of the new sailors stood out as the more vocal leaders of the southern crew. Ell passed by Kester—one of those leaders—and stopped a moment to chat.

She was not a Rimmer. She was taller and, while muscled, still leaner than those southern elves from the far western rim of the islands. Kester was likely from the area surrounding Dark Harbor or the Enclaves closer to the coast. She was strong from years spent pulling line, tying rope, handling oars, and in general, fighting the sea and all its glorious storms on a regular basis. Kester was also insane, or at least Ell believed that she was as close to crazy as an elf could be and still function somewhat normally. She laughed wildly in the teeth of storms, climbed among the mast and rigging as if she were a tree creature from the tropic islands, and rarely ever answered a question if it was posed to her.

"Nice day for a sail," she grunted to Ell as she tended a line that needed securing. She had seen his approach.

"Beautiful day indeed," Ell agreed, "thankfully, the storms have not returned to plague our voyage," he commented, referring to the few days of rough weather that had beset them upon departing the Southern Refuge.

Kester laughed as if what he had said was the funniest thing she'd ever heard. "Want to know a secret?" she whispered conspiratorially. "Every day is a good day for sailing. There are no bad days." She widened her eyes maniacally as if she had revealed the secret of existence to Ell. When he didn't react immediately, she pouted her lips in a mock impression of a little girl and didn't speak any further. Ell rarely knew what to say or how to act around her. His first impression of her had been of her standing in the prow of the ship as the *Water Wasp* crested a wave, spraying her with cold seawater before surging down the steep face of the stormy trough. She had been screaming with glee while the rest of the passengers clung to whatever they could grab for dear life.

Ell had wondered then if Piripeos had made a mistake, thinking he'd somehow managed to secure a crew consisting of lunatics, but the captain had quickly reassured Ell of his faith in Kester. Apparently, she was renowned for her fearless nature, and was known as one of the best sea elves to crew a ship. Ell had no choice but to trust the captain. In any regard, she did seem to know what she was doing, even if having a real discussion with her was difficult. When he'd initially asked her why she'd joined them to sail across the Fracture, Kester had stared at Ell as if he were the insane one and responded, "Sail the Fracture. Nobody has ever done it, nor attempted it for as long as I can remember. Why wouldn't I want to be a part of that? The adventure alone is worth the risk." She had giggled her wild giggle, her dark eyes shining like opals amidst the black hair that whipped around her face. "I should be paying you just for the opportunity to be a part of this venture."

Ell strolled further along the deck, leaving Kester in his wake. He passed two other sailors with significant enough reputations to warrant the crew's admiration. Rikiol and Baerg were a couple—or at least Ell imagined they must be since they spent nearly every moment together when they weren't working. Although, come to think of it, he had never actually seen them touch or kiss.

Baerg was a solemn, sober Departed. He was heavily muscled and looked like he'd have been more suited to the military than life as a pirate, but Ell was glad to have another fighting elf aboard should they run into trouble. He handled his cutlass with ease. His motives for joining seemed to be almost the exact same as Kester—the thrill of the adventure, the desire to do something impossible, to undertake a voyage never completed before and write himself into the histories. Yet, his mannerisms and the way he expressed that sentiment was the exact opposite of the half-mad Kester. Rikiol, Baerg's companion, had different reasons for joining. She was shorter, possibly having some Rimmer blood in her, and the way she handled her knives reminded Ell of Rihya. In fact, she reminded Ell of his sister in other ways too. She lived to fight, she never backed down from a contest or challenge, and her free time during the first few days had been spent competing with Rihya in the various blade-wielding competitions to which they could think to challenge each other. In Ell's estimation, his sister was only slightly more talented than Rikiol, which made him wary of the diminutive dark elf. Not that he planned on having any altercations with the crew, but it never hurt to have appraised those around you and be ready.

When questioned, Rikiol didn't seem to care a lick for the impossibility of the venture or the annals of history. She latched onto the destination. The human continent. She lived to fight, and had quickly grown weary of killing her own race and their kindred cousins to the north. Rikiol figured that if they were sailing to the human continent then there was bound to be a chance to fight. What grudge she bore the humans, or why, Ell wasn't sure, but he couldn't blame her. He'd taken enough joy in punishing the human invaders himself.

Ell approached the two of them, working side by side. He tried to make light conversation as he had done with Kester a moment ago, but was met by the typically stoic Baerg who did not wish to speak. It was Rikiol who responded to him with her normal, expected rudeness, telling him not to interfere as they were busy.

Ell let his sour expression show. He was curious about the three of the crew with reputations, and wished to know them better, but his curiosity was often met with disinterest in the case of these two, and with Kester it was simply too difficult to follow her train of thought to have a legitimate conversation.

Ell abandoned his hopes of conversation and meandered back along the deck the way he had come. The rest of the busy crew had joined the venture at Piripeos' bequest for similar reasons as Kester, Baerg, and Rikiol. Some sought fame and thought this a momentous voyage. Others, wanted blood, particularly human blood. Some hated the crown—hated Half-Mask—and what it represented, and they saw any venture helping the Northerners as an opportunity to spit in the face of royal authority. As pirates, this was practically their goal in life. Some few had joined the crew on the promise of loot to be had when they reached the human continent and these few were the ones that worried Ell. How was he to keep them happy and supply them with what Piripeos had promised? He would have to find an opportunity to loot when they reached the human continent or he might have an unhappy crew to deal with for the return voyage. Worries for later, for another day. Ell pushed those thoughts away from his head and sat down on a barrel outside of the aft cabin to watch the blue sky glide by the darker blue water.

Piripeos had left the tiller to one of the more able crewmembers and sat his short frame down beside Ell. The captain's various piercings glittered in the sunlight.

"Due for a rest?" Ell asked.

Piripeos grunted his assent. "Back aches if you stand at the wheel too long. Nothing to worry about now in good weather and open seas, but it's bad policy to allow a tired elf to steer the ship. It's all about principles."

Ell changed the topic. "The crew seems to be settling in well. They seem happy." It was half-statement, half-question. He left the running of the crew to the captain, because in most ways Piripeos was in charge while they were on board the ship. But when it came to the heart of it, this was still Ell's mission, his command, and he wanted to make sure all was well.

Piripeos assured Ell that all was going according to plan. "We don't need to worry about them—not yet at least. Most mutinies don't happen in the early stages of a voyage. Wait until you're out of food and clean water. That's the time to worry."

Ell didn't know if he was supposed to be comforted by the captain's statement or not.

"I cannot help but notice that you are somewhat… different than the rest of the crew." Ell didn't know how to put his statement more delicately than that.

"Different?" Piripeos asked with a smirk.

"Less rough around the edges. I can actually have a conversation with you. Dare I say, you're even a bit cultured."

Piripeos laughed. "I'll let you call me cultured just this once, but that's all you'll get. Next time I'll be forced to draw blood."

Ell joined the captain's laugh, enjoying someone who actually seemed to have good humor that he could understand.

"Truth is, I'm not exactly the typical type you find in the Southern Refuge. Nor in Dark Harbor, for that matter. Don't really fit in either place. I'm sort of on the fringe of both worlds, one foot planted on a ship sailing freely, the other foot aboard the deck of a ship making legitimate profit in accordance with the crown and society."

"What do you mean?" Ell asked curiously.

"I mean, I'm not the nasty pirate you assumed," Piripeos mocked good-naturedly. "Smugglers like to break the law, bend it, flout it, but we don't love the madness of complete anarchy on the open water. Pirates love the freedom, the hunt and kill, as much as the spoils from the ships and settlements they sack."

Ell nodded his head slowly. "So, you're more of a moderate, somewhere in between both worlds."

"Exactly," the Rimmer said.

Ell had begun to genuinely enjoy his interactions with the captain. What had started as just a business arrangement was blossoming into what might be considered friendship. Or at least, Ell hoped that was the case.

The two of them passed a few hours chatting idly while they watched the crew work, and Ell's family train lightly to keep their form and shape for the dangers ahead. All in all, Ell hadn't felt this rested, this relaxed, since before he'd set south on this venture. His summer with Miri had been breathtakingly peaceful, but the hectic search for his father had dominated his thoughts and time recently. Here on board the ship, there was nothing that needed immediate tending and it had been quite some time since there had been no immediate pressures weighing on him. Ell decided to make the most of it.

He watched with interest as Dacunda squared off in a duel with Dahranian, their swords flashing in the sunlight, their feet shifting and adjusting lithely to accommodate the swelling of the deck. Fighting on a ship was new to them, but they adjusted naturally in the way that only an elf could. Ell allowed himself to slip into a drowsy haze as he watched them cut and slash, testing each other without committing fully enough to do any real harm. It was only practice, after all.

Ell was nearly asleep when he was shaken from his drowsy state by the realization that Dahranian had handed his father the sword, and Adan was now squaring off with Dacunda.

Ell had never seen his father hold a sword, and he was curious to see if his father lived up to the legend—the shining defender of the walls of Verdantihya. It was enough to send Ell into wakeful attentiveness. Ell noticed that Rihya perked up, as well, at the sight of their father with a weapon in his hands.

Adan took the blade almost tenderly, the way one might greet an old friend or family member long thought forgotten or lost. Adan Wintermoon brought the blade up and let his gaze trail along the gleaming length of the sword. He swung a few lazy slashes through the air to hear the steel whip and rush in the wind. Adan smiled with pleasure and set his feet to square off with his brother, a look of anticipation and joy on his face.

Dacunda smiled also, but Ell noted a hint of wariness that he didn't have while facing Dahranian. Dacunda knew his brother as a sword wielder, knew his capabilities and was clearly cautious, even after a layoff of nearly twenty years.

They stepped fluidly into the mock duel, swords ringing with a clear metallic beauty that only those who love battle can truly appreciate. Dacunda moved with assurance, the confidence of an elf whose only profession for decades had been fighting. He attacked his brother with speed and accuracy. Adan blocked and parried, and edged backwards under the controlled onslaught. Ell's father fought like what he was—an elf who'd been enslaved for twenty years, an elf who hadn't held a blade in all that time. He was rusty, it was clear to Ell, as he parried those first few attacks. Yet, the light blazed in his eyes, and his joyous expression took on a focused mask. Ell saw him grow in confidence a minute into the mock duel, and Ell knew his father was finding his footing, knew Adan's reflexes and muscle memory were returning. Two minutes in, and Ell saw the grace returning to his father's movements, saw the duel become a duet of swords singing with beauty, rather than the clash of angry steel that inexperienced fighters employed.

It was a sight to behold. Adan quickly stepped forward to attack and as his confidence grew, his fluidity increased, and he fought like a snake, flowing from form to form, from attack to attack with an ease Ell had never seen. Arendahl and Ell were Water Callers. Their supernatural abilities afforded them power and agility and speed and strength. But theirs was a skill given by the magic of creation. Ell had never before seen an elf fight with such learned and practiced grace. It was incredible. He found tears welling in the corners of his eyes as Adan disarmed his brother and kissed the tip of his steel to Dacunda's throat.

They paused, panting for a moment, and then Dacunda let out a louder laugh than Ell had ever heard him emit before—a sound of the purest joy.

"By the First Days, you've still got it!" Dacunda declared breathlessly, pride streaking through his voice. It was the pride of a younger brother who had idolized the elder. "Twenty years a slave and you disarm me in a matter of minutes. I should be ashamed, but I just cannot feel angry." He laughed again.

Adan, the gracious winner, and beamed at his brother. "No hard feelings, Dac?" he teased his younger sibling.

"Never," Dacunda said with a serious smile. "In fact, I was half worried you might have forgotten it all. What a blow it would have been to have my one-time teacher and mentor be a husk of his former self."

A seriousness colored Adan's voice as he answered. "I was half worried myself, Brother." Relief was plain as day on his father's face. And for his sake, Ell was glad the memory of battle and blade handling had not abandoned his father.

The name of Adan Wintermoon was still to be feared.

Ell heard a spatter of applause from his family, saw Rihya's shining face, and imagined his own countenance must look similar. And then it was over. Too many congratulations were not the way of the Highest. Next up was Ryder and Rihya, two fiercely competitive fighters. Ell watched their duel with half interest. He caught his father's eyes on him as if Adan was wondering if Ell would take a practice bout himself. But for some reason, Ell declined to do so. Somehow he knew that the next time he took up arms in front of his father he would have to explain everything, his ability, his powers as a Water Caller. Ell was not ready to do that yet. He needed to sort through himself, sift out the strangely volatile emotions and desires he possessed in the wake of his defeat to Half-Mask. He wasn't ready to answer his father's questions because of the unanswered questions within himself.

Ell leaned back and closed his eyes, willing himself back into the dreamlike trance of drowsiness in which he had been earlier. Answers would come later. Both for his father and for himself.

A tap came on his shoulder, and Ell opened his eyes to see his father settling beside him.

"Well, fought," Ell congratulated. Adan smiled graciously.

"Thank you, Elliyar, it felt good to have a blade in my hand once again."

Suddenly, Ell was struck by a thought. He pulled both dueling daggers from his sheaths and extended them towards his father, hilts first.

"These were yours once, they should be yours again." It pained him to let them go, but they belonged to his father, not him. His father appraised him for a moment and then answered.

"No, Son. As you have seen, the sword suits me just fine. You keep them." He smiled again. Ell nodded in thanks. A sense of relief coursed through him as he realized he would not have to give up his blades. Though his family's blades were his father's by right, they were a part of him now and it would have been a pain to lose them.

Nothing more to say, the two of them settled back into a restful doze, letting the ocean wash past them and worries slough away for a time.

Chapter Thirty-Six

"The time is upon us! We must regroup, we must band together again and take a stand." Arendahl was standing on a large boulder, his feet level with most of the surrounding elves' heads, orating in his usual manner. His voice was loud, his emphasis hitting just the right mark to drive his points home. All in all, he was a good public speaker. Miri felt the surge of emotion course through her exactly as he intended. She watched the raptured gazes of the small crowd of elves gathered to listen and knew that the ancient elf's words were finding their mark in the hearts of the audience.

Arendahl addressed the small crowd standing around the boulder in the meadow for a few more minutes, uttering his cries for unity and courage, elaborating on why now was the time—two decades after the fall of Andalaya—for the Highest to join together once again and fight back against their oppressors. Miri had heard the sermon time and time again. Each time it lit a small fire of hope in her soul, but she also was accustomed enough to his speech to maintain control of her emotions. As such, she didn't join the cheer that arose as Arendahl drove his final points home with a resounding voice and a clenched fist.

The old elf hopped down from the boulder with a litheness that belied his age and clasped forearms and clapped shoulders of his audience.

"Our most ancient of Elders thinks a lot of himself, doesn't he?" Brie said slyly, with a bite of apple crunching between her teeth. A dribble of juice squirted from her mouth as she talked. Brie giggled and wiped it off her chin with the back of her hand.

Miri smiled indulgently at her newest and closest friend. They were opposites in almost every way and yet they were the fastest of companions, utter confidants. However, she didn't take the pixie blonde's joking bait.

"It's the cause he believes in so fiercely, thinks so much of, not himself." Miri's serious answer seemed to give Brie pause to think.

They did that for each other. Briesom emboldened Miri, taught her to use her knives to the best of her ability, gave her a new type of confidence that was rooted not in Miri's steadfast ability to endure hardship and find peace in life, but rather a confidence vested in a newfound ability to protect herself—or at least to attempt to protect herself. Miri was by no means a warrior, but the knives she threw no longer spun out of control to clatter harmlessly off their targets. Her grip on a bow was steadier than it had ever been. This wasn't to say that Miri had lost her desire for tranquility or her enjoyment of the simplicity of life. No, Miri still drew strength from her inner core of peace, yet Brie had helped her to add a new type of strength. For that, Miri was grateful. In return, Miri mellowed her brash, fierce, and irreverent companion. Miri gave Brie pause to think when she otherwise wouldn't. They were a good balance as each other's friends, and she could tell that Arendahl even approved of it.

"Well, whatever it is, I wish he would shut up about it every once in a while," Brie muttered. This time Miri, giggled with her. Arendahl just happened to glance over at them at that precise moment and caught their mirthful gazes upon him. His brow furrowed and his cheeks darkened for a moment until another elf placed herself in front of him and regained his attention.

Miri didn't begrudge Brie her little jests. The blonde fought more fiercely than most, and had been doing so for as long as she had been able to effectively wield a weapon. Brie believed in Arendahl's cause, heart and soul. She just liked to pretend she didn't care, liked the affectation of indifference. Miri wondered why that was. Perhaps it was a defense mechanism? Did it make it easier to cope with things that didn't happen if you acted like you never cared at all? Was Brie—a warrior who had spent years risking her life and fighting—so desperate to see the unification of the might of Andalaya that she had to protect herself against its potential failure by acting as if it meant nothing to her? Miri didn't ask her friend that question. She just allowed Brie her little games and enjoyed the company. You never knew exactly what you were going to get when it came to Brie.

Eventually, Arendahl made his rounds and spoke to everyone who wished a word with him. This gathering had been nearly thirty elves—which was slightly larger than the average group to which the old elf orated his tireless message of fighting back and banding together—and was mostly warriors.

Arendahl plopped down on the ground, leaning his back against the mossy log on which the two girls sat. He threw his elbows up behind him and reclined with a sigh, observing as Iyonei and the rest of her band set up camp and lit a cook fire.

"That went well," Miri ventured tentatively. His moods had been up and down of late and there was no predicting in which mood he would be.

"Too small."

"What was too small?"

"The gathering, girl. What else would I mean?" Arendahl said, in exasperation.

"It seemed to get you going well enough," Brie said, with a hint of a taunt in her voice.

The old elf pursed his lips into a grimace of sorts. "Girl, don't pretend you don't understand what I'm talking about. You're a warrior, you've seen the front lines of this conflict and it's only escalating in size. With the Unsired returned, we'll soon be fighting a full-fledged war on three fronts instead of two."

"What does he mean?" Miri asked, turning her gaze to Brie.

Brie sighed before answering, as if she was annoyed at the old elf for forcing her to drop her girlishly innocent and roguish act. With a serious face she said, "Like our grandest of leaders said, I've seen the front lines of this conflict and we are already losing ground—and fast. If we hope to make any headway, we are going to need to gather more elves of our kind than a handful here and a fistful there. Thirty more warriors isn't going to make a difference in the grand scheme." Arendahl gave her a look of approval as she elaborated on his point. For the barest of instants, there was a look of pride on her face as she saw his approval, but Brie quickly masked the emotion and regained her look of calculated disinterest, taking another bite of her apple and looking at the fruit as if it were the tastiest and most fascinating morsel of food she'd ever eaten. Arendahl shot a knowing look her way and let out a chuckle. He wasn't fooled by her charade. However, he didn't address Brie, but instead turned his face towards Miri.

"Like she said, we need more elves. We need to raise the whole of Andalaya, not just small pockets, here and there."

Miri thought for a moment. "What we need are runners. You should send those who are willing, out with details of a meeting—time and place set sometime in the near future—at which we could gather as many of the Highest as possible at one time to hear what you have to say, Arendahl."

"Not a half bad idea, girl. I'll organize that with Iyonei tomorrow." Arendahl gave her an almost impressed look, and for an instant Miri felt that fleeting feeling of pride she'd seen on Brie's face. She didn't hide it though, instead letting her grin show.

"Well, I'm not a half bad girl, am I?" she asked teasingly of the old elf who had become more important to her than she would ever have expected. Spending enough time with someone, even an elf as testy and cantankerous as Arendahl could be, inevitably led to strong feelings.

The old elf looked at her strangely and smiled, then answered in a surprisingly sweet voice. "No, you're not half bad at all."

Brie made a retching sound. "Are we done with these overt displays of emotion?" The little blonde warrior rolled her eyes suggestively, and Miri giggled again as an unusual rosy blush adorned Arendahl's face. Brie continued. "I get it, you guys are all big elf, baby elf now, but can't you act that way where the rest of us don't have to watch it." She smirked at the Elder's annoyance. Miri dug her elbow into Brie's ribs and the little blonde squawked in her own outrage. Brie made as if to wrestle Miri to the ground in some playful combat, but before they tumbled off the log in their exuberance, Arendahl cleared his throat to get their attention. It was odd. A month ago, Miri would never have thought to partake in a wrestling match, would never have even considered it as fun. Now, with a hint of confidence in her own physical ability, or perhaps just having learned to let go of her own shortcomings a bit, it was fun. It let her look forward to another aspect of Ell's return. Wouldn't he be surprised? Miri let that thought simmer as she and Brie turned their attention to Arendahl.

"How goes your training?" Arendahl asked Miri, but directed his question at Brie also. He knew she was overseeing Miri's practice.

"She can hit a target now from fifteen paces," Brie declared proudly before Miri could answer. "Her skill with a bow is also increasing, but her footwork is still sloppy in both activities and in her hand to hand combat. Hand to hand combat is her worst area—it helps to have her practice with the boy, Art," Brie finished with a faux conspiratorial whisper to the old elf who smiled.

Miri grimaced in annoyance. Sometimes she thought they forgot she was a cripple. Of course her footwork was terrible at times. There would never be any change to that weakness. But she didn't make excuses. Brie always told her 'a warrior never made excuses'.

The old elf nodded his head gravely, accepting the information and seeming to be glad of it. "And what of your other training?"

Brie narrowed her eyes slightly. Miri had not divulged the link she had forged with Ell's consciousness when she had Grafted him. In many ways, it was private. Maybe, one day soon, she would tell her friend. Brie was not stupid however. She'd seen Miri sitting alone on a log scrunching her face up in concentration as she attempted to access the link with Ell of her own accord. Yet the pixie warrior had the surprising tact not to inquire about it. Even so, Miri could see the interest in her eyes as she listened and watched the interaction between Miri and Arendahl.

"It goes much the same as before." Miri responded to Arendahl.

A faint look of disappointment flashed through the grey-haired elf's eyes but he quickly masked it.

"Keep practicing. It will come. I am sure of it."

Miri nodded. She caught a flicker of emotion here and there from Ell, but nothing powerful, not since that horrible experience when she had almost witnessed—no, experienced—his death. Everything since had been the faintest of flutters—a sensation of fear or joy, a hint of worry or relief. But nothing she could be certain was real, not in comparison to the powerfully charged emotions she experienced when something important occurred on Ell's end of the link and activated the Grafting between them. She told herself it would come, just as Arendahl comforted her in the same manner. Only, there were times, stretches of days even, when she feared precisely that. Miri wasn't sure she could bear to witness something as horrific as what she had seen before. Who knew what terrible things she might be forced to endure if she could access the link and peer into Ell's heart and soul at will? What if the daily struggle of his mission was too much for her? Miri knew that this probably wasn't the case. She tried to convince herself that it was silly to think such thoughts. Yet, there was a part of her that wondered, if perhaps she weren't so worried about it—afraid, she had to admit—that she might not experience more headway in her ability to access the Graft.

She looked into Arendahl's flint-grey eyes and he seemed to see to her core. Somehow, he knew what she was thinking, what she was wondering. He put a grandfatherly hand on her shoulder, but did not say anything. Brie's eyes were still narrowed, but she kept her silence, judging that now was not the time to ask for clarification.

Instead, the blonde elf asked in typical fashion, "Who's hungry?"

"Famished," Arendahl responded, clasping fingers across his belly. "Being a puffed up orator inspires such dreadful hunger pangs." His joke drew a surprising blush of its own on Brie's cheeks, as the old elf revealed his awareness of her tiny jibes at him from earlier. How he knew was a mystery, but it was clear he did. Brie managed to stare at him without blinking despite the blush. Miri covered her smile with a hand.

They stood together and walked over to the campfire where food was cooking. Smells wafted their way and Miri's mouth watered. Arendahl grabbed a haunch of meat and sliced himself a cut of the roasted meat with his belt knife. He forwent use of any utensil or plate and simply grasped it between his teeth and bit down, holding the rest in his hand. He didn't sit with them near the fire either.

"Where are you going?" Miri asked inquisitively.

"I'm off to tell Iyonei to follow your orders," the old elf joked.

"What!" Miri said, aghast at that prospect. Iyonei was a prickly one and

Miri didn't need the elf annoyed with her.

"Relax, girl," Arendahl barked in his stilted voice, "I'm only jesting. I'm simply off to relay your idea from earlier. The runners…" He let his voice trail off as her face cleared of confusion.

"It was a good idea," Briesom agreed, her mouth full again as she spoke, this time with supper.

Arendahl nodded. "Tomorrow, we'll send out runners to the four winds. We must call a large gathering, a gathering of all who will come. We are mustering for war, and all who wish to survive will need to stand together as one. The time for half measures is over."

A chill settled into the air as he spoke his words as the sun dropped below the ridgeline. Winter without sunshine was crisp and cold in the mountains of Andalaya, but his calm proclamation of war was colder still.

Miri shivered and tried to warm herself. But as much as the fire in front of her was hot and the meat in her hands was warm, she could not shake the foreboding chill from her bones.

War was coming and her people and her mate were at the center of it.

Chapter Thirty-Seven

The rains came at night. Southern rains, warm and wet, the drops fat enough to spatter in an elf's eye and blind him temporarily. Thunder and lightning accompanied the rain, a tropical storm which created troughs in the ocean big enough to swallow a ship whole. The *Water Wasp* wasn't a massive warship, it was a smuggler's vessel, a cutter, a slicer of the waves. Seas this rough sent the vessel surging up and down the face of swells hazardously. Ell would have been concerned for their wellbeing had it not been for Captain Piripeos' unwavering calm at the helm, steering their course and bellowing orders like it was any other day on the ocean. A couple of days out of the Refuge, and Ell was already missing land. He felt no seasickness, but there was an aching in his chest for hills and trees, for solid ground beneath his feet. Piripeos seemed to thrive on the weather, shouldering the responsibility for their safety as if it were the most natural thing to occur. And perhaps it was. The crew followed his orders without hesitation. It was a good sign, Ell thought, that a free willed bunch of sea elves didn't question the captain Ell had placed in charge.

Ell stood, soaking wet, on the captain's deck with the Rimmer.

"We are approaching The Point," Piripeos yelled at him over the roar of the wind and the crash of the waves pummeling the ship along its course.

The Point. Ell had seen maps. The Point was a peninsula of land jutting out into the southern sea surrounded by shoals and reefs. It was treacherous waters even without rough weather.

"Should we attempt passage in this type of weather?" Ell bellowed.

Piripeos shrugged noncommittally. "Not much of an option. No secure place to make port. In swells like these, we're better off trying to make headway than dropping anchor and waiting it out."

The answer didn't reassure Ell at all. He continued his raised voice. "Are you sure?"

Kester approached with some piece of information for the captain, interrupting their conversation. She delivered it and listened to Piripeos' directions before turning to leave again, to return to her post.

Before she left, she cast a wild grin at Ell. "I've never sailed The Passage in storm. Should be exciting. A thing to remember, eh?" And then the half-mad sailor disappeared back down the ladder steps to the deck, her wild-eyed enthusiasm reinforcing Ell's opinion that they were headed into trouble.

The Rimmer cocked his head at Ell and smiled ruefully. Had Ell misjudged the captain? Was he crazy too?

"Sometimes the only way to go is forward, however dangerous it is. There's bound to be pursuit on our trail, so turning north will do us no good. It won't do to get caught. Besides, we're crewed by pirates and they're not likely to enjoy sailing back towards Dark Harbor, the one port they're afraid to enter. No, that'll be mutiny for sure. The only way is onward." The captain finished his speech, and only barely managed to convince Ell that pushing through The Passage and around the tip of The Point was a good idea. Just barely. What finally tipped the scale was the fact that Ell knew nothing of the sea, and had to trust the instincts of his captain over the fears he might possess while being in unfamiliar territory.

They sailed onwards, and Ell descended from the captain's deck, leaving Piripeos to set their course in the building gale. Ell stepped inside the cabin and came face to face with Kalabi.

"Ah, Elliyar, just who I was looking for."

Ell tilted his head in unspoken question, waiting for the ex-slave to elaborate.

"I am worried with all this rain. Worried for my handfire. Is there a waterskin pouch, sealed from the elements in which I could place them?"

Are you worried, even with them safely stowed in the cabin?" Ell asked.

"I have been at sea before. Weather such as this tends to permeate all aspects of a ship. The handfire is delicately made with ingredients I do not wish to upset. It would set my mind at ease." Kalabi spread his hands almost regretfully as if he wished it wasn't so. He was probably no more happy about the storm than Ell.

"Very well," Ell agreed. It wouldn't hurt to secure something as valuable as their small cache of handfire, after all.

The two of them set off searching the cabin, and then the galley, and finally the storeroom in which Ell found what they were looking for: a watertight bag in which to place the handfire to protect and seal them away from the elements. Ell returned to the cabin with Kalabi and helped him place the individual erupting pouches into the larger watertight bag and then stow them in the corner.

Rihya wandered in, dyed green hair slicked against her head from the rain. She didn't seem concerned at all by the storm, her feet finding their footing with ease as the ship tilted up and then down, up and then down.

She grinned with excitement. "I didn't know sailing could be such an adventure. I would have done it sooner had I known!"

Ell couldn't help but laugh at her brash declaration. "If anyone seeks out a thrill, it's you, Rihya."

"Do not act like I am the only one, Little Brother. It was not I who climbed the crag and attacked the Pillar singlehandedly. Nor was it I who dueled Half-Mask."

"Matters of circumstance and necessity." Ell argued.

She shrugged. "If you say so, Brother." The twinkle in her eyes said she didn't believe him. Ell smiled. Maybe she was right. The responsibilities of leadership were weighing upon him, the success of the mission and the safety of his companions occupied his thoughts. Perhaps he should let that go for a time and enjoy the adventure, the wild ride of the tempest. Rihya certainly seemed to be doing so.

Impulsively, Ell caught Rihya in a rough embrace. She was bold and beautiful and someone to admire.

"What was that for?" Rihya asked quizzically, after he let her go.

"I am not really sure," Ell answered truthfully and a bit bashfully. Recovering his wits, he added, "Maybe I'm just hoping some of your rashness and arrogance will rub off on me as I leave this cabin to ride the storm from the ship's prow." Ell made as if to leave the room.

Rihya winked. "Whatever you need to do to gain a bit of boldness." Her eyes trailed to the watertight bag. "Good idea, securing the handfire."

And with that, Ell and Rihya exited the room and walked along the swelling deck. They reached the prow of the ship and rode the downward slope of the wave from the front of the *Water Wasp*, a front row seat on the wild ride of the storm. Rihya laughed delightedly and Ell smiled, even as her laugh mingled with the sound of Kester's hysteric giggle. Perhaps the insane sailor wasn't as crazy as he'd thought, Ell pondered, as he let himself enjoy the roiling of the ship beneath his feet. He'd faced death before, after all—many times in battle. How was it different to face the elements instead?

* * * *

The Passage was rough, but Ell forced himself to trust the captain. Piripeos guided the ship dexterously and skillfully through the dangerous reefs and shoals that marked the narrow passage around The Point. As they cleared the final shoal and entered the southern sea proper, Ell stared through the raging storm and saw another ship on the water. It was flying red flags from its prow and many masts. It was a massive war ship and it was surging their way, plowing through the swells.

Ell quickly climbed the steps to the captain's deck. "What is it?" He cried indicating the warship to Piripeos.

"It's from The Point—the sea fortress guarding our southern border from the humans."

"What do the red flags mean?" Ell was afraid he already knew the answer.

Piripeos shot a grim look at him as he navigated the last few rocky protrusions. "The red flags are meant to stop us. The Prince commands The Point, personally, and he operates with the full weight of the crown behind him. He can arrest any ship at any time. Likely our days in the Southern Refuge allowed a few ships to send word ahead of us."

Ell felt a chill of unexpected terror. "What do you mean, Half-Mask commands The Point? I thought he stayed in Dark Harbor?"

The captain shot him a strange look as if picking up on the frantic beating of Ell's heart at the mention of Half-Mask.

"The other prince, Half-Mask's older brother. He commands the naval forces at The Point and protects the southern seas from invasion. It's largely due to his presence on the southern front that the humans never tried to assault Dark Harbor."

Ell's mind was reeling. He'd never even heard of another prince. Half-Mask was the only one he had ever heard about. "What do we do—do we stop?"

Piripeos shook his head grimly. "We can't. I'm not the only fugitive on board. The rest of my mates from the Southern Refuge will never consent to surrender."

"Can we outrun them?" Ell asked.

"We could try, but the angle at which we are sailing means they'll likely be able to cut us off. Besides, out running a warship in heavy weather is difficult. No, a fight is brewing, Elliyar. Best to prepare yourself."

A fight. Ell knew how to deal with a fight. But fighting on water was unfamiliar territory to him. "What do we need to do? What's your counsel?" Ell immediately plied the captain for strategy.

Piripeos gave an approving nod as he acknowledged Ell's wisdom in deferring to his battle judgment, as they were at sea not on land. "A warship of that size will have mini catapults. Even in stormy weather, they're bond to land a missile or two, and even one lucky stone could crush a hole in our hull that would sink us."

"So…?"

"So we draw close. Let them board us and fight on deck, it's the only chance we have." The Rimmer shook his head grimly. Ell could tell that their odds were not good. Well, he'd fought and survived overwhelming odds before, this time would be no different.

"So we read our steel then." Ell stated. The captain nodded, and Ell departed to warn his crew of the imminent attack—although the crew seemed pretty much aware of what was about to happen. They were veterans of the sea and knew, as well as Piripeos, what the strengths and weaknesses of a vessel were. They knew they were outsized and out armed. Their only chance was to fight tooth and nail. Severe faces stared his way as he gathered his family together in the cabin and out of the pelting rain.

His companions filed into the room and looked to him for direction. Not for the first time, Ell felt a sense of astonishment that he was the leader of this venture. He'd strong-armed his uncle back in Andalaya at the outset of this journey, but Ell had not expected Dacunda to continue as his second for so long without question. Yet, unbelievably, Dacunda looked at him now for answers and with faith in his eyes.

"Well?" Dacunda asked.

"We fight," Ell answered simply. He relayed the plan to draw near and let their foes board the vessel in order to play to their strength, which was the skill of their warriors not the size of their ship.

Ryder cracked his knuckles menacingly—even eagerly—at the prospect of a fight, hefting his long axe with a practiced precision. Dahranian nodded resolutely, and Rihya flashed a thrilled grin.

"About time we saw some action. That scuffle at the docks wasn't nearly enough to make up for those weeks cooped up in the cave." Trust Rihya to make a joke on the brink of battle.

Ell looked at his father and Adan stared complacently back at him. Certainly a sea battle and possible death could be no worse than the hell in which he'd been imprisoned for the past two decades.

"We are with you, Son," Adan said simply.

Ell nodded, glad of their support. "Well then, arm yourselves and to your stations. The fight will be upon us shortly," he ordered, despite knowing that in what they were about to experience, battle stations and strategy usually disappeared in an instant, giving way to the free-for-all melee that accompanied close quarter fighting like on a ship's deck. Ell compulsively checked the dueling daggers strapped to his thighs and the belt knife at his hip. It was a habit born of years of battle—checking his weapons to make sure they were free and loose enough to draw quickly from their sheaths.

They left the cabin and returned to the deck. The roiling of the sea beneath them sent their vessel bobbing like a giant piece of driftwood. The warship had closed the distance and would be alongside them shortly. It was only a matter of minutes now. Their foes would soon be close enough to see that Ell and his ship were readying themselves for a fight not surrender, and that would set their foes' course as well. The warship loomed high and heavy upon the water. Even though a bulk of it was sunk beneath the waves, it rode the troughs of the stormy water like a water-soaked log, too buoyant to sink, but too heavy to be tossed around.

It closed the distance and Piripeos shouted orders for the crew to ready themselves to fight. The warship loomed closer and Ell could see the many Departed warriors scampering about the deck and eagerly preparing to fight. Surprisingly, despite the excited gleam of anticipation in their eyes and their fierce grins, he saw no teeth filed to points. Ell filed that bit of information away for another time because finally, the ship swung close enough and the warship rose up on a swell to sit above the *Water Wasp*, close enough that the hulls were nearly touching. Before the surge of the ocean could rip the two ships apart again, their enemies dropped grappling hooks from above and elves began shimmying down the ropes.

Twenty Departed warriors were on the deck amidst Ell and his family and crew before the ships broke apart. The fighting was savage. Cutlasses gashed limbs, swords, axes, knives did their part in the fray, and Ell fought with fierce energy, his body functioning by muscle memory more than any real decision of how or when to cut and attack. His body was a weapon all by itself—it had been for years. The fight raged, and elves on both sides fell. And all the while the two ships surged near to one another—one minute the warship was cresting a wave and high above, the next it was down a trough and the *Water Wasp* was riding high. On each high, the warship tried to drop more ropes and more elf warriors onto the *Water Wasp*. It was an effective tactic. The massive warship had dark elves to spare, while Ell and his ship had limited resources.

Ell chanced a glance over the few intervening yards of water between the ships and saw glowing braziers on the ships deck, warming dark warriors waiting in line to rope down and attack. Ell fought on, savagely gutting a southern elf as it tried to run him through with a sword. His crew and his family fought well, they always did, but even to Ell, the contest was inevitable. There was no victory here. Ell fought harder, and felt that dark side of himself float to the surface. He found a grim exuberance in eviscerating the next opponent he faced, but that ferocity did nothing to turn the tide of the battle. The *Water Wasp* crested high and Ell looked down from above onto the deck of the warship as he rode the stormy wave above and with despair he saw the true numbers of warriors that awaited. The battle was still raging, but the outcome was obvious.

Ell parried, blocked and kicked a dark elf over the rail into the gloomy death of the raging sea, a gaping wet maw waiting to claim any who entered. Ell looked up. His eyes caught Rihya's and while her brashness, her boldness, was still there in her face gleaming with exhilaration, there was a grim understanding, as well. She knew, as well as he, what was bound to happen sooner or later—their defeat was imminent. She disposed of an attacker and then dashed towards the cabin.

Ell felt a moment of surprise that she would run from a fight, but quickly enough she was back to the tempestuous battle, dodging blows until she reached Ell's side. They fought back to back for a moment, fending off opponents while more tried to board. Ell glanced at her and saw she was holding the watertight bag of handfire pouches. What could she possibly be planning? A sense of foreboding came across him as he saw her steel herself, saw a look of sublime grit and determination flood her face.

The *Water Wasp* rose high, crested a wave and hung for a moment of stillness above the warship sitting yards away but below it on the face of the giant wave. A rope dangled from the *Water Wasp*'s rigging and Rihya's gaze caught the rope.

In the midst of the battle she thrust her blade into the warrior that had been charging towards Ell, distracted as he was by what he saw in his sister's eyes. With a blazing look, she flashed a grin at Ell and all the years of her life, all the moments she had fought beside him, laughed with him, protected him, seemed to be encapsulated into that one fearless smile.

"Think fondly of me, Little Brother," she said.

And then she burst away before Ell could restrain her. Rihya leapt with all her might and caught hold of the rope dangling from the *Water Wasp*'s rigging. Riding high above the waves, above the warship, above it all, she soared through the air and let go, plummeting towards the warship riding the wave just below.

Ell saw her cast the bag of handfire with perfect aim, the focus of a true warrior facing death, into one of the glowing braziers full of smoldering coals.

The result was instantaneous and catastrophic for the warship. The explosive nature of the handfire thrown in bulk into the coals, ignited and erupted in a sudden explosion.

"Valerihya!" Ell screamed as the warship exploded into thousands of pieces, its destruction absolute. Ell screamed his sister's name again. He screamed and screamed until his voice resembled more of a broken wail, and an anguished numbness blocked out the battle around him. He supposed the fight continued—it must have. He supposed his crew must have finished off the enemy warriors still on the *Water Wasp*'s deck. But he had no recollection of it. All Ell could remember was the dark swirling water filled with floating debris, shattered beams and planks, bodies missing heads and limbs. The explosion had been utter and complete. There was nothing more than death and debris left of the warship and its crew.

And there was nothing to be seen of Rihya.

Ell vaguely remembered screaming some more. At one point he was fairly certain he tried to leap over the side and had to be restrained by his uncle and father. It was much like when he blacked out after discovering that Miri was taken all those months ago. Only this time was worse. Then, there had at least been the slimmest of hopes. But not now.

They circled the wreckage multiple times but there was no sign of life or of his sister. Hopefully, it had been as swift as it seemed. The massive, roiling waves made it hard to see and the darkness of night was approaching.

"We must go on," Piripeos was saying. "Elliyar, we must go on. I am sorry. But we cannot remain any longer—The Point with all its nearby shoals and reefs becomes increasingly dangerous at night."

Ell shook himself, tried to shake the fog from his mind. Numbly he agreed. They had to go on. That one thought was the only thing he clung to. They had to go on. Onwards. Away. Away from his sister, from Rihya. Ell swathed himself in numbness because the grief was too unbearable to confront.

Rihya was dead, and it was all his fault.

Chapter Thirty-Eight

His back ached. No, it seared. It felt like lighting from the sky was crackling across it every time he moved even a fraction. It had been years since Valdor had been lashed. And by the law, he had deserved it. The law of Lu Fang—well, of the entire human continent, probably—declared that if a slave verbally or physically opposed a guardsman or any non-slave for that matter, then they were legally subject to a whipping. Not that they needed to resort to legal measures. Humans had been beating their own for centuries, and elves as well for decades now, they did not need law to back them. The slavers had years and generations of tradition at their backs. What more could they need? And so, when Valdor had pleaded, begged the guardsman substituting for Engan on a sick day not to punish the child for accidentally spilling the drink on him, Valdor had opened himself up for this kind of abuse.

But he was the Sifra. He was grandfather to many here in Lu Fang. What else could he do but beg for the child? Better Valdor's back than the child of scarcely three name days who was already so disturbed by spilling his only cup of juice for the week that a wail had begun to burst from deep within his chest.

Valdor groaned and tried to adjust himself on the hard bottom bunk that was his bed.

"Here, Sifra." A human voice pierced the darkness, and Valdor opened tired eyes to see a hand extending its owner's only blanket to him. The voice continued. "Pad your bunk with this. I'll manage for tonight."

He almost resisted. The man would grow cold without the blanket. Winter was approaching. Almost. But he was getting too old to resist kindnesses such as this.

And so a heartfelt, murmured thanks was his response, and Valdor creakingly sat up to smooth the blanket flat on his bunk for padding and then pull his own blanket back over himself.

The mixed barrack in which Valdor resided and worked while watching his similarly mixed young charges was placed on the mountainous middle peninsula of Lu Fang. As such, he was known by both races of slaves.

The life of a slave conditioned many people out of emotion, burnt the sentimentality out of a person with hot, angry whips and blades, seared the compassion into the void with the burning shame of not being able to control one's destiny. Many who were born into this existence functioned in numbness. Even some of those who had become a slave partway through life lost their will to feel. Anyone could succumb, but those born free tended to cling to their emotions longer than others. There was something about the memory of peace, the recollection of free will that seemed to make a person more inclined to continue sharing what little they had. Valdor didn't know whether the human whose blanket on which he lay to cushion his flaming back was born into this life or not—there were many ways a human could become a slave: demotion, criminals, some even sold themselves into it to accomplish something that they deemed more important at the time such as finance a loved one's funeral—but he was grateful all the same.

This life hardened people. There were few precious things left, and hardly a person who could claim to be beloved by any, but Sifra—Valdor—was one of the few. When the lash had fallen, Sifra had heard the first angry mutterings he'd heard in years. It was strange to hear such a thing. There had not been a revolt on any scale since the first year in which the elves arrived, that miniature rebellion having been put down brutally enough to discourage any further attempts. Besides, the collars identified them. Any existence outside this one was bound to be short and highlighted by flight and hiding. He was one of the Highest, where could he go? There was no way to get home and nowhere to hide on this vastly populated and urbanized continent.

And so when the rumblings of discontent grew in the crowd of slaves watching his punishment, Valdor felt surprise for the first time in a long time. But that surprise was not accompanied by hope. There was no hope left to feel. The people might be angry at his plight—elf and human both—but they knew there was nothing to do but accept it. Unarmed and untrained and outnumbered any type of resistance and discord, or even simple displays of discontent could mean death. So they did nothing. They watched the lash fall and tear the aged elf's back. Valdor was glad. Long ago, he might have wished for a revolt to happen again, but not now. He was a realist. He knew it was pointless and would only result in their death. Perhaps if things were different. If there was something to turn the tables. If there was someone to inspire, to lead. Then, perhaps.

But for now, he had the children to care for and more pressing concerns than fancies. Concerns like how his weary body was going to manage a good night's sleep and get enough rest for tomorrow with his old back aflame as it was.

* * * *

Half-Mask sat in his tower, as he often did. However, this time he did not gaze out of its spacious, wall-sized, windows. The immediacy of his realm did not concern him. After all, it would soon enough be expanding—there was plenty of time to pay more attention to it when that growth began in earnest. No, the darkness in his cup was of much more interest to Half-Mask at the moment.

He swirled his finger idly, the habit he had picked up some years ago. The dark elf—no, he was something more than an elf now, was he not?—smiled as he swirled. He could bludgeon the boy into transition the way he often did with his own people who were affected by the darkness. He could usher that transition forth with hurried urgings, call to the deepest, darkest corners of the boy and command his allegiance. It would work. But where would be the fun in that? No, far better to coax the change forth. The subtlety of the boy's transformation would be its deliciousness, not the transformation itself—that was already a foregone conclusion. None resisted when the urgings began. But, knowing how Wintermoon would futilely struggle against it all, that was what put the ghastly joy in Half-Mask's heart.

He lifted the cup to his lips—the goblet of black liquid—but he did not drink. Instead, he whispered. He muttered quiet coaxings into the darkness, and presently into the boy's soul. Half-Mask murmured for quite some time, an endeavor of this prolonged and subtle nature required detailed attention and deliberateness. Half-Mask noticed some differences to when he normally urged the change on his own kind, but he shrugged them off. Those differences were likely a matter of process not content—the boy was not that special after all, their duel was an illustration of his inferiority. Half-Mask's plans for the boy were more a matter of gaining pleasure than any real necessity. It was always good to have a distraction he could play with idly. The quest for power could be all-consuming, and one needed balance.

The sun was setting, and Half-Mask watched the glorious picture of fading light painted before him. He did not see beauty in it—the Prince of Darkness did not often think in such terms as beauty—but there was an aptness to it. The encroaching darkness of night seemed to mirror perfectly what he knew was occurring within Ellilyar Wintermoon.

And that alone was enough to make Half-Mask smile.

Chapter Thirty-Nine

The numbness was all consuming. Ell functioned, but he functioned in a second hand sort of way. The way you told someone else's story, Ell felt as if he lived someone else's life. He ate when he needed, he spoke when spoken to, he worked to help the crew if it was necessary, but it was all done through a strange sort of daze. If he had been more present in the moment, he might have noticed his family's worried gazes and the way Dacunda slowly assumed more leadership—although there weren't many decisions to be made presently.

And so Ell allowed himself to be sucked in. The numbness was a paradox—it was blessed relief, sweet oblivion from the pain and the guilt. But it was simultaneously the most intense thing Ell had ever experienced in its consuming nature. He didn't try to shake it, partly because he wasn't sure if he could. Or if he wanted to.

The weeks blurred together as the ship sailed the southern sea. They passed no other vessels near enough for concern and all was relatively peaceful. It was as if the sea battle and Rihya's death was a storm that had finally blown itself out. For now.

Ell's mind shied away from thoughts of her demise. It was a slippery slope between those thoughts and the horrendous guilt he felt. If anything could shock him out of the numbness—or perhaps force him irretrievably deeper into it—it was that guilt. And so Ell avoided it and maintained the hazy status quo of his existence.

Although it was calm, it didn't mean that nothing of note happened between The Point and the Fracture, only that Ell functioned through it all as if even the more surprising events were normal. For instance, at one point during their voyage during another bout of rough weather, Ell had been assisting the crew in fastening lines near the rail when a sudden lurch of the ship from a particularly large wave sent one of the crewmembers careening into Ell's back. The suddenness of it, the swiftness with which Ell pitched over the rail and into the swirling, surging, depths surrounding the *Water Wasp* was enough to make

Ell react without thinking. He tapped his Water Calling ability instinctually, the way he had always done previously when first learning from Arendahl. Ell entered the water headfirst, feeling startled at the relative warmth of this southern sea compared to what he had been expecting. His instincts reached out immediately, and he felt the swell of power in his chest, felt the thunder of the roiling waves enter his mind, his consciousness. His eyes clouded over as they always did, misting his gaze in that strange half obscured, half clear vision. However, it didn't stop there. For the first time, he instinctively honed his power the way Arendahl had been attempting to teach him to do. This time, Ell's focusing of his abilities somehow made the water around him solidify. He bobbed upwards and gasped a lungful of rainy air, hearing the shouts and cries of the sailors and his family filled with concern.

He saw that he had somehow created watery steps for himself without even understanding how or why he was doing it. He gracefully stepped upwards and then upwards again until he stood on the surface of the ocean, gracefully riding the lurching motion of the stormy sea. He should have been surprised or shocked or even nervous at his newfound talent of standing on flowing water, but instead, Ell simply felt a cool detachment, a momentary sense of relief that he would not drown, replaced by the basic necessity of returning to the ship.

Ell stepped gingerly, but upon realizing that he could walk as well as stand upon the water, he then began to run easily and lightly across the surface, sending ripples and splashes out from his footsteps. The prints remained on the dark surface of the water for barely a moment before disappearing. He ran lithely along, gaining ground on the ship that had surged forward leaving him in its wake. Ell heard the shouts and the great swinging motion as the ship lumbered to change its course and return to search the watery troughs for Ell.

He saved them the trouble, running swiftly along until he reached the side of the ship. The crew, unaware of Ell's status as a Water Caller, was dumbfounded, and even Piripeos was shocked speechless. But Ell's family handled the matter more calmly, someone—Ell was too detached to register who—casually tossed him a rope over the rail, allowing Ell to clamber easily back onto the ship's deck.

Amazed, even frightened looks greeted him from the crew, but there were smiles of relief and clapped hands on his shoulders from his family. Yes, they were exceedingly glad. Another death, another Wintermoon lost overboard, would likely be too much for them right now.

Ell plastered a smiled on his face to look back at his family, showing a grateful—if half-heartedly sincere façade—for their concern. Yet, he could tell they weren't convinced. He was too calm about it all, too assured. Death didn't worry him within his numb confines—not that it had ever been a strong motivator for Ell. Therefore, his trip overboard and the subsequent discovery of his new ability to hone his power to a point and mold the very water beneath his feet, seemed less important to him. He brushed it off, but he could see the concern in his family's eyes. They hid it, but they were worried. He should have been more astounded with himself, or perhaps more proud of his skill. But he simply wasn't. His powers might still be growing, but the truth was, Half-Mask had dispatched him with more ease than he could knowingly admit to anyone. A tiny jaunt across the wave-tops was hardly a reason for celebration considering what Ell knew he truly faced. Not to mention what he could still feel lurking within him—that growing shred of darkness he could sense even through the foggy cloud of painless detachment.

More days passed and Ell heard the murmured conversations that they would soon be entering the coastal waters of the Fracture and not long after, would need to navigate its impossibly frozen and jagged waters. If riptides and currents didn't suck them under, they could always count on one of the many icebergs to gash a hole in their hull to bring them down.

Ell was standing idly in the prow, pretending to enjoy the unseasonably warm weather for this late in the year. He wasn't really feeling it, but he imagined it looked to the rest of them as if he was taking a moment to relax. It was all a ruse, and Ell wasn't sure entirely how clever a ruse it was, considering the looks he was beginning to finally notice. Nevertheless, he stared dully outward, lost in the nothingness of the absence of coherent thought. Focusing on nothing was the best way to avoid the pain.

A light step sounded behind him and Ell turned to see who was approaching. *Adan Wintermoon, your father, imprisoned twenty years a slave.* Ell's mind catalogued the information in that secondhand and detached way of thinking and living, as if this body, this life, didn't belong to him and he was just an impostor filling in.

Adan sauntered up. He had regained some of his lost confidence—lost during the years of beatings and chains, the decades of being told where to go and what to do. The flashes of his former authority had begun to solidify. However, there was still a hollowness to him that had nothing to do with his physical appearance.

"May we speak, Son?" The question sounded oddly formal.

Ell nodded his assent. "Of course, why would you need to ask?"

Adan paused. "You have been...different of late."

So. Confirmation. Ell's act had not been nearly as convincing as he had thought and hoped. "Come to tell me 'I told you so'?" Ell asked. "That we should never have attempted this venture?"

His father looked at him, a piercing gaze, and thankfully didn't answer that question directly. "I know it is hard, Elliyar. I mourn her too. But giving up on life is not the answer."

"I am not sure what you mean." Ell evaded, attempting to keep the disinterest from his voice, but not sure he succeeded.

"This," Adan said firmly, "this detachment you have cloaked yourself in. It is not the answer. I know you feel pain, pain so deep it has driven you to hide in this numbness, but it is not the answer."

For a moment, Ell felt emotion flash through him in the way that had been normal to him before her death. It was momentary, but even an instant of annoyance was cause for note.

"You think I hide from pain!" Ell asked strongly, as his frustration vented. It was fleeting, but then gone, and once again, all he felt was numb and the strange memory of that foreign emotion.

Ell's father looked at him strangely as if noticing that flash of passion and then seeing it slip away like grains of sand through a fist. "Tell me then, what do you feel?"

Ell answered with the same disinterest he felt at most things. He gazed out over the bow as he spoke. "I do not hide from pain Father, although the pain is more real than you can imagine. No, I feel guilt, a crippling guilt, but even that can be avoided."

Ell stared blankly at his father as if to prove his last point. Adan shook his head sadly.

"What happened to her was not your fault, Son. It was a battle. She sacrificed herself to save us. Don't cheapen her gift by giving up on the life she died to provide you."

Again there was a flash of emotion fighting to pierce through the fog of numbness. "Not my fault?" Ell practically yelled the question, but then felt the emotion ebb from him again. When he spoke further it was with his numb detachment. "Not my fault, Father? She was on this fool's quest because of me. I led her there. I am responsible."

"Fool's quest? Was it foolish to rescue me? Do you truly believe it is foolish to try and find your mother, your sister, and rescue them also? I do not believe you really think that, else you would never have begun this expedition in the first place."

Even through the daze, Ell noticed that the role reversal in this argument from weeks prior, was ironic. Ell gazed blankly at Adan again. "I have traded the sister I knew, the sister who cared for me, watched my back, protected me, and fought beside me for all of my life, for the sister I never knew, for the mother who I do not even know is alive. Tell me again how that is not foolish—no tell me how that is not wrong." Even through his numbness, Ell could recognize how strange it must sound to hear what should be an impassioned speech emitted from his dispassionate mouth.

Yet, to his credit Adan handled it well. "Not foolish, Elliyar, brave. Just as Valerihya was brave. And you traded nobody. Your sister was here of her own accord, she risked her own life to follow you. You must remember that if you are to be a great leader."

"I am not a great leader." Ell contradicted his father.

"One death, no matter how important that person was to you, does not make you a failure, Son. It. Was. Not. Your. Fault."

Ell shrugged his father away in annoyance. "If you say so, Wintermoon."

Perhaps it was the detachment or disinterest in his voice, or maybe it was the way he called his father by surname, as if he were a complete stranger. Whatever it was, it was too much for Adan.

Adan slapped him across the face. Not too hard, but hard enough to startle Ell.

"Snap out of it, Elliyar! Imagine how this is for me. Twenty years I lived, knowing I would never see or know the fates of my daughters or my son. And then I am miraculously able to meet the son I barely had time to hold and to know the daughter who had grown into a fierce warrior. I have lost her all over again, know not if I'll find the rest of my family even half as well, and am now watching my son waste himself away in self-pity. Valerihya was special, Son, but now she is gone and these people still need you. I still need you." He murmured the last sentence in a quiet, vulnerable voice.

Ell stared at him for a long moment. Adan seemed to take his lack of disagreement, lack of anger, and his apparent interest as a good sign so he continued.

"Son, we are approaching the Fracture. Piripeos says that by the end of tomorrow we will be amidst its icy waters. You urged this plan forward and only you have the ability to steer us through safely. You must return to us and lead again."

Ell stared at him again, really contemplating his father's words. Duty. Ell had a duty to this crew, to his family and friends. Duty was important. After a long silence, he nodded reluctantly at Adan. Then he nodded again more firmly. The answering smile from his father was almost warm enough to thaw the through the numbness in which he was cocooned. How to return from the brink of inner oblivion? Ell wasn't sure, but he tried. With every fiber of him he tried to feel again, tried to feel his emotions. It meant welcoming the return of grief and pain and guilt, but that was a cost he had to pay for his duty.

Ell dug for strength within himself. Somehow finally—he wasn't sure how—he managed to let the numb fog of anguish go. But in its disappearance, in the return of his emotions, Ell felt like a hollowed out shell. He had never felt so empty before, yet at the same time so filled with guilt. It wasn't a numb emptiness, no that sweet relief was gone. It was the emptiness of bereavement. Of loss. He fought back the tears.

"Come back, Son," his father was saying as Ell strained to free himself of the inner bonds he had forged.

"It is hard, Father," Ell choked out, fighting back the tears of grief as the pain washed over him again.

Adan grasped him in a firm embrace. "I know it is. I know."

Ell continued to struggle, to break completely free of the detachment with which he had shackled himself. He delved around inside of himself, looking for strength. He searched and finally he felt the old anger, the resentment, the bitterness of all those long years of struggle. Ell latched onto it, pulled on it, drew upon it as fuel. He needed the strength, something to keep him going.

Ell pulled on the old fire. It was familiar, yet accented differently now than before. There was a hint of bleakness, darkness, to it. Ell hesitated. It was risky, but he needed the strength, needed something to fuel him onwards if he hoped to help his family, if he hoped to finish this mission.

And so he let the darkness in—just a little bit. Just enough to tap his old anger for strength. It was only a tiny amount, but he felt it there now, lurking in the shadows of his soul. Ell felt the blackened scar beneath his eye tingle slightly, ominously. Ell ignored the worry and focused.

Adan smiled at him and Ell could see his father's eyes were moist with unshed tears. "Now. Now you are finally back, you are not the husk of my son anymore. I can see it in your eyes."

Ell nodded, not quite knowing how to respond. Not quite sure if he wished to travel too far down that line of thought, considering that bit of darkness he had pulled on, drawn on for strength. Was he still the same Elliyar? Would he ever be again? Ell wasn't sure.

"And now that you are finally you again, I have another question to ask of you," Adan said with a smile.

"Ask."

"I have heard bits and pieces of it all, seen some of what you can do. It is incredible!" There was pride in Adan's voice and in his face as he spoke. "Son, what exactly are you?"

Ell swallowed and spoke the words he was no longer sure were entirely true—not after his encounter with Half-Mask. "I am a Water Caller."

Adan nodded thoughtfully. Ell proceeded to tell his father everything— well almost. He spoke of last spring and the discovery of his power. Ell recounted the days in the north with Arendahl, and rescuing Miri, and saving Little Vale. He told of his duel with Silverfist. Ell compulsively told his father nearly everything he could think of except that one thing he was ashamed of.

As he drew to a close, Adan touched Ell's cheek lightly. "And what of this? What is the significance of this scar?"

"I told you, I dueled with Half-Mask and lost. His blades must have been tinged with poison." The lie came almost easily this time, despite the shame Ell still felt telling it.

"Ahh." Adan said sagely. "We all carry scars. Some of them more visible than others."

Almost. Ell almost caved and told his father the truth, about what had been done to him, about the strange exhibition of a new, more sinister power in his skirmish in the Southern Refuge. Ell tried to, he wanted to. But for some reason, he could not bring himself to do so. Not now, not after he had finally broken free of whatever prison of numbness he had been in. His father was too glad to see him back to normal to cause him even greater worry. It was Ell's burden, and for now he would bear it alone.

The following day passed in relative calm. Ell, free from the detachment, could actually recognize the relief and belief evident in his family members' faces as they saw he was back to normal after speaking with Adan—or at least that he appeared normal, despite whatever lay hidden and lurking beneath the surface.

Either way, they could not see the new danger growing within him—a danger that Ell was coming to fear. No, they only saw Elliyar, the young Water Caller. They saw their leader returned to them, to once again do what no one had done before—to once again attempt the impossible.

The Fracture approached and it needed to be crossed. It was not the last time Ell would be called upon to vanquish the impossible. He steeled himself for the task ahead.

Chapter Forty

"Piripeos says we are a matter of hours from the point in time at which you will be needed," Kalabi said to Ell, and to the rest of the group who were sitting on barrels or leaning comfortably against the exterior walls of the cabin.

Ell nodded his thanks for relaying the captain's message and turned to stride to the captain's deck. Kalabi and all the others had faith that Ell knew what to do to navigate them across the Fracture, and deep down, Ell believed he could also. But the difference was they thought he knew the how of it—or else they had the tact to not voice concerns that he didn't. Ell, on the other hand, believed he could do it, but had no idea how he was planning to do so. Truthfully, he often felt he operated better as a Water Caller on instinct at times. It was risky, it did not always work out, but there were times—like when he walked on water—where he was capable of achieving things it would never occur to his conscious mind to attempt. And so Ell had resigned to simply act on instinct as soon as the captain notified him that they would soon be entering the dangerously icy waters of the Fracture.

He paused, looking out over the rail as he stood. It was strange to imagine that such dangerously cold and icy waters, filled with riptides and maelstroms, could lie under such warm blue skies. Everything above the horizon would have one believe that the approaching seas were calm and smooth. But the incredibly strong northern current that surged southward all the way from the frozen lands near the Great Bridge kept this water icy cold and filled with frozen teeth and glacial blocks. It would not be long before they began to sight some of those icebergs. The riptides and maelstroms had nothing to do with the northern current, they were a mystery of the Fracture all their own. No explanation had ever been found. All sea captains simply knew was that the Fracture was a dying ground for ships, large or small. Only the insane or the desperate sought to enter those waters. Perhaps Ell, his family, and his crew were a little bit of both, all wrapped together with a healthy dose of faith—a faith that was placed largely on the shoulders of Ell and the power they knew he possessed.

It would not be bad for another briefing on what to expect. Ell felt more nervous than he let on. What if his powers didn't provide a magical fix to the dangers that lay ahead and he got more of his family members killed?

Before Ell could leave, Kalabi spoke again, this time with a hint of hesitancy, yet firm curiosity.

"If I may ask, Elliyar, where shall we go once we succeed in crossing the Fracture. Did your father tell you to which city your mother and sister were shipped?"

Ell glanced at Adan Wintermoon, who was one of the elves leaning against the wall of the cabin, eyes closed and basking in a free moment of sunshine—something he likely hadn't been able to do as a slave who worked from sunrise to sundown.

Adan opened his eyes as he heard the question and saw Ell's raised eyebrows questioning him. In truth, Ell was surprised that no one had asked this before. The Fracture had always stood as the huge barrier to overcome—knowing that the Great Bridge was too heavily fortified to sneak through unbeknownst to the humans. The Fracture had dominated everything and all conversations, leaving the not so distant future a seeming haze of success, but without any real plans or destination.

"I heard talk of a city by the name of Lu Fang," Adan answered slowly. "I do not know if it was their final destination, but I am sure that it was at least a stopping point." He pursed his lips and cocked his head slightly in apology at what he deemed a lack of information.

Ell turned back to appraise the dark skinned, ex-slave, the only human in their midst. Kalabi nodded slowly.

"That would make sense. It is a major recipient of the slave trade, being one of the greatest cities on Etheros—the human continent. It would not likely have been the first port of call for the slave ship sailing down from the Great Bridge, as it is further south, but it very well could have been a destination." The ex-slave trailed off thoughtfully, absently touching the gold collar that still wound around his throat—a habit formed over long years in the human tents. They had tried to find a way to remove it since he joined them, but without the proper instruments and a skilled metal worker, it was better to leave it in place. Ell wondered if Kalabi was worried to reenter his home continent with the mark of his slavery still prominently in place. Ell didn't ask however—a person's fears were private. He thought of his own dark worries.

Ell cleared his throat and spoke up firmly, dispelling the dangerous thoughts plaguing his mind whenever he gave it a free rein to wander.

"Well then, we start with Lu Fang. I have to believe that fortune is on our side. I found you after all." He smiled at his father who nodded back encouragingly.

"I have studied many maps of our coastline. I should be able to guide our course and sketch a useful map of our own," Kalabi said in response.

The rest of his family and friends calmly nodded their assent as well. When had they stopped telling him things were impossible? Ell seemed to remember a time not long ago when they had tried to convince him that finding his father in the heart of the enemy capital had been madness in the extreme. Now they were willing to simply accept his feeble platitude that providence was somehow on their side as they set their course to search a foreign continent for his two long lost family members. Ell wondered—feared, really—if they placed too much faith in him these days. He feared he would let them all down—and was beginning to feel certain that inevitably, he would.

Inevitably, *it* would happen. The darkness. When that occurred, it was a foregone conclusion that he would let them down.

But not before I find them, he thought determinedly. *I will make sure of this one thing before it happens.* Ell left them to discuss what tactics to employ in their coming search of the Lu Fang, as if their passage—his guidance—across the Fracture were a foregone conclusion and climbed lithely up the ladder steps to the captain's deck.

"About time," Captain Piripeos grunted. "We don't have much longer before we reach waters that sane captains avoid at all costs. You better have a plan." The Rimmer cast a shrewd eye on Ell as if he alone had guessed that Ell had no plan at all unless you could call it a plan to cast his hopes on a wing, and trust his innate skill, instincts, and no small amount of luck.

Ell shrugged off the question, ignoring it as if he hadn't heard the implication behind the captain's final comment. Ell didn't need a voice of concern to cloud his mind with doubt. He was committed. Rihya had died for this, and he would see it through. Determination welled inside of him and he felt a new, fresher sense of belief in his own powers. Yes, Rihya's memory was the key focus on which he could remain strong.

And then, a memory came to mind unexpectedly: Arendahl standing in flash flood waters of the rainstorm so long ago when he and the old elf had met with his family in Verdantihya after leaving the Barren Maze. Ell remembered Arendahl standing in the water and feeling through it, somehow using his ability to search for Dacunda and the rest of the band. And suddenly Ell had an idea. A smile began to form, and even the skeptical smuggler captain could see that Ell had the beginnings of a plan and he quit pestering Ell to reveal it.

They stood side by side on the captain's deck for another hour or so before they sighted the first small ice chunk floating in the water, contrasting strongly with to the blue sky above. Piripeos maneuvered the ship around it adroitly, leaving the floating frozen tooth of the sea in their wake. Within minutes, a few more icebergs had been sighted and the captain took on a focused look as he steered, leaving more icebergs in their wake, although the icebergs gradually became larger and more frequent, which meant that the captain was forced to navigate around them while keeping an eye out on the rest of the floating ice chunks. It meant that Piripeos began leaving only the barest of room for error. One wrong pull of the tiller and the *Water Wasp* would careen into a block of ice and gut itself. It was dangerous, but there was no other option, because to swing wide of an ice tooth, was to chance hitting another. So they cut it close, and Ell could see the nerves of his crewmembers and the worry in their faces, especially considering the fact that they had barely even entered the Fracture itself. This was just the entryway to the Fracture, the atrium so to speak.

Ell tapped his abilities. He felt the rush of power swell, his vision clouded in the familiar manner. Ell sent his focus out into the wealth of fluid around him and felt his power explode to life. He felt a strength of power that was foreign even to a Water Caller—it was the power that came to a Water Caller from being surrounded on all sides by water as far as the eye could see.

Ell remembered Arendahl in the floodwater in Verdantihya, remembered the old elf explaining what he had done, and Ell sent his consciousness out into the water around him once more—this time not to tap the power, but to feel it, to search the essence of the moisture around him for traps and dangers and for the safe corridors of passage.

"Give me the tiller," Ell said in a voice filled with detachment—this time not the detachment of grief, but rather the strange focus that often accompanied his Water Calling abilities.

"I don't think so," Piripeos stated grimly. "I'm the captain, and I have the experience."

"You just told me to have a plan. This is the plan. Give me the tiller." Ell spoke calmly, in a way he thought was reassuring, but as the captain grudgingly passed the tiller over to Ell, he looked anything but comforted.

Ell grabbed the wooden steering mechanism and once again felt. He felt the grain of the wood, once rough, but worn smooth after years of hands handling it. He felt the deck of the ship beneath him, felt the ponderous power of the ocean beneath the ship. He shut off the rational side of his mind and emptied it of everything but intuition and his desperate need to steer the ship safely somehow. Ell said a prayer of thanks that at the very least they had calm weather as they entered the Fracture, and he set his sights and his senses, both supernatural and physical, to navigating this ship through these most treacherous of waters.

It was like he was one with the ocean around the ship, Ell could feel the surges, the swells, could practically see through the murky depths enveloping the ship. It wasn't sight exactly, not vision per se, but almost like a new kind of sense, like sight and touch and feel and sound—all the senses—all wrapped into one, spurred on by his abilities as a Water Caller.

Ell vaguely heard the cursing and shouting from the crew as they tended to menial details necessary to keep a ship on course. All his focus was on the task at hand. He steered by instinct. He edged close to frozen hunks of ice, close enough that he heard Piripeos mutter a curse or a prayer, or perhaps both. But Ell's hands were sure as his instincts told him just the right amount to pull on the tiller or push, in order to avoid each berg when it passed.

And so it began.

Over the next few hours, Ell guided the ship past ice chunks, often passing dangerously close to them. Sometimes Ell split the difference between two floating boulders of ice, and Piripeos would bite back the urge to cry out as Ell took what appeared to be the more dangerous route. But that was only because the captain could not feel what Ell felt could not see beneath the waves, to the submerged bergs lurking in seemingly safer waters, the captain could not feel the riptides and currents that pulled and pushed and threatened to dash a ship to pieces like the tentacles of a beast determined to bring death to its unwanted visitors. No, Ell paid no heed to the captain, and focused on the minute motions of adjusting his course. He felt the pull of a riptide and shifted the tiller away, guiding the ship safely past it, past the danger—if only for a moment, because there was always another and another threatening current or ice block.

Eventually, the blocks of ice grew to the size of small hills and began obscuring parts of the horizon. Ell wasn't sure how long he'd been at his task, but he suddenly saw his father beside him. Without speaking or interrupting, Adan put a piece of food to his mouth. Ell opened reflexively and chewed. It was a hard biscuit, nothing tasty, but it was sustenance and Ell needed his strength to maintain his focus. He finished the biscuit, his father feedings pieces of it to him, so his own hands never left the tiller.

Night fell, and Ell kept his instincts honed, kept his heightened senses open to the sea, and steered the ship through the perilous night waters, now inky black around them. Yet to Ell, there was no difference. He still felt the ocean around him and navigated the ship away from the boulders and hills of ice. He should be tired, but he wasn't, the power within him helped keep his strength from failing. A small worry within him, however, noted that he'd never held his powers for such a prolonged period of time. What effects might that have on him? On his body and mind? Ell shoved away the worry and focused.

People kept quiet company with him, not speaking but refusing to leave him to vigil alone. They slept in shifts while Ell steered through the night and into the next day. It was days of this. All Ell was aware of were his heightened senses, his feeling of the sea, his consciousness in the water around him, and his hand on the tiller. Had there ever been a time when he wasn't behind the tiller of this ship? The idea of anything before or after this was a vague, foreign concept to him. He heard the worried whispers of his family as they observed him retreat within his shell and navigate, but they didn't interfere. They couldn't interfere, for fear of the consequences. Because regardless of how, Ell was achieving his goal. He was maneuvering around the jagged domes of ice that arose, he steered delicately between riptides and maelstroms, he took them down seemingly dangerous routes only to preserve their safety without fault. They were worried, but they feared what would happen should they ask Ell to rest. Could the ship survive such a break without Ell at the helm?

And so he steered.

On the third day into the heart of the Fracture, they began to see the gigantic, glacial walls of ice. The walls of ice blocked their path and Ell had to adjust his course north to sail along the edge, to find a way through. People whispered that there was none, that this was the end, this was the dying ground of so many ships who had tried to pass the icy waters of the Fracture. But Ell refused to give up, Rihya had died for this, and he would find a way. There had to be a way.

Eventually, he saw a gap in the glacier and navigated the ship into it. Ell could see the fear in the crew's faces as they entered a maze of ice, frozen walls thrusting upwards for what seemed like eternity around them, leaving only a hint of sky to show. Even Ell wasn't sure if this was wise. Would they ever return from the heart of this maze? Would they make it through to the other side? He didn't know the answer to that question, and yet he navigated on.

They wound their way between walls of ice, Ell steering their course on this fork or that as the watery maze opened up choices for their passage. They spent a full day in the maze and Ell could see desperation, even hopelessness, take root in the eyes of his crew, but he forged ahead anyways. Onwards, ever onwards. When it felt like they had been in the icy labyrinth forever, Ell finally saw a crack of light appear ahead of them. He steered the *Water Wasp* down one final fork and toward the hopeful crack of light in the dim blueish interior of the glacial maze. The crack of light drew closer and closer, but Ell worried as he saw their corridor grow narrower and narrower as they drew closer to the exit. What terrible fortune it would be to come this far only to be defeated by the simplicity of a passage too narrow to fit through. They could not turn around, as the room to maneuver was far behind them. Ell wracked his brain for answers. And instinctively again, he let go of all thought, felt the power that was still flowing through him. He often worked best when operating on instinct. They sailed closer to the crack and the walls threatened to bury them. The ship began to scrape against the icy walls, flaking chips of ice onto the deck. It was now or never, as they were about to grind to a deathly halt. Ell blanked his mind, searched for instinct. He was a Water Caller, it was who he was, his identity. His powers flowed from him naturally.

Ell remembered walking on water, how he had manipulated the liquid around him.

Ell flared his power.

He reached deep within his reserves of strength, and mentally lifted with his consciousness, and his abilities—or perhaps it was physical, who could tell, the way it strained his body and muscles as well as his mind. Ell strained with his Water Calling abilities to shift the water around them. The walls of ice were just frozen water, foreign to Elliyar Wintermoon, but not to Ell the Water Caller. He pushed outwards and, ever so slightly, the glaciers shifted. It was like moving mountains. No, it was like pushing on many mountains at once, but he did it anyways. Ell gasped for breath and gathered his strength. The ship crept forward, inching along the new room Ell had shifted for it. Ell gathered his strength for one final push—the crack of light, the exit was within reach.

Ell shoved outward with his powers, he thrust with all his abilities, all his strength, and with a dreadful groaning and creaking of ice, the glaciers moved and the crack widened.

They moved enough for the ship to scrape its way out of the icy maze and back into the world of riptides and maelstroms, back to smaller boulders of icebergs. But it was a relief. The crew cheered at the open sky around them. After the silent, suffocating walls of ice which blocked out everything but a sliver of sky overhead, these treacherous waters seemed relatively comforting.

Ell smiled grimly. The job was over half done now. They had entered the other side of the Fracture.

* * * *

There were three more days after leaving the labyrinth before they left the last ice chunk behind—three more sleepless days, three more days of Ell holding onto his power. Had he ever not been using his abilities? Had he not come from the womb tapping into them? It was strange. Ell had been holding his powers for so long, that he couldn't bring to mind a time when he had not. Did that make sense? The foggy mind of exhaustion threatened to overwhelm him. As they cleared the last riptide eagerly sucking at their rudder to draw them back to a watery grave, Ell finally let go of the tiller. Piripeos grabbed at it, immediately. When had the captain arrived?

Ell stumbled and would have fallen, all strength sapped from his limbs after the task was completed. Had he let go of the power, his ability? He thought so, but he couldn't think straight. How long had it been since he'd eaten? Since he had slept? How many days had he been awake now?

Ell's toe caught on a protruding lip of deck and he almost pitched head over heels down the ladder steps, only for strong, sure hands to catch him. Dacunda and Adan lowered him down from the captain's deck. Ell slumped half-conscious to the deck until they leapt down agilely and picked him up again.

They must have carried him to a hammock because the next thing he knew, he was enveloped in mind-numbing, soul-refreshing blackness, the kind of oblivion that only the truly exhausted sleeper understands. Sleep swallowed him whole, and for a time he knew nothing. It was a sweet time. No painful memories, no guilt, no strain, pain, or exhaustion. Just blessed relief, and sleep.

Chapter Forty-One

It was not hope, not quite. But something had changed in the weeks since his lashing. Valdor had watched malcontent grow among his brethren elves and among the human slaves as well. It wasn't enough. It would never be enough—he was sufficiently old and realistic to be resigned to that. But it was different. Beatings had increased, punishments were handed out with more regularity. There had even been a rash of deaths as a result of those punishments. There was still no hope in the slaves' hearts. Hope inspired, it carried people beyond their circumstances. Nothing else could accomplish that. As long as that was lacking nothing would change.

Yet, it was different. There was a simmering anger that laced nearly every interaction between guard and slave, owner and worker. So much so, that extra guards had been appointed to all areas, even to the children's ward, under Valdor's care—guards in shadowy dress with sinister, hard faces who appeared ready and willing to do absolutely anything. Still, the anger simmered. And anger was dangerous—for everyone involved. Valdor had an ominous feeling that many deaths were coming. In some ways, he hoped he wouldn't be around for the imminent bloodbath.

"Maybe I'm imagining things," he mumbled to himself, as he picked up a child. "It's probably nothing. I'm worried for nothing." He kissed the little girl.

"What was that, Sifra?" Anali said, as she nestled into his arms, her tiny, elegant features and pointed ears looking as if they would have been more at home in a wooded glen than a brick-walled barracks.

"Nothing child. I was only speaking to myself, as the elderly are wont to do." He crossed his eyes ridiculously at her, eliciting a silvery giggle, a happy noise that was mimicked by the human boy standing at his feet. All of them—human and elf children alike—loved it when Valdor poked fun at his own age. They were too young to grasp his meanings, but the young could see intuitively to the heart of matters in a way that bypassed rational thought and understanding. They understood the joy of a joke whether they knew its reasoning or not.

Sifra uncrossed his eyes and set the elf girl down. She was his blood, his kin, one of the Highest, but he had been here long enough that they all belonged to him, whether they were elf or not. A camaraderie born of shared plight joined them in a way that nothing else could.

Sifra gathered the children around him and directed them to sit cross-legged like him.

"Shall I tell a story?" Valdor inquired, already knowing the little ones' responses.

"Yes!" they screamed with glee—a delight they would shed before long, when cruel reality crashed down upon them after their fifth name day.

"Have I told you the story of the Willow and the Wandering Mist? Or how about the tale of our fabled home Verdantihya and the origins of the Source? Or perhaps I should tell you all of when Braemon climbed the tallest mountain?"

"The Mist," one child shouted.

"No, the Source," cried another.

"I want to hear about Braemon and the mountain!"

"We already heard that one, Anali," a self-important young elf chided the tiny girl.

"I know," Sifra said, settling on a tale that was particularly dear to him. "I'll tell you of the shining city of Akan Deraiya, so bright that the Sun itself grew jealous of its gleaming, pearly walls."

Valdor spoke, and all the while, a grim-faced and somehow regretfully wistful-looking Engan guarded the door to the room, accompanied by a shadowy slaver dressed in all black.

Chapter Forty-Two

The sun shone warmly, magnified through one of the porthole windows, creating a heat reminiscent of summer. So reminiscent, in fact, that Ell found himself confused upon waking. His consciousness opened up before his eyes did. Ell felt the bathing warmth of the light, and for an instant, just a moment, he forgot where he was and thought of warm summer days with Miri, of timeless naps and restful awakenings. So confused was he by the lethargy of his body upon waking, that he thought he was far to the north.

"Miri, why did you let me sleep so long?" he mumbled, still not bothering to open his eyes.

"Miri? Quit daydreaming, Ell," a voice snorted with muffled laughter.

Still confused, Ell opened his eyes and saw the beams of the ship above him, felt the swell and shift of the vessel upon the water, and the gentle swinging of his hammock bed. He groaned.

"Rihya?" he asked the source of that lightly mocking response.

Then reality crashed in on him. Ell's brain shied away from his longing for Miri, and he desperately fought to rid his mind of thoughts of his sister, lest the numbness consume him again.

"You're not delirious, are you, Ell?" Ryder's concerned face appeared above his own.

Ell stayed swinging gently in the hammock. How could he have mistaken Ryder's deep voice for his dead sister's? Had it been the mocking inflection? Rihya and Ryder had always shared a flavor for the sarcastic and witty. Perhaps he had simply wished it was so, and his mind had created the impression to suit that desire.

"No, Ry, just a bit groggy. I forgot that—," Ell's voice caught, and he couldn't quite manage to finish his sentence.

Ell's large cousin nodded in a moment of regretful commiseration. "You've been asleep for a while. It's no wonder you feel a bit out of sorts."

"How long?"

"About three days, give or take. We thought about waking you to make you eat, but Kalabi reckoned you needed the rest more," Ryder answered.

At the mention of food, Ell's stomach growled noticeably. Ell struggled to rise from the awkward lying position in the hammock so Ryder clasped his forearm and hoisted him out. Ell felt a surge of pain, and an ache ran throughout his entire body. He wasn't sure if the pain was a remnant from his extensive period of time using his abilities—who knew what that could do to a Water Caller?—or if it was simply a byproduct of three days spent sleeping in a swinging hammock. Hammocks were wonderful for naps, but Ell was beginning to admire the sailors' resilience in being able to sleep night after night in them without ill effects. Hammocks had a tendency to leave Ell feeling like strange muscles in his body were knotted. He groaned again and knuckled his back.

"Hungry?" Ryder asked in response to the growling of Ell's belly.

Ell nodded. They set out from the communal bunkroom towards the galley. It was afternoon and everyone was above deck, working or simply breathing in the fresh air. The galley was empty except for a few plates of food left over from the midday meal.

"Were you babysitting me?" Ell asked suspiciously.

Ryder shook his head dismissively. "Not exactly. We were worried at first when you collapsed, but you seemed to be breathing fine. Kalabi assured us you just needed rest, at least he guessed that was what it was. So we mostly left you to it. One of us checks in on you every now and then. You just happened to wake up right when I was checking in."

Ell began stuffing his face with food. He wasn't even sure what he was eating, it was some sort of southern stew, no doubt cooked up by one of the sailors. There was fish, however, but that was all he recognized. Someone must have dropped lines over the side of the ship. Ell picked out a few bones and thrust a spoonful of white fish into his mouth. He savored the flavor. Seasoned just enough with some spice—what, he wasn't sure—but it was enough to taste fantastic. Or perhaps he was simply so famished and that was driving his enjoyment of the meal.

"Is this how you feel all the time—ravenous?" he asked Ryder, with a sly glance as he stuffed more food into his mouth. "It's a wonder you don't get fat."

"Funny," Ryder responded in a flat voice. But then he winked, and Ell saw the humor that was lying just beneath the surface.

A footstep treaded just behind them. "So, our fearless leader awakes from his nap."

Ell turned and saw the half-mad Kester walking towards them with a strangely lopsided and sardonic smile on her face. The southern elf plopped down and dug into the food, as well, without a moment's hesitation.

"Nap?" Ell asked incredulously. "I slept for three days. I'd hardly call that a nap."

"Did you wake up at a specific time?" Kester asked innocently.

Ell narrowed his eyes in confusion. "No. I just slept."

"There you go, then."

"I don't really follow," Ell said to the southern elf.

Kester looked at him as if he were crazy, as if it was the easiest thing in the world to understand.

"When you sleep, normally you go to bed at night and you wake up at a specific time."

"When?" Ell asked.

"Morning, obviously." Kester raised one eyebrow as if she could believe how dense he was. She turned to Ryder. "Is he alright? Is he sick in the head after collapsing or something?"

Ryder covered a grin with another big bite of food. "No, he's fine. He's just always been a bit dense."

"Shut up, Ry," Ell responded in annoyance. "So, Kester, why don't you finish."

Kester finished chewing and swallowed. "I pretty much was finished. Normal sleep has a specific beginning and a specific ending—night and morning. Naps on the other hand, are defined by the lack of necessity for setting a beginning and ending point. You went to sleep when you were tired—or, in this case, just collapsed—much as someone who was really in need of a restful nap would do, and you woke up naturally when you felt refreshed enough to do so, just like a person waking up from a nap. When you wake from a nap, you wake when your body has had enough."

There was an odd logic to her statement. Ell wasn't sure if he followed her reasoning completely, but he chose not to press the issue further.

"In that case, yes, I have indeed awakened from my nap. What's the news above deck?"

Kester took the change of subject in stride. Ell noticed that she was surprisingly easy to talk with today. She was actually answering the questions posed to her.

"Not much to report. Captain has us sailing to the northeast, a course set by the human." Kester felt like that was enough information and went back to chowing down on her midafternoon snack—which was really more of a second lunch meal.

Ell glanced at Ryder, and his cousin shrugged his shoulders complacently as if to agree, that there wasn't much else to say. It sounded to Ell as if the last three days had been relatively peaceful. That peace was no doubt about to change, just as soon as they reached the shores of the human continent.

They went above deck, and Ell met the relieved looks of his family and friends. Even some of the crew cast relieved glances his way. Apparently his performance of guiding them through the Fracture was enough to inspire the wild crew of pirates to believe in him and his abilities.

Adan hugged him with one arm around the shoulder and his uncle and Dahranian and Kalabi clasped his forearm firmly. Piripeos gave a nod from the captain's deck where he stood holding the tiller in one seemingly-negligent hand.

Ell found himself once again thinking thoughts that he would give anything to forget. He wished Rihya could have been with them. He missed the way she never wasted a chance to needle him, to tease him, her blunt sarcastic jests that never quite masked the mothering look she got in her eyes whenever Ell was anything other than perfectly healthy. Ell swallowed. He couldn't ignore his emotions again, couldn't force them aside for a better time. There would be no better time. But he didn't have to deal with them now. Not right this instant. Ell forced a smile and murmured platitudes that he was fine and of course he was alright. He could see, yet again, the relief in their eyes. Most surprising, perhaps, was the relief in his uncle's eyes. Whether Dacunda was relieved to see his nephew well, or if it was more of a relief to see his leader well, Ell wasn't entirely certain. If it was the latter, it was a strange shift in events. It showed just how much the structure of their unit could change in only a few short months.

"Where are we?" Ell turned the topic back to business and looked at Kalabi.

"A few days north of where we left the ice flows. And still a few days out from Lu Fang by my calculations and my roughly sketched map."

The ex-slave toyed with the gold band of worked metal at his neck, reflexively as a nervous habit. Ell realized just how much his human friend was risking by returning to the human continent with the collar around his neck. It marked him not just as a slave, but as a highly prized and valuable slave that many would go out of their way to recapture should they notice. The risk of capture was there for everyone on their venture, Ell supposed, but for some reason the truth was more evident for Kalabi. At least, now it was. Perhaps it was because the man had been born a slave and had only known a few months of freedom. Maybe that was why Ell perceived him as risking so much on this mission. Ell felt a rush of warmth and pride toward the ex-slave—toward the first human he had ever thought of as a friend.

Ell nodded his approval of Kalabi's direction during his absence and clapped a hand to the tanned human's shoulder.

"Lu Fang, what do you know of it?"

"Know of it? A lot."

Ell tilted his head questioningly while the rest of the group remained silent and eager, listening for Kalabi's response.

Kalabi volunteered further information freely. "It is the city of my birth. I lived there for the first half of my life before I made the trek north and across the Great Bridge to arrive in Andalaya."

Realization dawned on Ell. Kalabi was going home. But whether that homecoming was filled with good or bad memories, Ell wasn't certain. He suspected the latter, by the carefully composed look on his friend's face.

"So what is there to know?" Ryder asked.

Kalabi took a deep, steadying breath. "Lu Fang is built on a bay and has three major peninsulas jutting into the water. The city is populated on the shore, but the settlement also extends out onto those peninsulas. It is heavily populated."

Then the barrage of questions began. Ell figured perhaps that would be the best way to go about it. A sort of question-and-answer time with the human, which Kalabi took in stride, answering questions in the way an instructor speaks to students.

Dacunda was the first. "What sort of military presence is there?" Trust Dacunda to see to the heart of matters and ask the important questions.

"Lu Fang is a huge destination for slaves, due to its size. As such, there is a noticeable guard presence. After all, slaves require masters, and armed ones at that. However, other than the slave guard, there isn't much of a standing military presence. Lu Fang is a city of commerce, not war. It has no wall and hasn't needed to protect itself for centuries. In fact, many of the human cities are similar. The empire hasn't seen more than a minor rebellion for years and years. The farther north you go—and the closer you get to the Great Bridge and the passage across to your continent—the more militarized the settlements become. These serve as training grounds for the army before they mobilize and cross over into your country, and also to be closer to the few rebel factions that still exist in the northeast of Etheros."

"Etheros?" Ryder asked.

"The human continent," Kalabi responded. "We humans tend to name the entire land mass, as well as small countries and provinces."

Ryder made a thoughtful face. "Andalaya has a name, but we sort of just accept that things just are. The southern kingdom is just that, the southern kingdom, and the continent as a whole doesn't even have a name, does it?"

Ell's cousin directed his last question towards the group.

"Perhaps now isn't the best time to be discussing the nominal natures of our two races," Dacunda remarked, guiding Ryder back onto the subject at hand.

"So, Lu Fang isn't far enough north to be a military settlement?" Adan prompted.

"Right," the ex-slave affirmed. "It's a city of merchants and great wealth. However, that doesn't mean it will be without danger. The Lashers are highly trained, in fact, they are some of the most skillful soldiers in the empire and we will need to be on our guard against them."

Adan nodded. He was never one to display worry, but twenty years a slave seemed to have supplied him with a healthy dose of caution when it came to expectations. He knew danger, he knew pain and hopelessness.

"So where do we begin to search for my mother and my...sister." Ell's throat caught just a bit as he said the word sister. For so long, his "sister" meant only Rihya, and now the same, exclusive term defined a stranger. Allowing his grief to touch and him was better than the dysfunctional numbness he'd embraced earlier, but it was becoming inconvenient how frequently he felt the grief welling up inside him at the smallest of things. It was a painful distraction from important issues at hand.

Kalabi nodded as if his question was the next topic he had been about to address anyway. "The slave barracks are situated on the three peninsulas. North Barracks is the slave quarters for elves, since they arrive from the north, transported down from the Great Bridge. South Barracks is purely humans. And the middle peninsula is a mixture of the two."

"So my mate and daughter will be on either the middle or the northern peninsula." Adan breathed his words with the tender anticipation of an elf who'd not seen his mate in two decades, and did not know if she was alive or dead. Ell thought of Miri and couldn't imagine what that must be like. Just being separated from her for a few months was difficult enough

Dahranian narrowed his eyes shrewdly. "Kalabi, my friend, how do you know this? You have been gone from your homeland for fifteen years. How do you know the layout?"

"Good question. In the years just prior to my departure for the coasts of Andalaya, a few shipments of elves, your kinfolk, began to arrive. This is how they situated the new slave arrivals. Lu Fang may be a city of commerce and money, of sales and negotiations, but the empire as a whole, Etheros, is originally built upon the military practices that carved it out. Human military is nothing if not routinized and even ritualized. The army of Etheros is a slick and well-oiled mechanism. But they do things the same way without great innovations, even if they deem change unnecessary. They would have seen no reason to shift anything in the intervening years. At least, that is my best guess."

"And your best guess is what we have to go on, and we trust it as we trust you," Ell affirmed Kalabi. "At least, until we have a chance to do a bit of our own reconnaissance."

"Speaking of which," Dacunda said, "do you have a plan in place for when we arrive?" He directed his question towards Ell.

The question hung in the air. There it was. Did Ell have a plan? His lack of planning had led to Valerihya's death. With all his heart, Ell wished he could answer with a firm yes. But the truth was, he'd been asleep for three days and had hardly thought about anything other than simply crossing the Fracture. Plans of what to do once they had reached the human continent had felt like questions for later, for 'if' rather than 'when' they arrived.

"Not yet," Ell answered regretfully. "But I'm working on it. This seems like as good a time as any to bring up another matter."

The rest of the group turned a keen eye to his face.

"I was talking with the captain some days ago now and he helped me realize an important point. Our mission must be about more than rescuing my family. We are once again striving to do, and so far accomplishing, the impossible. But, we must aim bigger than simple a rescue. We are risking our lives for this. This venture should strike a blow at the heart of the human continent somehow. If we can accomplish that, we'll strike a blow at their allies, the Departed, as well—and by doing so, we strike a blow at Half-Mask."

"What did you have in mind, Son?" Adan asked cautiously.

"I don't know exactly," Ell admitted, "but I'm open to suggestions. All I know is that..." Ell paused again, choking on the words. He steeled himself and spoke slowly, deliberately. "All I know, is that Valerihya died for this. For us. Her death should mean more than a small fleabite on the backs of our enemies. Her sacrifice should mean more to us, should inspire us to dream to accomplish something greater." Ell's voice gained passion. "We've fought from hiding with our black arrows in the shadows, with quick ambushes for too long now. It ends here. We strike a blow that they will actually feel! We honor my sister's memory by making her sacrifice count!"

There were nodding heads and mutterings of assent. Ell had never thought himself much of a public speaker, but his small speech seemed to have galvanized his family well enough.

"So what do you have in mind?" Ryder repeated the question, similar to what Ell's father had asked, which had spurred this topic forward.

"I don't know," Ell admitted again. "We are doing this together. I need you all to help me to determine our aims."

The moment stretched on in silence as people thought. A miniature eternity. Then it was broken.

"An uprising." Dahranian spoke with a calm certainty and purpose. "We start a revolt."

Chapter Forty-Three

The day was not warm. Fall was beginning to hint at a cold winter to come. Crisp leaves and brown needles sifted down from the trees on the edge of camp. Miri closed her eyes and sought to access the link with Ell's mind. However, the fear that had plagued her recent attempts to access the Graft did so again. It had been almost two weeks since that terrifying onslaught of anguish that had rendered her nearly incapacitated. Strangely however, Miri hadn't witnessed whatever incident had caused Ell's grief; she had only experienced the brutal aftermath. The Graft was a relatively unknown phenomenon, so perhaps inconsistency was to be expected. Sometimes Miri only saw into Ell's emotions, as she had when they'd been together when the link first formed. Others, she saw as if through his eyes, his experience taking over and clouding all else out of her vision and focus until it was as if she *was* him. Other times, it was only the aftermath of a moment, emotions and thoughts swirling in a jumbled attempt to make sense of something. Miri wasn't sure what had happened on the day when she had felt Ell's grief, but she was nearly positive that someone had died.

She had not been seeking the link that day, but it had found her anyway. The grief had been overwhelming beyond belief. It had not been hers, but even now, the memory of it was enough to crush her soul. And even after the link had stopped relaying Ell's feelings, the memory of that pain was enough to leave a dull, steady ache as if her heart was being carved out with a blunt instrument. More and more, Miri was beginning to understand Ell's initial fear and aversion to the Grafting. It could be a wondrous gift, catching a glimpse of your lover's soul, but the link also provided a window into a person's darkest, most miserable moments, and Miri was beginning to wonder if perhaps some moments were not best processed alone. It hurt her just to think of the numbing pain Ell had been forced to endure. She was afraid to consider the one person whose loss might elicit that type of grief. Her mind shied away from the realization. She didn't know exactly what happened. And to be honest, she was just as happy living in denial, hoping against hope that what she supposed had happened actually hadn't.

And so today, Miri closed her eyes and sought the link, sought to somehow activate the Graft she had forged with Ell's consciousness so many months ago, now. But the fear clouded her focus, and made her question whether she really wanted to activate the link.

Miri took a deep breath and thought. She had seen Ell's heart during their first Graft, and she had known his mind even before then, before she had Joined with him. Had the best parts of this Graft already been experienced, with only pain to come?

"What's wrong?" The stilted voice didn't frighten her so much as startle her.

With her eyes closed, Arendahl had snuck up on her. Once again she was surprised by just how light his feet could be. Miri opened her eyes and looked the old elf in the face.

"Didn't you hear me?" The old elf asked gruffly.

"Stop that, I'm thinking of how to respond," Miri adopted a tone of exasperation.

Arendahl raised his eyebrows and cocked his head in mute question, waiting for her to answer. When she didn't, he prodded her further.

"I've seen you scrunch up your face and act like you're training—or trying to train—for the past couple weeks now. What's going on? What the problem?"

Miri sighed. She might as well tell him. He could be stubborn as a badger when he felt like it. And in those instances, his insistence usually paid off. Better to open up and be done with it quickly.

"I'm frightened," she admitted in a smaller voice than she intended.

"Why?" Arendahl asked, still speaking in his blunt manner.

"Well, I told you something bad happened a couple of weeks ago. I'm fairly certain someone died."

Arendahl nodded gravely. "That happens girl, we're in a war, whether you want to admit it or not." He wasn't trying to be cavalier. The old elf had simply seen more death in his long life than Miri cared to imagine.

"It was the aftermath that was so hard," Miri said. "It was like his soul was crushed, like he couldn't breathe, and so I couldn't breathe. I don't want to go through that again."

The old elf shook his head. "You have to move past it. Pain is pain, whether it's now or later. You'll find out sooner or later what happened and you'll feel the pain of that loss anyway. You're the mate of a Water Caller. You aren't avoiding anything by not connecting to his mind, girl. You're just putting it off not avoiding it completely. "

She nodded reluctantly. He was right, of course. Arendahl usually was. But it didn't really make it any easier to accept. Arendahl seemed to realize what she was thinking.

"Alright, Miri, think of it this way. What would you do if Ell was here with us and he lost someone right now, would you ignore him?"

"Of course not," Miri said indignantly.

"Why?"

"Because I love him. I'd want to comfort him."

Arendahl narrowed his eyes and led her further along the line of thought. Miri had the unsettling feeling that the old elf was laying a trap for her.

"What if he was beyond the ability to comfort, just for a time, that is? What if he seemed to be immune to your comfort? Would you ignore him then, or abandon him?" The old elf prodded.

"You know I wouldn't," Miri protested weakly, her mind starting to see where he was leading. "I would want to be there for him, no matter what."

Arendahl shot her a muted triumphant look. "Exactly. How is that any different than what you're doing now? He may not be able to feel your comfort, and it may be hard for you to bear, girl, but at least you're there for him, when he needs it. He may not even realize it, but you will."

Miri pursed her lips in thought. The old elf was right. Again. Arendahl was annoying that way. She didn't really have a rebuttal, other than the fact that the immensity of Ell's pain scared her at times. For a young warrior, baptized in the fire of battle from a young age, he still maintained a depth of emotionality, something she was only now beginning to realize.

Arendahl stared at her for a time. He knew that deep down she agreed. "You have to get over your fear, girl. I trust my intuition. We don't know much about this Graft—I don't know much," he said, taking responsibility where it was due. He was the one they counted on to know these things. "But I do know one thing, and that is that I have the feeling, call it a premonition, call it what you will, that this Graft, this link between you, is going to be important. And the more you know about it, the more you discover, the more you are able to control it, the better it will be for everyone. It's important for us all, girl." He finished with a simple and solemn statement.

Miri inhaled deeply. She composed herself and nodded. He was right, she had to get over this fear. At the very least, for no other reason than to convince herself that she had done everything in her power to be there for her mate when he needed her.

Arendahl saw her determination return and patted her on the cheek tenderly. He was softer than anyone gave him credit for. He pretended to be hard, all brittle bones and jagged emotions, but he had lived long enough to

327

fully understand the wealth of emotions that accompanied all sorts of situations. She knew he understood. Miri regained control of her emotions as the old elf strode away to handle business elsewhere. He had a lot on his mind. Runners had been sent out. They had already attended one large gathering with many hundreds of elves in one place and there was more to come. Arendahl would see to it, would make sure that their attempts to gather a host of warriors did not fall short.

She stretched her mind out and sought to connect her consciousness to Ell's. The worry and fear flickered in her mind for a moment, but she snuffed it out the way you might a candle.

The breeze swirled and Miri drew her cloak about her more closely and pulled the hood up to protect herself against the wind and to seclude herself in a solitude that would keep out everything around her. The edges of her hood obscured her vision like blinders. She was alone, it was just her and her emotions, her and her Graft. Just her and Ell, a million miles away.

She controlled the Graft, not chance. She willed it so. *She* controlled her fears, not the other way around. She brushed them aside, dispersed them with a focused thought. Those worries that she couldn't quite shed, she shunted away, crammed them so tightly into the furthest corners and reaches of her mind so they could cause her no more concern at the moment. She did it again and again, cleaned her mind of all distracting thoughts.

What was there to fear, after all? She was already separated from her love, which was bad enough. Besides, there had been excitement and wonder at first. Fear hadn't always blocked her ability to link with Ell at will. Something else was inhibiting her progress.

Miri delved deeper, past the fear and the worry, past the excitement from early on, past it all right to the bottom of herself. And there it was. Resistance. Something that had been there from the first Grafting. It wasn't fear, not exactly. It was more like aversion. But to what? Miri focused. She searched more introspectively than she'd ever done before. What aversion had she had to the Grafting?

And then it clicked. It slid into place. Miri remembered memory after memory, dating back to the very first day discussing the Grafting with Ell, hearing him recount what Arendahl had told him of the linking. Since the first conversation, the old elf had stressed the importance of this, the need to understand it, how useful it could be. Not intentionally, she knew him better than that, but somehow right from the start, Arendahl had turned something precious, something intimate and private and wonderful into a tool to be used. And somehow, subconsciously, even before any fear had set in, Miri had formed a resistance, an aversion, to that idea of turning something so private and beautiful into a tool to be used—and if she was honest, Arendahl wanted it for a tool for war. He wanted to make this precious gift a tool for conflict.

Anger welled in her, rash and impulsive. It wasn't wrong, but she knew it wasn't right either. Rationality was important here. The inner struggle continued. Miri forced down what anger she could and accepted and dealt with the rest. It wasn't Arendahl's fault that a war was happening. It wasn't his fault that this intimate and precious bond was an important and useful tool. She might not like it in principle, but she knew her mentor was in the right. Miri fought for acceptance. It was the instinctive, childish refusal to accept that the world wasn't perfect. Crippled since childhood, considered passive by most, Miri had avoided anything to do with violence until recently. She had done so by choice and by necessity. Her body hadn't allowed her to do what others could, and so she had rejected violent means and turned to the opposite, convincing herself that the world was safe and tranquil. And she wasn't wrong, it wasn't about right or wrong. But she had to accept the other side. Just as she was now learning the knife and the bow, accepting that she might be called upon to defend herself—cripples or not—in a less than perfect world, so too she had to accept that her precious Graft with Ell needed to be mastered and controlled as a tool for the conflict. It helped that she wanted to control it for herself also, which gave her strength and focus, but Miri had to come to terms with the initial aversion she'd felt at using something so intimate for such a deliberate purpose.

Something flickered in her mind. The flash of blue water meeting blue sky, the scent of cold and warm strangely mixing in the air whipped across her vision and senses. There was no immediacy to the thought, no intensity.

Miri focused. Something was happening, something was shifting.

She blinked. But her eyes were closed. She blinked and then opened her eyes again and she saw sailors and masts. She felt exhaustion deep within her bones, her limbs, receding a little bit each day. She blinked again. Or rather, Ell blinked. This was it. She was in his mind, seeing through his eyes, even though nothing of note or importance was happening. It was a first. After the initial forging of the Graft, she had only ever accessed his consciousness accidentally during times of importance. This was different.

Ell was lounging, sitting on a rail of some sort, leaning back, his eyelids drooping and his innate agility keeping his lazy body from falling from his perch. All the while, sailors shouted and cursed in the salty air. The sun drifted downwards behind him, heating his neck and the left side of his face. Afternoon sun on his left cheek. Sailing north then, and east.

Miri smiled. This was the joy she'd been anticipating with the Graft. She was in his head, his mind, his heart. She sent all the love in her soul his way, even though she knew he couldn't feel it or sense it.

He blinked again, and then the connection evaporated. But this time, Miri wasn't frustrated at the loss. Something had changed. Whatever block had been created by her subconscious in response to Arendahl's intentions was gone now. Miri felt certain that with some practice, she could do this again, whenever she wished.

Miri opened her eyes. The sun felt pale and almost chill on her cheek. So he was farther South than she. It was time to talk to Arendahl again. The old elf would want to hear about this. With a victorious smile, Miri went to speak with her friend and teacher.

Chapter Forty-Four

Kalabi knew about a stretch of coastline of what he said was a day's journey or so south of Lu Fang that consisted mostly of secluded coves and rocky headlands, so they dropped anchor off that rough, windswept shore and rowed to land on skiffs the *Water Wasp* possessed. Captain Piripeos left a handful of sailors on board to guard the ship and have it ready to sail when they returned. If they returned. Ell wasn't so sure everything would work out anymore. Rihya's death had firmed the reality that good fortune ran out, and even when things appeared to work out, that wasn't always the case.

After they went ashore, it took a few minutes of searching to find a ravine that wasn't too steep for them to climb. Small rivulets of water trickled down the cliff face, and tiny waterfalls like falling streams made the climb mossy and slick with moisture. However, they managed it without any mishap and reached the top of the cliff to an outstanding view. The Fracture stretched west from their position for endless miles. It was strange to realize he was standing on foreign soil. Even in Dark Harbor, there had been a familiarity to the land. One continent, one people—elves were kin, even if the schism had fractured the two societies beyond recognition. This was different. They stood now upon the shores of Etheros, a continent wholly populated humans, by a separate race.

"Ready?" Kalabi asked.

Ell nodded silently and followed the human's lead as he set their course north. Every so often, a fjord appeared, its watery scythe cut deeply into the landscape, forcing Ell and his companions to turn inland for a ways until they had reached a small enough body of water to cross. It was time consuming. Ell realized now that the "day's journey" about which Kalabi had spoken was by ship. They would be a few days, at least, in journeying overland to Lu Fang through this countryside.

As they trekked, they talked. They discussed possibilities. Ell mostly listened at first, letting the others have their say and voice their opinions on how to find his family or how to go about instigating a slave rebellion. As they went, two groups formed within their party. Sailors made up one group and the other was his original band plus the more vocal of the sea elves—namely, Piripeos, Kester, Rikiol, and Baerg.

As luck would have it, the landscape was fairly rough and uninhabited, which was why Kalabi had volunteered it as an approach point to Lu Fang, and as such, they didn't encounter anyone. It was strange. Kalabi spoke of how populated the human continent was, but it seemed he'd led them to a miniature desolation, populated only by trees and rocks. Either way, Ell wasn't about to complain. It meant they could hope to reach the city unnoticed.

"What if your mate isn't there?"

Ell snapped out of his reverie when he heard Dacunda plying his elder brother, Adan, with somber questions.

"She will be." Adan said, more forcefully than necessary. He was clinging to the hope of seeing his mate and daughter again. Adan had left no room in his mind for failure. In some ways, it reminded Ell of how he'd approached his time searching for Adan in Dark Harbor. He'd had an unflinching resolve and belief that all would turn out right in the end. Rihya's death had ruined that for him. Oh, he still had the unflinching resolve, but not the faith in the positive outcome.

"But what if she's not?" Dacunda pressed. "What then?"

Ell's father opened his mouth to retort, but Ell smoothly interjected, "Then we do what we came here to do anyway. We spark unrest. This is bigger now. It's about more than just what I or my father need or want. We start something here that has the potential to strike a real blow at the enemy."

The others listened with quiet attention while Dacunda appraised him for a moment and then nodded. They'd heard a similar monologue of Ell's before. But each time he spoke of striking a blow at the enemy, it was as if the steel in their spine and the mettle in their gazes hardened and firmed slightly. They would need determination for what they hoped to accomplish.

Ell continued to speak. "It seems to me that the first thing we will need to do in either case—whether searching for my family or sparking a rebellion—is to send out feelers and make preliminary contact with the enslaved population. My lost family might be among them, and even if they aren't, that population is the key to starting the revolt. We must find out if they even have the courage to do so."

Ell had directed his comment at his uncle, an automatic reflex after so many years of running his plans and actions by Dacunda, but it was Kalabi who answered.

"You speak correctly, Elliyar. We will need to make contact. But I fear your questions of valor are apt. Many slaves in Etheros have never known a life other than slavery. Your kinfolk were brought here twenty years ago. There may be youth among them who were born here, but the majority will at least remember freedom. That is not so with many of the humans. We will need the entire slave population in Lu Fang to aid us if we hope for success, but I am certain that many of the humans may not be so easy to convince to join our cause." The ex-slave trailed off, again absently toying with the golden collar around his neck.

"You were born a slave and yet you desired freedom." Dahranian had a way of speaking briefly, but often his words carried weight and required attention. One ignored Dahranian at their own mistake.

Kalabi smiled ruefully. "I saw an opportunity and ran. I did not fight. Do not confuse the two scenarios."

"What's the difference?" This time it was Ryder, brow furrowed, who addressed the human.

"The difference, my friend Ryder, is that I was in a land where, should I escape, there was hope of finding a place of freedom, a place not under the dominion of slavers. Andalaya, your land, whose name I heard in whispers. But here in Etheros, there is nowhere to run. Slavery exists everywhere and slaves themselves are marked with a collar we cannot easily remove," he said, indicating his own golden band. "That means that in Etheros, to revolt means almost certain death. A free death, but demise no less."

"Then we must offer them another alternative." Adan Wintermoon joined the discussion abruptly. For a moment, as Ell had noticed in moments passed, his father's voice took on a note of authority, an ironclad expectation to be listened to, likely a remnant from his years helping command Verdantihya's defense.

"What do you mean, Father?"

Adan looked at Ell. "I mean, Kalabi speaks correctly. Slaves need hope, for without hope, the world grows bleak. They will never fight back if they have no hope. We must give them another option, a place, something in which to hope." His words carried the force and weight of personal experience.

They all gazed at Adan, waiting for him to continue. They could see he had more to say.

"Andalaya." Surprisingly it was Baerg, solemn, stoic Baerg who spoke. The sailor followed up that one word with another sentence. "The sea would work also, if there were enough ships for an entire population, but there isn't, so Andalaya will have do."

Adan smiled at the dark skinned elf in agreement. Comprehension lit in Ell's mind and he could see it bloom in the faces of his friends and family, as well.

"An amnesty then, between the races?" Dahranian asked.

"Not really an amnesty, since I would not say we were ever truly at war with the human slaves, but for the sake of easy terms, yes." Adan responded to his nephew. "The hopelessness Kalabi spoke of has a solution—or at least the potential to be a solution. Slaves who revolt will be given sanctuary in Andalaya."

"It's a brilliant idea. It strikes a blow at our enemy and swells our own ranks in the process." Dacunda breathed.

Ell found himself nodding excitedly along with the others. "It's a good start."

Kalabi once again was the voice of reason, stalling the conversation in its tracks. "I foresee only one problem." They waited for him to continue. The human obliged. "We are not in Andalaya, in fact, we are nowhere near it."

Adan again took the lead in answering. "Nobody claimed it would be easy to revolt or easy to convince people to do so. Rebellions carry great risk, but also great reward. But if slaves revolt here they could fight their way north and back across the Great Bridge."

Kalabi looked skeptical. "What you are describing is unlikely. The military controls the Great Bridge. It will not fall with even close to the—dare I say—ease of Lu Fang."

"It might if the army grows." Dacunda supported his brother.

Adan nodded. "A slave army would have to fight its way to freedom, without doubt, but its losses could be balanced by a swelling of numbers as they pass cities and towns along the way. So it always is with armies."

Suddenly, Kalabi didn't seem so convinced that their proposed plan would fail. A speculative look grew on his face. Even a hint of a smile.

This time it was Rikiol who spoke up for the Departed pirates. "Besides, if the fighting got too hot, they could always steal ships and sail the army back to our continent."

"You're forgetting the Fracture," Kalabi said absently, almost lost in thought. "We only made the crossing because of Elliyar and his abilities."

Rikiol shook her head impatiently. "I have heard stories. It is said that the humans clear the ice in the waters far to the north and near the Great Bridge. Ships can make it across."

Ell cut in, heading the conversation back towards the present. "All of this is good to ponder, but I think we've outlined enough of a plan to establish that it's not outside the realm of possibility to offer the slaves in Lu Fang hope that a future exists for them, albeit with trials and obstacles between them and that future. But we can ignite hope for a free future all the same. Wouldn't you agree, Kalabi?"

The dark-skinned human nodded slowly, his close-cropped beard catching a ray of sun, causing his face to glisten slightly, the way a raven's glossy feathers shine. "I admit this is beginning to seem feasible. Improbable still, but possible." Kalabi grinned wryly in an uncharacteristically fatalistic manner. "You know, we'll probably all die in the endeavor."

Ell grinned back at him wolfishly. "I think I may have heard that before."

Kester, the half-mad sailor, threw back her head and cackled maniacally. For some reason, her crazy laughter sent the rest of them into fits of mirth. Ell felt a release. It was necessary to laugh at life sometimes, to look death or the impossible in the eye and tell it that it didn't matter. He felt like he had been doing that a lot lately.

* * * *

Lu Fang was an impressive sprawling city built in a crescent shape around the edges of a bay. It was built on hilled land, and the city had hardly a flat space to be found, though it had three mounded, finger-like peninsulas jutting out into the water. According to Kalabi, there were slave quarters throughout the city, but the three largest—in which the majority of the slave population resided—were on the peninsulas.

Ell and his companions crouched low on a mountain ridge just to the south of Lu Fang. They were still far enough away to not be seen by wandering eyes, but caution was ingrained in Ell and most of his companions. They were careful to hide their presence. Bodies held low, they surveyed the area. They were high up, so the city appeared smaller than Ell knew it was in actuality and even so, he could still see how large it was. It was larger in scope, if not necessarily in population, than Dark Harbor—the elven capital of the south was piled and built upon itself in a haphazard way due to its confinement to its island—and Ell had come to realize just how big even the island capital of the southern kingdom was.

Lu Fang didn't seem to be constructed of beautiful architecture or flowery design the way Verdantihya had been, yet this human city was impressive in its own ways. It was large, Ell had already established that in his mind, but that was only part of it. Whereas one could lose themselves in the warren of side streets in Dark Harbor or get lost gazing at the sweeping terraces and walkways of broken Verdantihya, such was not the case in Lu Fang. There was a formidableness to the straight streets, the carefully planned and executed organization of this human city of commerce and trade. Looking down upon Lu Fang, Ell was struck by the impression that not a road, not a building, not even a cobblestone was out of place from where the creators had intended it to be. There was the immaculate sense of a well-oiled mechanism to the city, and even as Ell watched, the bustle of tiny figures moved in rhythmic patterns along its thoroughfares and avenues and treed boulevards. This was a city that knew its identity, knew its place in the world and how it functioned. This was a city that had not needed to break from routine for a long, long time. Perhaps that was its strength. But maybe it could also be a weakness.

"It's built on the bay without a major river," Kalabi spoke quietly into Ell's ear, despite their distance from the city, "yet there are enough minor streams to more than make up for that."

Ell glanced around at the mountainous features surrounding the city and saw what Kalabi meant. Hundreds of small waterfalls caught the glimmering light of the afternoon sun and twinkled, reflecting the light as they cascaded to the earth and trickled toward the city. It might be troublesome if the city fell under siege to have so many of its water sources on the outskirts of the city, but Ell had a feeling that this was a city that had not been under military threat in a long time—if ever. Some of the waterfalls carried enough water to cascade with force from high upon the cliff sides, others simply trickled down, like the wet, clammy hands of nature clinging to the rocky, mossy walls.

"I suggest we make camp just on the south side of this ridgeline, in that thicket of trees for now, and hold off on our first approach to the city until tonight." Kalabi spoke a little louder than he had before, loud enough for all to hear.

"Good idea," Ell said. "Let's make camp. Tonight, I'll lead a few of us into the city to scout."

Kalabi pursed his lips and grimaced slightly. "I do not mean to offend, Elliyar, but I am not sure you are the best to guide us."

"What do you mean by that?" Ell asked, feeling startlingly defensive.

Kalabi spread his hands peacefully. "I simply wish to point out that you bear the tattoos upon your cheeks."

Ell narrowed his eyes as he waited for the human to continue.

Kalabi obliged. "In Dark Harbor, the Traitor's Tears gained you entrance. Here in Lu Fang, there has never been a free elf of any kind. Those tears will only draw attention to you I fear."

"It will be dark. I'll keep my hood up." Ell responded, feeling frustrated. He could see the swarthy ex-slave's point but he was itching to get into the city and search for his family and weigh the situation as a whole.

"A hood might hide those distinctive ears your kind possess, and your fair hair. It might even cast enough shadows across your face to partially conceal your exotic features when compared to a human's. But I fear the bright red of those tattoos will still garner attention should any torchlight lighten your face."

It was Ell's turn to grimace. "I'll take my chances, Kalabi."

Kalabi put forth one last argument. "How do you suppose those elves enslaved here will react when you appear with the traitor's tattoos? You have no father to see himself in your visage. We do not even know for certain that your mother and sister are here. You will need to make contact with someone to gather support for a revolt. I do not think one branded a traitor to his kind—false or not—will be able to initiate the types of encounters that we will need."

Dahranian placed a hand on his shoulder. "He is right, cousin. You and I will have to wait until the action begins." Dahranian also had the false tears on his cheeks from when they had slipped everyone into Dark Harbor.

Ell's resistance wilted.

"A good leader knows what he cannot do." Dacunda was there as always with a word of wisdom. Ell nodded his acceptance.

"Looks like you're the one stuck outside, waiting this time," Ryder threw a roguish wink in his direction and Ell shot his cousin a flat, unhappy look.

"Don't blame me, Ell, it's not my fault that you marred your pretty little face with those hideous markings." Ryder adopted an airy tone to cover the smirk playing at the edges of his mouth.

And so when evening approached, Ell, Dahranian, Piripeos, and most of the sailors sat in the fireless camp in the thicket on the ridgeline. Of the crew, only Rikiol had demanded to go on the scouting trip and Baerg had suitably followed her.

It was torture. Just hours into waiting, Ell could appreciate the difficulty it must have proven for his family to wait for him in the cave outside Dark Harbor. Rihya, especially, would have found it hard. No doubt, Ryder was having the time of his life, larking about Lu Fang right now. The thought made Ell grit his teeth in frustration. Dahranian must have heard the grinding of his jaws.

"We'll be down there soon enough, Ell. When the fighting begins—whenever we manage to spark a revolt—the plan will need us down there in the thick of things. You especially."

"It's just hard. I'm not used to sitting around and waiting."

Dahranian laughed, mirth breaking through his characteristically somber demeanor. "You've had more excitement in the last six months than many elves dream of. You faced Ghouls and Ogres, flown on an Icari, and toppled a Pillar. You even dueled the Prince of Darkness, cousin. I think you can afford to sit one out."

Ell felt a tremor of fear run through him at the mention of Half-Mask. A sliver of doubt gnawed darkly in his belly. It bloomed as if just mentioning Half-Mask was enough to elicit some kind of response from Ell's subconscious. An irrational urge to fight something, to kill, to squeeze the life out of some living thing and watch the light drain from its eyes, threatened to overpower Ell's consciousness. He tightened his jaw even more and willed the darkness within him to recede.

"Are you alright, Cousin?"

"I'm fine," Ell just managed to respond to Dahranian, without panting. The struggle to control his emotions and his thoughts was relatively new. Before, it had just occurred occasionally in the midst of a fight.

Dahranian seemed to accept his declaration at face value. But out of the corner of his eye, Ell saw Kester, a pirate from the area around Dark Harbor, staring keenly at him without any of the madness she usually bore. Perhaps her proximity of origin to the southern capital afforded her knowledge of the process of becoming an Unsired—what did they call it there, the Blackness? Ell glanced Kester's way, but decided to ignore the sea elf's gaze. Regardless of what she did or did not know, his own worry was enough to deal with without having to field another's questions.

The rest of the evening and night passed without much to disturb their camp. It was quiet, but not a peaceful quiet. Sailors were naturally boisterous and loud, Ell had seen that from his time in Dark Harbor and the Southern Refuge, but these sailors knew when to be quiet. So they all passed their time in tense silence until it was time to assign watches and get some sleep. Kalabi and the group that had gone down into the city, might arrive back only just before dawn, so there was no point in waiting up for them.

Dahranian took the first watch while Ell curled up under his cloak and tried to sleep. The night air was chill and a steady, whistling breeze billowed up over the ridgeline and threatened to disrupt any hope of rest Ell had for the night. After an hour of fitful dozing, Ell eventually surrendered and joined his cousin.

"Couldn't sleep?" Dahranian grunted.

Ell shook his head. "I'll take over your watch if you like, Dahranian."

Ell's cousin pondered the idea for a moment but decided otherwise. "I think I'll keep you company a bit. I'm not sure I could sleep myself just now." Dahranian's eyes had the wide watchfulness of a warrior on duty in enemy territory. Ever responsible, ever cautious, ever concerned with duty, Dahranian was very much his father's son.

They gazed down from the ridge top toward the city below. The basin in which the city lay had darkened, but there were torches still lighting many of the streets, homes, and buildings. The peninsulas jutted out into the blackness of the bay below like three fiery, flickering claws.

"There are so many people down there," Ell murmured, half to himself.

Dahranian nodded. "I wouldn't worry about the population fighting us though. Kalabi seemed fairly convinced that the average person in Lu Fang doesn't have much in the way of military training."

"So he expects it will be easy? He didn't seem to think so in our discussion earlier," Ell said.

Dahranian shook his head slightly. "Not easy, no. The common folk are harmless enough, but he said there's a city guard that is fairly numerous. However, the real danger is the Lashers."

"Who are they?" Ell found himself whispering his question into the night.

Dahranian answered without turning toward him, keeping his face obscured by shadow, "I asked Kalabi some questions days ago, while you were sleeping and in recovery. He said they're a special unit of soldiers tasked with controlling the slave population. They're given the highest military training available and then sent into the cities to manage the slave quarters. Kalabi didn't come right out and say this, but from the look on his face and the tone of his voice, I got the impression that the Lashers are fairly brutal. He is afraid of them."

"We'll deal with these Lashers when the time comes," Ell said resolutely.

"Do not be overconfident, Cousin. Some of the humans know how to fight, and these Lashers are reputed to be far and away the best of them."

Ell nodded. Dahranian was right. An arrogant leader got his people killed. "Did he say why they were called Lashers?"

"They carry whips," Dahranian answered simply.

That explained it. Whether these special units of soldiers were dangerous or not, they had likely been free with their whips, earning them their name. Ell felt his emotions seethe at the thought of so many of his people suffering under the whip for so many years. To occupy his hands and hopefully quiet his mind, Ell pulled out his belt knife and began to sharpen it. The methodical motions calmed him somewhat, but he still felt the age-old anger that had burned in his chest since before he could think. Anger that had been born of a child growing up without his parents, of one of the Highest reaching adulthood without the opportunity to see Verdantihya's splendor alive and flourishing rather than in ruins.

The moon was pale and bright, and Ell's work sharpening his blade filled his senses. The whisk of the knife against the whetstone, the gleam of the blade as it caught the moonlight. In a moment of uncharacteristic clumsiness, Ell nicked his finger on the edge of his belt knife. The blade didn't cut deeply, but a thin strand of blood appeared.

Ell swore and looked at his finger closely. As he did, a chill ran down his spine. The blood was dark, almost black. He quickly popped his finger into his mouth to suck the blood away, hoping Dahranian hadn't noticed. The blood tasted bitter. Ell almost gagged, but before too many moments passed the usual tang of metallic blood filled his mouth. Nervously, he pulled his finger out and looked at it again by moonlight. This time the blood was red, the usual color. Ell popped it back in for one last suck and then wiped it on his pants. They were far from home and with little Source Water available to them. A nick didn't merit anything more than a lick and a wipe. The Source Water and its healing properties had to be saved for any emergencies that might arise.

Ell shot a glance at his cousin. Dahranian's eyes had a narrowed and there was a worried look on his face. Ell felt the clasping hand of fear on his heart. What was happening to him? Why had his blood been black? Irrationally, he felt shame. Ell felt the powerful urge to do anything possible to prevent anyone from discovering his secret—that Half-Mask had warped his body and mind somehow, that he was destined to become something ugly and vile. Ell steeled his resolve as he attempted a rueful smile to Dahranian. All he had to do was fulfill the purpose for which they had come to Etheros—find his family, set in motion the wheels of revolution. After that, whatever happened, happened. He could face whatever might come, knowing that he'd freed his family. Anything except Miri. Cold panic suddenly shook his heart as he thought of what she might think of him.

"Nothing to worry about, Cousin." Ell faked a smile at Dahranian. Dahranian peered at him closely for an instant, but seemed to accept his statement.

They chatted idly far into the night. Finally, they roused one of the sailors to take a turn to watch. Ell and Dahranian slept back to back, warming each other with their presences. However, Ell's sleep was fitful, plagued by dreams of dark thoughts and black blood. Dreams in which Ell was the villain and people ran screaming from him.

A hand shook him. Ell awakened with a start, one hand impulsively feeling for his belt knife.

"Easy, Son." Adan knelt over him.

The grey of morning had already reached this mountain ridge. It was a dark, wintry dawn, but morning nonetheless. Ell pulled his cloak about his shoulders and stood up. Most were still asleep, and Dahranian was snoring quietly at his feet.

"When did you return?"

"Just now," Adan said. "I wanted to wake you and report first thing."

Not for the first time, Ell's head spun at the concept of others, especially Dacunda and his father, reporting to him, but he had come to accept it now. He had chosen to lead after all, so many months ago in Andalaya when he had boldly declared to Arendahl and Dacunda that he would lead the expedition. It seemed so long ago. Would he ever see Miri again? The thought came unbidden, followed by a bleaker thought. Did he want to see her again? Judging by last night's incident with his blood, he was frightened of the future. Ell wasn't sure a future in which he might become a danger to Miri was one in which he wanted to exist. Ell shoved those thoughts brutally from his mind and focused on Adan.

"We scouted most of the city. It took all of the night because we avoided the ferry services and their potential attention to us, but it's done," Adan was saying.

"Is it as Kalabi described, Father?"

Adan nodded his affirmation. "Yes, the north peninsula is elf slave barracks. Heavily guarded. The middle is a mixture and the south is purely human."

Ell paused before speaking. "Did you... did you see any sign of Mother?" Ell could hardly keep the wistful tone from his voice. He wasn't sure he'd ever actually used the word mother as a pronoun before, to describe someone particular rather than a mother in general. Rihya and he had always avoided the topic.

Adan took his question in stride, business-like and efficient. Ell could see where Dacunda had learned some of his focus and attention to duty.

"Not yet, Elliyar. But we only scouted the outskirts of the barracks. Located them for future reference. Next time, we will attempt infiltration. That will give us a better idea of whether or not she is here and alive." Ell noted his father's steely tone. It was the only clue as to the powerful emotions he must be feeling. Ell couldn't imagine two decades separated from Miri. His father's worry and anticipation must be unbearable.

"We'll find them," Ell stated. Adan smiled.

The rest of the camp began to awaken. Still without fire for fear of discovery, even high up on the mountain as they were, Ell and his band broke their fast on cold rations. Kalabi, Dacunda, and the others who had gone down into the city quickly found their blankets—mainly cloaks they used to wrap themselves—and closed their eyes for a few quick hours of sleep before they would wake again and deliberate on the information they had gathered.

Ell spent the hours in solitude, gazing down upon the city of Lu Fang from his perch on the mountain's shoulder. Last night, the city had been illuminated here and there by the orangey glow of fire and torches. In the daylight, it looked much cleaner, almost pretty. Ell was forced to admit that if cities were your preference, then Lu Fang appeared a pleasant one. It had none of the sinister and dirty streets of Dark Harbor, no grime and crime to contend with. Of course, from a distance, anything could look pretty. Perspective changed upon close inspection. Nevertheless, Ell couldn't help but look upon the tree lined avenues of Lu Fang and think they were beautiful in their own way. Tree leaves having lost their greenery to late autumn had taken on a dark, brilliant red. From afar, it looked almost like a festival.

The time passed slowly as Ell impatiently waited for the members under his command to awaken. Adan was first of the scouts to rise. He made his way over to Ell again and they talked, just the two of them, as they waited for the rest to rise. It was nearly midday.

"You miss her." It was a statement, not a question by Adan.

"Yes," Ell said, "very much. Rihya always had my back. She had a barbed wit and quick knives that drew my blood on more than one occasion, but until recently, she was the closest person I had in the entire world."

Adan put a comforting hand on his shoulder. "I did not know her well. She was a hardly more than a babe when I was taken. But I know enough to be proud of her. As should you, Elliyar. She did not die without purpose."

"It will mean all the more if we can accomplish what we have set out to do here." Ell spoke with determination.

"Lliaria—your mother—is strong. She will have survived. Valerihya's death will not have been for nothing." Ell could hear the faith in his father's voice and his own hope swelled with it.

"What was she like? Mother, I mean."

"You'll find out soon enough, Elliyar."

"Humor me, Father."

"Very well," Adan said with a smile. "She was—is—blonde like you and I, with eyes that looked at everything with joy. I pray captivity has not stolen that from her. She was not unskilled with a bow or a sword, but that was not her calling, not like you and I and Valerihya. She fought when necessary, but she preferred other activities, like singing or telling tales. Your oldest sister, Delle, was five name days old when we were captured, and was already more like your mother than me."

"Lliaria. Delle." Ell breathed the names the way you would strange, foreign words. He had heard them spoken of course, Dacunda had not completely left his and Rihya's family history unsaid, but it had not been something of which they had spoken regularly. Certainly not for years. As soon as Ell had been old enough to fight, that had become the focus of everything.

"You will like them." Adan smiled to himself. Again Ell heard an unshaking belief in his voice. Sometimes Adan appeared a broken elf, his confidence and pride wrecked by his years of slavery. But at other times, Ell could almost see his father's resilience to it all—to the years of harsh labor, the pain and agony of being torn from his family—to shake it off and still believe in the world was almost tangible. His rescue had been a miracle in Adan's mind, Ell supposed. What was one more miracle added to that?

They chatted for some time more, and Ell was filled with a profound sense of gratitude that this chance to get to know his father had been provided him. He'd never even imagined something like this would be possible. If only Rihya could be here too. They talked until the others woke.

Suddenly, and somewhat off topic, Adan asked a question as Ell was watching the rest of his family and friends wake from their slumber.

"What do you make of the scar on your cheek?" Adan's voice was deceptively innocent, yet Ell could hear the undertone of intensity in the question. What did Adan know? After two decades living in Dark Harbor, something about the Unsired and their attributes must have filtered down into the slave ranks.

Ell felt a flash of shame. What would his father think of him if he knew what Half-Mask had done to his son? Ell swallowed.

"It's nothing, Father, a mark on my cheek to match the scars all over the rest of my body. And I would have had more if Source Water had not been used to heal many others over the years. What is one more?"

"Still, its black color is something to note, do you not think, Elliyar?"

Why was Adan pressing this now?

"I said it's nothing!" Ell spoke more sharply than he intended. Adan gave him a strange look, but Ell was saved from further discussion by the arrival of the others.

Ryder had a hard biscuit packed from the ship's galley and was glumly gumming it as best he could to soften the hard exterior.

"If I'd known food on the sea was so terrible, I would never have agreed to follow you on this cockeyed adventure, Ell." Ryder said with a sour twist to his mouth.

"We are not on the sea, Brother, we are on firm land. A mountain actually, or hadn't you noticed." Dahranian spoke smoothly, placidly.

Ryder glowered and then raised one skeptical eyebrow. "Was that actually an attempt at humor, Dahranian? Maybe you should stick to poking people with your sword instead. I think you're better at that."

Dahranian's mouth quirked into the smallest of smiles, but he declined to respond.

Ell received a full report from the night's activities—fuller than the brief information Adan had given him upon his arrival back to camp.

From their report, Ell found that his and Dahranian's discussion from the night before had dealt with accurate information. The city guard was present and while not a standing army, it was numerous enough to merit concern. The common folk however were not warlike—not like the average elf who could take up arms along with any other warrior—and Kalabi suspected that should any violence break out then they would likely shutter themselves up in their houses and avoid involvement in the tumult.

"It is the Lashers we must worry about." Kalabi had a fretful look on his face. "The Lashers are—"

"Dahranian filled me in on the Lashers, Kalabi," Ell said brusquely. He didn't have time to deal with fear. "Specially trained units of soldiers tasked to quell the slaves into supple submission. Does that sum it up?"

"Not really, they are vicious and more dangerous than you might believe, Elliyar. I think they might even give you and your family a good fight at even numbers," Kalabi paused and took a deep breath. "But for now, yes, I suppose we do not need to deliberate upon them any further."

"Soldiers are soldiers no matter how they are trained," Ryder said with a shrug. "I'm with Ell on this one."

"That isn't exactly true, Ryder," Dacunda said reprovingly. "Elliyar is proof of that."

Ryder turned back to Kalabi. "Do these Lashers have magic?" He wiggled his fingers mysteriously.

"No," Kalabi answered slowly.

"Then there's no problem, really. I stand by what I said. Soldiers are soldiers, if they're the normal kind."

"That's just it, they may not be supernatural, but they are hardly normal," Kalabi disagreed. Ell saw the look of fear on his face that Dahranian had mentioned last night.

"What do you mean?" Dacunda asked.

"Fear," Adan supplied his brother with a terse answer.

Kalabi turned in surprise to Adan. "Exactly. I suppose I shouldn't be startled that you see to the heart of this so quickly while the rest cannot. You are the only former slave other than me, after all."

"What am I missing?" Ell asked impatiently. He didn't want to have to pick through a conversation with only educated guesses.

Kalabi looked at Adan to see if he wanted to answer.

"What our human friend is alluding to, Elliyar, is that slavery changes a person—that's not even taking into account those born into slavery. People have courage, and dignity, valor, even faith at first. But that changes. Fear and pain changes a person, strips away all the characteristics that made you who you were before, until you're not much more than a husk, a shell of a person." Adan swallowed as if uncomfortable with revealing so much. Ell hadn't really heard him speak of his tribulations as a slave.

Kalabi cleared his throat, taking over from Adan. "What I think your father means, Ell, is that slavery changes people. And often those responsible for that change are the people—the guards—with whom one comes into immediate contact with daily. Slavers are typically brutal. They instill fear and condition their captives to relinquish hope. Lashers are a particularly savage group of slavers. They inflict pain for fun." Kalabi paused. "The point of all this is to say that they may only be men, but they are far from normal. They are ruthless, and the fear that the slaves in Lu Fang have been conditioned into feeling at the sight of the Lashers will be difficult to surmount."

"You're saying the Lashers will make it difficult to convince the slaves to revolt." Ell said shrewdly.

"Precisely."

"So how do we overcome that?" Dacunda asked.

The ex-slave shrugged apologetically. "I am not sure. I'm not sure it can be overcome, speaking from experience."

The group discussion trailed off for a moment as they all thought. Baerg, the stoic and stalwart pirate, broke the silence.

"If they are so afraid of the Lashers, then we must show them something even more frightening. Greater fear can conquer lesser fear." The pirate spoke hastily and then clamped his mouth shut as if not accustomed to speaking much. Ell wasn't sure what he said had made sense.

Adan seemed to agree with Ell's sentiment. "I do not believe we will inspire these people by frightening them."

"Hold on," Dacunda said, looking thoughtfully at Ell with that speculative look he sometimes got when a plan was forming. "We don't have to frighten them. We just have to show them something more dangerous than the Lashers, something to overcome their psychological block that's been conditioned into them."

"What do you have in mind?" Kalabi asked intently.

But Ell already knew where his uncle's mind was going.

"I'd think it was obvious," Dacunda said gesturing towards Ell. "We have the most dangerous thing right here with us."

If only you knew how truly dangerous I am, Uncle, Ell thought. *I'm changing and there's nothing anyone can do about it.* For a moment, the hidden blackness deep in his soul threatened to explode, to overflow, just at the simple thought of it.

Adan looked at his brother. He almost whispered. "Is my son really that dangerous, Dac?" There was a strange note in his voice, pride, mingled with a hint of fear. He did know something, the black scar on Ell's cheek had him worried.

Dacunda nodded to his brother. "Ell is more than a match for these Lashers. We just need to convince the slaves of that."

"It could work," Kalabi mused.

"Right, so that's it then," Ryder said impatiently. "We just persuade them of Ell's terrible prowess and scour the city for my aunt and cousin." His matter of fact tone jogged them all into action.

"Right, grab some food and we should start out. There's no real hurry, but we want to be around the outskirts of the city by dusk so that we can make the most of the night." Ell said.

Dacunda raised his eyebrows. "We?"

Ell grimaced as he remembered. "I wish I'd never put these false marks on my cheeks!" he growled.

"It will not be forever, Son. But for now, it will be best for those of us who do not resemble traitors to initiate the contact with the elves in the slave barracks." Adan spoke reassuringly. "Besides, you would not want a repeat of the first encounter that we had with your mother and sister, would you?" Adan had a half smile on his face, but Ell took the warning to heart.

"True," he muttered grimly. "I'm trusting you to handle this, then." Ell directed his comment somewhere between the two elders—his father and uncle.

"I handled business for years before you ever took charge, Nephew," Dacunda said with a slight smile. "Everything will go well."

Ell nodded. "Very well. Make contact. Feel the slaves out. And ask after my family. You'll have to infiltrate some of the barracks, so by the First Days, be careful!"

* * * *

The following days were torture. Ell and Dahranian were sidelined from the action, needing to wait until morning for reports of their group's activities fomenting unrest in the city by night. With the exception of the wonderful news that Ell's mother and sister were indeed still alive and living within the mixed barracks on the middle peninsula, the reports the band brought back to Ell were disappointing. They split up and infiltrated the barracks by night to ascertain leaders within the slave ranks, but there was little encouragement. The slaves were beaten down, hopeless. Not many were as brutalized as Ell had witnessed with the slaves in Dark Harbor, but there was still a pervading hopelessness to the slaves in Lu Fang. Their lives were just bad enough to keep them broken and hopeless, with just enough comfort to give them something to lose if they did revolt and lose.

Dacunda, Adan, and Ryder spoke of their frustration in trying to inspire their kinfolk. Adan had a joyous look about his eyes when he spoke of seeing

Lliaria and Delle, but other than that, a vexed expression adorned his face. Kalabi's interactions with the human slave barracks were no different. Four nights of this passed before they met again in the dull light of morning to discuss.

"Discontent is there, simmering beneath the surface, but I fear it is too deep, still. They simply do not believe," Kalabi said. "They fear the Lashers too much."

"With good reason," Piripeos grunted realistically.

"They will not believe, not without seeing him in action, and they will not see Ell fight without first committing to action. We do not want to start a rebellion that they cannot, will not finish," Adan responded.

"Perhaps they cannot see him fight, but they can still see him," Dacunda mused.

"What do you propose, Dac?" Adan asked.

"They know of us now, Brother. They know we are here and they know of Elliyar, for we have spoken of him. Perhaps now is the time to bring him down. His Traitor's Tears will not surprise them the way they might have upon first meeting."

Kalabi nodded. "I do not think it will hurt at this point."

Ell's heart leapt at the realization that he was finally about to join the action. The days of waiting had been filled with pining for Miri—which, while it was enjoyable to think of her and her sun kissed face, it was totally unproductive—and worrying about what Half-Mask had done and when it would take full effect. Some action would do him good.

"Alright, then. Tonight, I'll go down with you."

Ell was finally going into Lu Fang.

Chapter Forty-Five

They were in far northwestern Andalaya, not far from Little Vale, actually. The runners sent out over the past weeks had been productive. Elves had been gathering for days now at Arendahl's summons. Miri glanced down from her boulder perch on the hillside. Art sat on a slightly smaller rock nearby, mimicking her. Arendahl stood readying himself on another boulder a short way down the slope from her. There was a buzz in the crowd that was gathered. People could feel the energy, the changing times. Miri had been around greatness. Ell was challenging in many ways, he wasn't fully in touch with his emotions—she supposed killing for a living could do that to a person—he was rash at times, and prone to overconfidence. But Elliyar was great. There was a greatness to his person, his nature, that was impossible to deny. And it wasn't just his powers. He'd attempted and succeeded at the impossible even before he'd ever mastered his abilities as a Water Caller. Yes, Miri could sense greatness. She felt it when she spoke to Arendahl, felt the years and weight of his knowledge and ironclad, unrelenting resolve. And she felt it now. The rest of the crowd could feel it too. Something momentous was happening.

Not wishing to be in the milling throng below, Miri and Brie had decided to sit above the action and watch as Arendahl orated. She had heard him speak before, but never to this many people. Once again, she was astounded by the number of her people filling this valley. There were thousands upon thousands of Highest! They were gathered, readying themselves to listen. Readying themselves for war.

Almost idly, Miri accessed the Graft into Ell's mind. She couldn't do it perfectly, or with full accuracy yet, but more and more she was beginning to be able to reach out on command and merge her consciousness with Ell's. As always, she smiled. She couldn't help but do so when she felt his presence, even if he couldn't feel hers.

Surprisingly enough, he was bored. She almost laughed. He was supposed to be off having adventures and rescuing people. He was on another continent

348

and he had the temerity to be bored. He was waiting. She could feel his irked impatience. This time, there was a vision with her merge. He was gazing down upon a city of some size. Miri had never been in a city, only the ruins of her people's glory—Verdantihya being only the largest of those. She wondered what it was like. He was waiting for people, coiled and ready for action.

"Did you go wandering off into lover boy's mind again, Miri?" Brie asked with a mischievous twinkle in her eye.

Miri had finally sat her friend down and explained to her. Now that she had broken through whatever block her subconscious had erected, she felt more free to discuss Grafting. Arendahl had been overjoyed to hear what she had accomplished and from the information she could now give him, they pieced together that Ell and the rest of his family were no longer in Dark Harbor. They had sailed across the Fracture—once again doing something no one had ever done—and were now on the human continent, Etheros, Arendahl called it. They couldn't tell exactly where, but Miri checked in on him multiple times a day so she knew he was safe for the moment.

"Stop it. You know I do it all the time. Quit teasing." She smiled at Brie.

Brie shook her head in disgust. "If I ever become besotted as you are, promise me you'll stick a knife in me."

"You have my word," Miri promised with exaggerated seriousness.

"Shh, he's about to start," Brie cut her off as if Miri had been making more noise than a storm. As much as she needled the old elf and made fun of Miri and Arendahl's relationship, Brie looked at Arendahl with something akin to worship—an irreverent adulation, but adulation nonetheless. Miri supposed it was something to do with the way the ancient elf fought. They all knew he was special, possessed Water Calling powers like Ell, but that wasn't what kept them impressed. And Miri thought she understood. To be a warrior and see someone as old as Arendahl and still functioning at the highest skill level and physical prowess, must be inspiring.

Miri and Brie quieted their chatter and listened as the old elf began to speak in a hollow, booming voice to reach out over the valley and the mass of elves gathered before him.

"Long ago, when creation was young and new, there was a plague upon the land. Creation spun us into existence to right that wrong. And we did!" Arendahl raised a clenched fist. He was wasting no time building up this crowd. It had already attended to that itself in the time leading up to his speech. The crowd let out a rumbling murmur of assent as it recognized the ancient tale relating the history of the Highest.

Arendahl continued while Miri and Brie listened with intent ears and rapt gazes, "In the First Days, our people were one. Distinction of north and south did not exist. We were unified and we crushed the darkness before us. It was a long and bitter battle, but we emerged utterly victorious, or so we thought. And we were for a time." Once again, the crowd swelled with excitement at the story, not recognizing the ominous warning at which he hinted.

"But over time, our people splintered, factions formed, enmities arose. Our cousins to the south departed from our ways, left their connection to the earth, to creation, to the Source behind them. With that separation, the enmity and conflict increased. War was waged, battles were fought. It grew worse and worse, until only two cities remained in our land, Verdantihya in the north, and Dor Khabor in the south.

"For a time, it seemed there was an equilibrium reached. But then the humans came with their teeming multitudes and their mechanisms of war. They swamped the eastern moors with their numbers, they logged the eastern plains. But worst of all, they strong-armed our cousins in the south into an alliance against us."

This time, angry mutters arose. Arendahl was playing the crowds emotions. He was entering into present difficulties. There was not a family in Andalaya who had not lost a member to the slavers or to battle.

The old elf strutted across his boulder as he spoke. "They reached the glorious walls of our capital. Verdantihya, in all its green splendor, had never been breached—its walls impregnable. But we had not counted on a traitor amongst us."

Arendahl's voice dropped to barely more than a whisper and the crowd silenced with him.

"We had not counted on the Original Betrayer. With vile conspiracy, he contrived to burst our gates from within and as the battle was lost, so was the kingdom. And so were many lives and friends and family. "

Miri could hear the real emotion in Arendahl's voice. As much as he was performing, molding the crowd to suit his will, he believed in what he was saying, felt it to his core.

"Twenty years we have been beaten. We have been bruised and bloodied, our people stolen and enslaved. For two decades, we have tucked tail and ran at the sign of battle, lived as nomads, surviving just for the sake of surviving."

"Not all of us did," Brie muttered fiercely, ever the warrior.

As if in responding to the pixie warrior's quiet, unheard reaction to his statement, Arendahl plowed forward.

"But not everyone ran. Some fought from the shadows, with dark Dreampine arrows to blend into the ambushes by night. Some struggled valiantly and refused to give up, making our enemies bleed for every step they took into our shattered kingdom. For anyone who knows what it means to be of the Highest knows that though Andalaya might be broken and her people scattered, she is not gone she is not lost!"

The crowd rumbled a little louder.

Arendahl continued. "Some who fought were present when recently a young and immensely talented warrior by the name of Elliyar Wintermoon slew that traitor, Silverfist, and put to flight a small horde of his slavers. A warrior bearing the gifts of our forefathers, a warrior behind whom a standard could finally be raised." Arendahl carefully hinted at Ell's powers, gave reason for the Andalayans to find hope again in a figurehead, without ever really revealing any specifics.

"And I have fought with Wintermoon. All the while, some few of us kept up the fight, not just the southern battles, but the ancient fight against our weakened foe in the far north. Against the Ghouls and Ogres they fought, only a few, but they fought."

Arendahl's voice took on a particular ferocity as he spoke of his personal battle, of his countless years spent ranging the northern marches, cutting his way through Ghouls in great swathes.

"It is a bleak time for the Highest," Arendahl conceded sadly, and the crowd hung on his words. "We are scattered and desperate, fighting for our very existence. But as if that were not enough, as if the struggle to avoid enslavement and domination were not enough, something even worse is brewing. The ancient foe is rising."

Arendahl let the crowd ponder that lingering thought. The crowd muttered worriedly, angrily, and the greying elf let them simmer. When he had them where he wanted, he continued.

"The First Days are come again. Our foe has returned, but in a new form and in a new location. Our cousins to the south have been warped by their leaders, their minds poisoned beyond anything we could have ever imagined. The Bonewinds blow again and the Unsired have returned!"

He let the last bit out in an angry shout. Miri could see his anger, and surprisingly, she could feel her own rage seething just below the surface. She was not a warrior, and despite her recent practice, she never would be. But something deep inside of her cried out for the destruction of her people's enemy. Sure, Miri had been confronted with the atrocities of the Unsired face to face, but it was more than that. Some innate element of her being called for vengeance, for justice. Creation had spun them out for a purpose, had it not? To right its wrong. It had created them for this battle.

"Our kin from the south are perverted even beyond their alliance with the human invaders. We fight a foe that has morphed and changed over the millennia but remains as dangerous as ever. I tell you, my friends, my people, my kin, that we fight for our very existence! How many of you have lost loved ones, how many have cried as your friends and family have been hauled away or buried. The slavers raid from the south and the Icari fly again by night. A time to fight is upon us again. We must put away our fear and arm ourselves once more. The time for war is now!"

Arendahl ended his speech with a roar and fists lifted to the air. The crowd roared with him. Miri felt the earth vibrate with the noise of shouts and the stomping of feet. Ululating cries pierced the air as thousands upon thousands of the Highest had gathered in one spot to take a stand once again. Perhaps it would be a last stand; time would tell. But they would fight. She could feel the certainty in that one thought.

She would fight.

Miri felt her own surprise overwhelm her for a moment as she realized that. But then she shoved the emotion aside and gave herself over to the moment. Brie was already on her feet and Miri joined her, joined her voice with her friend's and the thousands of voices down slope from them.

Resistance had been reignited in Andalaya.

Ell might be a world away right now, but the elves of Andalaya were flocking to his cause. And she was one of them.

Chapter Forty-Six

Moving felt good. Instead of sitting and waiting, he was now engaged in action. Even the light running they were doing had Ell feeling better than he had all the days cooped up in the camp on the ridgeline. Everyone was together now. Ell, his family, Kalabi, and even the pirates. Everyone could feel that tonight was a night of action, one way or another.

The breeze was cool on Ell's cheek. Dusk was falling and the air hinted at a chill almost-winter night to come. It didn't have the bite of Andalaya's far northern reaches, but it was cold enough that it gave Ell another reason to appreciate their motion. They ran down the sloping mountainside, their lithe feet delicately picking a path the way others struggled to do. They paced themselves, however, as Kalabi would not be able to keep up with them at full speed, and even Piripeos and the Departed sailors would struggle to maintain the pace, should Ell and his Highest kinfolk move as fast as they could. They were born for this after all. His kind were fashioned to run along mountain trails and dodge between trees.

Downward, off the mountain, they ran until they reached the edge of the city. The glow of torchlight emanating from within the city limits was a harsh contrast to the starlight by which they had been navigating.

"We're on the south side of Lu Fang. We need to get to the middle peninsula." Kalabi took charge now that they were in his homeland.

They silently followed the ex-slave's guidance. Hoods up, they slowed their pace to a fast walk and stayed in the shadows that clung to the walls of buildings. Men and women passed in the night, but it seemed that Lu Fang was much more law abiding and reputable than Dark Harbor had been, for the city watch patrolled at regular intervals and Ell had to strain his eyes to catch a glimpse of anything that seemed out of the ordinary or suspicious. Lu Fang was ruled with a structured grace. It was a city of order and business, a city where the people worked by day and slept by night. It was a city without crime—although the ethical implication of slavery clouded that pristine facade.

It took them nearly an hour of a fast moving, weaving pace to avoid the patrols before they found themselves striking out onto the middle peninsula.

"Why the middle peninsula? I thought the main elf slave barracks was on the northern peninsula." Ell asked Kalabi at a moment's pause during which they waited for a patrol to pass by before pressing forward.

The swarthy human whispered his response. "It is, but there is a combined slave quarters in the middle—both elf and human. If we wish to incite a revolt, we will need all the slaves not just your northern kinfolk. That means if a revolt were to ignite, its logical inception point would be here in the overlap of slave races."

Ell considered this for a minute, but could find no fault in Kalabi's logic.

"Besides," Adan interjected, "Lliaria and Delle are in this barracks." Ell's father had a youthful gleam of excitement at the prospect of seeing his mate again. He'd only seen her a couple times since they'd discovered her location, sneaking in at night to visit, but he was dying for more.

Ell felt a strange lurch of anxiety at the thought. He was excited also, but his meeting with Adan had gone so terribly wrong in that first moment in Dark Harbor that he was almost afraid to imagine what his reunion with his mother might be like.

Adan seemed to read his mind. "It will go well, my son. Put it from your mind."

They slunk forward through the night until Ell and the group reached an alley running up to a huge building. It was larger than any of the slave quarters Ell had seen in Dark Harbor. Apparently, most of the slaves in Lu Fang lived in a few major locations. Dark Harbor kept its slaves separated in small pockets all throughout the city, making it more difficult to incite a revolt.

"Now we wait here for the present," Dacunda said for Ell and Dahranian's benefit since they had not accompanied the group on previous infiltrations. "We gauge the patrols and then go over the wall in a gap between patrol passes."

Sure enough, a few minutes of waiting in the darkened side street yielded two sentries passing in front of Ell and the group's position. They waited until the sentries made a pass back, calculating how much time they had between patrols.

"We have no more than a few minutes, so let's move." Dacunda was already leading the way, slinking out into the street and then across to the wall encircling the slave barracks.

With a few sprinted steps and a bounding leap, Dacunda's fingers gripped the upper ledge and he hauled himself up and over.

"Who's next?" Ryder whispered.

Adan followed his younger brother. Then the pirates. Then Dahranian. Ell,

Kalabi, and Ryder waited in the alley as another patrol passed then followed the rest of the group up and over the wall. A few abrasions on his palms from the rough stone wall were all Ell had from the first step of this infiltration.

Ell dropped to the ground in an outer courtyard of sorts. No, not a courtyard, he thought, more of a walled enclosure. For letting slaves outside under a watchful eye perhaps? It didn't matter what it was. What mattered was what lay inside. Months of searching and at great cost, Ell was finally about to meet the rest of his family and get them to safety.

Ell followed his uncle who was still leading the way, to a locked door.

"We don't have much time, there's bound to be an inner patrol sooner or later," Dacunda was saying. "Rikiol, you're up."

The female Departed bounded forward with a grace that almost looked like it should belong to one of her northern compatriots and pulled a set of slim metallic tools from a pocket. In a few quick motions, Rikiol picked the lock and held the door open nonchalantly for them to enter.

"Do we need to worry about guards inside the building itself?" Ell asked to no one in particular.

Ryder spoke up to answer. "Not really. The humans aren't the most thorough thinkers. They worry about escape by slaves. But they can't imagine anyone trying to sneak in, so once we avoid the guards and get inside and as long as we keep relatively quiet, then we won't have to worry about the guards until we try to sneak back out. That can be tricky."

They padded silently along darkened corridors, Kalabi leading the way, whether by memory of the barracks or by some innate slave sense human slaves had in barracks of their kind's making, Ell didn't know. They reached two large doors and paused once again for Rikiol to pick the lock. Kalabi grabbed a torch from the sconce on the wall near the doorway.

The great doors swung inward with a deafening creak. Ell winced, hoping it hadn't alerted anyone outside. It certainly woke the inhabitants of what was an enormous dormitory room. Bed upon row of bed stacked upon each other, sometimes three or four levels high, filled the room endlessly. The back of the dormitory was lost in total darkness.

"Who's there?" a frightened voice whispered. Another and another whispered the same thing. The air of fear in the atmosphere was palpable. The Lashers had done their work well.

"It is I again, Adan Wintermoon," Ell's father whispered in response.

"Wintermoon…" A few voices murmured in the darkness as if they half remembered hearing that name in a place and a time long forgotten.

Another voice spoke up with a modicum of authority. "Wake Valdor."

There was a shuffling of feet as someone went to wake this Valdor. By the flickering light of the solitary torch, Ell could see bodies beginning to wake from slumber. There was no surprise, however. Clearly his family had visited this barracks before in their days of trying to promote the rebellion, and Adan certainly must have visited his mate and daughter.

After a long pause during which no one spoke, an aged elf strode wearily towards them from the back of the room. He was the oldest elf Ell had ever seen apart from Arendahl. But whereas Arendahl had the vitality of his Water Calling powers to keep him hale and healthy, this elf looked grey to the point of collapse. Oh, he moved well enough, Ell supposed, but elves always did right up until the moment their bodies gave out, and his looked like it might do so soon.

"You are back," the wizened elf said simply.

"We are, Valdor," Dacunda responded.

Valdor smiled sadly. It was a genuine smile as if he were truly happy to see them, but also sad as to what he must say.

"I told you the last time, it will not happen. It is useless. It is death to revolt. We learned that in the early days when many of us died in vain." Valdor spoke plainly, but he spoke with a hopeless authority and Ell could feel the room in agreement with him. Voices muttered assent.

Valdor continued. "It warms my heart to see those of my kin who are still free, still un-collared." He toyed with the copper band around his neck almost as Kalabi often did. "But you should leave while you can."

"Come with us!" Dacunda interjected in frustration.

"We cannot all go without raising alarm, and I would not leave anyone behind."

"Then fight," Adan spoke up grimly. "You are right, you cannot run. You must fight."

"I told you, we learned our lesson in the early days. Fighting is useless. We have no weapons, and even if we had them, many of us have not held a spear or a sword in two decades, what good would that do us." Valdor shook his head politely and sadly. "No. I am afraid this is our plight in life, until such time as creation sees fit to free us, in life or in death."

Adan snorted angrily. "I was a slave too. For twenty years I labored in Dark Harbor. I understand your minds, but you must overcome your fear." The crowd murmured in surprise.

Ell surveyed the crowd. A look of mingled fear and respect filled their eyes as they looked at Adan. Slavery might be more widespread in Etheros, an empire, a continent built upon the backs of forced labor, but everyone had heard the stories, the tales. They had heard of Dark Harbor and knew it was a singularly terrible place to be enslaved.

"Do you not work with shovels and picks as you construct for the humans who control this city?" Adan raised his voice slightly to carry over the crowd of mixed elf and human slaves alike. "Those are weapons if you so choose, for how different is a pick from an axe, a shovel from a war hammer?"

There was a murmur of assent, but it was small and died out quickly. That was the simmering anger below the surface that they had reported back in camp. It was there, but it was not strong. Not enough to support outright revolt. Fear quenched the tiny flame of resistance like a bucket of water dowsing a candle.

"We will help you fight!" Adan declared.

"You are only a handful," Valdor responded calmly, unmoved by Adan's comments. "What help can you possibly be?"

Ell put a steadying hand on his father and held back Adan's angry retort. Ell saw Valdor's words work like a stifling, smothering wind. He was the unspoken leader in this hopeless environment. Valdor bent down to pick up a child who had wormed her way to the front. The old elf smiled venerably at the girl and held her close. Valdor was leader here, and from the looks on the faces of those around him, he was respected and loved. As he went so would go this crowd, so would go this conversation.

Ell stepped forward and pulled back his hood.

"I am Elliyar Wintermoon." Ell heard a small gasp from off to the side, but he didn't turn his head to look. He had to address Valdor here and now, and hopefully win the old elf over.

"I am pleased to make your acquaintance, young elf." Valdor said, and once again Ell heard the ring of truth. This was a good elf, a kind elf, an elf who had loved and lost and was trying to protect who he saw as his people. But he was a hopeless elf and one who had long ago stopped believing in anything beyond the walls of this barracks.

"If you will trust me, I will help you free yourselves." Ell promised with as much vehemence as he could manage. "I swear to you, that we will win. Many will die, I do not dispute that, but we can fight our way to victory, it is not impossible."

Valdor shook his head in wistful disbelief. "You are one elf, what possible difference can you make against hundreds of Lashers and thousands of guards?"

"I am not just an elf, I am a Water Caller," Ell let his voice ring out.

There were a number of curious and confused mutters but many did not know what that meant. Arendahl had told Ell long ago that the secret of the Water Callers had been lost in the memory of most of their kind. However, Ell saw the flicker of recognition in Valdor's eyes, but it was just as quickly suppressed by the dour hopelessness of enslaved mentality.

Ell tapped his abilities. He hadn't done so since the Fracture, but his powers came to him easily enough. The familiar cloudiness filled his eyes, at once making it harder and yet easier to see at the same time. It was so familiar in fact, that Ell hardly noticed it. Mist wisped around him as he pulled upon all the latent moisture in this water-rich coastal port.

"I am a Water Caller," Ell repeated. "I can do things you would not believe. I will deal with these Lashers, if you will but join with us in striking back at our enemies!" His promise rang out.

Ell saw a few faces lift in hope, for a moment the fear was replaced and a light of wonder and hope filled some eyes, but once again Valdor stifled it.

"You are still one elf, Water Caller or not. It will not happen," Valdor finished with regretful resolve.

Ell saw the light fade from eyes and the simmer of discontent wilt back to nothing. These people were conditioned. They would not change their minds and hearts for anything he could say. And he would not attack the guards and Lashers without their approval because without them a revolution would never succeed, no matter how many Lashers Ell killed. He needed their belief—Valdor's belief—to earn the opportunity to prove himself to them, but he would never earn that belief without first showing them. It was a circular trap from which there was no escape.

Valdor watched him, saw the understanding dawn in his eyes. Sadly, again, the old elf smiled.

"Please, while it has warmed my heart to see members of my race who are still free, I must now ask you to go, before you bring trouble down on all of us."

Ell stared at the old elf for a long moment before finally acquiescing with a nod.

"Fine. Have it your way, Valdor. We will leave you in peace. But we are collecting my mother and my sister before we go and there is nothing you can do to stop us, whatever harm their disappearance might cause you." Ell spoke with sad determination.

Valdor opened his mouth as if to debate Ell's choice to free slaves, but then closed it again and smiled that genuine sad little smile. "Of course. I would not keep long estranged family apart."

Dacunda grabbed Ell by the shoulder and spun Ell around. "That's it? We're giving up?"

"Nothing we say will change their minds, Uncle. They will have to come to the conclusion to fight back all on their own. I only pray that there will be someone to help them, someone with a plan to get them home, when the time comes."

Adan was nodding to himself as if he saw the truth in Ell's words and was turning to his right, searching the crowd with his eyes. "Lliaria! Delle!" he cried out.

Two shapes pushed their way through the crowd of people toward them. Two blonde females, one only a few years older than Ell, appeared. They were worn and tired–looking, but the joy and the hope in their eyes as they saw their salvation before them was enough to quench the pain Ell felt at the all-prevalent hopelessness that pervaded the rest of this barracks. Ell smiled. He still held his power, but even through the calm detachment that often accompanied his abilities he felt the joy.

The elder of the two walked up to Ell, hands trembling with the sheer weight of the moment. Ell gazed into the eyes of his mother, the mother who he'd long thought dead, the mother for whom he should have long ago given up hope. He looked into her eyes in beautiful silence. No words were necessary. Lliaria didn't even see the fake tattoos on his cheeks, she didn't mention his black scar, or the strange mist still swirling about him from tapping his abilities, dampening his clothes and hers.

Lliaria leaned forward and pulled his forehead to her lips. Ell felt her lips smiling as she kissed him.

Pulling apart after an interminable moment Ell broke the silence and held out his hand. Lliaria grasped it in her work-callused palm.

"Come, Mother, it is time to take you home."

* * * *

They exited as quietly as they had entered. Ell still held his abilities, having seen no cause to drop them after tapping his powers to show Valdor. He would hold them until they were clear of the city. He wanted no mishaps with his mother and sister around. There was a lot he wanted to ask her, them, but now was not the time. They were relying on silence to see them out safely.

They reached the outer enclosure and hopped the wall into the street adjoining the alley. The group was almost into the dark recesses of the side street, torch abandoned so as to blend into the shadows, when misfortune struck. Ryder was in the rear and he was just dropping down to the ground from the top of the wall when a patrol turned the corner. Not just any guardsmen. Ell hadn't seen them before, but he knew that these were the feared Lashers. Whips coiled at their hips and armed with a variety of weapons they looked positively fearsome. The array of swords, axes, halberds, and spears, lent them a mercenary air as opposed to a uniformed look. They wore hardened leather and straps with small studded spikes worked into their black clothing to tear at the flesh in close quarter fighting. Some wore chain mail shirts, but most just had black leather protecting their bodies—less protection but more mobility. These were hardened fighters and from the look in their eyes and the instantaneous recognition of a dangerous situation they were not to be taken lightly.

There was no choice but to engage. The fight was short and brutal with blood shed on all sides. Ell's band suffered no fatalities although that was likely due to the fact that he was still holding his Water Calling power and scythed through the Lashers like lightning.

His dueling daggers came free in one fluid motion and Ell was already ducking into the crowd of his enemies before anyone else had time to react. He cut low and hamstrung one, and then opened up a vein on the interior of another's arm before his companions joined him. Then Dacunda was in the fray, with Adan, Ryder, Dahranian, Piripeos and the rest of the pirates behind. Ell's mother and sister hung back since they were unarmed, but Ell saw them kick a few downed Lashers in the face. Whether it was a modicum of vengeance exacted after two decades of slavery, or a simple precautionary action to ensure that their enemies wouldn't rise, Ell wasn't sure. But he would have understood either.

The skirmish was over almost as soon as it began. The Lashers were all dead or down, while Adan and Kalabi had picked up a few wounds of their own. The rest of the band appeared unscathed.

Adan held one hand to his side and blood was seeping out slowly, but steadily. Lliaria was at his side in a heartbeat.

"Do not worry, my love, I will be fine," Adan said through gritted teeth, accepting a flask of Source Water from Dacunda and taking a small sip.

Still wrapped in the cocoon of his Water Calling detachment, Ell focused on the task at hand. Escape.

"Come on," Ell said brusquely, "we don't want to wait around for more guards to arrive. The noise was bound to attract attention. Let's go."

And they set of into the night.

Chapter Forty-Seven

Valdor awoke with the sun. Although in this windowless room there was no way to tell for sure if that was the case, yet his internal rhythm told him it was so. Sounds of wakeful movement from around him told him that he wasn't the only one. A human arose and clambered down from the bunk above him and hastened to use a chamber pot—one of the few dignities still allowed as a slave. Valdor hadn't eaten much the last few days—having given his rations to some of his favorite little ones—and would not likely need to do the same.

He sat on the edge of his bed for a moment, wondering. Was last night a dream? Had that boy really exhibited such mystique and power? Should he have listened?

No.

Valdor reassured himself of his right decision. There was no use fighting anymore. One had to accept their lot in life. What little joy was left to them here would evaporate in an instant if one harbored futile aspirations of freedom. He heard the murmured conversations talking of last night's encounter with the free elves cut short as the door creaked and ground open. Torches filled the entry way and more guards than usual appeared in the dormitory. Lashers also. Even so, they were still greatly outnumbered by the slaves.

"Form up for count!" A stern voice bellowed from the doorway.

Valdor sensed something. A tinge of anger, was it, maybe a hint of uncertainty in the shouter's tone. But he lost himself in the shuffle as he made his way to the front. He was the designated counter. The guards would come get him if he didn't present himself.

"Hello, Engan," Valdor said politely and with a smile, as he reached the front of the room. "How is your family?"

Guardsman Engan almost smiled. Almost. "Fine, Valdor. Now lead the rest of your companions outside into the outer enclosure and form up for count." Engan spoke gruffly, and Valdor was certain now that he detected a real note of worry.

"As you wish, Engan."

Valdor organized the departure from the dormitory. It was standard procedure. Every month, they did a count so every slave knew how to line up. Eventually, everyone was where they were supposed to be. All but two. Two who would never return.

Valdor began his count even though he knew it would fall short. Some time later, he returned to Engan, walking with the tired limbs of old age. "We are two short, Engan."

Engan paled slightly. A Lasher stepped forward and stood parallel to Engan.

"Engan? You let this slave call you by name?" The Lasher's tone was incredulous. Engan swallowed nervously and did not reply. Valdor remained silent not knowing how to fix his mistake. He wished no harm to come to Engan.

The Lasher elevated his voice for all to hear, his shout echoing into the dawn stillness.

"Two are missing! And last night, a cohort of my men were found murdered just outside these walls! I doubt that is a coincidence. There must be a consequence for such actions. A reprisal is necessary."

The Lasher turned to Engan with a silky smile on his face.

"Sir?" Engan responded to the attention.

"Guardsman Engan. This elf is the leader within these walls, chosen to oversee the count. A position of honor. Is he not?" The Lasher had a cruel smirk on his face. Valdor caught a premonition of his impending doom.

"He is," Engan said as he swallowed again.

"Make an example of him."

"What?" Engan blanched this time.

"He calls you by name. Is he your friend, is that why you hesitate?"

Terror laced Engan's face. "He is not a friend, Sir." Engan avoided looking at Valdor.

"Good. Prove it. I want you to make an example of him. Kill him."

Engan turned to face Valdor with regret in his eyes, but a snarl of fear and survival on his lip. With only a moment of hesitation the man grabbed the cudgel from his hip and in one swift motion clubbed Valdor across the side of his head with vicious force.

Valdor fell.

It did not take him long to die. At least he didn't think it did. As he lay on his side, gazing vaguely at the legs of his fellow slaves, he thought wistfully of the meadow in Andalaya near the home of his far distant youth. A roaring sound filled his ears. His thoughts were fuzzy. Why was there thunder? The sky had been grey but hardly stormy, especially for the morning. What was that noise?

It took him a moment to realize in his dying state that it was the sound of yelling, of screaming. Rage filled the air around him. Something was happening.

So this is what it felt like to die.

He had thought there would be more pain.

Feet rushed around him and the sounds of fighting reached his ears as if through fog. Engan fell with blood trickling from his ear as a swarm of angry slaves surged forward.

Valdor stared at Engan since there wasn't anything else to look at. They both lay on their sides. The human was dead, the glaze of the beyond filling his eyes.

Valdor's legs twitched as his body weakened. His vision darkened, and all the while the sounds of battle raged around him.

Death came.

Chapter Forty-Nine

The mountain slope felt particularly steep and tiring this morning. No sleep combined with the emotions of the night left Ell feeling drained. He'd let his abilities go as soon as they reached the trail on the outskirts of the city. Dawn's light crept up and by the time it illuminated the land they were halfway back to camp.

"At least we did what you set out to do initially, Elliyar. You rescued them—rescued us." Adan placed a hand on Ell's shoulder as they paused for a brief respite. Kalabi and Adan needed the rest since they were still bleeding. The small portion of Source Water had helped Adan somewhat, but Kalabi would have to heal on his own.

"We did, Father, and I am glad of it—beyond glad—but I had hoped for more. I had hoped to strike a blow at our enemy in more than just principle."

As if in contradiction, or perhaps in conjunction with his statement, an explosion concussed the air and shook the hillside. They looked down at Lu Fang. Gouts of fire and billows of smoke were pouring forth from the middle peninsula. Another fire started and another. Even from far away they could hear the ringing of alarm bells, tolling for warning. Black figures poured into the streets, many of whom went right back inside, but others formed up and made their way in units toward the middle peninsula where the fires were starting. City guard.

More fires lit and Ell could see them spreading quickly. Shapes met in streets and alleys and fell, some surged onward. They were too far away to hear anything other than the bells, but Ell was certain that had they been closer they would hear the screams of agony and the clash of steel that always accompanied battle.

It had begun.

Against the odds, somehow the revolt had started. Without them. It had started despite the fact that they were leaving.

"What do you think happened?" Ryder asked with a grunt.

"I don't know," Adan said slowly, still clutching his side, "but I have a feeling it was nothing pretty. Revolts are like fire, they don't start without kindling and a spark."

"We have to go back!" Ell declared.

"Why?" Piripeos debated, "You've accomplished your goal, saved your family, and started a rebellion. All the better that you aren't in the middle of it as it begins."

"I gave them my word," Ell said solemnly. "I promised them that if they fought, I would fight with them. We cannot abandon them now." His hands were gripping the hilts of his blades so tightly that white was showing on the knuckles.

"We're hours away. Do you really think you can get back down there in time to make a difference?" Kalabi asked, his face unusually pale from his wounded shoulder.

Ell felt a small smile curl his lips. "I can move fast. You have no idea."

"So we go back," Dacunda said grimly.

Ell nodded, and Ryder hefted his long-axe in agreement. Adan stepped up to join them in their momentary gaze down the hillside.

Ell shook his head at his father. "No, Adan. You're wounded and you need more Source Water and rest. You can get both back at camp."

"I've gone twenty years without Source Water, boy," Adan barked, suddenly sounding like Arendahl.

"I need to know that they are safe," Ell said to his father seriously, glancing at his mother and sister. "I didn't come all this way to free them, just so that they could die in some dirty alley." They stared at one another for a long time.

"Please, Father." Finally, Adan Wintermoon nodded, although accepting that he would not join them in battle seemed to cost him more than the small movement it required.

"Take them back to camp," Dacunda said, clasping his brother's forearm. "If we aren't back by nightfall, take them back to the ship and try and make your way home somehow."

Swift goodbyes were said but there was no time to waste on long departures. Adan, Lliaria, Delle, and Kalabi headed back to camp while the rest of them turned back downhill.

"Ready?" Ryder asked, his eyes alight with anticipation.

"Ready," Ell affirmed. With one last lingering glance at his mother and sister, Ell tapped his abilities. Seizing his Water Calling powers, he leapt forward in a huge bound and was followed by Ryder, Dahranian, Dacunda, Piripeos and the pirates. They tore forward at a breakneck speed, determined to reach the city before it was too late to make good on their promise of aid.

Ell ran. As he ran, he thought of Miri briefly and wished to hear her laugh one last time before battle. He ran. Ell ran like the east wind, light and fresh and full of energy. His people ran behind him.

They covered the distance to Lu Fang in a third of the time it had taken them to leave it. Racing into the streets on the southern edge of the city Ell and his band wove their way through milling people, many of whom were leaving the city. Civilians who had no wish to be anywhere near fighting. However, the further toward the city center, the emptier the streets became. This close to the revolt's epicenter, people were barring doors and boarding windows the way a seaport battens down the hatches in a storm, looking to ride out the revolt like rough weather.

The sound of steel and screams echoed from the north, and Ell and his group charged onto the middle peninsula. Finally, they were nearing the combat. Fires were sending smoke to drift like serpentine tendrils along streets and alleys, clogging the air making it difficult to see and breathe.

They rounded a corner and came face to face with a company of Lashers. With a roar of fury, the Lashers saw them and charged. Ell and his family cut into them. Ryder hewed like a tree-feller and heads went flying. Ell ducked and weaved and sliced open his opponents, followed by Dacunda and Dahranian who grimly wielded their swords as if the steel were extensions of their own arms. The pirates, led by Rikiol, Baerg, and Kester, followed and they screamed their angry defiance as they cut through the human cohort.

Ell felt a black fury, an urge to kill welling up from some unknown place inside of himself. He surrendered to it for the duration of the short fight. As he did, wisps of black haze trailed from his fingertips, mixing with the mist surrounding him. His blackened scars burned as if newly given. He fought with a lust to kill, to win, to dominate.

When the Lashers were dead, they took a minute to wait for a few of the pirates who were looting the dead.

"Good fight," Rikiol said with grin.

"It isn't even near over yet," Ell responded, and found himself relishing the thought of more death. He shook his head to clear his thoughts. Why was he thinking like that?

Ell froze. A waft of something dead and putrefied wafted across his nostrils. Ever so slightly, so slight nobody but him noticed. Bonewinds!

But there couldn't be any Unsired here in Etheros, could there? Had Half-Mask sent his people across the sea to aid his allies? It didn't seem likely. Confused, Ell paused, but the scent drifted on and he had to ignore it for the moment. There were no Unsired in sight and there was a battle to fight.

They continued forward, rising up on the hill as they climbed the sloped streets of the hilled, middle peninsula. They crested a rise and looked down the street onto the backs of a unit of human soldiers, city watch and Lashers alike. They had a mixed mob of slaves retreating ahead of them, who must have raided work sheds in their barracks to have armed themselves with shovels and picks and wooden handles fashioned into clubs. Some had picked up weapons from fallen soldiers and wielded swords and spears, but most did not. They were hard pressed.

Without even thinking, Ell charged down the hill into the backs of the enemy. The human soldiers never saw him coming and by the time they realized what was happening he was already among them, slaying like a tornado, a hurricane of death. Ell fought with a strangely dark glee verging on madness. He had to save the slaves—he'd promised them. He had to kill the soldiers—he wanted to. He wanted to?

Ell shoved the odd thought away and kept fighting. Killing, really. They were not much of a challenge. Ell tore into the foe like the Water Caller he was, with his strength and agility heightened, and he moved like no one they'd ever faced. Not even the Lashers stood a chance against him. He slashed veins, and severed throats, he infected arms and faces with disease, and the wispy blackness mingled with the mist. And all the while, his family mopped up behind him. He took a few minor cuts but paid them no attention. His body was strong. His Water Calling abilities made him strong. But his new powers made him dominant.

His new powers?

The thought from his subconscious stopped him in his tracks. He looked at the swath of death and disease around him. Ell swallowed in fear.

He turned to look at his family following behind and for the first time ever he saw fear in their eyes.

"Elliyar, you're bleeding." Dacunda said slowly, gazing at a shallow gash on Ell's forearm.

"It's nothing," Ell shook off his uncle's worry, unnerved by their expressions. He didn't feel the pain. They had to keep going to help the slaves.

"Your blood, it's black," Dacunda stated, staring at Ell with a dire almost accusatory look on his face.

Ell was saved from answering by the arrival of slave troops who were opposite from the human soldiers they had just crushed like a hammer and anvil.

"It's you," one of the elves at the fore breathed.

Ell nodded, not knowing how to respond to that statement.

"We were hard pressed, desperate, for a time until you showed up. Thank you."

"I promised you my aid," Ell said, as graciously as he could. "Now can you tell me how all this started? I thought none of you wanted to fight?"

"They killed Valdor," the leader answered grimly. "After he died, it just sort of happened."

"I am sorry," Ell said, his senses feeling more normal now that he'd stopped fighting for a moment. The delight he'd taken in killing was gone replaced by only revulsion at the death in his wake.

The collared elf nodded his thanks. "He didn't want this, Valdor, but we didn't want that death for him. He was a good elf. And we certainly don't want a death like that for any others. It was time to do something. We've been fighting to consolidate the middle peninsula for hours now and then we'll push into the rest of the city, work our way towards the other two slave barracks. There are factions of us all over, fighting in pockets like this."

An idea hit Ell. "We can move fast and accomplish more with fewer people than you," he said. "Why don't we help you out by releasing the other slaves from the barracks. That will help this revolt spread all the faster."

"It's a good idea, Elliyar," Dacunda said, stepping up to his shoulder. His uncle was still looking at him strangely, carefully, but he seemed to have put his questions on hold for the moment.

"Right then, we'll keep consolidating while you spring the others from their cages," the elf said with a grin. He hefted the pickaxe he was wielding. "By the First Days, it feels good to hold a weapon again, even a makeshift one. You know, I was a defender of the walls of Verdantihya when I was your age. I served under your father."

Ell gave him a wolfish grin. "Make them remember who they tried to enslave, friend."

"Djedian."

"What?" Ell asked.

"My name is Djedian."

"Elliyar Wintermoon."

They clasped forearms and then Ell and his band set off back toward the main city center to circle off to the northern peninsula and release more slaves. They passed pockets of fighting, but unless the slaves were especially hard pressed, they didn't pause from their task. The slave revolt needed to have its numbers swelled more than anything, and that meant freeing the other two thirds of the slaves in Lu Fang.

* * * *

Half-Mask sat looking at the stars. He placed a thumb in front of his vision to blot out a few. He liked doing this. Not the star gazing part, but the imagining part, imagining a world where blotting out every winking, twinkling light was possible. It made him hopeful of a darker future. He would make that future happen. The Prince of Darkness sat up with a jolt. Another of his kind—a new equal—was fluttering at the edge of existence. Not a paltry Unsired, but one like him, like his father. He'd been more than glad to transform that Wintermoon boy into an Unsired—a subject—but he hadn't expected this. He hadn't expected the boy to become a Spectralist—hadn't wanted that.

Half-Mask experienced a strange sensation of anticipation—even, admitting to himself, fear—as the felt the boy dabbling with becoming. It would not take much more before the process was complete.

* * * *

Ell stood amidst a pile of bodies. The Lashers had been particularly numerous around the slave barracks on the southern peninsula. He had freed the Highest slaves from the northern peninsula hours ago and moved on to the south.

He breathed heavily. Once again, he'd given in to the strange dark compulsion to kill simply for the sake of destruction as he fought. He could pretend that he was doing only what was necessary to survive and win this battle, but that would be a lie. Especially considering the fact that the last dozen or so he had killed had been trying to flee in terror from the menace fighting before them.

Edgy glances and shifty looks were all Ell received from his tightlipped family members. Although a few of the Departed pirates eyed him with some mingling of revulsion and awe. Death incarnate had a way of inspiring that reaction and that was exactly what Ell was this day. He'd lost count of how many he had killed after losing control to the darkly dangerous glee he felt deep within his soul. Ell felt the urge to weep. What had Half-Mask done to him? He felt the urge to scream a bloodcurdling yell and find more enemies to fight. He was a paradoxical being. A Water Caller…and yet, something else. Something worse. But that something had been necessary today. Hadn't it?

Ell fought down the questions and strode to the gated doors to the southern slave barracks. He bent down and hefted a massive war hammer wielded by one of the larger Lashers in the now-dead cohort. With a tremendous swing fueled by his supernatural abilities, he shattered the gates to the slave barracks.

The doors crumbled upon impact and the slaves having heard the ruckus were waiting within—all human—and ready to partake in the fight. They could hear the bells tolling, hear the screams and clash of battle. They knew it was now or never to fight for their freedom.

"Are you ready?" Ell asked, handing the war hammer to a particularly large, collared human.

The man took the weapon almost reverently. "I think so," he said, sounding a lot less sure of himself than Ell would have wished.

The wind played across Ell's face and suddenly the rotted scent was there. The Bonewinds, again! Ell whirled, searching, looking for his ancient foe, the enemy of the Water Callers, of his people the Highest.

Enemy? Why had he thought that?

Wait, why had he questioned the original thought—that the Bonewinds signaled an enemy?

Ell's confusion brought a sudden, terrifying clarity. He almost wilted under the realization.

The smell of the Bonewinds was coming from him.

* * * *

Miri lazed on her cloak, alone in the meadow. It was probably too cold for a nap. Winter was almost upon them, but she closed her eyes and allowed herself to at least try and doze. On impulse she reached out as she had been doing during the days since she had unblocked her ability with the Graft. Merging her consciousness with Ell's was one of her daily pleasures and she didn't even have to feel guilty about it because Arendahl appreciated her steady updates. The army was growing and Ell would need to lead them eventually. Arendahl liked her keeping tabs on what was happening across the ocean.

Miri sent her consciousness out and merged with Ell with ease. She was getting better and better at it.

Her eyes were closed as she lay in the meadow in Andalaya, but across the sea she opened them. Acrid smoke filled her nostrils. The scent of blood and fire was in the air. Miri felt the urge to kill. She wanted more blood. Miri fought down the impulse and handed a war hammer to a human. She pushed at the darkness inside of her, willed it down, willed it away. She fought with every fiber of her being and contained the vileness that had been implanted in her— that was taking her over. For a moment, Miri considered killing the human who held the hammer. Just because. Red blood looked so pretty against skin so pale. Again, she quashed the impulse.

Barely.

Miri blinked and opened her eyes in the meadow. She was up in a flash, limping her way back to camp. She needed to speak with Arendahl.

Something was very, very wrong.

* * * *

Djedian stood wearily on the hill top. He'd fought all day for this single peninsula. So many others had gone out and spread throughout the city, liberating captives, punishing those who deserved punishing. Mostly Lashers and a few guardsmen who refused to throw down arms. However, there had been some atrocities. Events he would rather not think about. It wasn't right. But it wasn't as if Lu Fang—its apathetic, self-righteous people—didn't have some measure of justice or even vengeance coming its way.

Either way, there was nothing he could do about it now, even if he wanted to. The grey skies of morning burned away. It would have been a clear blue sky if it weren't for the haze of smoke clouding the air. Djedian said a prayer of thanks for Wintermoon and his company. They had been integral in freeing enough slaves for them to overwhelm the army. Divided between the three peninsulas, the guard and the Lashers would have likely been able to deal with each threat one at a time. But the near-simultaneous freeing of the slaves had released a slew of captives, too many for the defenders of Lu Fang to stand against. Many had thrown down arms. Only the Lashers had fought until the bitter end. Better that they had, it gave the slaves—ex-slaves, he corrected himself—an excuse to kill them all.

Djedian gazed almost blankly over the city that had been his home for over a decade. He missed Andalaya, missed it with a fiery passion. But a part of him would never leave this place. A piece of his soul had been shaved off and would remain in Lu Fang, wherever he went next. The smoke filled his nostrils and the scent of death wafted on the air.

Nevertheless, Djedian smiled.

A revolution had begun.

Epilogue

The sand was coarse and rough on her skin, but it was the most wonderful feeling she'd ever experienced. So long without solid ground beneath her, lost in the delirium of swells and waves, she'd wondered if land even existed any more—if she'd entered a reality where there was only driftwood and water.

She hauled herself halfway out of the rippling, tiny waves to lie face down on the wet sand, her cheek pressed to the grainy earth. She tasted grit in her teeth and it was the best thing she'd ever tasted. Unbidden, she closed her eyes as exhaustion overtook her and fell into unconsciousness with the gentle lapping of waves around her feet.

A boot turned her over, and only half-awake, she opened her eyes, squinting against the brightness of the sun. She felt considerably worse than she had when she'd first washed ashore. Then all she could feel was gratitude. Now, every ache and pain was magnified by a more steady alertness, an alertness she'd been lacking before.

"Is that seaweed on her head?" a rough voice asked.

"I think it's her hair."

She blinked and tried to focus. She was lying on her back staring up at a dark-skinned elf with regal features, almost haughty. But there was an understanding about his eyes, a weary knowledge that did not speak of cruelty. His teeth were unfiled.

A swarthy hand reached down to help her up, while simultaneously the same elf held a long, elegant sword, the tip of which was nestled against her neck.

"That's an odd combination, one I've not seen before," she said with a quirked eyebrow and a mocking look, belied only slightly by her sea-worn, parched-throat voice. Her gaze indicated to the elf above her, that she meant the sword and the helping hand together.

The regal-looking Departed smiled. His teeth were not filed to points. The sides of his head were shaven, leaving a mane of lustrous black hair trailing down his back.

"I am polite, but cautious." He also let his eyes speak volumes as he glanced down towards her waist.

A belt knife was still sheathed at her hip. Despite the endless days of floating and exhaustion, of breakers and troughs the knife had managed to remain in its sheath. It had survived the ordeal. Like her. Against the odds.

Somehow she summoned a laugh. "I don't think I'm in much condition to do you any harm right now." She struggled weakly to grasp his hand, but didn't quite manage. "At least, no blade-wielder worth his salt would have any trouble with someone in my position."

"Perhaps not," the Departed allowed, again with a polished smile, although his eyes remained searching, penetrating. "But as I said. I am cautious. And I have heard the tales of you wild northern females who fight in every battle along with your mates. Are you a warrior?" Genuine curiosity tinged his reserved veneer.

She didn't see much point in lying and nodded wearily.

"Any good?" he probed.

A flash of her spark remained, yet unbedraggled by her ordeal in the ocean.

"Good enough to sink one of your warships, virtually singlehandedly," she responded with pride and a challenging look. He was Departed and the enemy. If this was the end, she would meet it with her dignity intact.

"I see," his face hardened. "So that was you."

However, the moment of anger passed and his curiosity returned.

Again he held out his hand, and this time she managed to grab it as he hauled her to her feet with ease.

"What is your name?" He asked.

She shook the dyed green hair from her face.

"Valerihya Wintermoon."

"Well, Valerihya Wintermoon, welcome to the Point."

About the Author

Mathias Colwell grew up in far Northern California exploring redwood forests and cloudy beaches. He loves God, his family, and friends. Mathias has been a writer for most of his life, drafting his first stories as young as eight years of age. His desire to write fantasy was inspired by such authors as J.R.R. Tolkien, David Eddings and the late Robert Jordan. He is an avid traveler and all-around adventurer, having visited or lived in 27 countries. His travels have led him around the world to five continents including stays in Siberia, Spain, and Chile, and he attributes many of his passions and goals in life to these experiences. In his free time he enjoys reading, outdoor activities such as soccer, snowboarding and water sports. Mathias has a passion for issues pertaining to social justice and human rights and hopes to influence these areas in the future.

Other Works by the author at Melange, And Fire and Ice for Young Adults

An Age of Mist
The Collector
A Burning Hope

Dusk Runner, Boook 1 of The Dark Arrow Trilogy

www.ingramcontent.com/pod-product-compliance
Lightning Source LLC
Chambersburg PA
CBHW031100030726
47496CB00002BA/303